The Flying Fish

Eduardo Zayas-Bazán and Robert J. Higgs

www.trafford.com
North America & international
toll-free: 1 888 232 4444 (USA & Canada)
fax: 812 355 4082

Epigraph

Whereof what's past is prologue, what to come
In yours and my discharge.
The Tempest, Act II, Scene I

This novel is dedicated to the frogmen at Playa Girón: José Enrique Alonso, Jesús "Chiqui" Llama, and Jorge and Felipe Silva, who chose imprisonment in order to stay with a wounded comrade, and to the memory of Professor David McClellan, who knew a good story when he heard it.

Contents

Part 1

The Promise in the Mountains
The "Horse" Versus the "Sergeant"

Chapter 1
Havana, March 31, 1958

Luis Recio realized he had little time. If the Batista police were on to his fund-raising activities in Camagüey, they would soon be looking for him in Havana. They would have known of his political activities at University of Havana, but Luis was sure only Enrique Bueno knew about his mission. It was possible someone had tapped their telephone lines or talked too much; even worse, there could be a traitor among the recruits. The cell members under Bueno were not supposed to be aware of Luis' identity, a fundamental code of the cell organization. In any event, their organization was probably compromised, and Luis moved quickly to warn Alberto Sánchez that the Havana police might be searching for him as well.

That night Luis had dinner with his father at his estate on Fifth Avenue and filled him in on the situation. Fidel Castro was calling for a general strike April 9th, but Luis' group was not involved. Luis had been told that the government was aware of his financial activities in Camagüey and that the police would soon be questioning him in Havana.

"I'm considering several options, but I would prefer not to leave Cuba. However, I have to make sure my passport is current, and I'm going to the U.S. Embassy to secure a 6-month tourist visa."

The next morning, Luis put his affairs in order at his law office and then informed Francisco Uría, the senior member of the firm and a man he trusted, of his plans to join the rebel forces in the Sierra Maestra.

"We've been very impressed with you and your work, Luis," said Dr. Uría. "Take a leave of absence. If I were a young man, I'd be going to the mountains too."

Everything up to this point seemed easy compared to breaking the news to his wife Laura Ramírez. Their relationship had deteriorated since their last confrontation. Using the pretext of the recent birth of their son, she more often than not rejected Luis' amorous advances, and her lack of ardor opened Luis's eyes wider to their differences. Still, Luis wanted to believe they had a strong enough love to make their marriage last, but Laura admitted she did not want to share him with nebulous political groups.

Luis had also noticed a new subtle hostility toward him on the part of the Ramírezes. There were hints that he was not spending enough time at home with their daughter and grandson and suggestions he should avoid taking sides in the political mess.

Luis could not find the words to respond. Unbeknown to Laura, he had spent many sleepless nights debating his participation in the underground and worrying about its consequences on his family.

During breakfast on the morning of April 2, Luis finally told Laura of a warning from his friend, Gaspar Betancourt, that the Batista regime was aware of his activities and of his decision to join the guerrillas in the mountains. After a stunned silence, Laura screamed at him, "How could you? You bastard! Don't you realize you might be killed? Luis, how could you possibly do this to your son?"

Luis did not answer, knowing no matter what he said, Laura would not listen to him now. They had argued over the same story many times since he had begun his work in the underground. Now her worst fears were becoming a grim reality.

"Both your parents and mine will be around to help you look after Luisito," Luis said. "I've spoken to Papá, and he's promised me he'll check on you every day."

"How long are you going to be away?" she asked with an air of dejection.

"I don't know, Laura. But the situation can't continue forever."

"When are you leaving us?"

"In a few days. Just in case the Havana police are on to me, we'll move to my parents' house today and leave the maid here. We'll instruct her to tell the police we're vacationing in the United States if they should come looking for me."

When the Ramírezes learned of Luis' situation, they were, to Luis' surprise, more concerned for him than reproachful. He expected a royal rebuke from his father-in-law, who, while not exactly a Batista supporter, was unsympathetic to the rebels. Ever since Castro's failed attack on the Moncada Barracks, Mario had criticized the rebels and continued to argue that Castro was a communist. Luis had not eased family tensions any when he remarked at a family gathering that perhaps the country needed a healthy dose of socialism. On top of everything else, Luis was now abandoning Mario's "little princess" to follow a quixotic cause in the wild mountains of Cuba. Still, all Mario said to him was, "Take care, Luis. Your wife and son need you."

That night, Luis met with Gaspar at the Recio mansion and asked Gaspar to take him to the mountains with a load of arms in a car owned by Gaspar's father, a pro-government senator.

"Gaspar, I really need your help."

Gaspar pondered a moment and answered, "I'll help you out. I would even join you in the mountains if my father were not a member of Batista's government. I can't believe that my own father backs a regime that has suspended civil rights and imposed press censorship. When I reminded him even the Church had called for Batista's resignation, he said the Church hierarchy was made up of a bunch of naive fools who ought to stick to spiritual matters," Gaspar confessed.

Luis patted his friend on the shoulder. He had grown up with both Gaspar and Alberto Sánchez in Camagüey and ended up in law school with them in Havana. He knew how much easier it was for Alberto, who had leftist leanings to start with, to work for Castro than it was for Gaspar to embrace the cause against Batista. It was tragic they were being forced to take sides, but Fidel Castro represented the only viable opposition to Batista.

Chapter 2

Luis Recio's life had always been anything but predictable. His mother, María Luisa Heymann Recio, had been told by her obstetrician in Havana she had a narrow pelvis which might make childbirth dangerous. Since she was of delicate nature and did not want anything to happen to her firstborn, she persuaded her husband to take her to Johns Hopkins for a thorough checkup. They traveled to Miami by ferry, boarded a train, and arrived in Baltimore in the middle of a snowstorm. The next day extensive tests confirmed that María Luisa's narrow pelvis made it impossible to give birth naturally, and the specialist at Hopkins recommended a cesarean-section delivery upon her return to Havana.

Fate, however, intervened early the next day. As Rogerio and María Luisa were leaving the hospital, María Luisa slipped on the ice outside of the train terminal, and her fall forced a premature cesarean operation that afternoon. Thus, Luis Recio was born in the Johns Hopkins Hospital in Baltimore on December 22, 1933, making him the first direct descendant of Martín Recio born in the United States.

Two years later, his sister Isabel was born. In this manner, brother and sister became members of the fourteenth generation of Recios in Cuba. Their ancestor, Martín Recio, left Spain during the first half of the sixteenth century, and one of his grandsons, Captain Jacinto Recio, was the first member of the family to settle in Puerto Príncipe, a village in the center of Cuba founded in 1528.

As a young child, one of Luis Recio's first vivid memories was sitting in the living room of the family's ancestral colonial home in Camagüey and listening to stories about two of the family's most famous members, his grandfather, Bernabé Recio Betancourt, and

Bernabé's brother, Manuel. Papá Bernabé owned and operated the Tamarindo Sugar Mill and surrounding sugar cane plantation, forty kilometers east of the city, just off the central highway that bisected Cuba from East to West. In 1895 during the Cuban War for Independence, young Bernabé rose to fame when he led a machete charge on horseback and defeated the Spaniards near the city of Morón.

Luis loved to gallop on his broomstick horse around the screened-in porch of the spacious wooden house at the sugar mill. Brandishing his toy machete, Luis relived the heroic feats of Papá Bernabé in his mind. Shouting orders to his imaginary troops, Luis frequently ambushed the family's servants and held them prisoner in the kitchen pantry until his mother came to their rescue.

Bernabé's older and more famous bachelor brother, Manuel Recio, was known as *"El Honrado"* or "The Righteous One." He was wounded while fighting near Bayamo, and for his valor he reached the rank of Colonel. After the war, Manuel joined the Liberal Party and was elected first governor and then senator from the province of Camagüey. By 1918 he was a leading contender for the presidency of Cuba. Unfortunately, a few months later Manuel died during a pistol duel with a political enemy.

The seven-year old Luis imagined that he would continue the family legacy, and with Papá Bernabé's encouragement, he appointed himself president of Cuba with the platform of shortening the school year to three months and using 20% of the sugar harvest for the manufacturing of candy.

As he grew older, Luis treasured the time he spent with his paternal grandparents, Papá Bernabé and Mamá Celia at the Tamarindo sugar mill.

Many evenings over the years Luis and his grandparents would sit in comfortable rocking chairs on the patio after dinner and enjoy the gentle evening breeze. During those special moments, Papá Bernabé loved to share details of the family history. As his beloved grandfather answered his many questions, Luis learned that Rogerio Recio de Varona, his father, had studied in the United States, first as a high school student at Southern Military Academy in Tennessee and later as an undergraduate at Louisiana State University. Papá Bernabé wanted to groom his son to follow in his footsteps. When Rogerio returned to the Tamarindo Sugar Mill after college graduation with a degree in agricultural engineering, his newly acquired knowledge was instrumental in doubling the yield of the cane. Over time, Rogerio rotated through the different departments at the mill, and when he turned twenty-nine, Bernabé Recio proudly appointed his son general manager of the mill.

In time, Luis learned the story of his mother's family as well. In contrast to the Recios, his maternal grandfather was a newcomer to Cuba. Luis' mother, María Luisa, was the daughter of Moisés Heymann, a young Jew from Hamburg who came to Cuba as a tobacco dealer in 1905.

On a visit to one of his supplier's farms, Moisés met Rafael Luaces's only daughter, Cecilia, and the two of them were immediately attracted to each other. From then on, the ambitious and love-smitten young businessman tried to buy more tobacco in the Camagüey region than elsewhere, always finding time to pay a visit to the Luaces family. Cecilia's family viewed the budding courtship with ambivalent feelings. On one hand, Moisés Heymann was an attractive and well-to-do young man; on the other, he was Jewish, and the Luaces did not know his family.

Moisés won his future in-laws over by converting to Catholicism. The decision scandalized his family in Hamburg, but Moisés never regretted it, for in Cecilia he gained a loving and loyal wife who gave him with two daughters and two sons. María Luisa Heymann Luaces, Luis' mother, was born in 1912.

However, the story of greatest interest to Luis was his parents' courtship. Rogerio Recio de Varona met María Luisa Heymann Luaces on one of her family's periodic visits to Camagüey. Only nineteen years old and a gentle beauty with long, black hair and a flawless, creamy complexion, María Luisa studied English at Havana University. Rogerio's interest sparked when he noticed the beautiful stranger with flirtatious eyes playing cards with other young women in the ballroom of the Camagüey Tennis Club. María Luisa had been aware of the frequent glances of the tall, handsome man, and she inquired about him.

Shortly thereafter, they casually drifted toward each other at the club's bar and struck up a conversation. Although on first impression Rogerio found the young woman to be somewhat fragile and naïve, he soon discovered she possessed a strong will and a mind of her own. When Rogerio learned that María Luisa and her family were in Camagüey visiting relatives for Christmas vacation, he invited her to the New Year's Eve dance, and much to his delight, María Luisa graciously accepted.

In the next few days, the couple saw each other constantly at the club. They played tennis, discussed political ideas, and talked about their families. They discovered they both belonged to the Havana Yacht Club and had mutual friends. Rogerio found María Luisa to be the ideal woman: beautiful, refreshing, intelligent, and quite refined. The young woman from Havana simply knew she had fallen in love.

For the traditional Christmas Eve dinner, Rogerio invited María Luisa to his home. As was the custom, Rogerio came to pick her up with his mother serving as chaperon. By the end of the evening, María Luisa had thoroughly charmed both Bernabé and Celia. After Midnight Mass, "The Cock's Mass" as it is known in Cuba, Celia took Rogerio by the arm and whispered to her son, "I think she's lovely. She would make a fine wife and daughter-in-law!"

Chapter 3
Havana, April 3, 1958

Luis knew his father to be an honest, hard-working man who had inherited Papá Bernabé's large, muscular bone structure and Mamá Celia's delicate features. Rogerio's personality more resembled his mother's than his father's, and he was a gentle, rather reserved man. Rogerio, a fair disciplinarian and loving father, played an integral role in his children's lives.

Shortly before noon, Luis heard an unexpected knock at the door and was surprised to find his father and Dr. Uría. When he saw their faces, Luis knew they had important news.

"I've talked to some of my friends at the American Embassy," said Dr. Uría. "You can pass the word to your comrades that Batista has fallen from grace with the Americans. The U.S. has decided to stop the shipment of arms to Batista, and without American support, Batista won't last. There's a strike planned for day after tomorrow which will further complicate Batista's problems." It was the best news that Luis had heard in a long while.

That night Laura again turned her back to Luis and pushed his arm away when he reached for her. Neither spoke.

As the Recio household came to life the next morning, Laura made a final appeal, "Luis, don't you realize you're abandoning your family? What are you trying to do? Become the next family hero? It's all so stupid and selfish!"

Luis wished he had shown her Herbert Matthews's article in the *New York Times* with its photographs of Castro and his guerrillas in the Sierra Maestra. Many young men and women like him were joining the rebel leader, yet Luis decided not to challenge his wife.

When he got out of bed, he went directly to Luisito's bedroom. As he bent over the crib to pick up his son, Laura interrupted the moment with a stern command. "Don't wake him! He needs his sleep." Luis glanced at Laura and then gently stroked his son's hair before sadly turning away from the crib.

When Luis left the house with his father, Laura, fighting back the tears, gave him a perfunctory kiss as cold as the marble stairway behind her. "Luisito and I are going to stay at my parents' house this week," was all she said. The tone of her voice left little doubt that as long as the future of Cuba was in limbo, her marriage to Luis Recio would be also.

As Rogerio backed out of the driveway, Luis caught sight of his mother standing beside Laura in the doorway, and for a moment his decision to join the guerrillas seemed ridiculous to him. He came close to asking his father to stop the car, but he knew there was no turning back.

Their destination was Varadero, the legendary beach resort two hours from Havana. It provided an ideal hiding place because of the thousands of American tourists who enjoyed its white beaches and crystal clear water. The house where they stopped, as with most other private houses in Varadero, was closed for the winter months, so Rogerio helped Luis open the windows and put away the food Luis had brought. After a stroll on the beach, they ate broiled red snapper at one of the seaside restaurants and reminisced about their fishing trips to Santa Cruz del Sur on the southern coast of Camagüey. When Rogerio departed, they gave each other a long embrace as tears flowed down their faces. Seeing his father drive away, Luis was overcome with the same loneliness he had experienced when his parents had left him at the military academy in Tennessee.

Luis now had time to think about the details of the last few days, the unrest, and loss of life caused by the failed general strike the previous day, and the details of tasks that lay ahead--receiving the guns and ammunition on the twelfth of April and transporting them in Gaspar's car to the rebels. Reflecting on the difference between revolution in town and country, Luis concluded it was really safer to be a guerrilla fighter than to be a member of the underground in the cities, particularly the sabotage groups that risked their lives every time they went out on a mission. Sometimes these men were caught and tortured, and later their bloody bodies would appear in the outskirts of the cities. Still, he had been told the toughest part of being a guerrilla was to survive in those mountains.

As Luis waited for the arrival of the weapons, he noted how peaceful everything seemed. Somewhere he had read the two most pleasant sounds were of waves breaking on the seashore and wood crackling in a fireplace. He had rarely heard winter fires, but he was well-acquainted with the soothing cadence of the waves.

This wait gave him time to relax and think. Among the books he had thrown into his canvas bag was a copy of Steinbeck's *Of Mice and Men* that Mrs. Russell, his high school English teacher at SMA, had given him when he graduated. He had never taken the time to read it until some years later at the university. When he finally finished it, he was so taken with it that he became absorbed with Steinbeck, reading his favorite, *The Grapes of Wrath*, in just two sittings. Steinbeck led him to discover Hemingway. In law school, the intellectuals among his colleagues, such as Gaspar, read and talked about Jean-Paul Sartre and Albert Camus, but Luis had not been impressed by either of these French writers. He was too much of a social animal to identify with alienation, and his Catholicism reacted against the idea of existentialism. When he had time to do some reading, he opted to return to American classics such as *Grapes* and *For Whom the Bell Tolls*. The authors might be sentimental, as Gaspar argued, but to Luis they grappled with the one basic issue that the whole world needed to address: Which side, brother, are you on?

On the morning of April 12, 1958, a young couple in swimsuits knocked at the door of the house. Luis, who was waiting for the arms, wondered what they wanted. The young woman smiled, extended her hand, and introduced herself, "I'm Consuelo, and this is my friend, Armando. We have a present for you from Alberto Sánchez."

Hearing the name of his friend and the word "present," Luis immediately understood why they were there, and he followed them to the side of the house to a 1952 Wayfarer Dodge. In the trunk and back seat of the car, there were several wooden boxes covered with folded beach chairs and deflated floats. It was a simple guise, probably even unnecessary, since no one would be apt to question two youths who were on their way to Varadero for a day at the beach. When they had moved the boxes inside, the young couple bid him farewell.

"We wish we could accompany you!" Armando said, embracing Luis. "Tell the rebels we're doing our best to create chaos in the cities!"

"And good luck!" said Consuelo, kissing him on the cheek.

Gaspar Betancourt arrived as planned on the thirteenth at noon in his father's Bel Air Nomad Chevrolet station wagon with government license plates. They loaded the car without ceremony and closed the house. As they drove away, Luis informed Gaspar that rather than drive to Bayamo, they were now going to Santa Cruz del Sur via the city of Camagüey.

The trip was uneventful. It took them less than an hour to get from Varadero to the central highway, and from then on it was smooth sailing on the two-lane highway that had been built by General Machado in the late twenties. Luis recalled traveling to Havana by car as a teenager with his Grandfather Bernabé Recio. The old man told tales about Machado, summarizing his administration by saying, "Luis, that old goat might have turned out to be a dictator the last four years he was in power, but before that he was the best president Cuba has had. During his tenure, there was a lot of construction in Cuba, and this highway we're traveling was part of it."

On the outskirts of Santa Clara, the army had set up a roadblock.

"Be cool, and let me do the talking," Gaspar said.

When they stopped at the barrier, the soldiers glanced at the government plates and looked at each other in hesitation. It was then that Gaspar flashed a smile and greeted them in the friendliest voice, "I'm Senator Betancourt's son. I'm on my way to the farm with some feed and fertilizer. I bet it has been a long day for you."

"We just started our shift a little while ago."

"And how is Colonel García treating you fellows?"

"He's a fine man." As he spoke, the corporal deferentially signaled Gaspar through with a forward wave of the right arm and saluted him on the return motion.

Driving away, Gaspar turned to Luis, who had kept silent, and gave him a smile and an exaggerated wink.

"Am I not a good actor, brother? Jot it down so you can tell your grandchildren about it."

There were no more roadblocks until they reached the Agramonte Barracks in Camagüey. Gaspar was set to repeat his previous performance, but since they were now in Camagüey, the senator's home city, the soldiers were familiar with the senator's car and waved them on through without hesitation.

"Only two more hours," said Luis.

To help his son, Rogerio Recio secured a shrimp boat named *Cayo Largo* from his good friend, Thorwald Sánchez. The sixty-six foot craft was the pride of Sánchez's fleet. When they arrived at the pier in Santa Cruz del Sur, the captain of the shrimper was waiting for them.

"I'm Vicente Juan," he said as he shook their hands. He had a cart into which Gaspar and Luis put the boxes from the station wagon. In less than an hour, they were sailing the shrimp route toward the Gulf of Guacanayabo. They slept that night in the only cabin of the boat as Vicente and his first mate took turns piloting, and the next day Luis and Gaspar joined the crew in fishing for shrimp in the muddy waters of the gulf in order to disguise their intentions.

That night after dark, the boat entered the port of Manzanillo. Luis and Gaspar walked from the boat to *El Bar de Pepe* and ordered beers from a fat, bald man who fit the description of the person they were instructed to contact.

"I'm Gonzalo," said Luis, using the code word sent to him by Alberto Sánchez.

"Oh, *sí*," replied Pepe as he patted Luis on the back as if they were old friends. "I've been expecting you. My son, Pepito, will be your guide. Give him an hour, and he'll meet you at the boat. Which one is yours?"

"The *Cayo Largo*, the large shrimper at the end of the pier."

The boat had its motors running when Pepito arrived. They departed immediately and rounded Cape Cruz that night and turned east.

Early in the morning, they docked at the pier of the Beattie Sugar Company and spent the rest of the day conspicuously repairing the nets and snapping off the heads of the shrimp caught on the trip. At nightfall, Pepito left the boat and returned two hours later with a powerful-looking peasant. "This is Prudencio," he said to Luis, "the man who will take you to the Sierra. The soldier who is guarding the pier is one of our men. Prudencio has a horse for you and mules for the boxes. Let's hurry, and keep quiet."

Gaspar and Luis gave each other a farewell embrace, and Luis followed Prudencio.

In twenty minutes, they were riding the horses and leading pack mules through the Beattie village. By nine o'clock, most of the lights of the *bohíos* were out. Apart from the noise of a few domino players in a bar, there was a deep silence. Out in the country, only the sounds of insects and barking dogs could be heard.

In the distance Luis could make out the sharp contours of the Sierra Maestra which came closer as he and Prudencio rode through narrow canyons and rocky creeks.

They arrived at the camp around 3 a.m. in a torrential rain, and Prudencio, as he had done at check points all along the way, gave a low whistle to the guards on duty near the first *bohío* they came to. Luis was wringing wet, and his butt was chaffed and sore from the ride. Still he was not about to complain. Luis wondered how many "city boys" Prudencio had led into these mountains. Prudencio himself was not too worried about Luis' discomfort, telling him to wait on his horse until he and one of the guards unloaded the mules and put the arms in one of the *bohíos*.

At last they returned, and Prudencio directed Luis to the *bohío* called the armory where he found a mat and, of all things, a faded color print of the *Virgen de la Caridad del Cobre*. Luis did not mind where he slept. Exhausted, he collapsed on the mat without removing his clothes. As he drifted into sleep, he remembered how the eyes of that same Virgen of Charity had scrutinized him the night he lost his virginity as an adolescent. In what seemed only minutes, a harsh voice awakened him, "Get up, Recio. Fidel wants to see you!"

Chapter 4

During World War II, Luis and his family tuned into the radio every day for news of the war in Europe, and afterwards the adults discussed the latest events. In those days Churchill, Roosevelt, Stalin, Hitler, Mussolini, and Hirohito were household names. María Luisa recounted how the events abroad directly impacted the Jewish side of their family. Her Uncle Heinrich, a professor of economics, Aunt Rebecca, and their three children, Heinrich, Jr., Philip, and little Rebecca, fled from Germany in June of 1937 because of Adolph Hitler's anti-Semitism and after many difficulties reached Havana early in 1938. They stayed at Moisés' home for five months until Heinrich and his family obtained visas for the United States. Moisés sent his brother money every month until American University in Washington, D.C., offered Heinrich a teaching position.

About that time, Luis started to accompany his father on rides to oversee the work performed by the laborers in the *cañaverales*, or cane fields--Rogerio, on horseback, and Luis, on his black and white pony, Daiquirí. Rogerio loved to stop and chat with the workers, and he and Luis were often invited to enter their humble *bohío*s or huts for a sip of the strong Cuban coffee. The children of the cane workers became Luis' first friends, and they always accepted Rogerio's invitation to play with Luis at the rambling two-story house at the Tamarindo Sugar Mill.

On one occasion, Rogerio allowed Luis to stay overnight at Ramón Blanco's *bohío*. Ramón, a plantation worker, served as one of the Recio's gardeners in his spare time, and his son, Ramoncito, was one of Luis' frequent playmates at the mill. There, Luis observed first-hand how the sugar cane cutters lived.

The *bohío* was a small wood-framed structure with a thatched roof and primitive windows on the front and back. When Luis entered his friend's house, he saw cardboard dividers that served as the walls of three small rooms, the largest, a rudimentary kitchen, and the other two, the living quarters. The earthen floor, the sagging and tattered furniture, and flies everywhere starkly contrasted to the comfort and elegance of the Recio home at the mill. All of this vividly touched Luis' sensitive nature.

At supper time, the boys sat at the table with Ramón, and Clemencia served them a tasty beef stew with rice. Remembering his manners, Luis commented, "Clemencia, your stew is excellent," which brought a smile of appreciation to her fatigued face.

While they ate, Clemencia nursed Ramoncito's younger brother, Ignacio, who had been sleeping fitfully on a pile of burlap sacks that served as his crib. It was obvious the child was sick. As he cried, he choked at his mother's breast and gasped for air. Luis could tell from the wheezing and rattling sounds in his chest that the little boy was struggling to breathe.

Over the course of the evening, Clemencia attended to the baby and wrapped his chest with rags steamed in eucalyptus water, but Ignacio's condition continued to deteriorate. From the bed they shared, Luis and Ramoncito could hear the worried conversation of the parents as the child's condition worsened. Fearing that Ignacio was going to die, Luis turned to Ramoncito and whispered, "Get up, we need to get help."

Without telling Ramón and Clemencia they were leaving, the boys ran the two kilometers to Luis' home without stopping. Rogerio, who was awakened by their pounding on the door, met them and instantly saw the panic in their faces.

"Luis, what are you doing here? What's wrong? Has something happened?"

"Papá, you've got to come and help Ignacio," Luis begged, gasping as he tried to catch his breath. "The baby is dying. He can't breathe. Please, Papá, we have to get Dr. Crucet. Hurry!"

Rogerio responded without hesitation. The tears which spilled from the young boys' eyes convinced him of the gravity of the situation. Within minutes, the three of them got into Rogerio's car and drove directly to Dr. Crucet's home. Luis had been right. Dr. Crucet diagnosed Ignacio with an advanced case of pneumonia and took him immediately to the mill's hospital.

The next day, as Luis shared his experiences with his parents while being served lunch by a servant at their large mahogany dining room table, Rogerio listened with a proud smile on his face. María Luisa then reminded Luis of his good fortune and told him to thank God every night for all he had been given.

The following week, Luis accompanied his father on a business trip to Camagüey. The outing broke the monotony of his provincial life at the sugar mill, and Luis patiently tolerated those moments when his father felt the urge to stop by the side of the road and lecture him about sugar cane and cattle.

In the city, Rogerio first took care of business matters. Then, Papá Bernabé and Rogerio took Luis to the Liceo Club for a drink with their friends. The landed aristocracy of Camagüey composed the Liceo membership. Most members were cattle ranchers although quite a few also owned sugar plantations.

When they walked into the bar, Rogerio proudly showed his son their family's two brands: an "R" for the Recio name and the Star of David for María Luisa, who had cattle of her own. Looking at the symbol, Luis wondered why this star had six points.

Just about everybody at the Liceo, including his father, had a nickname which pertained either to animals or vegetables. Luis would chuckle when Rogerio addressed some his friends as "Mule," " Peacock," or "Sweet Potato." Other names, such as "Vulture" and "Snake," did not seem as humorous to Luis. When Luis asked his father what Rogerio's nickname was, his father replied, "Colt."

"What will I be called?" Luis wanted to know.

"Maybe we will call you 'The Pony' since you love your little horse Daiquirí so much."

"I would rather be a lion like one of those in our coat of arms," said Luis with a combative edge that surprised his father.

"I wouldn't worry about it now," Rogerio answered with a laugh while passing his hand over his son's hair.

María Luisa also cherished her trips to Havana with her children. Since she had been raised there, María Luisa missed the excitement of the metropolis. Soon after her marriage, her father purchased a house for her near the beach, and she took Luis and Isabel to the capital for sea baths every summer. Each June, María Luisa made elaborate preparations for the nine-hour trip by car to Havana. Once there, the children had a quick breakfast every morning, and then Antonio, the chauffeur, and their nanny took them to the HYC for swimming lessons. They returned to the house on Fifth Avenue for lunch, took a nap, and spent the afternoons playing with the neighbors' children.

Since María Luisa wanted Luis to learn a sense of right and wrong, she enrolled Luis in catechism classes when he was seven, and soon thereafter Luis had his first communion. María Luisa and Rogerio had come to an understanding years before. His mother would guide Luis' spiritual upbringing, and his father would teach him about the life in the practical world. Thus, María Luisa determined Luis would go to his first Catholic retreat when he turned thirteen.

Luis found the retreat a powerful experience. The director, Father Amando Llorente, was a Jesuit with a persuasive personality. The hardest part for Luis was maintaining silence in the monastery during the three days of the retreat. A strapping, energetic boy on the threshold of adolescence, he loved to socialize, and although he was the youngest of the group of thirty, he knew more than half of the participants as schoolmates or friends of his parents. He found Father Llorente's homilies a bit insipid, but since he was there to please his mother, he tried to make the most of the required meditation periods which followed Father Llorente's talks. It was useless. More real than Jesus was the warm stirring between his legs as he remembered the sight of that voluptuous woman a few steps ahead of him on Comercio Street the week before.

Luis left the retreat vowing to live a life of continence. He was going to eradicate impure thoughts about females from his mind, and above all, he was going to refrain from masturbating. His resolution lasted fewer than twenty-four hours, for the next day, when he went downtown, he saw a very beautiful young woman and he couldn't help getting excited over her sensual body.

When Luis was ready to begin his formal education, Rogerio bought a large house in the Garrido subdivision of the city of Camagüey. Several boys and girls of Luis' age lived close by. Alberto and Juan Sánchez lived across the street, and Enrique Bueno and two younger sisters resided two houses to the west of the Recios.

With his new friends, Luis rode the bus to Colegio Maristas, a prestigious all-male school run by the Marist Brothers.

On Saturday mornings, the boys gathered at one of the empty lots in the barrio to play baseball, their favorite pastime. The two oldest players were always the captains and selected the teams. Initially, Luis only got to play because he owned a bat, a glove, and several balls, but as time went on, Luis improved and was often the captain's first choice. After baseball later in the afternoon, Luis and his friends usually went to see a Hollywood picture with Spanish subtitles, always preceded by an episode of Superman, the Lone Ranger, or a similar series which, like baseball, inspired Luis to dream of becoming a hero. If he could not play for the New York Yankees, he wanted to be a brave general or, even better, a famous politician like his great uncle, Manuel *"El Honrado,"* who might have been president of Cuba had he not been killed in a duel.

Among Luis' friends was Pepe Fernández, who appeared to be older than his thirteen years. Pepe's father, Pedro, a well-established cattle rancher, fancied himself a ladies' man. In reality, he regularly frequented the city's red-light district. One day Pedro decided to take his son to one of the houses of ill-repute, and Pepe told his friends every detail of his memorable experience. The group did not believe Pepe's father would take him to such a place, but Pepe's vivid description finally convinced them. When Pepe proposed a visit to the whorehouse to his friends, Luis and Alberto Sánchez took him up on it.

"Cachita's House," as the place was called, was located in the west side of the city, two blocks from the main highway. It was a plain, one-story brick structure on the corner of a long row of adjoining houses.

The trio prepared for their escapade by telling their parents one Friday night they were going to the movies. Then they took a bus to the café located two blocks south of Cachita's. An effeminate man in his early twenties with bleached hair greeted Pepe, the first to knock at the door.

"Well, well, what do we have here?" the young man asked as he placed one hand on his hip with an exaggerated gesture while looking approvingly at the timid young men.

"We'd like to come in for a while," Pepe answered nervously.

"But you're too young."

"Cachita said I could come any time. I'm Pedro Fernández's son."

"Welllll, that's another matter. Pleeeeasse come in," the man purred as he turned and sashayed down the hall.

Inside the forbidden place, they entered a large living room where a couple, quietly talking, stopped to look at them and snickered. Pepe, Alberto, and Luis hurried to the next room where several couples were engaged in animated conversation with a well-preserved and saucy older woman around a large, well-stocked bar. When the woman saw the boys, she approached them.

"*Buenas noches, muchachos.* Aren't you Pedro's son?" she asked Pepe.

"*Sí*, Cachita."

"And who are these handsome young fellows?"

"Alberto Sánchez and Luis Recio."

"I have many Sánchezes as clients," replied Cachita. "And you," she said pointing to Luis, "are you by any chance related to Bernabé Recio?"

"He's my grandfather."

"Welllll, I'll be darned," said Cachita with half-amused, yet tender eyes. "Your grandfather was my first lover. He took away my sweet virginity. What a persuasive rascal he was!"

Luis knew Bernabé had earned a reputation as a womanizer during his bachelor days. Tall and handsome with large, captivating green eyes and beautiful long eyelashes, Bernabé learned early in his life that those eyes could cast a spell on any woman, and he exploited their seductive power shamelessly. By the time he was twenty-five, Bernabé had fathered several illegitimate children, all of them with the Recio hallmark--those unmistakable emerald green eyes.

Looking at his friends, Luis didn't know how to react to Cachita's revelation. Cachita continued in a light tone, "And you, little devil," she said affectionately pinching his cheek, "have inherited Bernabé's eyes. But enough of that. When you're ready, let me know if you feel like visiting with any of the girls. They're all very sweet and obliging." She winked at the boys and returned to the bar where other clients waited.

The trio stayed for twenty more minutes, making nervous conversation while sipping their drinks and glancing from the corner of their eyes at the goings on around the whorehouse.

It took three trips to Cachita's house before Luis and Alberto got up the nerve to select a partner. Luis chose a small-breasted young woman named Carmen because she had made eyes at him on his previous visit and her feigned interest excited him. After two stiff drinks of rum and coke, better known as *Cuba Libre*, Luis took a deep breath and courageously announced, "I'm ready."

Luis approached Carmen, who sat on a lavender sofa on the other side of the room with some of the other girls, and asked her, "Are you free?"

Carmen smiled as she stood up and motioned for Luis to follow her. They walked down a dimly lit narrow hall and entered a dark, humid room which smelled of stale perfume and which Carmen illuminated by turning on the light, and after latching the door, Carmen took Luis' hands in hers and looking him in the eyes, asked sweetly, "Is this your first time, darling?"

"Oh no," said Luis hurriedly, shaking his head.

"Let me undress you, sugar," said Carmen, who proceeded to take off his clothes. "What a lovely body you have," she exclaimed admiringly when she had finished. "I'm gonna have some fun with you!" Then removing her clothes, she threw back the spread, jumped into bed, and signaled for Luis to hop in.

Before he complied, Luis picked up his pants from the chair, took a condom out of a pocket, and handed it to Carmen as if he were presenting her a gift.

"Oh, *mi amor*," said Carmen holding the condom like a cherry on a stem as she looked up at Luis standing beside the bed.

""Don't you know you've got to get it up before I can do anything with this? This is your first time, isn't it?"

Smiling timidly, Luis assented.

"Don't you worry about a thing, my precious one," Carmen said. Tenderly, she reached up and pulled him onto the bed, and she patiently proceeded to guide him through the labyrinth of lovemaking.

When Luis' initiation was completed, he disengaged, turned over on his back, and closed his eyes as if to savor the experience. When he opened them again, he noticed a statue the Virgin of Charity, the patron saint of Cuba, on a shelf on the opposite wall. Peering down at him benignly, her gaze penetrated his body and soul.

Rolling out of bed, Luis grabbed his clothes, ran into the small bathroom, and became sick. When he came back fully dressed, he asked Carmen if the statue ever bothered her in her work.

"No," answered Carmen sitting in a robe on the side of the bed with her legs crossed, "*La Virgen* keeps me healthy."

Reaching into his billfold, Luis gave her two *pesos* and left the room a bit ashamed. He had been naked in front of the Virgin, and he had paid for sex, something he was sure his Grandfather Bernabé had never done, not even with Cachita.

Chapter 5
Sierra Maestra, April 17, 1958

Luis Recio jumped to his feet and splashed his face with water from his canteen. Excitement swept through him, even pushing away the soreness in his thighs and groin as he recalled the high purpose for which he had come to this strange, secluded place. In an instant, he felt invigorated and ready for his first meeting with Fidel Castro, the enigmatic leader of the Revolution.

Following the guard up a steep trail, Luis inhaled deeply to savor the full effect of the rarefied mountain air and the aroma of exotic plants and flowers. Luis could identify the fragrant smell of the red hibiscus whose leaves yielded their fragrance after showers and the now familiar odor of horse and mule manure. In the early dawn, as the fog fought a losing battle with the sun, Luis saw the grandeur of the Cuban jungle for the first time, a wild array of trees, bushes, ferns, bamboo and vines-- beautiful and ominous vines wrapped around other vines and around tree trunks--the perfect place to spawn a revolution. Above the sounds of insects which he had heard since coming into the jungle, he now heard a hum of a different sort.

"A generator?" he asked the guard.

"It came last week. Things have really improved lately around here. It was tough when we had to get by with pine torches and candles and do without salt for our food!"

For a moment Luis thought of the flat acres of sugar cane under sunlight, morning *café con leche,* and crackers with butter on the veranda, the symmetry and simplicity of his other life, but these images vanished when the jungle opened onto a small clearing where the *bohío* which served as headquarters stood. The guard might have thought that conditions had improved, but to Luis the *bohío* seemed crude and primitive with its straw ceiling, wooden walls, and square openings for windows on either side of the door. Approaching it, Luis smelled the familiar and pungent odor of a cigar, and upon entering, he saw in the dimness of the morning light a scene that made his heart leap.

There, before a makeshift table sat Fidel Castro himself, studying a map under a pale electric light. He was smoking a cigar and gesticulating excitedly to two others who, like Castro, were dressed in olive green fatigues. They were discussing plans for an attack, and Luis knew instinctively the man smoking a pipe was "Che" Guevara, whose wispy beard and searching eyes made him look more like a student actor than a soldier in a revolution.

While Luis was wondering if the man he had come to see was going to recognize him, Castro leaned back from his map, took a puff on his cigar, turned toward the door, opened his arms wide, and with a smile bright enough to disperse the remaining fog on the mountains, greeted Luis as if he were the prodigal son.

"Ah, Recio!" he pronounced, motioning with both hands for Luis to come and receive his embrace.

"We've been waiting for you for two days. The arms you brought came at just the right time. Let me see if I got it straight: a tripod machine gun, two Mazden automatics, five M-1's, three Johnsons, and a total of two thousand rounds. Recio, you're a mobile armory. Che, here, I want you to meet one of the members of Cuba's oligarchy."

As Guevara tentatively shook Luis' hand, Castro went on, at first addressing Che more than Luis. "Here is the great nephew of *"El Honrado"* Recio, one of the most honest politicians Cuba ever had. Had Colonel Recio not died prematurely, the history of Cuba might have been different. Still, the Recios are oligarchs. Your family has what, Recio, thirty thousand acres of land?"

Luis assented and to his own surprise found himself saying, "Yes, Dr. Castro, we have thirty thousand, and I believe your father has ten thousand."

Castro roared at the comparison. Even the solemn Guevara smiled.

"Regardless of our fathers, the guns you have brought make us brothers in the revolution. Here, I want you to meet Ramiro Valdés, one of our best soldiers."

Luis reached out across the large-scale map of Cuba to shake hands with a cold-faced youth with short, kinky, reddish hair. Neither of Castro's lieutenants seemed eager to welcome him, but Fidel made up for their sullenness with his own extravagant hospitality.

"Sit down, Luis," he said, and turning his head to a side door added, "Ofelia, bring our newcomer coffee." To Luis' surprise, Castro wanted to talk about the strike in Havana.

"Faustino Pérez has told us why he thinks it failed, but I want your own impression. Tell me what happened."

The attention focused on him immensely pleased Luis, but at the same time he was a little ill at ease since Castro was set to devour his every word. Leaning forward in his wooden chair with one hand on the table and the other on his right knee with the cigar, Castro gave the impression of a bearded lion ready to leap upon its prey.

"Well," Luis began, "I think it failed because the Communists sabotaged it. There were other minor reasons of course-- poor planning, lack of arms, the failure of student directorate and the Auténtico Party to support us, and the fear of Batista's reprisals. Only the 26th of July really took part."

"Goddamn it, Che," Castro uttered, leaning back, hitting the table, and covering a sizeable portion of the Windward Passage with the palm of his left hand. "You can't depend on those fucking Communists for anything."

"As I tried to tell you, we should have made a pact with the Communists," Che replied.

Castro, irritated by subject, took off his glasses, threw them on the table, and rubbed his eyes vigorously with the palms of his hands. Breathing deeply, he questioned Luis about the underground finances in Havana.

As Luis responded, making the report as rosy as possible but still keeping his assessment realistic, he noticed the entrance into the room of a woman whose large penetrating almond eyes scrutinized him. The subtle curves of her body exuded a natural health and radiance, but her smile hinted of sadness. Her clean freshness, her soft demeanor and beauty sharply contrasted with the primitive surroundings of the camp and the sweaty figures seated around the table. She timidly acknowledged Luis when Castro stopped Luis' financial report to introduce her. "This is Ofelia Reyes, one of our volunteers," Fidel explained. After serving coffee, she walked back across the earthen floor, her slim, rounded hips moving with seductive grace. She may make *El Comandante's* coffee, Luis thought, but she could easily be the wine bearer of the gods.

Castro sensed his interest. As she left the room, he added, "Ofelia Reyes and her brother have been with us for two months. They joined us after the army slaughtered their family for giving us food. She's one of several women in our camp. We treat them with respect here."

After dinner, Luis recounted his experience in the underground. It was raining outside, and in the *bohío* that served as a mess hall, a group of men had gathered around him. Appreciating their interest in the exotic life in faraway Havana, Luis regaled them with vivid descriptions of how the underground operated in the cities, and as he talked, it dawned on him how totally foreign his life was to most of these peasant fighters. While he was giving his opinion of what went wrong with the Presidential Palace attack, he noticed Ofelia and two other women seated at a table in a corner. In the twilight he could see she was closely following his every word as he spoke about sabotage in Havana.

He made a point to find out more about her, and the soldiers supplied the details. A few weeks earlier, on February 16 near Pino del Agua, a small village located on a slope of the Bayamesa Mountain in the middle of the Sierra Maestra, there had been a skirmish between Raúl Castro's column and the army. When Raúl's column retreated, the army, suspecting some of the peasants were collaborating with the guerrillas, ordered them outside their *bohíos* and machine-gunned them to death. Ofelia and her brother, Teófilo, had gone to a well for fresh water and were returning with full buckets when they heard the shots. They fell to the ground and lay under bushes as if dead until nightfall when they returned to the village and learned their parents and older sister were among the victims. When their dead were buried, they sought out the rebels.

That night he could not fall asleep for thinking about Ofelia. He was concerned for her plight and supportive of her role in the Revolution. But the last memory in his mind before he succumbed to sleep was the way her hand smoothed the already tight denim covering her lovely bottom as she left the room that morning after bringing the coffee.

Chapter 6

Early in his life Papá Bernabé took it upon himself to teach Luis how to appreciate beautiful women. Luis remembered strolling down Comercio Street in downtown Camagüey when he was seven with his grandfather, who always pointed out the many attributes of attractive women as they passed by.

"Luis, look at those two beauties coming toward us. What do you think, my boy? Which one do you prefer? The one with the long legs or the other with the exquisite hips?" Bernabé took off his hat as the women passed by and with a slight bow and a devilish smile on his lips greeted the pretty women, "*Buenos días* to you, lovely damsels."

Bernabé was a master at the *piropo*. He told Luis that women were not supposed to acknowledge *piropos* from a man, for if they did, the man would understand the woman was giving him "the come on," and he would behave accordingly. Luis learned from his grandfather how witty *piropos*, as delicate and seductive as flowers thrown at the ladies' feet, delighted women, and later had the opportunity to experience a *piropo* from the female perspective. He had gone shopping one morning with María Luisa and Isabel, and as they were about to enter *El Encanto* department store, a middle-aged man standing by the entrance commented graciously, "I do believe the mother is as beautiful as the daughter." Luis, who had been following his mother and sister, shot a nasty look at the man and proceeded to hold his mother's hand in a protective gesture. When he looked at his mother and Isabel for approval, he could see they both were making an effort not to laugh, for they had enjoyed the *piropo*.

Bernabé's tutelage continued through Luis' teenage years, and his grandfather encouraged him to go out with girls from the Camagüey

Tennis Club. "Ah, Luis, look how pretty she is," Bernabé would say of a friend's granddaughter. "You should meet her at the movie some afternoon or take her to a dance."

María Luisa openly objected to her father-in-law's involvement. "Rogerio," she complained, "Luis is only thirteen. He's much too young to begin dating. Your father will only succeed in molding our son into a spitting image of himself. What do you think?"

Rogerio made light of her concern, "*Mi amor*, Luis is handsome and well-built. He looks older than thirteen, and he's much more mature than most boys his age. Let him be."

Unconvinced, María Luisa continued to argue that Bernabé's behavior was in no way worthy of imitation by her son.

According to tradition in Cuba, an older member of the family always accompanied couples on their dates. The presence of the chaperon distinguished a young woman's reputation since no family of standing would ever approve their son or daughter to date without a chaperon. The chaperon guarded the young couple's virtue and guaranteed the good behavior of young women and men.

After dating several young women in Camagüey for more than a year, Luis was frustrated. In order to kiss and fondle them, he would have to become their *novio*, or boyfriend, but Luis had no desire to commit to any one girl. There had to be some middle ground between Cachita's girls and those from reputable families. Margarita Pérez, daughter of Catalina, the Recio cook, offered still another possibility. He had never thought of Margarita as anything but a friend, with her black hair and eyes and olive skin, but she unfortunately fell into a disreputable status by accident of birth. She was also four years older than Luis.

Catalina, like most of their other half-dozen servants, had been with the Recios as long as Luis could remember, cooking for them wherever they lived. She came from Barcelona, Spain, widowed in 1934 by the Catalan workers' revolt against the Madrid government. Luis associated the mother with the aroma and taste of food and the daughter with the smells and charms of the opposite sex. Both he and Isabel played with Margarita, the leader in all their games.

One summer afternoon when Luis was nine, Margarita took him into her mother's bedroom in the servants' quarters, threw him upon the bed, and covered him with her body, uttering "Oh, you sweet little thing. Come to me. Let me hold you close!" Luis had no idea how long the rolling and tumbling and sweet talk went on; experiencing a strange yearning concentrated between his legs, he only knew he loved every minute of it. For months later he asked Margarita to "please play house," but she always replied coldly, "No, we can't do that anymore."

After several visits to Cachita's place, the sight of Margaritas's well-proportioned body working around the house drove Luis mad with desire. He would initiate pillow fights with her in the upstairs hallway with the purpose of brushing against her breasts and pinching her curvaceous fanny. One day in the hallway he whispered, "Margarita, remember when we were children? Remember when we played 'house'? Let's do that again, Margarita." While she giggled, Luis pleaded with his green eyes flashing, "Let me make love to you!"

Initially Margarita refused Luis' suggestion, but, undeniably attracted to him, she knew sex between them was only a matter of time. After several furtive petting sessions in the pantry, they agreed to meet at 3:00 a.m. one morning in a room formerly occupied by one of the nannies. Catalina would be sound asleep by then and not likely to hear her daughter's departure.

Luis had been eagerly waiting for fifteen minutes when Margarita arrived. She was dressed in a light robe, and as they embraced and started to kiss, he realized that under her robe she was naked. When he untied the robe, it fell to the floor. How lovely she was! Her breasts were firm and inviting. Cupping each in his hands, he was overcome with pleasure. He took off his robe and began to suckle her breasts, evoking soft moans from her. Consumed by desire, they fell into the small bed. "I'm ready for you," she whispered in a hoarse voice. It surprised Luis how easily he entered her, and the next instant he exploded inside her. They roamed over each other's bodies until the coming of dawn.

After each encounter with Margarita, Luis was lost in sensation. For hours afterward, he felt her presence on his skin, and at the Marist Brothers School, radiant images of her luscious body filled his mind during the long hours of classes. How was it, he wondered, that such a treasure had been in his own house all those years while he had gone traipsing off to a whorehouse with his friends and to movies and dances with stiff-armed debutantes? From this point on, there would be no need for him to look elsewhere.

Luis often wondered how long the affair with Margarita would go on, but he would never know since neither he nor Margarita had any choice in the occurrence that brought it to an end.

"Luis," a serious voice greeted him as he entered his darkened bedroom after an early morning rendezvous with Margarita. His father, standing just inside the door in his bathrobe smoking a cigarette, was obviously perturbed.

"Close the door and sit down, Luis," Rogerio ordered in a stern voice as he turned on the bedside light.

Fearing the worst, Luis obeyed.

"We know what you're doing," his father began. "Your mother went to the bathroom to get some toilet items, and when she happened to look out the upstairs window, she saw Margarita going across the lawn toward the empty servants' quarters. She checked your bed . . . and . . . well, Luis... she's very upset. How long has this been going on?"

"Only two or three months," Luis answered defensively.

"Son," Rogerio began again, "your behavior is completely unacceptable. As a result, your mother and I have decided to send you to Southern Military Academy. I'll inform the director at your school I'm transferring you in the middle of the year. As far as Margarita is concerned, she too will be sent away. I'll find her a good job in Havana."

"Oh, Papá, don't blame her!" Luis exclaimed. "I was the one who started this!"

"Sit down, Luis," Rogerio said firmly. "Don't raise your voice at me. Let me tell you something, Luis. Catalina's husband wasn't killed in the fighting in España. She was never married."

"I don't care!" Luis said, emphasizing each word. "What does that matter, Papá?"

"Over a year ago, Catalina told your mother you were making passes at Margarita. María Luisa wanted me to talk to you then, but I never did. Damn it, Luis, I never thought you would actually bed one of our servants!"

Long after his father left, Luis Recio sat on the side of the bed with his head in his hands, his mind awhirl with images of a shattered world and fears of what his future held.

Rogerio, María Luisa, and Luis left Havana Harbor late on a February afternoon of 1948 on the *Florida*, the Miami ferry.

How cruel, Luis thought, as he lay awake in his bed on the ferry. His parents' decision to imprison Luis in a military academy for falling in love with Margarita seemed totally unjust.

Luis had barely closed his eyes on the ferry when Rogerio shook him and told him to get up and get dressed. It was time for breakfast, but Luis refused to eat.

While his parents waited in their cabin for the *Florida* to reach Miami, Luis stood on deck at the gunwale and stared at the beautiful, calm sea. He was thinking about Margarita Pérez and her unfortunate birth legacy. No matter how intelligent she was, Margarita would struggle all her life.

As Luis was leaving the deck, he saw a huge blue marlin leap from the water in chase of a shoal of flying fish. The large-finned fish devoured its catch in mid-air, and the unexpected scene was over with in a second, the sea again tranquil as if nothing had happened.

At that moment, however, Luis Recio was struck with a profound revelation. Luis noticed the shape of the marlin as it went sailing through the air-- the big, beautiful, sun-lit, sea-drenched marlin reminded him of Cuba! Cuba, long and slim, rose from the blue-green sea, and, like the marlin, her oligarchy fed on smaller fry, people like Ramoncito and Margarita.

Luis turned his gaze to see if anyone else witnessed the scene. The reaction on the upper deck convinced him he was not dreaming. Both passengers and crew had seen the drama, one or two still pointing to the spot where the leap had taken place. Luis heard one man nearby say the prey was definitely flying fish which, he went on to say, were also devoured by large birds.

As he watched the Florida coast come into sight, Luis realized he had a better nickname for himself than Pony. He was tempted to tell his father: "Papá, from now on call me The Flying Fish!"

Chapter 7
Sierra Maestra, April 1958

As the days wore on, Luis saw more and more of Ofelia. In the absence of her brother, Teófilo, who had joined Raúl's column in the Sierra Cristal mountains, he felt the need to protect her. Her eyes gave away her interest in Luis. To him she was like a wild, delicate flower in a beautiful but savage country of men at war. He often visited the kitchen to see her on the pretext of offering his advice on the preparation of the simple food she and the other women cooked for the rebels.

Ofelia found it hard to believe that a man would have such knowledge about food, but Luis would humorously comment that many great chefs were men. The kitchen staff laughed when he inquired if they had herbs for the black beans, and it became a joke around camp when Luis put in a request to carriers for cumin, oregano, and olive oil. The head of the kitchen staff, Ana, a heavy peasant woman, was very taken by Luis when he made one of his regular stops to check on the cooking. Luis promised the women that after the Revolution he would invite them to Havana for the most magnificent meal they would ever have.

Early one morning, Luis was surprised to see Ofelia standing by a table under a tree with several of the men listening attentively to her. Curious, he approached and realized she was teaching them how to read. It didn't take him long to recognize she was a talented teacher. From seeing her work in the rudimentary kitchen and knowing she was from the mountains, he had taken for granted she was not well educated. That evening when he saw her outside the mess hall, he took the opportunity to seek more information about her.

"I was a school teacher for a year until our school in Pilón was closed because of this war," said Ofelia.

"Tell me about it," Luis requested.

"Life works in strange ways," she said with a sigh. "My parents and sister were murdered by Batista's army. But it was Batista, while he was head of the army, who started to build Civic Rural Schools in backward areas to improve conditions because some of the teachers did not want to come to the countryside to teach us peasants. They all wanted to go to the big cities, or at least to towns not too far from them.

"I was fortunate. I was able to go to the normal school in Pino de Agua where I had a dedicated teacher, José Amaro, who inspired me to learn. Under his tutelage, I completed my first six years of school, and he helped me get a scholarship to a vocational school in Santa Clara. After graduating I returned to Manzanillo, and later I came back to Pilón to teach at the one-room school which closed when the fighting got bad. So I went to live with my parents, stupidly thinking I would be safe out in the middle of the mountains."

"Ofelia, it's a small world," Luis said, taking her hand. "The man who started the Culture Corps of the army is General Arístides Sosa de Quesada. His two sons, Ari and Rafael, are friends of mine, and I've heard them tell me about sergeants who used to teach in the Civic Rural Schools. After the 1940 Constitution went into effect, civilian teachers like you replaced the sergeants. It has always puzzled me how Batista, who started as a defender of the people's interest, could change so much."

"Power corrupts," Ofelia commented.

"Ofelia," Luis replied, looking into her lovely eyes, "when you brought us coffee the other day, I thought you were beautiful, and I also sensed you were an intelligent woman."

"You see," Ofelia interrupted, "here we all do menial tasks, but I'm also in charge of teaching soldiers how to read."

Luis admired Ofelia for all she had endured. She was wise beyond her years because of the misfortunes in her life. He understood and honored her conviction to the Revolution, not only as a mean of avenging her family's death, but also because she wanted to improve life for her people. Beyond that, her beauty and sensuality compensated for this god-forsaken place.

They talked for hours, and when Luis went to his *bohío* for the night, he thanked his lucky stars for placing this remarkable woman close to him in such an unusual setting. He knew he could easily fall in love with Ofelia.

During Luis' first week in the mountains, Castro urged him to learn all he could about the operation of the camp, the columns, and the use of weapons. Luis cooperated gladly, realizing the difference between smuggling weapons and using them. He had never had a fondness for firearms and had always thought rifle training at SMA was the most boring activity in the world. Now, though, the M-1 looked different, and he came to know it again. He also learned about the strategic uses of mines, grenades, home-made bombs, and other weapons.

The discipline, camaraderie, morale of the soldiers, and the relative sophistication of the camp surprised Luis. A radio station regularly broadcasted news; generators satisfied their electrical needs; and a blacksmith shop had been set up to repair damaged arms. A crude bomb factory had recently been started. There were also a tannery, a butcher shop, and even a crude hospital.

Food was plentiful. Beans, corn, and rice were staples, as was pork. Beef, while not so abundant, was regularly confiscated from the big landowners, the *latifundistas*, and shared equally with the peasants in the Sierra. Luis thought it wise to enlist them to the guerrilla cause, and Castro's policy of returning prisoners unharmed to Batista's bewildered army was inspiring. It was a fairly efficient and well-run organization, considering the ruggedness of the terrain and the difficulty in obtaining supplies.

As Luis wandered about the camp, he discovered he and Castro were not the only lawyers around. The other was Dr. Humberto Sorí Marín, the auditor general of the rebel army. He was an efficient and affable man who knew several of Luis' friends. Castro had asked him, he said, to begin thinking about the land reform law that would be implemented after their victory. Luis thought the idea a bit premature, but a good one, nevertheless. Luis told Sorí Marín of his arguments with his father over that very topic, agreeing with Sorí Marín that an equitable redistribution of the land was needed. The question, they concluded, was how to go about it without jeopardizing agricultural production.

One of the most colorful of the unusual crew of officers in the mountains was Captain Miguel Ochoa, by his own admission a playboy from a well-to-do family in Santiago. He had joined the guerrillas six months earlier and by his acts of valor had risen quickly to the rank of captain. He had brought a guitar with him, and after the establishment of a base camp in La Mesa Valley, he entertained the troops by playing and singing for them. Luis found himself singing duets and parodies with Captain Ochoa to the delight of their comrades. A couple of times they were joined by one of Fidel's confidants, Camilo Cienfuegos, who, in addition to his reputation as a fearless fighter, was also known as a free spirit.

Of all the people Luis met, Major Che Guevara intrigued him the most. A physician, intellectual, and combat strategist, Guevara was difficult to approach. Luis had heard tales about his exploits in the field and his struggle with asthma. He had been so weakened during some operations by the mere effort to breathe that he was forced to use his rifle as a walking stick.

As a newcomer, Luis heard Che lecture about the fundamentals of guerrilla warfare which could, he said, be reduced to three principles—constant mobility, constant mistrust, and constant vigilance. Luis approached him after his presentation but found him aloof and, Luis believed, suspicious of him.

"I noticed, Doctor Guevara, that you emphasized constant mobility in your talk, and I was wondering if a camp such as this contradicts that idea?"

"You sound like a lawyer," Che said with a weak smile, "I don't like the idea of permanency until the final goal is reached. In the meantime, there ought to be continuous struggle and sacrifice. I think it's possible to weaken the revolutionary spirit with prosaic activities like singing and laughing. There seem to be two types of rebels—those who keep their uniforms clean and ready to go to Havana to cash in on the glory, and those who are willing to go out to the actual combat."

Luis knew he had been speared, and Che's eyes made it clear he was not one of the Argentine's favorites.

In spite of the uniqueness of the place and the personalities living there, Luis soon became fidgety with inaction and asked Castro for a specific assignment. Castro replied that he had plenty in mind for Luis and would let him know soon what his duties would be. Luis knew something big was about to take place. All of the columns were returning to the headquarters east of Pico Turquino for some sort of concentrated action in which he, too, would have a part, as he inferred from Castro's remark.

Two days later, Castro summoned Luis to report to headquarters in the late afternoon. There, Fidel ordered him to put together a firing squad to execute a prisoner returning with one of the columns. When Luis inquired about a trial, Castro looked at him incredulously and said, "You idiot, what do you mean 'trial'? The bastard is a stool pigeon, and that's all the evidence we need. He's already had all the trial he's going to get."

"*Comandante*," said Luis, "I can't condone killing a man without a trial."

Castro pounded on the table in disgust. "My dear Recio, you're not up here to play a damn lawyer. You're here to obey orders! This worthless traitor has already received his sentence!"

"Then I respectfully decline to participate," Luis responded.

"Hell, Recio!" Castro shouted. "We've just barely been able to stay alive and ahead of the army, and you come up here and ask us to worry about legal niceties. I'll get someone with more balls than you to do it. Get the hell out of here!"

Trying to control his anger, Luis and left, went back to his *bohío*, threw himself into his hammock, and stared at the thatched ceiling. Many questions rolled through his mind: What else could I have done? Should I have tried harder to reason with him? Don't I have the right to question him? These questions took on more urgency when an hour later he heard distant shots. Goose bumps popped out all over his body.

He lay in the hammock through the evening meal and dozed off to sleep. When he was awakened by one of the soldiers asking him if he wanted to participate in a game of domino, he politely declined and took a solitary walk. Luis had not gone far when Captain Húber Matos, appearing out of nowhere, joined him. In mid-April, Luis and Matos had spent a day together learning how to detonate mines.

"I heard about your encounter with Fidel," Matos began, going right to the point.

"I respect what you said to him. I've had the same problem with *El Comandante.* Apparently Fidel feels he has to put down his subordinates, particularly if they question his judgment or challenge his authority."

"Well, I couldn't help speaking my mind. I refuse to kill anybody without a fair trial," answered Luis.

"I don't blame you, but we walk a fine line between life and death here in the Sierra. Furthermore, I've come to the conclusion that Castro expects total loyalty from us. Don't take it personally, Luis. I bet this won't be the last time you clash with him." Patting Luis on the back, Matos left Luis and returned to the camp.

As Luis was about to come back to his quarters, he saw Ofelia approaching him, her face indicating she had learned of Castro's outburst with Luis as well.

"Luis, I'm sorry for what happened, but you did what was honorable. Since the army murdered my family, I get sick to my stomach when I hear the firing squad. In the eyes of the army, my parents were guilty because they helped the rebels with food, but they never had a chance to ask for mercy. The soldiers shot them like dogs."

As she spoke, Luis saw her face tighten and her eyes moisten.

"Let's go where we can talk," he suggested. When they were outside the clearing of the camp, he put his arm around her and guided her to a smaller clearing which had been partially filled by a huge fallen tree, a victim of lightning. It seemed designed to stop any traveler from going further and to demand a look at the sweep of the mountains bathed now in the blue haze of the twilight. At the tree, they turned not toward the majestic view of the Sierra but toward each other. As they embraced, Ofelia began to cry. Tenderly Luis passed his hand through her hair. "I wonder if all this struggle is worth it," Ofelia said in desperation.

They talked, kissed, and caressed each other until darkness covered the scene they had not come to see.

Chapter 8

Though a native of Baltimore, Maryland, Luis Recio returned to the United States for the first time when the limousine in which he sat rolled off the *Florida* and the ferry slip in Miami. Riding north on up the interminable Highway One, Luis looked out the window and gazed at the Atlantic whenever it came into view. There was little reason for him to talk but plenty of cause for reflection. Who were these people in front of him? They seemed like strangers. María Luisa, the force behind his banishment, rarely spoke. His father, who was caught in the middle, remained uncharacteristically silent.

Slowly but surely, María Luisa had spiritually emasculated "The Colt," stripping him of his natural energies and filling the vacuum with silly notions of family honor and tradition. But, how could he think such things of his parents? A hundred memories of their affection flooded Luis's mind: Rogerio placing him on Daiquirí, taking him to the races in Havana, going with him on fishing trips to the keys off the coast of Santa Cruz del Sur, showing him off at the bar in the Liceo; María Luisa holding him in her lap reading stories, inspecting him before a date or mass with the fussiness only a mother could show, taking him and Isabel to the Havana Yacht Club, kneeling between him and Isabel at prayer in church, and most cherished of all, kissing him goodnight throughout his childhood.

How could he dare accuse her of coldness and Rogerio of spinelessness? They had done many charitable deeds for house servants and sugar-mill employees, and Rogerio, instead of toeing some domestic line defined by his wife, did what he wanted. Though her sense of duty to family and church sometimes seemed exaggerated,

María Luisa could display spontaneous love that came straight from the heart.

Luis came within a hair of crying out an apology, but thoughts of Papá Bernabé held him back. Yes, Luis regretted disappointing his parents, but, no, he would not apologize for what had evoked their stern reaction. Dear old Bernabé was still with him, steadfast in his defense of love.

Travelling northward toward Tennessee, the Recios spent the first night in Jacksonville, Florida, and the next in Greenville, South Carolina. When they left Cuba, the temperature was in the low seventies, but the farther north they moved, the colder the weather became. The January landscape of the Carolinas appeared desolate and lifeless.

In Cuba the land always vibrated with life, but here winter took its annual toll, stripping the trees, searing the grass, and leaving animals in a suspended state between life and death. Horses and mules stood like statues in the open fields. Herds of dairy and beef cattle huddled around barns and haystacks, the warmth from their own bodies their only protection against the elements.

As they ascended the mountains near Asheville, North Carolina, Luis saw snow for the first time in his life, not as it was falling but as it lay on the distant peaks, giving the impression those giants had been knighted by nature for their eminence. He had been to the Sierra de Cubitas Mountains in Camagüey Province on weekend trips with the family, but he had never seen anything as majestic as the Appalachian Mountains. For the first time, Luis Recio heard the heater come on in the limousine, Rogerio remarking he should have checked it before leaving home to see if the system worked. Thankfully it did. As Luis listened to the howling wind and looked at the awesome sights around him, he shuddered and wondered if he could survive in this land.

They slept in Asheville at the Grove Park Inn Hotel and began the last leg of their journey the next day, passing through Knoxville and arriving late in the afternoon in Lewiston, some twenty miles southeast of Nashville. Luis felt as though he had traveled through eternity and arrived at the end of the universe. Is this where I am to spend the next three and a half years of my life? he thought as he surveyed the sleepy-looking little town of wooden houses and tree-lined streets at dusk. "It doesn't look like much in the winter, but in the spring, it's charming," Rogerio acknowledged, as if reading his son's mind. "You'll come to like it. The people here are down to earth and very nice. They get along well with the school too. Little country towns like this have made the United States the great nation it is."

The next morning the Recios headed west down the main street of Lewiston and turned onto a narrow, tree-lined avenue running through a campus. The complex of fortress-like buildings with towers and parapets reminded Luis of buildings he had seen in storybook pictures of foreign and ancient places. At the end of the street, Rogerio drove the limousine under the arcade of the administration building and parked in front of the main doors.

Getting out of the car in the arcade, Rogerio ascended the steps of the main building with a cigarette in his left hand as if he were coming into his own home in Camagüey. Luis waited in the car with his mother. "Luis," she said, looking straight ahead through the windshield of the limousine, "I want you to promise me two things. I want you to write as often as possible, and I want you to go to mass regularly."

When Luis did not respond, María Luisa looked back at him and asked, "Luis Recio, did you hear me?" "*Sí*, Mamá," her son muttered.

Within a few minutes, Rogerio descended the steps of the building with an aging gentleman in uniform. "This is Colonel Whitney, Superintendent of SMA, and this, Colonel Whitney, is my dear wife, María Luisa." It was rumored among SMA cadets that Colonel Whitney, nicknamed "Sleeping Jesus," had never uttered a word in his life, but Luis was positive he took his mother's hand in both of his own and said, "It's such a pleasure to meet you, Mrs. Recio." Then, when Rogerio asked Luis to step out of the car and meet the Superintendent, Luis heard "Sleeping Jesus" say softly, "This is a momentous occasion, having two generations of Recios join us here at SMA. It confirms my belief we must be doing something right to enroll so many sons of fathers who came to SMA."

As his father and mother left him in his room with his unpacked bags, Luis had never felt so forlorn in all his life. In his rebellion, he resolved not to watch them leave, but after a moment he walked to the end of the dormitory hallway and followed them with his eyes as they entered the limousine and drove away.

Less than a week later, Luis talked to his father again, this time by phone. It had taken him half a day to get his call through. Rogerio and María Luisa were vacationing in Williamsburg, Virginia, which somewhat infuriated him, but the effort in reaching them would have been worth the trouble if he had been able to convince them how bad his situation really was. He had located his parents through his Great Uncle Heinrich Heymann who lived in Washington, D.C. since they had left an itinerary of their trip with the Heymanns. Homesick and frightened, Luis made his predicament sound as unbearable as possible.

"I'm miserable," he told his father. "Please come and take me back to Cuba *por favor*, Papá."

"I'm sorry, son, you'll just have to grin and bear it," Rogerio answered with finality. "With time, I'm sure you'll come to like the school."

When Luis hung up the receiver, the silence that followed was the loneliest sound he had ever heard.

Chapter 9
Sierra Maestra, April-June, 1958

E arly the next morning, Luis was called into Castro's *bohío*. As soon as he entered, Castro turned his attention away from Ramiro Valdés and, pointing a finger at Luis, said, "You're going to join Ramiro's column. The army is moving in for the big offensive, and we need everyone. The next few days are critical for the Revolution. Any questions?"

As Luis silently shook his head, Castro resumed his discussion with Valdés, whose focus did not waver from the heavily marked area on the topographical map spread out on the long table.

Later in the week at a meeting in the operations *bohío*, Luis was given command of a squad of eight men. There were several squads of eight to twelve men in each platoon and three platoons in each column, totaling some seventy-five to one hundred twenty men per column.

Castro reminded Luis that although most squad leaders were sergeants, he was giving Luis the rank of lieutenant because Luis had served the Revolution well in the underground. Luis had also succeeded in delivering badly needed arms and ammunition. Deep down Luis wondered if the real reason for his officer's rank was, as Dr. Sorí Marín told him, that ancestral family names, such as Recio, impressed Castro, and he wanted leaders with those names to give the armed struggle an aura of prestige.

Here at last was the chance to see some action. The task assigned to his squad was to plant a mine in one of the roads on the perimeter of the mountain and to ambush the advancing troops once the mine was tripped. Luis listened to the details of the planned maneuver attentively, taking careful mental notes and visualizing the event.

After the briefing, Luis stopped by the kitchen to look for Ofelia. The other women were preparing lunch while Ofelia was setting the table. Drawing her aside, he told her he had received his orders and he wanted to see her before he left.

"Whose column?" Ofelia asked above a whisper, trying to look busy by wiping a plate with a cloth.

"Ramiro Valdés'," he answered, "Why do you ask?"

"I'll tell you later," she said. "Meet me tonight in back of the blacksmith's shop at nine o'clock. Walk past it. Don't hang around. I'll be there."

After supper, Luis tried to kill time as best he could. He played domino in his *bohío* until shortly before the appointed hour when he quietly excused himself and headed for the door.

Ofelia was waiting for him as promised, materializing out of the moonlight. She touched him lightly on the arm and whispered, "Come with me."

Taking him by the hand, she led him uphill along a winding path that soon came to an end against the stone face of a mountain. Undeterred, she guided him along the side of the cliff through patches of brush that blocked the way. The brushes gave away, and as they moved along the rocky terrain, Luis could not keep from noting the spectacular fireflies. He saw them as his allies in their secret rendezvous. There were hundreds of them, darting in all directions, soaring and descending without a care.

"Where are you taking me?" he asked, holding her waist.

"To a cavern where we used to keep the supplies before we moved into the camp. Now it's my secret hideaway."

Shortly she stopped and parted some bushes, and there, as if by magic, was an opening in the side of the mountain. Nature conspired in her secret; the bushes knitted back together as if to conceal their entry. The moonlight filtering through the bushes left moon shadows on their bodies and the hard floor of the cave.

"Here," she said, guiding Luis to a mat. Within an instant, they were entwined on the ground, kissing, fondling, and undressing each other. Soon they were naked, Luis gratified and surprised by Ofelia's lack of inhibition. His hands traced the contours of her hips and breasts while he marveled at her beauty. Wanting to give each other pleasure, they kissed every part of the other's body as their passion came to a peak. "Now, darling, now," she cried out, and Luis and Ofelia became one.

Afterwards, when the sweat had dried on their skin and their breath slowed to a comfortable rhythm, Luis broke the womblike silence of the cave, "What did you mean earlier about Ramiro Valdés?"

"Before you arrived, he made a pass at me, and I told him off. He kept on for several days until I threatened to go to Fidel. That made him mad, but he stopped. Recently he mentioned to Ana you were spending a lot of time in the kitchen and he doubted you were there just to sample the food. He also told her you were married. I know he suspects there's something going on between us. Please be careful. I couldn't bear it if something happened to you."

The idea of being watched infuriated Luis. "I'll be careful, I promise you, but Ramiro Valdés doesn't intimidate me."

After a pause, he added, "Ofelia, what Ramiro told Ana is true. I've been married for almost two years, and I have a small son, but I haven't felt close to my wife for a long time. There are such stark differences between us that I doubt our marriage will survive."

"I knew what I was doing when I brought you here," she answered, caressing his face. "When Ana told me, it was too late. I was already in love with you."

They slept and made love until a camp rooster crowed at dawn. As they headed back to camp, each took a separate route.

Over the course of the two months Luis remained in the Sierra, he and Ofelia spent many nights of similar abandonment in the security of the cavern. The cave became like their home, a hallowed place where their physical unions gave birth to a much deeper connection in which their souls bonded in unconditional love. With Luis, Ofelia allowed herself to believe that her world need not be defined in terms of tragedy and sorrow, and with Ofelia, Luis came to know a simple sweetness and beauty in loving that he had never given nor received. Neither would argue that their love had its genesis in a source greater than themselves, for were it not for many unpredictable circumstances, their paths would never have crossed.

Chapter 10

Luis tried to push Margarita from his mind and concentrate on coping with the rigor of the military academy. Day after day he was placed on report for offenses which seemed petty and unfair to him. His stack of demerit slips included every possible violation from offenses such as "shoes not properly shined" to "corners of bed sloppily folded." From his second day there, he found himself waiting in line with other delinquent cadets after the evening meal outside the office of the no-nonsense commandant who wrought holy fear on the corps.

To ease his loneliness, he frequently wrote to Enrique Bueno in Havana and Alberto Sánchez in Camagüey. Luis described how difficult things were but hoped somehow they could find a bit of humor in it all.

> *Dear Enrique,*
>
> *Let me tell you about my roommates, Jonathan Burleson and Clifford Manning. I call them "Tennessee" and "Kentucky," after their home states. They know as little about Cuba as I know about the states they come from. Tennessee had never been to a movie until he got to Lewiston.*
>
> *Kentucky knows more about movies but not much about geography. He thought Cuba was in South America! Students here ask me if we have radios in Cuba, and one imbecile wanted to know if most Cubans were Indians. If it weren't for the other Latin Americans here, I couldn't survive!*

Tennessee is unbelievably fat. He comes from a farm in the middle of nowhere. He said it took nearly two hours to get to his school. He had to cross a river in a rowboat going and coming. What boat could hold a whale like him?

Tennessee eats like a horse, and although he hates the cooking here, he eats everything in sight. On top of that, his "mama" sends him food all the time. She sends him shoeboxes full of ham biscuits wrapped in wax paper, and he eats them as soon as they arrive. When he gets the box open, he shoves it toward me and Kentucky and says, "Have some of these fine ham biscuits!"

I really don't know much about Kentucky since he rarely talks. He's mad at his parents, who own a racehorse farm in Kentucky. He's fifteen and has flunked out of a high school in his county and a military school in Virginia. The commandant makes him stay in study hall all the time, but his grades haven't improved.

I've learned that of all the military schools in the country, SMA is supposed to be the toughest, known as the "Alcatraz of the South." The Latins say the school motto is "Abandon all hope ye who enter here!" This time, my friend, I'm out of luck. Send help!

A warm embrace,
Luis

Dear Alberto,

Would you believe I'm the only person in my room passing English? It doesn't surprise me in the case of Tennessee who doesn't even speak English! If what Miss Pickford taught me was English, then what he speaks would be closer to Chinese! He puts an 'R' in everything he says, like "Cuburn," "Americar," "Panerma Kernal," and calls me "Luris."

The southern boys love country music and play it all the time. ¡Es terrible! All of their songs are about religion, car wrecks, and love gone wrong. They sing about little

*footprints in the snow, dust on the Bible, and hearing
a crash on the highway! Every Sunday night they have
vespers in the chapel and sing such songs as "What a
Friend We Have in Jesus," "Beulah Land," and "Throw
Out the Life Line." We Latin Americans call it "The
Protestant Hour!"*

*I think you can see why the Latinos call this area
"The Buckle on the Bible Belt." Religion here is all
protestant, hillbilly religion which in some places includes
snake handling and "holy rollers." I haven't seen any
of it myself, but some cadets tell me it happens in the
backwoods. The Catholics in this state are outnumbered
by a million to one.*

*As I write, I look out of my window and see nothing
but snow. It's pretty, but there is nothing as beautiful to
me as the green royal palms and the blue sea of Cuba.*

*I'm doing all right, but continue to remember me and
write often.*

Receive a tight abrazo,
Luis

Dear Enrique,

*One bright spot in my life here is my swimming. The
coach brags on my strokes and says I have a good future
as a swimmer. Most of the Latinos here go out either
for boxing, wrestling, or swimming, and, in the spring,
baseball.*

*Guess what? The commandant put Jonathan on a
diet, and his parents came to complain. When she saw
me, she said, "So this is the Mexercan you've been writing
me about!" "Not Mexercan, Marma," Jonathan said,
"Cuburn!" "Mexercan, Cubarn, Jew, A-rab, or I-talian,"
she said and laughed. "They all look the same to me!*

*When Tennessee left, Clifford told me an
unbelievable secret. He's fathered a son! That's why his
parents sent him to SMA. So many of the students here*

are problem cases, and according to my parents, I'm one
of them!
    Un abrazo,
    Luis

When Luis returned home from the military academy after his first year, it was not as a conquering hero, but as one who, sexual matters aside, had conquered himself. At peace with his parents and with a new appreciation for his homeland, he began the daily routine of the previous summers: touring the mill with father and grandfather, visiting with his friends, going on occasional dates, and swimming every day to stay in shape.

"Hey, Alberto," he said to his friend one day at the pool at the Camagüey Tennis Club. "Look at all those girls! I'd like to catch a piece of those asses."

"Let's go to Cachita's," Alberto said.

"I can't," Luis answered.

"Why not?"

"Because I've vowed never to pay for sex again."

"I'd like to be that strong," said Alberto, "but I'm just too turned on. Remember how we used to call ourselves 'horny little sinners'? Well, what are we now? No less than 'horny big sinners.' I'm sure I'll grow up to be a dirty old man."

"We'll open a whorehouse," Luis laughed. "I can see the sign now: 'Home for Horny Old Men, Proprietors Alberto Sánchez and Luis Recio: Filthy Pictures from Paris on Constant Display and Pornographic Movies Every Night from Seven to Midnight!'"

"There's no escape," Alberto replied, and the two friends headed for the bar to have a beer.

One afternoon later that summer, Luis and his father were seated in wicker rockers on the veranda of the Liceo when Rogerio, prodded by the display of posters for the 1948 election, began to discuss politics with Luis.

"It's dirty business," Rogerio warned him. "Most politicians are demagogues who have utter contempt for public opinion. The public remains indifferent, and this lack of interest is pathetic. I only know a handful of honest políticos in our country.

"One of them is Eduardo Chibás. I pointed him out to you last summer when we were at the Havana Yacht Club. Remember the funny-looking man with thick glasses and the old-fashioned two-piece swimming outfit? That was Eddy Chibás. He's a firecracker who attacks corruption and gangsterism on his radio program.

"Chibás favors a revolution which would change our economic structure. Though incorruptible, he has vague ideas that can't be implemented. I respect him, but one I really admire is Manuel Antonio de Varona, a senator from our province. He's sincere and down to earth."

"I've heard of Tony de Varona," Luis said. "So, Papá, if you don't like the way things are, why don't you get involved in politics?"

"My son, you don't understand the system. We're talking about an evil that has been around for centuries. Greed and corruption have been a way of life since the Spaniards landed on this island. Look at what happened to my uncle, Manuel Recio. Well-intentioned politicians such as Uncle Manuel don't stand much of a chance.

"It would take a new breed of men to change things, and I'm not about to waste my energies on such a frustrating enterprise. I do what I can. I'm backing Senator Tony de Varona in this election although there are quite a few crooks in his Auténtico party. I prefer to use my influence and money from behind the scene."

Luis had known through the years of his father's generous contributions to the arts in Camagüey and Havana, but this was the first time he realized his father was also directly involved in politics.

Two weeks after that conversation, persuaded by Senator de Varona, Rogerio hosted a political rally at the Tamarindo Sugar Mill for Senator Carlos Prío, the presidential candidate of the Auténtico party. Having told his father he wanted to meet Prío and de Varona, Luis volunteered to bring some of his friends to the rally which took place at an old warehouse that once served as a movie theater on Saturday nights.

Luis got up very early that day and rounded up Ramoncito and several of his old playmates at the mill. When they arrived at the warehouse, the festive rhythm of conga drums greeted them. Two distinct groups of people packed the warehouse: those who were anxiously waiting to see the leaders, and those who went to have fun and were already dancing to the congas and drinking the beer and rum Rogerio provided.

Suddenly, word spread that Prío's entourage was arriving. The volume of the music escalated as the políticos struggled to enter the packed warehouse. Rogerio spotted his son in the crowd and motioned for him to come to the stage, and after shoving and pushing his way through the excited crowd, Luis managed to climb the three steps and join his father and Papá Bernabé on the platform.

Roberto Pérez, the mill's Auténtico leader, introduced the candidates. Tony de Varona gave a short speech which served as the introduction to the presidential candidate, and after prolonged applause, Prío took over the microphone. His account of the accomplishments of his party during the Grau administration impressed Luis. No wonder the polls placed Prío as the favorite to win the election.

After the rally, Rogerio hosted a dinner at the house for the dignitaries, and there Luis finally got to meet de Varona and Prío.

"Senator Prío," Rogerio said, "I want you to meet my son, Luis. If ever there is a future político, he is it."

"I think he might have some of '*El Honrado*'s' blood in him, Senator!" added Bernabé.

Prío laughed and warmly shook Luis' hand. Luis closely observed Carlos Prío as he talked to those who came to congratulate him on his speech. He makes everybody feel important, Luis observed.

Rogerio introduced Luis to Tony de Varona, who acknowledged him with a big smile.

"So you're Luis! I've heard many good things about you."

Then he winked at Luis and asked, "How are you making out with those American *señoritas?*"

"Not too well, Senator. I've gotten to know detention hall much better than American girls!" Luis replied jokingly.

De Varona laughed and commented, "Your father tells me you're interested in politics."

"I suppose so, although this is the first time I've attended a political rally."

"Well, it's never too late. I trust you like Carlos Prío. We need bright young men such as you to join our party. When you finish high school, do you know what you want to study?"

"I imagine I'll study law at Havana University," Luis answered.

"An excellent idea. That's the way I became involved in politics, and I hope you do the same. You must come to see me when you start law school."

That night Luis was not able to sleep. The rally had been very exciting! After meeting two senators, one of them the leading presidential candidate, he lay awake remembering what his father had told him about politicians, and he couldn't reconcile how someone corrupt could get to be president. It seemed to him that pride and honor would override whatever temptation might come one's way. He earnestly hoped Prío would be an honest president.

Years later, Luis would recall the rally at the mill as the day he became hooked on politics.

Chapter 11
Sierra Maestra, June, 1958

At 10 a.m. on June 19, Luis and his squad left the camp with the rest of Ramiro Valdés' column. The mission of his squad was to lay a mine in the road running from the town of Santo Domingo to the Sierra. Their intelligence reported that Batista's army under the command of Sánchez Mosquera was making a pincer movement from east and west on both sides of the obscure valley town of Las Mercedes which the army had controlled for the last twenty days. Luis' squad moved on the eastern flank toward Santo Domingo. The objective of the army was to penetrate the perimeter of four square kilometers that Castro controlled.

On the road to Santo Domingo, Luis was reflective and quiet. Here in the Sierra he had been in uniform for only a month and a half and now faced the distinct possibility of baptism by fire. The prospect of his own death frightened him, but more terrifying was the idea of taking someone else's life. If the TNT mine worked, he would almost certainly kill others. He had chosen to push the plunger on the detonator himself instead of delegating the responsibility to a veteran in the squad. He admitted, though, that perhaps he had chosen that task as the lesser of two evils since the squad had orders to open fire on the enemy from their heights above the road immediately after the explosion. All of this, he knew, was the essence of guerrilla warfare he had learned in sessions from Che Guevara and other seasoned fighters. They talked of taking human life as others might of killing rabbits.

Midway in the afternoon, the squadron reached the point in the road where the convoy was expected to pass and set about the task of planting the mine, working to get it in the ground quickly so that the inevitable rain would wash away any evidence of their presence.

Luis observed more than directed the work of a young peasant by the name of Joseíto, who dug a hole in the muddy road, expertly laid the explosive, unrolled the wires, and then covered up the disturbance in the road with natural debris.

Luis remembered films he had seen of soldiers eating K-rations in World War II and thought how tasty such food would seem compared to the cold kidney beans and crackers he ate under his poncho. The prospect of battle and the long march had made him ravenous. Fulfilling his duty as squad leader, he ordered the guards to keep watch during the night, taking an early turn in the rotation himself. By the end of his watch, he was having trouble keeping his eyes open, and as soon as he his relief arrived, he fell asleep on his bed of wet leaves and branches.

The rain poured hard throughout the night and eventually eased to a drizzle, ceasing in the early hours of the morning. As the sun rose, Luis wanted to see troops coming up the road or hear the sound of trucks. He grew tired of waiting and wished the ordeal were over. Just as those under him were better soldiers than he, so were they more patient. Not one gave any hint of anxiety. He remembered painfully an old saying, "*La espera, desespera*," or "waiting unnerves."

The ubiquitous gadflies, the *macagüeras*, and the huge mosquitoes were everywhere. The repellent which he brought to the mountains only lasted a couple of weeks, and although he had become somewhat acclimatized to the incessant buzzing and biting of the insects, they now attacked in force. Luis missed the netting and the screens his family had used at the Tamarindo sugar mill to keep out the insects.

Toward noon Luis and others washed their hands in a nearby stream and made sandwiches of *chorizos* and stale bread. Neither exercise nor labor had ever made him this hungry. The guerrillas ate as if each meal was their last, and no doubt Batista's soldiers did the same.

In spite of his fear of combat, the food and heat lulled Luis into drowsiness. He even thought about a siesta as a way of escaping the boredom, but his waiting was near its end. Sergeant Nasario was the first to hear the approaching enemy, pointing down the mountain toward the hum of motors. No one spoke; no one needed to. Luis' initiation into combat was only moments away.

Within seconds, Luis was more fully awake than he had ever been in his life. He did not need to give orders to his men. All knew their assigned posts from the moment Luis first identified the curve in the road where the mine was to be buried and the ambush set up.

The hum of insects was in tune with the droning of trucks as the enemy's vehicles inched up the muddy mountain road. It would be the sounds, not the sights or smells which Luis would remember from the jungle, and those sounds were all strangely similar-- the hum of insects, of Castro's generator, of roaring rain, and now of army trucks geared down for the climb up the mountain. The trucks slowly inched nearer and nearer, obstinately refusing to come into view.

Sergeant Nasario Blanco waited, his eyes ablaze with anticipation. He was thirty-five but looked much older. Nasario had worked on a farm of a *latifundista*, milking cows since he was a child, rising at four in the morning and going to bed shortly after dusk. His only leisure consisted of listening to the radio and playing domino.

The Revolution promised Nasario many things, but the real attraction, Luis suddenly realized, was the power his M-1 gave him. As Nasario listened to the trucks with the attentiveness of a hound, the glow in his eyes intensified, contrasting sharply with the gap in his teeth and the stubble of his beard. My God, Luis thought, he really likes this. If we succeed, this one will never milk cows again. Sergeant Nasario was smiling when he said with a gleeful whisper, "Here they come."

The lead truck came into view as it rounded the mountain, and, Luis got a glimpse through its windshield of the man he would try to kill. Did he have children? What led him to this remote mountain road where in a few moments he would pass into eternity? For a second, Luis felt like untying the wires from the generator. Instead, he pulled the handkerchief from his back pocket and wrapped it around the handle so as not to lose his grip.

Some two meters before the truck reached the mine, Luis pushed the handle to set off the explosion under the truck just as Sergeant Nasario reached out to restrain him a second longer. That was Luis' plan too; at exactly the right instant, he would push down on the handle, and the front end of the truck would rise up in the air as if it were sneezing, scattering mud, rocks, and debris in every direction.

From the rear end of the truck, tilted now at an angle, troops would spill out onto the road so surprised and confused they would surrender with their hands in the air as soon as they got to their feet.

Those in the other trucks would follow suit, and the battle would be won without a shot having ever been fired. Even the driver would only be slightly wounded, and after their arms and other gear were taken, the soldiers and the rebels would all embrace as comrades. Some soldiers would join the rebel forces, and others would be set free to go back to the government units and tell the others just how civilized the guerrillas really were.

Luis' wishful thinking was far from the reality of the moment. Instead of destroying the truck, his premature action only succeeded in covering the windshield in mud, and the driver, instead of being wounded, had another fate in store. As he jumped out of the door of the truck and scrambled for the ditch, a squad member cut him down. Luis saw the driver's arms jerk up, his body twitch, and then fall theatrically into the mud.

The troops in the back met a similar fate. As they spilled out with rifles at the ready but not knowing where to shoot, they were perfect targets for the guerrillas, who raked the entire column with machine gun fire.

Surrender seemed the only sensible choice for the soldiers, but in an instant, some of them managed to return fire, though so randomly as to be ineffective. Amid the cracking sounds around him, Luis took aim with his own M-l. His bullets downed one of the enemy. He wondered if he could get the order, "Hold your fire!" out of his mouth when he saw a number of the soldiers with their hands in the air, making signals for the guerrillas to stop. His mouth was drier than a rock in the desert sun, but he managed to shout the order over and over and was relieved when his men obeyed.

Luis scrambled from his position and jumped down on the road to survey the bodies that lay in the road and the ditch. It was as if he were drawn to them by a morbid curiosity. He counted eleven bodies. One young soldier whose face had never met a razor had been shot in the center of the forehead, as if someone had hit a bull's eye. Here, Luis thought, is a *casquito*, the derogatory term used in Cuba for the young recruits in Batista's army. Luis felt pity, thinking the youth had surely joined the army because he was poor, unemployed, and without any other recourse.

To Luis' dismay, the young man was the one he himself had shot. Reluctantly Luis moved toward the body and stood over it. The young soldier's legs were twisted in the shape of the number four, and his mouth was open. Insects were already on the scene, one fly claiming a whole cheek for his domain and another ready to enter the mouth cavity for better hunting. Afraid of what his men might think, Luis fought back an impulse to shoo away the flies as well as an urge to vomit, visualizing the maggots and vultures fasting on the bodies before the army could recover them.

As the squad was getting ready to move back to the camp with seventeen prisoners laden with the supplies they had hoped to use in an advanced outpost against the rebels, Luis and others heard a moan in the ditch behind him and went immediately to its source. There, still alive, lay another young soldier with a grazed head wound. Judging from the holes in his uniform, he had also suffered grave wounds in the chest. Tearing back his jacket, Luis saw how extensive the damage was to the torso and called for first aid. The first to reach him was Sergeant Nasario who, however, did not have first aid in mind.

"Lieutenant Recio, that man is beyond help. There's nothing that can be done for him."

As if by way of argument, the man opened his eyes and looked at Luis imploringly.

"The hell there isn't," Luis shouted. "Get a hammock here, and we'll take him with us."

Within a matter of seconds, Luis' men had the prisoner on a canvas hammock and were ready to move from the battle area. They had not gone far into the jungle, though, when they encountered other elements of the column and Ramiro Valdés himself.

"What the hell are you doing?" he inquired of Luis. "We didn't bring hammocks out here for the enemy."

Cursing Luis for his ignorance, Valdés ordered Luis to shoot the man where he lay, but Luis refused.

"Fine," said Valdés, "you can explain this to Fidel yourself when we get back."

Luis expected Valdés to shoot the man, but to Luis' surprise, Valdés ordered Sergeant Nasario to place him under a tree and to roll up the hammock.

"If you had left him at the scene of the ambush, he might have been found by the army and given a proper burial," said Valdés, looking at Luis. "Now when he dies, only the buzzards will take care of him--thanks to you! I'll let you decide, then, if you think it best to let him linger here with the insects or put him out of his misery."

Luis opened his mouth to speak but nothing came forth. Valdés had taken charge anyway, ordering Luis' squad and his own men to move out.

Luis stayed behind to weigh the predicament of the dying man. Why did Valdés have to mention buzzards? The scene that came to his mind was one Papá Bernabé described when vultures attached young Americans who died at the Battle of San Juan Hill. Two of them were not quite dead when the scavengers started to peck at their flesh. The following day these men were found dead with their hands gripped tightly around the buzzards' necks.

Luis saw scores of flies beginning to gorge themselves on the injured man's exposed wounds. Taking off his cap, he tried to disperse them, but they returned as soon as he stopped. Knowing he could not stay with the man indefinitely and realizing the buzzards would soon arrive, he made his decision.

Staring straight in the man's face, Luis asked, "Do you hear me? Can you understand me?"

The soldier blinked his eyes.

" I can't take you with me. You're going to die here. Do you want me to leave you for the vultures or end your suffering now?"

As the man attempted to speak, Luis understood only the word "now."

"May God save our souls," Luis prayed. He then put the gun to the dying man's temple and pulled the trigger.

Strangely at peace with himself, Luis made the sign of the cross, closed the soldier's eyes, and hurried to join his squad.

Chapter 12

During Luis' second year at SMA, the roommate situation was reversed. Instead of Luis living with two North Americans, Kentucky now had to share a room with two Latin Americans. Their new roommate for the rest of their time at SMA was Cadet Julio Cubillán from Maracaibo, Venezuela. Short, square, and swarthy, Julio appeared older than his fifteen years and showed the varied strains of his ancestry. With deep, dark eyes and coarse black hair, he was part Indian and proud of it. His goal was to attend West Point. The son of a general in the Venezuelan Army, he was at home at SMA from the beginning. He accepted the rigorous routine and the first year paddling with such stoic calm that the upper class hazing for him ceased almost before it began.

In his freshman year Luis' room had a reputation for being disorderly, but the next year it became known as a room of athletes. Julio won a position on the boxing team as a welterweight, Clifford took over as top man in the 145-pound division on the wrestling team, and Luis excelled in freestyle swimming. The cadets on their hall held nightly bull sessions in their room. Luis liked SMA more and more, and as he made close friendships with both the Latins and North Americans, he took special pride in his dual citizenship.

As soon as he enrolled at SMA, Julio Cubillán subscribed to the Nashville *Tennessean* and once a week received the Sunday edition of *El Mundo* from Caracas. Luis had never been much of a reader, but under Julio's influence he kept up with current events in two languages.

Julio's digestion of news took the form of self-briefing, but Luis contemplated world affairs from a different perspective. Questions arose in his mind. Why were nations set against one another? Why had Russia, Spain, China, and even "the good old U.S.A.," as Clifford would say, suffered through revolution and civil wars? Why was there so little stability in Latin America? Why must people go hungry while others prosper? Why was there so much corruption in Cuban politics, and why in America were Negroes denied basic rights?

Most of the cadets of whom Luis would ask questions had neither knowledge nor opinions about issues that Luis wanted to discuss. Clifford knew a lot about socio-economic groups, but he got tired of trying to explain them to his roommates. So, in order to give them a first-hand taste of life in the South, he invited Luis and Julio to his home for Thanksgiving of their junior year.

The Manning's family chauffeur met the boys in front of the main building after noon meal on Wednesday. During the drive to the Manning's horse farm that afternoon, Luis, intoxicated by the change of scenery, drove Clifford crazy with question after question. How was bourbon whiskey made? How much did it cost to raise a thoroughbred? What was burley tobacco? What was the average size of a Kentucky farm? Did most of the farmers raise dairy or beef cattle? Had Kentucky ever seen a hog butchered? Samson, the driver, joined in the conversation. After two hours of constant interrogation by Luis, Clifford had his fill. When Luis asked him if he had ever skinned a skunk, his roommate turned to the back seat and replied, "Jesus Christ, Luis! Go to sleep!"

Mr. And Mrs. Manning, by contrast, appreciated Luis' interest in their way of life and queried him about Cuba. Luis shared that his mother's folks were jewelers, his father a sugar mill owner, and his grandfather the owner of Serapio, the champion racehorse of Cuba.

On Friday, after a traditional southern Thanksgiving feast, Clifford took Luis on a jeep ride over the family farm, showing him their stallions and cattle and remarking how aroused it had made him as a boy to see a bull or a studhorse at work. Clifford's father's dream was to breed and run a winner of the Derby. Their wealth, Luis learned, came from the bank Mr. Manning owned. On the Saturday after Thanksgiving, he took them bird hunting and later that night to dinner at his country club where Luis surprised them by asking if he could order a mint julep. Mr. Manning honored his request and laughed when Luis, after taking a sip of the drink, rubbed his lips together, and announced it tasted like a Cuban drink known as *mojito,* which consisted of white rum, mint, angostura bitters, lemon, soda, and sugar.

It did not take long for Luis to win the hearts of Kentucky's mother and father. He was, Mrs. Manning told her son, "a most charming young man." Clifford passed on the compliment to Luis but not in the presence of Julio, who, his mother described as "nice but quiet." On Sunday Samson took them on the long ride back to SMA, all three cadets sleeping for most of the trip.

Luis wrote to Enrique about his trip to Kentucky, but he did not add that while looking at the splendid stallions on the farm, the grace and beauty of these magnificent animals sent shivers up his spine. He did not confide to Enrique that while leaning on the white wooden fence of that farm in the Bluegrass State, he thought of "El Honrado," Papá Bernabé, and his racehorse, Serapio. What he did mention to Enrique was the realization that if there was a race for a democratic Cuba, victory could only be declared if those who had to struggle like Margarita crossed the finish line at the same time as people like himself.

Luis had learned about affluent southern society, but little about the larger South, as he discovered in the spring of his senior year. That education came when he spent the weekend with Joe Williams, the catcher on the baseball team, at his family's farm in the foothills of the Cumberland Plateau. He recorded his visit in a final letter to Alberto shortly before his graduation.

> *Esteemed Alberto,*
>
> *It has taken me three years to understand the true essence of United States. I now realize most of the boys here come from well-to-do families, but they don't make up a true cross-section of this great land. Joe Williams, my friend on the baseball team, is an exception here. Joe Williams' family farm should be an example for Cuba.*
>
> *The Williams are truly self-sufficient, producing almost everything they need to live on their 150-acre farm in the Tennessee hills. When I met Joe's father, I asked Mr. Williams what a hillbilly was, and he replied, "You're looking at one!"*

It's spring now, but Mrs. Williams still has enough home-canned food to last until the next harvest. They kill their own pigs and share the sacks of sausage and ham with their family and neighbors. Everything she puts on that table came from the farm, except the salt and sugar.

How different with us in Cuba! What we eat comes from someone else's hard work. Alberto, everyone here works with his hands! You should see the tool shed on the Williams' farm!

The U.S. is the largest producer of the world's tools, and its people know how to use them! I'm going on seventeen, and I can't do anything except shave, shine shoes, and hit a baseball. I have no practical skills!

All the Williams's neighbors are self-sufficient as well. Most of them make their money from dairy cattle, and on both sides of the road, grazing herds are all you can see.

The Williams have a tenant who helps them with milking and other work. Mr. Williams gives him one-fourth of the milk check, one-third of the corn, one-half of the tobacco, the bull calves born to cows in the herd, a garden spot, and three pigs to kill every year. The tenant house is modest but warm and comfortable. When we contrast this with the conditions of farm laborers in Cuba, we don't look so good!

On Sunday I attended the Methodist church with the Williams family. Their churches are simple, plain white wooden buildings where the people love to sing, stand around in the churchyard after services, and talk. The most obvious thing about their services was the absence of black people.

On the surface, the Negroes and whites seem to get along and treat each other with respect in the U.S., but its obvious whites consider the Negroes inferior. Blacks and whites have separate churches, schools, rest rooms, and even buses. After church on Sunday afternoon, Joe took me to visit a Negro family so I could see how they lived.

We visited the Johnsons, who used to be the Williams's neighbors and were tenants on an adjoining farm. Although the Johnsons welcomed us, I saw Joe slightly stiffen and force a smile when Mrs. Johnson gave him a warm hug. Obviously, Joe's attitude toward the Negroes is something he has grown up with here in the South.

As Joe talked on our way back to the Williams farm, I was feeling proud because of our acceptance of people of different races. Then it hit me! Sure, in Cuba we don't see people in terms of their color. Negroes can sit anywhere on the bus and rise to positions of power in the government. Blacks in Cuba have always had free access to public education through the university and have played a role in politics since our independence from Spain, but think about it. How many Negroes are there in our exclusive clubs and private schools? How many black families own homes in neighborhoods like ours?

The black man's struggle in our country is economic, not racial. Who has money in Cuba? Not the blacks and mulattoes. Who makes up the bulk of the menial labor force in our country? Not people from families like yours or mine. The blacks and mulattoes struggle for things you and I take for granted. Darn it, Alberto! We have our own problems to solve in Cuba.

You know what also crossed my mind while Joe and I were visiting the Johnsons? The batey! Yes, the colony of workers' huts on my father's sugar mill. The living conditions of blacks in the South are better than those of the batey--all those straw huts and earthen floors! Papá thinks my grandfather did a great thing by building the school at the mill, but the people he really built it for were his own children. Papá went to school with poor children, yes, and takes pride in being liberal-minded, but he and his workers live in separate worlds.

This visit to a Tennessee farm has opened my eyes to many things about the United States and Cuba. Both

countries need to concentrate on helping the poor, and I
plan to do my share!
   Un abrazo,
   Luis

At SMA Luis had accomplished more than he dreamed he would. He was secretary of his senior class, president of the Latin American Club, an All-American in swimming, and captain of the team. During Honors Night, Luis went forward to receive his letters in swimming and baseball and then again for the best all-round athlete. The Latin Americans were ecstatic over the announcement. Rogerio, María Luisa, and Bernabé stood with the rest of the audience and proudly applauded as Luis received the award from Colonel Whitney.

Among the Latin Americans, Luis was called "The Flying Fish of Cuba," as he on more than one occasion had dubbed himself and as the Nashville *Tennessean* had referred to him in a special sports article on his swimming record. He was at once a solid student, a prankster, a team man, and a leader. More significantly, however, as one cadet wrote in his yearbook, Luis Recio had "a heart like the great outdoors."

When the flag was lowered in the Circle of Cannon following graduation of the class of 1951, Luis Recio felt a knot in his throat, and his eyes moistened. When he came to tell Julio and Clifford farewell, it was more than he could bear. He hugged them and walked away without saying a word, tears trickling down his cheeks.

Now at the wheel of the car, with his father in the front seat and his mother and Bernabé in the rear, Luis steered down the same tree-lined avenue that only a few years ago they had driven in the dead of winter to deposit him in the hands of others. Sending him to SMA, Luis now realized, was a wise decision. At the highway, he turned left toward Knoxville, and began the journey back to Cuba. "The Flying Fish" was returning to the land he loved.

Chapter 13
Sierra Maestra, June, 1958

Fidel Castro called Luis to the *bohío* on urgent business the day after their return. The matter did not seem too critical, though, since Castro was happily reviewing the results of another battle with Ramiro Valdés and other column leaders. As Luis listened at the door, only Valdés acknowledged his presence, doing so with an icy smile. From the animated talk, it was obvious the perimeter skirmishes of the past few days were the most important of the war. Castro's men were still counting their gains in terms of prisoners and weapons and commenting enthusiastically upon the demoralizing effects the fighting had on Batista's troops. Later Luis would learn the real cause of the jubilation was the capture of short-wave radio equipment and an army code that greatly increased the effectiveness of the rebels' intelligence. An elated Castro declared, "Now we have those fucking sons of bitches where we want them!"

When those around him had dispersed, Castro signaled impatiently for Luis to come over to the map table, his happy mood of a moment earlier obviously evaporating.

"Recio, you damn fool," Castro began, raising his eyebrows as the smoke from his eternal cigar rose before his face, "once again you committed an act of insubordination, this time in battle. What do you have to say?"

"*Comandante*, we have been told we must treat our prisoners with utmost respect. It was my judgment that the wounded man had a chance to survive."

"Since when did you, a stupid neophyte in combat, become an expert able to judge the gravity of wounds?" Castro asked. "You don't know shit compared to veterans such as Sergeant Nasario and Ramiro who are fully aware of my policy toward prisoners and know the practicalities of war!"

Without giving Luis a chance to respond, Castro continued, "Furthermore, it is my understanding you damned near botched the whole operation by detonating the mine too quickly, almost giving the enemy a warning instead of blowing up the truck. I'm not about to put you in the field again because you're a fucking coward. You've blown it on three occasions within a short period of time—in your effort to play lawyer, in your rush in exploding the mine, and in your insistence upon bringing back an enemy soldier who didn't deserve to live."

Luis tried to interrupt, feeling he had never had the opportunity to defend himself, but Castro was not through.

"You're not fit for combat. Sure, there have been others before you who haven't succeeded in this business, but I will not tolerate your repeated insubordination and, worse, your self-righteous attitude.

"Your individualism, has gotten you into more serious trouble." Castro went on. "It has just come to my attention you seduced Ofelia Reyes. I won't ask how long this has been going on-- once is enough!"

"*Comandante*, I must tell you . . ."

"Don't tell me a goddamn thing!" Castro erupted. "Shut up until I finish. You, a married man and a father, are having an affair with a woman in our camp. Seduction in a war situation is as serious an offense in my view as insubordination, and I could charge you with both."

Luis waited until he was sure Castro's rage had subsided before speaking. Waiting gave him time for his own temper to cool. Still, he did not mince words though his tone was calm and his manner discreet.

"*Comandante*, with all due respect, I don't see how you can accuse me in the way you have when everybody knows I'm not the only one in this camp involved with a woman."

Looking back on that moment, Luis would conclude it was the audacity of youth that made him speak out about Castro's affair with Celia Sánchez. I may not have been brave in my first combat, he would reason later, but for one instance I had balls as big as a bull's.

Luis would never forget the change of expression in Fidel Castro's eyes. The large, liquid orbs which seemed to see and understand everything and could register broad human sympathy as well as outrage glared at Luis, giving him the feeling he was looking down the barrel of a rifle. Castro put out his cigar on a wooden tray and drew a breath before speaking in the calmest manner.

"Recio, your stay here has come to an end. You don't fit in. You're too outspoken for the common good. If you wish to continue to serve the Revolution, you can go to Miami to promote the 26th of July Movement there. Your command of English and your connections there could help us."

"*Comandante*," said Luis, "you haven't heard my side of the day's events. My part of the operation was in fact a complete success. It was my first outing, I didn't lose one man. Furthermore, my squad inflicted significant losses on the enemy. I feel…"

"There . . . you . . . go . . . again," Castro interrupted ever so slowly, making a concerted effort to control his rage. "You have perfectly illustrated my very point—you're always trying to second-guess me. No . . . revolution . . . on earth . . . can . . . succeed . . . with . . . people questioning every . . . fucking . . .decision!"

As Castro talked, Luis was not so much aware of the control Castro was trying to exert over his emotions as he was of the volcano in the man, which Luis knew would erupt if he so much as uttered another contrary word.

"As you wish, *comandante*," he said backing off. "I'll be glad to serve the Revolution in whatever capacity you choose."

Castro smiled faintly and rising, stated in a low and patient voice, "Recio, let's forget the past and look to the future. I have important messages to send to David Salvador in Miami. You'll leave tonight. A guide will take you down to the Beattie plantation. You'll make your way to Miami by way of Jamaica. You'll find the Jamaicans sympathetic to our cause. Prepare your things now."

Luis answered, "*Sí, comandante*," and left the *bohío* hastily. Careful that no one was following, he made his way to the kitchen tent and managed to get Ofelia's attention. After explaining the situation to her, they shared one final kiss. Ofelia heard her name called out from the kitchen and broke off from Luis in an instant. Luis knew better than to resist. He whispered hurriedly to her, "We'll be together again, I promise."

After supper, Luis shaved off his beard and put on the civilian clothes which he had brought to the camp and kept rolled up on his hammock to use as a pillow. He felt reasonably safe about the trip down from the mountains since the rebels controlled the south side of the mountains, but there was no need to take unnecessary chances by sporting a rebel beard and fatigues.

As Luis was leaving the camp, Ana intercepted him. "I'm sorry you have to leave. Don't worry, we'll take care of Ofelia. And don't you dare forget the dinner you promised to cook for us."

"Believe me," Luis said, "nothing will give me more pleasure. Goodbye, Ana." They hugged, and Luis spoke softly into Ana's ear, "Please tell Ofelia I love her."

Prudencio was waiting with two horses near the camp. He had brought Luis to this high, remote place, and now he would take him down again. "Recio," he said and smiled, "you've lost weight and toughened up." Not feeling talkative, Luis patted Prudencio on the back and simply replied, "Good to see you, Prudencio."

As they moved down the mountain path, Luis' mind ping-ponged from one thought to another. "How will this whole thing end?" he asked, as if the remote surroundings could predict the answers to his questions. "Are the recent victories the beginning of the end of Batista, or will the struggle go on for years?"

Castro had proven to be a real disappointment. Luis would never again put such blind faith in a leader. He would embrace a worthwhile cause again but without falling into the trap of hero-worship. The idealism that had driven him to the mountains had in some strange way melded with the image of Castro.

Castro was on target about one thing: Luis was not a soldier. He simply did not have the steel required of the military mind. On the other hand, Luis was certain neither Valdés nor Castro genuinely respected human life. In spite of Castro's much touted magnanimity in his treatment of prisoners, it was in reality a purely tactical gesture. Castro was still using him under the banner of the Revolution, and because he still believed deeply in its causes, he would continue to work on behalf of the changes it promised. For better or worse, the difficult and sometimes irrational *comandante* was the undisputed leader of the opposition to Batista.

As he followed Prudencio's shadowy figure through the jungle, Luis let his body sway with the movement of the horse and his thoughts drift to Ofelia and Laura. He had deceived them both. He searched deep within himself and found little he could be proud of. Looking back, he realized many things he could have done differently in his relationships with Fidel Castro, Ofelia Reyes, and Laura Ramírez.

Staying awake meant thinking, and thinking produced even greater confusion. Just as his parents had sent him away from Cuba, Castro had banished him again. In both cases illicit love played a role, but Castro was also sending him away because he did not have the constitution of a military man. While his parents tried to instill moral values in him, he inherited the willingness to fight for his ideals from *"El Honrado"* and Papá Bernabé.

"El Honrado" was the honorable politician, and Papá Bernabé was the warrior. It was his grandfather who chided his father and his friends for not taking action against Batista. Papá Bernabé had set an example for Luis long ago by showing him his uniform, sword, and medals from the war of Cuban independence as he told him gripping tales of heroic combat.

Luis' father was not a warrior but a caring man. The two, Papá Bernabé and Rogerio, earned Luis' deep admiration and respect throughout his life. Now Rogerio had won at least one clear victory: Luis might never play soldier again. He would have to work behind the scenes like his father if it would help bring about a change in Cuba. In spite of his differences with Castro, Luis still wished he had been the leader of one of the columns so one day his son could take pride in his achievements and carry on in his great grandfather's tradition. Old Bernabé would expect no less.

In the early hours of the morning, the rain came, and Luis and Prudencio put on their ponchos. Luis was careful to protect the two envelopes Castro gave him before leaving camp, one with a hefty sum of U.S dollars and the other with sealed orders for David Salvador in Miami. Luis wondered what those orders said and if they mentioned him. He could not escape feeling mistrust; Castro would not be above discrediting him with a damaging letter.

In the downpour, the path became soggy. The horses' hooves made splashing and sucking sounds in the mud. Luis wondered what the chance might be to be hit by a random bolt of lightning since there was no metal anywhere except for that on the horses' hooves and the guns on their backs. He passed the time trying to judge the distance of the lightning by counting the seconds until the thunder rolled above the majestic Sierra.

He remembered hearing tales at his father's plantation of how men were sometimes struck down while working in the cane fields. Once a peasant out in a field was about to stab another when a lightning bolt melted the knife in the man's hand. The impact of this experience made the former enemies friends for life.

Perhaps it would take something close to divine intervention to bring Cuba to its senses. He recalled what his father told him one afternoon when they were caught in a thunderstorm while inspecting the fields, "Don't be afraid, son, because if lightning were to strike and kill us, we would never see it. So thank God for all the beautiful flashes you see." So many things, even the thunder and lightning, reminded him of home, but as the storm subsided, so did his thoughts of the past.

They arrived before dawn at the outskirts of the Beattie *batey* and went directly to Prudencio's *bohío*. Exhausted from the experiences of the last several days, Luis instantly fell asleep on an old cot. Though tattered and sagging, it was still the best bed he had known in weeks. It was a bed the guerrillas in the mountains might well dream of. His last conscious thought was of the amazing hospitality of Prudencio, his peasant guide to the Sierra.

Chapter 14

In June of 1951, Luis' return to Cuba was a happy one. In the family home on the exclusive Fifth Avenue in the Miramar section of Marianao, a city adjacent to Havana, he had the whole summer at his pleasure. His most pressing matter was to pass the compulsory entrance test to law school which students who had graduated from high school in the United States had to take.

Although Luis loved the Miramar subdivision with its broad tree-lined streets, splendid homes, and fine beaches, he now made a point to reacquaint himself with Old Havana. Once again he relished walking through its narrow streets and hearing the cries of the ambulatory fish and ice cream vendors and the noisy exchanges in the corner *bodegas* where ladies would do their daily shopping. He enjoyed the aroma of freshly baked bread, roasted peanuts, and the smell of salt water as the waves, which on windy days hit the Malecón sea wall and splashed the passing cars.

At the HYC, Luis renewed old friendships and marveled at how well those flat-breasted girls with braces had developed into shapely young women with photographic smiles. After being away for over three years in Tennessee, it occurred to him he had missed two precious parts of growing up--not living with his parents during his high school years and not spending time with those lovely, dark-haired, brown-eyed girls.

While Luis enjoyed his carefree summer in Havana, he could not keep from wondering what Margarita looked like now and thinking of the circumstances that led to his banishment from this marvelous city. Long ago, he reconciled his time away as a consequence of his actions, and in his last year at SMA, he resolved to make amends to

Margarita and Catalina. One day as he was returning his breakfast dishes to the kitchen, he approached the family cook and smiling apologetically said, "Catalina, I'm really sorry about what happened between Margarita and me."

Looking into his eyes, Catalina replied deliberately, "Luis, as bad as things may seem at times, they often are blessings in disguise. Your father sent Margarita to a nun's school here in the city where she studied to become a secretary. Now she works in a bank and is happily married."

"I'm so glad for her. I knew that Papá had sent her to school in Havana, but I didn't know what had happened later. I guess I was embarrassed to ask."

"Luis, you know that you have always been like a son to me," Catalina said lovingly. As she patted his cheek, both of them were on the brink of tears.

"One more thing, Catalina. I've wanted to apologize to Margarita for a long time. It's really important to me that she knows I regret my actions. I've written her a letter. Would you make sure she gets it?"

Taking the letter from Luis' hand, Catalina assented.

Making peace with Catalina and Margarita lifted a big burden from Luis' shoulders. Luis knew, though, that there was another aspect of life he could not ignore—politics! Three years before he had been thrilled when Prío was elected president in 1948, and he kept up with his presidency while at SMA. Now he followed the conflict between the Auténticos and Ortodoxos closely. The Auténticos had been the dominant force in overthrowing the Machado dictatorship in 1933, but after seven years in power, the party had become corrupt, though with freedom of press, and open elections, as his father pointed out. The Ortodoxo Party was a splinter group of the Auténticos, formed and led by Eddy Chibás.

Though respectful of the 1940 Constitution, the Ortodoxos were oriented toward the left and revolutionary change. Their leader, Eddy Chibás, opposed the communists, but he did not hesitate to use Marxist rhetoric at times. Prío won the election by pooling 900,000 votes, with the runner up, Ricardo Núñez, a prestigious surgeon who ran as the candidate of the old Liberal party, receiving 600,000. Chibás came in a weak third place with only 325,000 votes. The

Communist party was a distant fourth with 142,000 votes, and it lost its three seats in the Senate while retaining nine seats in the House of Representatives.

A number of Prío's promises of change did not materialize. After four years of disappointment with the administration of Ramón Grau, his Auténtico predecessor from 1944 to 1948, the people hoped for a better performance from Prío. Although the high export price of sugar contributing to rising prosperity in the country, political gang-war continued under the indifferent eyes of the government, creating a political climate which brought about a feeling of hopelessness.

Eddy Chibás, who in his weekly Sunday night radio program denounced the government's corruption and the gangsters' groups, exacerbated this chaotic state of things. His hot-headed speeches made him the most powerful voice of the opposition. His party's symbol became a broom, which would be used to sweep "the scandalous administration notorious for its mismanagement, robberies and crimes" out of power. The party's motto, "Honor against money," appealed to Luis since it reminded him of his great uncle, "*El Honrado.*"

Although Chibás lacked a coherent platform, a number of the Auténtico leaders who felt Cuba needed an end to the political corruption joined his party. The accusations of graft increased. Toward the end of June, the government retaliated through its spokesman, Aureliano Sánchez, who accused Chibás of being a liar and a would-be dictator. Chibás, in turn, countered by charging Sánchez with stealing public money to develop land in Guatemala. The exchange lasted weeks, and the media gave it detailed publicity.

Luis and his family followed this war of words. Luis was aware of Sánchez's reputation as an honest politician, and soon it became obvious Chibás did not have proof of Sánchez's corruption. Finally, on August 5, Chibás went to the CMQ radio station to present what he said was new evidence. Everybody in the country listened to the radio that night. Chibás talked for a few minutes, and rather than detailing the alleged evidence, he rambled about people refusing to see the truth. Then, to the surprise of his largest radio audience ever, he shot himself at the end of the program. The shot, however, went off after he was no longer on the air. Ten days later, surrounded by admirers, Chibás died in a hospital. His suicide further discredited the Prío government.

It was in this atmosphere that Luis Recio began law studies in September of 1951. Although he agreed with his father that Chibás was an agitator, the fact that Chibás killed himself made him a martyr in Luis' eyes. Chibás made a strong case when he argued that Cuba needed a revolution in order to bring about change. With a heightened sensitivity created by Chibás' broad and fiery accusations, Luis became increasingly disgusted with the Auténtico leaders. Government had to guarantee more than open elections and freedom of the press; it needed to cultivate a social conscience among the people.

Law school at Havana University was a new experience for Luis. After the discipline of the military school, the informal atmosphere of the university took him by surprise. In order to obtain his Doctor of Jurisprudence degree, he had to complete five years of studies requiring six subjects for each for the first three years and seven for the last two, but he had not expected the freedom given to law school students. There were no attendance requirements for classes, and as long as he knew the subject, all he had to do was pass comprehensive examinations at the end of the school year. Many students only took the comprehensive examination since they had jobs that often conflicted with the regular classes scheduled three times a week during the day.

Legal Anthropology became Luis' favorite class. The study of criminal traits in man intrigued him, and he liked Dr. Morales Coello, a jolly man in his seventies who was notorious for two things. He was the son-in-law of General José Miguel Gómez, an ex-president of Cuba, nicknamed *"Tiburón"* or "Shark," who coined the saying, *"El tiburón se baña, pero salpica."* "The shark bathes but splashes" indicated that General Gómez knew how to take care of himself and his friends. Dr. Morales also had an obvious preference for attractive female students, and he had an ample supply since almost 30% of the freshman class was women, the largest group ever.

A number of old friends started law school with him, among them Alberto Sánchez, his lifelong pal from Camagüey. Alberto, who always had a plan for his friend, persuaded Luis to run for student delegate of the Legal Anthropology class.

"It's no big deal," Alberto said convincingly. "You serve as an intermediary between the professor and the students, you find out from the professor what material will be covered on the final exam, you see that it's scheduled so as not to conflict with other examinations, and most importantly, you have to call the roll during tests."

Luis remained undecided, but the next day, Dr. Morales Coello brought a human skull to class and placed it on the table beside the podium.

"I'd like to find out if any student knows the difference between a male and female cranium?" he asked and looked around to see if any hands were raised. Seeing none, he continued.

"Please notice this male cranium sits perfectly as on a tripod." Then he reached into a bag and brought out another skull which he set on the table. "On the other hand, this female cranium oscillates. That's why *la donna e mobile* or "the lady sways." With a mischievous grin, he wiggled his hips and rolled his eyes, and the class roared in approval.

Whatever doubts Luis had about running for delegate, the *la donna e mobile* story took care of them. He liked a professor with a sense of humor. After a few days of politicking, his classmates elected him student delegate of Legal Anthropology. Alberto Sánchez ran and won as delegate of Roman Law I.

Classes at Havana University soon became routine. When they were over for the day, Luis would join classmates at the law school basement bar for refreshments and conversation. It surprised Luis how articulate his friends were. When he brought the subject up, they came to the conclusion the *Bachillerato en Letras*, the degree his friends had received before entering law school, was more comprehensive than his high school studies at SMA.

Toward the end of October, his father urged Luis to schedule a meeting with Tony de Varona. Although Luis was disappointed with the Auténticos, he loved politics, and the thought of sitting down with the Prime Minister excited him.

De Varona received him in his spacious office with the same cordiality Luis experienced when he first met the veteran politician at the rally at the Tamarindo Sugar Mill. He gestured for Luis to sit in a chair next to him.

"So, you finally paid me a call. I expected you at the beginning of the school year. I had to ask your father about you."

"I meant to contact you, but I've been very busy. It's quite a change from a U.S. high school to a Cuban law school, and I'm having to hit the books."

"Well, it's all right to keep up with your studies, but don't overdo it. You must also have some fun. Single and without major responsibilities, a good-looking man like you should enjoy all Havana has to offer. Have you been to the nightclubs? I swear, those chorus girls are sexier now than in my time."

De Varona laughed and added, "Luis, tell me, what's your opinion of the Prío administration?"

Luis pondered a moment before answering. He highly respected Tony de Varona, who was a good friend of his father, but he decided to answer the Prime Minister's question quite candidly.

"Dr. de Varona, I'm disappointed with the Auténticos. I had hoped when President Prío took office, he would try to fulfill his campaign promises. As of now, not a significant promise he made has been realized."

De Varona blinked at Luis' remarks and after a moment's pause, replied, "You know, Luis, you're right. Prío hasn't turned out to be what many of us hoped for, but he has accomplished several good things: the establishment of the Central Bank, headed by Felipe Pazos, and the Land Law, forcing absentee owners to lend land to local farmers for cultivation. He has appointed impeccable men such as Juan Antonio Rubio Padilla, Carlos Hevia, Aureliano Sánchez, José Andreu, and Luis Casero, to the cabinet. As you know, Hevia is our presidential candidate for the coming election.

"Did you know Hevia graduated from Annapolis? If he gets elected, he'll try to eliminate government corruption. As for Prío, he has been no different than our previous presidents! It's sad to say, but we've only had one honest president, Cuba's first, Don Tomás Estrada Palma, who later unfortunately started us downhill by preferring the first American intervention in 1906 rather than turning power over to his opposition. I am sure Carlos Hevia will restore some basic decency to government, and I would like for you to take part in our government. Would you like to work in this office?"

Luis responded without hesitation. "I appreciate your offer, Dr. de Varona, but I'm not prepared to work. I need to concentrate on my studies."

"I understand, Luis, but I want you to know you have a job here whenever you want."

They shook hands, and as Luis left de Varona's office, he muttered under his breath, "If I had accepted such an offer, my friends would think I'm an Auténtico with a sinecure."

A few days later, Luis went to the Students' Federation offices on the campus of the university to meet the student leaders in the other colleges. Julio Castañeda, a friend of Luis from Camagüey in the College of Business, introduced him to Álvaro Barba, the president of the University Students' Federation. After several minutes of small talk, they decided to have coffee together.

When they entered the cafeteria, they saw some twenty students surrounding a distinguished-looking man in his middle fifties who was lecturing to the group. They listened attentively to Dr. Jorge Mañach, a professor at the College of Philosophy and Letters who taught History of Philosophy and who was considered one of Cuba's leading intellectuals.

Luis and Alberto approached the group quietly and heard Mañach say, " . . . the main problem with Latin American politicians has been that they turn to politics as the fastest means of becoming rich. The process starts right here at the university. The ambitious but poor student becomes a student leader as his first step toward building political recognition. When he returns to his province to run for public office, he is already well- known for his university activities.

"This young man might be well-intentioned at the beginning, but once he's elected to Congress, power and greed corrupt him. He'll be offered pay-offs to vote for or against certain laws, and since most of his fellow legislators gladly accept any money offered, he'll see nothing wrong with it either. As the years pass, he'll become rich. I ask you, do you for a second believe this person will try to bring about reforms that will diminish his wealth? On the contrary, he'll do everything within his power to maintain the status quo. Otherwise, it would be like *pedirle peras al olmo* or "asking for pears from an elm tree.""

"The main difference between politics in the United States and Latin America is that in the United States a man turns to politics after he has achieved financial success. Having his economic well-being secure, he now craves prestige and power, and he runs for office after having spent many years building political support by working in civic organizations. There're many well-known names, such as the Roosevelts and Rockefellers, which illustrate my point. Interestingly enough, since they are already millionaires, they consistently support liberal social and economic legislation. Take, for example, Franklin D. Roosevelt and his laws--the Social Security system, the New Deal, etc. . . ."

At this point, a tall, thin student interrupted Professor Mañach, "That's all very well, Dr. Mañach, but these American imperialists have also been exploiting Latin America for decades."

"That's true," replied Mañach, "but American foreign policy has changed. Remember the Marshall Plan."

"So what's the solution?" the student retorted.

"The solution lies in education, my friend, and in an unselfish desire by young men and women like you to improve the welfare of the country. You must possess a spirit of sacrifice and be willing to work with unwavering determination for necessary changes without expecting material benefits in return. The Ortodoxo party platform advocates this level of commitment. Unfortunately, however, since we lost our beloved leader, Eddy Chibás, we now find ourselves divided and faction-ridden, a sad situation with elections close at hand."

Later Alberto informed Luis that the student who challenged Dr. Mañach's ideas was Alfredo Guevara, the president of the student body of the College of Philosophy and Letters. "He's a well-known communist," Alberto told him.

Jorge Mañach's perception of the political differences between the United States and Latin America lodged in Luis' mind. The call for commitment and sacrifice to a just cause appealed to his idealistic nature. When he inquired further about the Ortodoxo Party, Luis learned there was to be a general meeting the following Friday at the party headquarters. He persuaded Alberto to attend with him.

At the meeting Luis got a glance of the Ortodoxo leaders. He had already met Jorge Mañach, but now Alberto pointed out to him

Roberto Agramonte, Emilio Ochoa, Carlos Márquez Stérling, and Herminio Portell Vilá. It was a rowdy meeting with many people from the audience demanding to speak. Luis noticed a tall, broad-shouldered young man standing behind Professor Portell Vilá. He appeared to be impatient with the disorganized manner in which the meeting was being conducted and made several boisterous remarks to those beside him. He finally asked for the floor and proceeded to give an emotional call for the end of the division among the Ortodoxos.

"Whoever thinks that up until now everything has been done well, that we have nothing about which to reproach ourselves, such a man is very tender to his conscience. These sterile fights which have followed Chibás' death, these colossal commotions are scarcely ideological but are purely egotistical; they resound like hammer blows in our conscience. We're facing grave symptoms of irresponsibility and lack of discipline. We must once and for all eradicate the petty rancors and the private empire building. Let's make ourselves the promise to end these stupid quarrels forever . . ."

The audience applauded his stirring words. Luis learned the speaker was Fidel Castro, a twenty-five year old lawyer who was a candidate for the House of Representatives from one of Havana's districts in the upcoming May election. His reputation while studying at Havana University Law school, Luis later found out, was somewhat tainted. Castro was a member of one of several violent university-based groups which disrupted political life in the city with their gang-like warfare. Castro came across as a forceful person, and he made a number of enemies who considered him power-hungry and unprincipled, a revolutionary who lacked respect for the democratic process. However, the intensity of Castro's sentiments captivated Luis.

Election fever had been growing since the beginning of the year. Although the Ortodoxos had finally rallied around the leadership of Roberto Agramonte and were confident of winning the May election, it was by no means a certain outcome, as Agramonte lacked Chibás' charisma. On the other hand, the Auténticos, who were in power and spent election money generously, made a strong alliance with the Liberal Party, and most importantly, had a viable presidential candidate in Carlos Hevia, an engineer who had an untarnished reputation. Batista's hopes for a comeback to the presidency had fizzled when his party could not establish a coalition with another major political party. During February, another round of violence by gangster groups had erupted in Havana, and both the Ortodoxos and the Batistianos continued to accuse the government of maintaining an anarchic state.

Much to everyone's surprise, General Fulgencio Batista staged a coup on March 10, 1952. Batista served as head of the armed forces in the thirties and president of Cuba from 1940 to 1944. In 1948 he had been elected senator from Las Villas Province and was now one of three presidential candidates in the upcoming election.

Army officers, many of whom had been retired when the Auténticos came to power in 1944, led the coup in Batista's name. Thus, although their stated aim was to save Cuba from "a government of thievery and chaos," it was safe to assume the officers could not resign themselves to four more years without sharing in the spoils of power.

The morning of the coup Alberto Sánchez abruptly awakened Luis at 6:00 a.m. at his parents' home. "Batista has taken over the government. The son-of-a-bitch couldn't even wait for the results of the election! Something has to be done!"

Alberto's news astounded Luis. The upcoming election was to be the first in which he would take an active part. Since Luis had made up his mind to work for the Ortodoxo party, he had gone with Alberto to see Álvaro Barba, the president of the University Students' Federation, to sign up as a volunteer. The idea of a possible coup had never crossed his mind. What a mockery of the democratic process! How could Batista be so duplicitous!

As soon as Luis got dressed, he and Alberto hurried to the university. Luis decided to park his car by one of the side streets three blocks from the main entrance in case they had to make a hasty retreat. When they arrived at the Students' Federation headquarters, they found the place in ferment. Julio Castañeda informed Alberto and Luis that a delegation of students led by Barba had just returned from the Presidential Palace where they had talked with Prío and several of the members of his cabinet.

"Barba offered the president our support," Julio said excitedly. "He told Prío that although the students disagreed with the conduct of his government, they still considered him the legitimate leader of the Cuban people, and thus the students supported him. He also told the president that in order to defend his legal power, they were prepared to fight. Prío thanked him and promised to send a cargo of arms to the university. We're waiting for them now."

Elated, Luis realized the students would have the opportunity again to lead a revolution to restore democracy as they had in 1933. This time they would be successful!

Alberto and Luis were asked to organize the law students who were beginning to gather in the building, and they decided to go to the law school to wait for the arrival of the arms. They waited in vain. By noon, it became clear Prío would not keep his promise to send guns.

At 1:00 p.m., a spokesman for Batista announced the new cabinet of the government on the radio. Soldiers and police were positioned in front of government buildings, banks, and stores. Except for the disgruntled students at the university, the new government appeared to have things under control. When Batista promised to abide by the progressive labor laws which had been legislated during the previous years, labor leaders cancelled a general strike planned for the next day.

The apathy with which the people of Cuba regarded the coup shocked Luis. It appeared to him no one, except the students and the middle class, cared that a legitimate government had been toppled. Perhaps Batista was still popular with the working class. Perhaps the apathy of the people was the direct result of the corruption which permeated the discredited government of Prío. For whatever the reason, it was obvious to Luis that a new political era had begun in Cuba, and although it saddened him, it was also clear that the majority of the people accepted the coup with relief and resignation.

Chapter 15
Departure from Sierra Maestra, June, 1958

When Prudencio woke Luis, it was night again, and Luis gladly accepted Prudencio's offer of *arroz con pollo*, a chicken and rice dish his wife, Eloísa, had prepared. Such a meal was a real treat, but Luis knew the generosity of his hosts was typical of Cuban peasants. His hunger, like his need for sleep in the morning, was overpowering, and he devoured the plain but tasty food.

"By the way," Luis said between bites, "I've invited the women at the camp to eat a meal I'll cook at my home in Havana once the Revolution triumphs, and I'd like for you to be there also." Prudencio looked at Eloísa and grinned.

"We would love to come to Havana," replied Prudencio. "I've have never been outside of Oriente Province."

When he had finished the meal, Luis inquired. "What are your plans after the Revolution?"

The *campesinos* looked at each other as if the question opened the door to possibilities they had never considered. "I've always wanted to own my own land and have a home for my children and their children," said Prudencio, gazing off into the distance.

"As for me," Eloísa added, "I just want peace."

Later in the night there was a knock on the door, signaling them to go to the Beattie dock. There in the moonlight, Luis saw an old fishing boat sitting high in the water. Shaking hands with the middle-aged captain named Juan, whose beard looked more like a Van Dyke than a Castro, Luis asked, "How long will it take us?"

"Anywhere from eighteen to twenty hours," Juan said. "We'll arrive tomorrow night."

The reply depressed Luis. Perhaps now that he was down from the mountains, he wanted some kind of regularity in his life, and another night of travel seemed synonymous with eternity. He thought how odd it was his life was in the hands of so many strangers. He had no options, however, and he thus had to put his trust in Prudencio. After embracing and thanking his friend, Luis jumped on board the *Santa María,* a vessel that seemed as ancient as its namesake.

When they were at sea, Luis discovered Juan came from a large family and had been a fisherman since he was a teenager. He had been all over the Caribbean, and his face reflected a salty weariness. His beard was like those of the *conquistadores,* not full and fluffy like Papá Hemingway's nor thick and scraggly like Fidel's. From certain angles in the thin light of the cabin, he could have passed for the urbane commander of an ocean liner or even a splendid demonic figure, like the captain of the Flying Dutchman. To Luis' inevitable question about life after the Revolution, Juan said he wanted to establish a cooperative of fellow fishermen so they could build a warehouse for refrigerating fish. The Cubans, he said, did not eat much fish, and he wanted to be able to sell fish to foreign markets.

"You sound like an old-fashioned capitalist, Juan," Luis joked.

"Whatever makes a better living for me," Juan replied, shrugging his shoulders.

The soporific puttering of the engine made Luis drowsy, and lying down on the green-padded bench at the back of the cabin, he fell asleep. He was awakened hours later by the yawing and pitching of the boat in the downpouring of rain.

"It's just a little storm," Juan said calmly.

Luis was reassured by the captain's confidence, for never had he seen such waves. The lightning was continuous, and the thunder became a steady roll across the horizon instead of the periodic booms he had heard in the mountains. The large swells made him nervous in spite of the relaxed manner of the captain.

When the storm subsided, Luis asked Juan for food. Juan pointed to a cabinet, and inside Luis found a jar of boiled eggs in vinegar and a tin box of crackers. Taking down a small bowl from the same shelf, he shook pepper and salt on the bottom of it. He fished three eggs from the jar, put the eggs in the bowl, and rolled them around in the salt and pepper. Then he surrounded them with crackers and sat down on the swinging bench for a private feast.

When he finished his meal, Luis lay on the bench and put his hands under his head for a pillow. Sleep would not come; instead, his mind wandered over his past, trying to make sense of the present.

On the choppy seas the *Santa María* rocked like a cradle, and Luis finally let himself be lulled to sleep. When he awoke several hours later, he saw Juan at the helm of the boat. It was nearly noon, the sea was calm, and the sun blazed overhead. Luis wiped away the sweat from his face. When he started out of the cabin to get fresh air, he noticed a black and white magazine photograph of the Black Virgin of Regla, the patron saint of Cuban sailors, on the rear bulkhead. Instinctively he crossed himself and thanked her for guiding him through the voyages of the night.

Luis had not been awake long when he asked Juan if he could have a couple more eggs. Juan replied he could have the whole jar if he wanted. "We don't always get fish, but our chickens never fail us," Juan joked.

Juan sat down to eat with Luis. "Juan, are you going to Kingston just for me?" Luis asked.

Juan took several bites before answering, "I'm taking you to Kingston because my orders are to deliver you to Jamaica and return with the supplies Prudencio requested."

Luis sat quietly. He wondered what Prudencio would take to the rebels. Fidel and his band lived simply, but they constantly needed all kinds of supplies for the hospital, tools for the shops and tannery, paper for propaganda purposes, new parts for the radio, ammunition, and arms. Keeping the columns going for an increasing number of men was no small logistical task, and it would become more complex as time went on.

Pondering the matter of supplies and communications, Luis saw further proof of Papá Bernabé's claim that history always repeats itself. In the War of Independence, sloops made similar runs from Jamaica to Pilón, and even Lieutenant Rowan, the man who carried "the message to García," had come to Oriente by way of Kingston and Montego Bay. However, he had not, as the legend claimed, landed on the north of Cuba and spent three weeks making his way across the island.

His own situation was quite different. Rowan was carrying a message from President McKinley to General Calixto García, Commander of Oriente Province, informing him of the United States' intention to enter the war. Luis, in contrast, was carrying a "message to Salvador" in Miami from an upstart revolutionary.

The afternoon wore on, and when the eggs and crackers had settled in his stomach, Luis surprised Juan by saying, "If you don't mind, I'm going to take a little dip. I'll swim alongside if you'll slow down a little. Just toss me a line when I'm ready to come back."

Smiling, Juan shrugged his shoulders as Luis stripped down to his underwear, stepped outside the cabin door, and plunged into the sea. With the ease of a porpoise, he took a course parallel to the *Santa María* while Juan cut his speed so Luis could stay abreast.

After a couple hundred meters, Luis signaled Juan for a line. Holding on to it as Juan pulled him back on board, Luis was glad to finally feel clean again. One of the things that bothered him in the mountains was the smell of unwashed male bodies. He could count on the fingers of one hand the times he had bathed in a creek, and he was sure his comrades bathed even less. He had been embarrassed to have deodorant in the Sierra since such an amenity went against the Spartan revolutionary spirit, but after he came to know Ofelia, he was thankful for this underrated import from the U.S. While Ofelia did not have deodorant or perfume, she always exuded a fresh scent of soap. That scent sparked his fondest memories of the Sierra.

Chapter 16

Havana University closed temporarily, and feeling helpless in the face of events, Luis heeded his mother's advice and began to attend the *Agrupación Católica Universitaria*. The *Agrupación* was a religious organization headed by Jesuit Father Amando Llorente, the director of Luis' retreat as a teenager and confessor and friend of his mother and his aunt, Ana María Recio. The *Agrupación* maintained a clinic and a school in barrio Las Yaguas, the poorest section of Havana, where Ana María had served as a volunteer for many years.

The mission of the *Agrupación* was to mold the cream of Catholic university students into political activists, who, by their example, would bring ethics back to politics. To become a member or *Agrupado*, Luis not only had to go to Sunday masses at the *Agrupación* but attend retreats and seminars on a regular basis as well. While he treasured the recently discovered freedom from SMA and the beautiful *señoritas* who enjoyed partying as much as he did, he respected the ideals of the *Agrupados* and felt the need to become involved in their efforts.

Discovering that many of them taught underprivileged adults at San Lorenzo School, a continuing education institution run by Augustinian priests, Luis suggested to Father Llorente that he would like to teach English classes there. With one phone call from Father Llorente to the Augustinians, the approval was immediate. Luis began the next week and was surprised at how much he enjoyed being in the classroom and getting to know the students on a personal basis. For the rest of law school, he met three times a week with them at night for an hour, concentrating on vocabulary and basic conversation. The students' motivation gratified Luis, and by the end of the first semester he found himself staying after class at their request to lead informal conversation groups to improve their fluency.

As much as he loved working with students, Luis was not attracted to the pietistic regimen an *Agrupado* had to follow, as evidenced by his lack of attendance at masses and scheduled meetings.

Since Luis had ample time while the university was closed, he decided to take up cooking. Under Catalina's watchful eyes, he tried old-time family recipes, and improvising here and there with different spices, he managed to improve some of them. Papá Bernabé, his severest culinary critic, commented favorably on the delicious meals and gave Luis a new insight into the pleasures of gourmet cooking.

"My son," Bernabé said as they were cooking a shrimp *enchilado.* "I'm sure you know the old saying, 'The way to a man's heart is through his stomach.' Well, let me tell you something else. This is also the case with women. As a good cook, you hold one of the keys which unlocks the door to their heart." And with a wink, he added, "The other key you hold as a sensitive lover."

Luis' new found interest in gourmet food inspired his family to frequent the best restaurants in Havana, where Luis, following the example of his grandfather, made a point to befriend the chefs, complimenting their specialties and exchanging recipes. In spite of the wretched political situation, life in Havana could still be quite pleasant.

The Havana Yacht Club became Luis' second home. At 6'2" and 180 lbs., Luis was well aware of the attention his broad-chested, long, well-defined and muscular body attracted. He appeared older than his eighteen years. He had inherited Bernabé's seductive green eyes and flawless tan complexion and the curly dark hair of the Heymanns. The carefree smile on his full sensual lips highlighted his warm personality and good looks. Luis had come of age, returning the flirtations of the many attractive young women at the club with gusto.

In April, he started to take long swims in the calm, clear sea that faced the beach in front of the clubhouse. His powerful strokes would soon take him to the anchorage of the club's sailboats. Boarding one of them, he would lie on his back with his eyes closed as he breathed deeply to take in the smell of the salt water and the sound of the wind against the folded sails. What a life, he thought. I could do this forever.

One day, as he rested on the deck of a sailboat, Luis heard the splash of an oar close by, and before he could open his eyes, the prow of a boat hit his. As he sat up, he saw a beautiful, bronzed woman in her late twenties in a black swimsuit which accentuated her lovely body and matched her dark wavy hair.

"Well, hello there, Luis. Fancy meeting you here," and thinking Luis did not recognize her, she added, "I'm Olga Loynaz, the wife of Senator Sócrates Miranda. Don't you remember me? I've known you since you were a baby."

"Of course," Luis replied, "I remember you from the Camagüey Tennis Club, but I didn't know you were in Havana."

"I come to Havana whenever I get bored in Camagüey. I enjoy coming to the club, bathing in the ocean, and getting some exercise. It's great to get into a boat and row for an hour or so."

While she talked, Luis eyed her, trying not to be too obvious. There was a certain intimacy in her voice that suggested more than a mere social acquaintance.

"What are you thinking?" she asked with a giggle, as she got up and extended her hands to jump into Luis' sailboat.

"I'm thinking I'm a lucky fellow to have someone like you drop in on me like this." What the hell, he was really thinking, this gorgeous lady is obviously wanting attention, and moments like this don't come around often.

"You flirt," she replied with dancing eyes while she sat down next to him and started splashing her feet in the water. "You know I could get in trouble if my husband saw me with someone as young as you."

"Believe me, dear lady, he has nothing to fear from me."

"Come on, Luis, your reputation is pretty well-established," she teased.

"And how is that?" Luis inquired with a grin.

"Let me just say I know more about you than you think," Olga answered.

Luis looked at her openly now. The contour of her hard breasts was perfectly defined under the black swimsuit. He felt a stir between his legs and taking a deep breath added, "And what would you say if I told you I've watched you many times at the club in Camagüey. I've noticed you since I was a kid. You were always surrounded by young men and oblivious to us brats."

"Oh, but you're so wrong," replied Olga. "I remember you quite well. You were the handsomest boy in the group. Don't you recall one day I held your face between my hands and told you I wished you were ten years older?"

The memory flashed in his mind. How embarrassed he had been in front of his playmates!

"Then, dear Olga, don't you think it's time we do something about it?" Luis ventured in a moment of daring,

Olga's face turned serious for a moment. She rapidly looked around to be sure they were alone and then broke into an inviting smile. "Am I supposed to take the initiative?" she seductively inquired.

No further words were needed. Pulling her inside the boat, Luis took her in his arms and, first gently, then passionately, kissed her. She responded with unexpected hunger. In an instant, they took off each other's swimsuits, and locked in each other's arms, they rolled on the narrow deck. The boat rocked on the placid sea.

Thus began a relationship that to Luis was like a course in the art of lovemaking, Luis, the eager student, and Olga, the experienced instructor whose knowledge was like a bottomless well. Although Olga's sensuality awed him, he feared being consumed by her desire. It was too much of a risk to meet every day, and Luis knew he had to maintain a normal social life.

As a result, he began to date the young women at the Havana Yacht Club. On Saturday afternoons, several couples would get together and after securing the indispensable chaperon, they would decide which nightclub they would go to, usually the Tropicana. They would get a large, round table and spend the night dancing while they waited to see the two choreographed shows of dancers on an open-air stage surrounded by tropical trees. When Luis danced with his virginal dates, he could hardly help thinking about Olga's voluptuous breasts, hips and thighs. How sensual the dance would have been if Olga had been in his arms!

The Tropicana and the other nightclubs could afford the best entertainment in the world from the revenues obtained from their gambling casinos. At times, Luis would play "21" to please his dates, but he really didn't care for gambling. He remembered his father's warning, "Don't become addicted to it, for it will ruin you." Luis knew there was no danger that he would succumb to this common vice of Cuba, for he had too much to accomplish to waste his time playing poker every afternoon, like some of his acquaintances at the Havana Yacht Club.

After the Batista coup in March, 1952, life in Havana settled down to politics as usual. The passivity of the population was a direct result of the low opinion the people held for the Prío government. In April, Batista issued a constitutional code with 275 articles which claimed to be the essence of the 1940 Constitution. Elections were to be held in November, 1954, and the new president was to take office in February of 1955. The government, however, suspended political parties as well as the old Congress and appointed a new consultative council composed of eighty members to temporarily take over the legislature. The middle class soon rallied around the economic and political stability the Batista regime appeared to offer, while the students remained the only real opposition to the government. The Auténticos, the Ortodoxos, and other political parties were also hostile to Batista, but since they were disorganized, they did not present much of a threat.

As soon as classes were reinstated, Luis went back to law school. He remained active in university politics and on May 20 participated in a student-sponsored rally at the stone staircase, the principal entrance to the university, to commemorate the 50th anniversary of Cuban independence. On June 14, after classes ended for the academic year, there was another protest demonstration under the pretext of commemorating General Antonio Maceo's birthday.

Meanwhile, Luis' love affair with Olga was in full bloom. Olga persuaded Senator Miranda she needed to remain in Havana until the end of the summer in order to take tennis lessons at the club. They were idyllic months for Luis and Olga. The lovers would plot elaborate schemes not to be seen together more than casually at the Havana Yacht Club. Luis decided to confide in Guillermo Fernández-Quirch about his affair with Olga so Guillermo could pass the word among their friends that Luis and Olga were distant cousins. It was perfectly natural to talk at the pool and occasionally to be seen together on a sailboat. It was out of the question for Luis to go to Olga's home, so when they wanted to make love some place other than on a sailboat or in the ocean, they would go to one of the many *posadas* or secluded motels located in the outskirts of the city.

The reality of the political situation at the beginning of his second year of law school contrasted with Luis' romantic escapades with Olga. The military did not perceive the Batista regime as tough and puritanical as it had hoped for, and the middle class was becoming impatient with the slow process toward democracy. The masses remained indifferent to the whole situation.

In the months that followed, the government began to tighten its reins. In January of 1953, Rubén Batista, a student, was shot during a demonstration in memory of Mella, a university student leader who had been killed by the Machado regime. On March 10, the anniversary of the coup, there were student riots in protest, and the government discovered a student plot in April in which a large number of students planned to march to Camp Columbia to try to convince the military leaders to rise against Batista. The leaders were arrested, and other student demonstrations followed. The university was again closed for a few days.

To Luis, the situation appeared to be deteriorating for the Batista regime. His observation was confirmed when on July 26, Fidel Castro and his followers came out of nowhere and attacked the Moncada and Bayamo barracks in Oriente Province. The news of the raid shook the country. The attacks failed, but the attackers, outnumbered ten to one, were proof of the growing political frustration on the island.

Luis contacted the Ortodoxo headquarters to ask if there was anything he could do, only to be told the best thing for the moment was to watch and hope. He learned Dr. Emilio Ochoa, the Ortodoxo leader from Oriente, had been taken prisoner, but after being questioned, he was set free. Soon the news was out that Batista's soldiers tortured and later shot many of the prisoners. The savagery of the soldiers caused public opinion to shift in favor of the insurgents. Luis was revolted when press censorship was lifted and the magazine, *Bohemia,* published pictures of the bodies on August 2.

Thirty-two prisoners, among them Fidel Castro, remained alive only because they had been captured several days later. The trial of

Castro and his group took place in October. Luis followed it closely and discussed it daily with fellow students and professors. They were not surprised when Fidel was sentenced to fifteen years in prison and his brother, Raúl, to thirteen. The atrocities committed by the army and Castro's trial made him a hero in Luis Recio's eyes. Luis regretted being a mere spectator of the budding struggle against the dictatorship. His relationship with Olga was undeniably self-indulgent compared to the bold action of those who assaulted the military barracks in Oriente Province. Luis knew that sooner or later he would have to rearrange his priorities.

Chapter 17
Jamaica, June, 1958

They arrived in Kingston Harbor at dusk. The setting sun bathed the Blue Mountains behind the city with a golden hue as the shadow of night pushed against the evening glow on the crown of the mountains. Beneath the shadow, like a string of sparkling pearls, the lights of the city shined at the water's edge. Stars popped out in the east while in the west Venus offered her blessing on the entire scene.

Juan moored the boat at a deserted pier on the western end of the harbor, and just as Juan was about to say goodbye, an idea occurred to Luis.

"Hey, Juan, let me treat you to dinner and a comfortable bed in a nice hotel," Luis suggested.

It took Juan only a few seconds to agree. "Recio, it's the best idea I've heard in a hell of a long time."

They checked in at The Paradise, a modestly priced hotel near the waterfront. Luis found out from the hotel manager that the best restaurant in town was called Pierre's and it required a coat and tie. Luis made reservations for dinner later that evening and had the desk clerk call the owner of a clothing store nearby to make an appointment to buy new clothes. For both of them, Luis chose white linen suits, black Italian shoes, a red tie for him, and a blue one for Juan. Luis reassured Juan the cost of both outfits was on him and not Fidel Castro.

Though Juan had not understood a word of native speech since leaving the dock, Luis was very much at ease with Jamaican English and conversed freely with the solicitous waiter at Pierre's. After Luis ordered drinks, he chose onion soup and a pepper steak for Juan, and for himself a paté and red snapper almandine.

Luis could never offer a logical explanation for his motivation in taking Juan to an exclusive French restaurant in a British colony, but there were few things he had done in life which provided him greater pleasure. Juan wiped his plate clean with the bread and finished the last cup of the bottle of Chablis which they had ordered.

In the back seat of a taxi on the return to The Paradise, Juan asked where he got the money to spend on food and clothes. Luis answered he was fortunate to come from a wealthy family.

"Then, why are you a revolutionary?" Juan inquired, the tone of his voice indicating he would not place his life in jeopardy if he were in Luis' shoes.

"I'm a revolutionary," Luis explained, "because I want everybody to be free and to have the opportunity to enjoy the good things in life."

"I understand. Thanks for doing this for me," replied Juan, patting Luis on the back.

Back at the hotel, Luis called his father in Havana. Rogerio was thrilled to hear from his son but surprised the call came from Kingston.

"I'll save the details for later. Now the most pressing matter is to help me get out of Jamaica. Papá, will you go to the American Embassy tomorrow morning to see Ambassador Earl Smith? Ask him to arrange with the U.S. Consulate in Kingston for me to be given political asylum to enter the United States.

"Of course, I'll take care of everything and call you back as soon as possible. I'll also make arrangements for you to pick up some money from a Kingston bank tomorrow."

As soon as he hung up, Luis called Laura at the Ramírezes. Overjoyed at hearing his voice and learning of his safety, Laura wept openly, but her emotions changed when he told her he wanted her and Luisito to come live with him in Miami. In the silence that followed, Luis could hear her old familiar question, "When are you going to get out of politics so we can have a life together?" She surprised him, though, by saying she would join him but it would be several days before she could move. Pleased and relieved the conversation was free of argument, Luis asked her to hurry because he was eager to see them. Just as he was about to hang up, Laura asked, "Where will we stay?"

"I'll get an apartment," Luis answered, "but first I must get out of Kingston. Papá is making the arrangements."

Laura did not say whether the idea of an apartment pleased her or not, but she did not ask any more questions, assuring Luis she loved him and looked forward to seeing him.

Overcome by fatigue and with a full stomach, Luis stretched out on the bed. It far surpassed the comfort of the hammock in the Sierra Maestra, the humble frame at Prudencio's, and the green leather bench on the *Santa María.*

The next morning, Luis walked with Juan to the pier to say goodbye and offered the crusty sailor his thanks, "Take care, *mi amigo.* There are only a few of us good people left." Juan embraced Luis, who then watched as his friend boarded the *Santa María* carrying his white linen suit rolled up under his arm and his Italian shoes in a brown paper bag. Little did Luis know the story of their white suits and night on the town would get back to Castro via Prudencio. He would later learn gossip traveled as fast in the mountains as in social club.

Rogerio's call at the hotel came at 11:00 a.m. "Here's what you need to do. Go to see a Mr. Edwin Williams at the U. S. Consulate. He'll take you to the proper British authorities who will grant you temporary political asylum. You're booked on a commercial flight to Miami. I've sent you two thousand dollars to Kingston's Royal Bank of Canada. I'll be leaving Havana this afternoon, and I've already made reservations for us at the Columbus Hotel in Miami. If anything should go wrong, call me there."

Listening to his father discuss the arrangements, Luis remembered it was Rogerio who had insisted Luis secure a U.S. visa in case he had to make a quick getaway from the Batista police. Ironically, he would be using it to get out of Jamaica on a secret mission for Fidel Castro. Now Luis understood his father's true talents did not lie in grandiose acts but rather in thinking about details and solving bureaucratic problems. Papá Bernabé and his great uncle *"El Honrado"* had inspired him to go to the mountains, but it was his father who was pulling the strings to get him back to safety.

Chapter 18

Despite a growing sense of political awareness, Luis continued to go to the Havana Yacht Club in the afternoons. He started to play squash and, a good athlete with a long reach, he soon became quite adept at the game. He played with men of all ages, and he struck up friendships with a number of professionals with whom he would have lively talks between matches. It was during these conversations that Luis began to understand the importance of social status in the organization of Cuba's clubs.

At the Sacred Heart Academy in New York, Isabel had made friends with Laura Ramírez, whose parents were members of the HYC. Isabel had raved to Laura about Luis, and when Isabel returned to Havana for Christmas, she hosted a party at the Recio's and persuaded her brother to bring several of his friends. Although they were older than his sister's friends, it was quite proper for young men of twenty to date seventeen-year-old girls.

Luis had only seen Laura from afar at the HYC, having paid little attention to younger women of his sister's age. But when Laura entered the living room arm in arm with Isabel, he was immediately taken by her beauty.

"Luis, this is Laura Ramírez," said Isabel with a sheepish grin. "Do you remember her?"

"Of course I do," Luis replied chivalrously as he smiled and extended both hands to Laura. "I never forget a divine face."

Laura was striking. The teenager Luis vaguely remembered had blossomed into a radiant young woman. What a magnificent figure she had, this tall, olive-skinned girl in the blue silk dress. Luis eyed her discreetly while they chatted and sipped their drinks.

She looks feline, he said to himself, with her almond eyes, full lips, and sleek charcoal black hair. His eyes caressed her face as he asked her about her life at the Sacred Heart Academy.

As they danced the entire evening together, Luis luxuriated in her sensuality. He had never felt this way about any other woman. It was not the same as with Margarita or Olga, for whom he had felt sexual passion more than anything else. Here in his arms was the girl of his dreams, someone who was sexy and virginal at once. By the end of the evening, Luis felt as if he had known Laura all of his life. She was easy to talk to and very natural in her manner.

After that night, Luis tried to see Laura at every opportunity. Although it was December and past the swimming season, he went to the HYC regularly and took Isabel with him so Laura could join them. With politics upstaged by a young woman, the days were idyllic, Luis and Laura entranced with each other. Their first kiss took place during a sailboat ride with Isabel and Guillermo. Luis was handling the tiller, and Laura sat close to him. With a steady wind at some fifteen knots, the boat was navigating beautifully. Luis devilishly made a 45-degree turn which forced Guillermo and Isabel to change the jib, and while they were busy pulling the sheet, Luis kissed Laura softly on her cheek. The sparkle in her big almond eyes invited him to reach for her full-parted lips.

Although it only lasted a few seconds, Luis fully understood the underlying message this first kiss revealed. Laura, by reciprocating, put herself in his hands. By the end of the ride, Luis asked Laura to become his *novia* or sweetheart, which entailed a commitment not to date anybody else. Laura responded with a demure nod, and she followed by timidly touching her lips on his smiling mouth. Guillermo and Isabel's laughter broke their rapture.

"What's this I see?" cried Isabel. "Could it be my big brother is taking advantage of my best friend?" she added with a mischievous smile.

"Not at all," replied Luis, "I'm just crazy about her." He winked at Guillermo with a grin.

The dilemma Luis now faced was to untangle himself from Olga Loynaz. It was a touchy situation he wanted to overcome without Laura's knowledge and without hurting Olga's feelings.

The opportunity presented itself the day after Christmas. While Luis was having breakfast, the telephone rang once. The single ring signaled Olga had returned to Havana from Camagüey. Luis waited the pre-arranged half-hour before he rang Olga's number once. They met an hour later at the Laguito, a small lake in the country club subdivision.

Olga was waiting for him when he arrived. She eagerly jumped into his Buick and embraced him.

"I missed you, darling," she said after she kissed him. Realizing Luis was not responding as usual, she backed off and looked at him with serious eyes.

"What's happening? You know our understanding."

Luis took her hands in his and began, "I need to tell you something. I've met a very special girl, and I'm in love with her. From the beginning you and I agreed to be honest with each other and not have expectations about our relationship."

After an awkward moment, Olga replied, "It's all right, Luis. I've always known someday it would end."

"I want you to know I care deeply for you, but I want to start things right with Laura," Luis said.

"So, Laura is the name of the lucky one. Tell me more about her."

"She's Laura Ramírez. I think you know her parents. Her father owns the Ramírez Supermercado market chain."

"Oh, yes, I think I met them at the club. And how did you get to know her?"

"She goes to the Sacred Heart Academy with my sister, Isabel."

"Well, Luis, I'll try to be gracious about it and leave you alone," Olga said affectionately, "but it's going to be hard on me. I've gotten used to you."

"And I to you, but this is best for all concerned," Luis answered softly.

Olga gave Luis a long look and broke into a sad smile while saying, "Well, I wish you the best." She hurriedly reached for him, kissed him on the cheek, and walked away, fighting back the tears.

Luis and Laura enjoyed being together every day of her Christmas vacation. At the New Year's Eve dance at the HYC, the young couple sat at the same table with Laura's parents. Laura looked incredibly beautiful, and Mario Ramírez was pleased with his daughter's *novio*.

When Laura returned to school in January, Luis went back to the routine of classes at Havana University, and half-heartedly followed the unfolding political scene. Former President Ramón Grau announced he would run for the presidency under the Auténtico party banner. The Communists, realizing that they did not have the strength to come up with a winning candidate, allied themselves with the Auténticos. Most of the Ortodoxos refused to participate in the campaign on the grounds that Batista would not permit honest elections. Thus Luis found himself belonging to a party that did not have a candidate. True, the Ortodoxos had selected Raúl Chibás as their new head, but the brother of the dead leader did not appear to have the ability to control the party.

From February to June, Luis counted the days left until Laura returned with her high school diploma and spent May preparing for final examinations. With examinations over, Luis looked forward to being with Laura more than ever. He resented the two-week trip to the New England states his father gave Isabel as part of a graduation present because it spurred Mario to do the same thing for Laura. Both families traveled together while Luis waited impatiently in Havana.

The Recios and the Ramírezes returned to Havana the third week of June, and from then on, Luis and Laura saw each other every day. They usually met at the club, Laura bringing her mother as chaperon. Once at the club, Elsa would leave Laura with her friends at the swimming pool, and they would sit and talk at one of the tables with umbrellas. For Luis, it was a time of renewal, of holding hands and of enjoying her company. To Laura, being in love with Luis was beyond imagination. Until she met Luis, she had never felt that way about any man.

During those summer weeks, Laura developed a certain possessiveness toward Luis which amused and pleased him. Whenever an attractive woman would make eyes at Luis, Laura would pinch his arm to remind him of her presence.

"Whom are you looking at now?" she would ask with a half-serious smile on her face. Luis would play innocent in return, thinking that from now on he would need to be careful where he looked. It did not bother him since he knew in the Latin culture jealousy was expected of people in love.

Luis and Laura soon discovered a secluded spot at the end of one of the two concrete piers which delineated the club's boundaries. Under one of the piers, their first extended kissing took place in the water. These moments of exquisite lust led to further intimacies as they explored each other's bodies.

Fidel Castro's stirring defense speech, "History Will Absolve Me," was published as a pamphlet in June, 1954. When Luis read it, he agreed wholeheartedly with the five laws which Castro wanted to proclaim: first, a restoration of the 1940 Constitution; second, an agrarian reform which would hand over land worked in lots of less than 150 acres to planters and squatters; third, a profit-sharing system between workers and employers by which one-third of the profits of all sugar mills would be shared; fourth, a guarantee of a minimum quota of 450 tons of cane a year and a right to 55% of the total sugar production for the sugar plantation owners; and fifth, government seizure of all illegally obtained land and property or cash obtained by fraud. In addition, Castro proposed the nationalization of utilities and telephones, as well as educational and housing reforms. All these ideas appealed to Luis' awakening sense of social justice.

They did not impress his father, however, and shortly after Luis gave Rogerio a copy to read, they had their first serious ideological confrontation. It occurred one morning after breakfast on the patio in the presence of Luis' mother.

"Son, you're siding with the radicals. Castro's a communist. He's talking about an agrarian reform that will take away the property your Grandfather Bernabé developed."

"But there's a need for a land reform, Papá. The land reform Fidel mentions has to do with idle land. Since our land is well developed, we have nothing to fear."

"Son, can't you see this is only the beginning? That gangster is also talking about profit sharing by workers and the plantation owners having a guaranteed percentage of their sugar cane processed by the owner of the sugar mill. Not on your life! I believe in capitalism. I'm not about to support a government that's going to tell me how to run my business."

"Papá, I also believe in capitalism, but the economic sector must consider the general welfare of the people. I know you're generous with your workers, but there's so much poverty in the countryside that only the government can deal with it."

"We don't need a bureaucracy to take care of the poor," Luis' father argued, forcefully setting his coffee cup on the table. "I'm much more concerned with having free elections. You know how I feel about the way Batista took power. No matter how corrupt the Prío government might have been, it was elected by the people, and they would have had an opportunity to reject it in the next election. Batista chose to bypass the democratic process because he knew he couldn't get elected, not to end corruption and gangsterism. True, the gangster groups appear to be under control, but I doubt corruption will end."

"But Papá," interjected Luis, visibly irritated, "we probably would've had four more years of Auténtico government if Batista had not taken over. As you know, I've joined the Ortodoxo party, but we were too divided to beat the Auténtico machine, especially with all the money it had to buy votes."

"Luis, you made a mistake by joining that party. I know the Auténticos have had corrupt leaders, but I had faith in Hevia and his new team."

"Papá," said Luis, pacing from one side of the room to the other as his frustration escalated. "Cuba needs something much more radical. Cuba needs a revolution. How else are things going to change?"

"Son, if there's going to be change, I'd like it to be done in a democratic manner."

"It won't happen," Luis replied, raising his voice.

"Are you suggesting the only option is armed struggle?"

"I think so. I don't believe Batista will surrender power in the next election. I don't think the opposition parties will even participate, at least not the Ortodoxos. I seriously doubt the Auténticos will. The Liberales and Demócratas will support Batista, but the Communists won't this time. I see no other option but armed struggle." Having stated his case, Luis sat down again at the table.

"You're influenced by leftist professors at the university," his father objected, throwing his napkin on the table. "I'd like to believe you could think for yourself rather than be taken in by all this demagogic talk!"

"Yes, son," interjected María Luisa, who until that moment had anxiously kept quiet, hoping the subject would be changed. "Listen to your Papá. You're young and idealistic. You swallow those ideas without fully understanding the issues."

"Mamá, please respect my opinions," Luis replied angrily. "I can think for myself. Papá needs to accept the notion of constructive change. In any case, let's drop this conversation. We're getting nowhere."

From then on, Luis avoided discussing politics with his parents. If this was a touchy subject with them, he could just imagine what it would be like talking about agrarian reform with Papá Bernabé!

Chapter 19
Jamaica-Miami, June, 1958

Everything in Jamaica had run as smoothly as at the Tamarindo Sugar Mill. His father was waiting for Luis when the Pan American plane landed at 5:00 p.m. at Miami International Airport. After an emotional embrace, they went directly to David Salvador's apartment on Flagler Street. Luis had hoped to meet David and bring him up to date on recent activities in the Sierra. Unfortunately, David was not at home, so Luis left the envelopes Fidel Castro had sent from the Sierra with his wife.

From there, Luis and his father went to Rogerio's suite on the top floor of the Columbus Hotel. They talked about events of the last few months over cocktails. His father told him Laura had distanced herself from the Recios, visiting periodically only to allow Luisito to spend time with his grandparents. Rogerio wanted to know more about their relationship. "Papá," Luis said, "I'm afraid we're mismatched. She can't accept my commitment to the Revolution. The only thing that we have in common is our son."

"He's beautiful!" the elder Recio beamed after a moment, as if trying to lighten the mood. "He's got those green Recio eyes and your complexion. He's about to start walking too. He and Laura should be here in a few days, God willing."

Inquiring about his mother and sister, Luis learned Isabel was now engaged to Jorge León whom Luis knew from the HYC and who was working in the underground against Batista with Manuel Ray's People's Revolutionary Movement, better known as MRP.

"Well, how does Isabel feel about his activities?" asked Luis.

"She's a true Recio, Luis. She thinks for herself, and she believes Batista must go."

"Your mother has been very worried about you," Rogerio continued. "She prays for you at mass every day. She and Isabel can't wait to see you."

After sharing all his news, Rogerio asked Luis about the Sierra. When Luis confided his disappointment in Castro, Rogerio responded, "I told you this man was not to be trusted. Too many people have had negative things to say about him, and it's not all Batista propaganda."

"But Papá, he's still the only realistic alternative to Batista." Luis insisted. "None of the other leaders is in the mountains, and, apart from the underground, that's where the action is."

"The action may be in the mountains now," Rogerio said, "but I'm not sure Cuba's future is there. Luis, I'd rather have a more moderate government like the Auténtico Party with Prío, who should have been allowed to finish his first term. Had Batista not pulled his coup, we wouldn't be going through all this hell."

Rogerio went on to say he planned to support Carlos Márquez Stérling for president in the election in November because Márquez Stérling was really the only sensible alternative to Castro. He told Luis Ambassador Smith did not believe Castro was the answer to Cuba's problems since Smith was firmly convinced Castro was a communist.

"When I asked him to help get you out of Jamaica, I'm sure he had his suspicions, but since he's a gentleman and a friend, he didn't ask questions. We owe him one."

To avoid a political argument, Luis started talking again about life in the mountains, but when the steaks arrived just as Luis was about to describe the details of the fighting, he steered the conversation back to the family and asked his father about Papá Bernabé.

"Lately I have been spending most of my time in Havana," his father answered, "and he's been keeping an eye on the mill. What troubles me is that he wants to run a modern mill the same way he did the first one. When I'm not around, Papá constantly interferes with the work of Bernabé Morán. He goes into tirades about Batista and has chided more than one young man for not being in the mountains with his grandson! Of course, I haven't told him yet that you're now in Miami."

Luis chuckled at the information, but inside he felt like a failure and wondered what Papá Bernabé would think if he had witnessed some of Luis' actions in the Sierra Maestra.

"Papá, it might be best if you didn't tell Papá Bernabé about my troubles with Castro."

Fortified by after-dinner brandy, Luis returned to the story of his days in the Sierra, down to the last sordid details of the faces of the dead. Rogerio frequently shook his head in disbelief over the tragedy of it all.

After a while, they moved out on the balcony that overlooked the night skyline of Miami.

"The Sierra Maestra seems so far away from here," Luis reflected. "Americans are really lucky to have a decent government and peaceful transfers of power every four years. I guess I'm thankful to be alive!"

"Maybe your mother's prayers had something to do with your safe return," Rogerio added.

"It would be nice to think so," replied Luis.

Shortly after eleven, they went to bed. Unable to sleep, Luis got up and sat on the balcony in the summer night air. He remembered when he first came to America as a teenager and how his father insisted he get out of the car, stand on American soil, and give thanks for the land of his birth. He could see the general area of the old ferry slip where he had once disembarked, a time so distant and yet so recent. "Oh, *Dios mío*," he murmured, "thanks for protecting me, and please watch over those who are in the mountains, particularly Ofelia."

Chapter 20

Fulgencio Batista announced in August of 1954 that he would run for the presidency and began an aggressive well-funded electoral campaign. After the Batista coup, the Auténtico Party split into a Prío wing and a Grau wing. The Prío group opposed any accommodation with Batista. The followers of Grau, however, were willing to take a chance in the upcoming election, as were the Communists, who made an alliance with the Grau supporters. Many Prío politicos, realizing Grau was serious in his quest, abandoned their leader and shifted allegiance to Grau. Something similar happened within the Ortodoxos. Carlos Márquez Stérling, one of the leaders of the party who was unhappy with Raúl Chibás' leadership, decided to break away and enter the race.

Luis watched the last two months of this political campaign as an edgy spectator. This could have been his first opportunity to vote, but his allegiance remained with the wing of the Ortodoxos under Raúl Chibás.

Late in October, events proved the abstaining Auténticos and Ortodoxos right. The government decided to control the election boards by refusing to give Grau equal representation. Having no alternative, Grau withdrew from the election much to the chagrin of the Communists, who accused him of withdrawing to please the United States. Batista, perhaps to placate the Americans, decided to outlaw the Communist Party that had once supported him. Thus, when the elections were held on November 1, Batista won without official opposition, with less than half of the electorate bothering to vote. The Auténtico candidates running for office did earn the minority seats in the senate--three senators in each of the six provinces, and a total of 16 representatives.

On his twenty-first birthday, Luis went to the Municipal Court in Havana and officially relinquished his United States citizenship as required under the 1940 Constitution by means of a deposition. How ironic it is, he thought, that I'm obeying a constitution disdained by the very man, Batista, who was running the country when that document was conceived.

Batista was inaugurated in February of 1955, and his promise to return the country to the 1940 Constitution was allegedly fulfilled. The U.S. vice-president, Richard Nixon, visiting Cuba that month as part of a tour to Central America, appeared to give the blessing of the U.S. to the new regime. The economic situation steadily improved with additional sales of sugar to Russia, and the construction industry flourished. With this new prosperity, Batista was strong enough to declare an amnesty which included Fidel and Raúl Castro and eighteen of the men who had participated in the Moncada attack.

Castro left the Isle of Pines prison on May 15, 1955, and a few days later met with the National Committee of the Ortodoxo party to assure them he did not plan to start another opposition movement. On Cuban Independence Day, May 20, however, he tried to meet with students at the famous stairs at the main entrance of the university, but the police disrupted the meeting. Luis learned from Alberto Sánchez that a later meeting took place, but the students were not willing to acknowledge Fidel Castro as their leader.

"Why should we support Fidel?" Alberto asked. "He has a violent past, he's no student, and we have leaders such as José Antonio Echevarría of the School of Architecture who want to end corruption and gangsterism at Havana University. Echevarría is a moral and courageous leader around whom we can rally to put an end to bully tactics and pistol-carrying thugs."

Luis had to agree with Alberto's assessment. Furthermore, had not the amnesty proved that Batista wanted to accommodate the abstaining opposition? Maybe this was not the time to pursue revolutionary action against the government. Luis now favored a wait-and-see attitude.

Through an Ortodoxo friend, Luis later found out Castro had decided to leave for Mexico and that before he left on July 19, he had organized a group of supporters. Many participated in the Moncada attack and remained committed to the overthrow of Batista by force. The group was to be called the 26th of July Movement after the date of the attack on the barracks.

Luis understood Castro's impatience, but he did not think it was the proper time to fight Batista by violent means. Most politicians held the same view, and the most important one, Carlos Prío, the deposed president, decided to return to Cuba in August of 1955 and pledged to oppose Batista, but only through the electoral process.

Luis' fifth and last year of law school started routinely enough. José Antonio Echevarría was elected president of the Federation of University Students or FEU and joined other opponents of the government in a campaign to force Batista to hold elections in 1956. The new movement was named Society of Friends of the Republic (SAR), and Don Cosme de la Torriente, a venerable old man of eighty-three and a distinguished public figure, headed the movement.

Luis participated in meetings of the FEU since like other students, he was becoming disgruntled with Batista's apparent unwillingness to take the opposition seriously. The public high school students in particular were vocal in their opposition, and sporadic riots broke out in cities around the country. With each outbreak, Luis again felt the chances for an orderly operation of government decreased while the probability of armed revolution increased with each passing day. He did not dare to share his views with his father.

On November 19, the SAR organized a gigantic meeting attended by most of the opposition leaders. The Auténticos were represented by Carlos Prío and Ramón Grau, the Ortodoxos by Raúl Chibás, the Democrats by José Andreu, the National Bar Association by José Miró Cardona, the Radicals by Amalio Fiallo, and the FEU by Echevarría. The 26th of July Movement and the Communists were conspicuously absent at the platform. The meeting proved to be a huge success because the opposition rallied around a call for new elections, but its leaders failed to persuade Batista to hold elections before 1958.

Luis balanced his frustrations with the political impasse by focusing his attention on Laura. Not having any particular vocation,

Laura had decided to study art with the idea of specializing in interior design. Classes at Villanueva University were as uneventful as they were erratic at Havana University. The American Dominican order founded Villanueva in the late forties, modeling its curriculum after that of American universities, and it catered to middle and upper middle-class students who were serious about pursuing an education. Classes were compulsory, and although there was some interest in politics on campus in the law school, the great majority of the student body was not politically aware. Villanueva was the natural place to send proper young ladies who wanted to attend college and perhaps meet a suitable young man from the same social background.

Luis and Laura met every day, often in the afternoons at the club after Laura and Isabel finished classes. They played tennis or squash at the HYC with Isabel serving as the unofficial chaperon. Later they would join the Recios or the Ramírezes for cocktails either at the spacious bar at the club overlooking the swimming pool or at their parents' homes. Unless they went out to a movie at night with a chaperon, they stayed at the Ramírezes and entertained themselves by playing double solitaire and enjoying each other's company.

They soon found the small library that had been built by Elsa Angulo's father provided a place where the two of them could be alone. The room had a stereo, a television set, and a comfortable sofa. More importantly, it was located at the end of the first floor hall and gave Luis and Laura the privacy they craved. In their intimate moments, Laura would take the initiative with caresses that led to serious foreplay that became more and more intense with each encounter. Luis knew he would have to control himself to preserve Laura's virginity.

One afternoon Laura called Luis and invited him to her house. When he arrived, Humberto, the servant, informed him that the Ramírezes were out. Shortly after Humberto left the room, Laura summoned Luis from the top of the marble stairs.

"Come on up, Luis, I have something I want to show you," she said in an innocently seductive tone.

Luis hurried upstairs to her bedroom and found Laura in bed. Before he could speak, Laura put her finger over her lips and with a provoking smile motioned for him to join her in bed. Luis felt himself getting aroused as he bent over to kiss her. She was naked under the sheets, and before long his own clothes, with Laura's help, were at the foot of the bed. This is madness he thought, unable to contain himself as he kissed every inch of her body.

"I want to make love with you," she whispered in his ear as she responded to him.

"If only we could. There's nothing that I desire more than to make love to you, but now is not the time. We must wait until we get married."

"Then we must marry soon; I can't wait any longer," Laura replied in desperation.

"You know how much I love you," Luis countered, "but I have one year of law school left. I promise you we'll get married as soon as I finish and start to work. So, pleeease, my love, for the sake of your honor, don't tempt me like this anymore."

By restraining himself with his future wife, Luis was conforming to one of the most sacred codes of Cuban society, the respect of the bride's virginity. From then on, they regularly gave each other pleasure but in ways which circumvented the consummation of their desire.

Meanwhile, after much stalling, Batista was persuaded to meet with the opposition in March of 1956. Several cursory sessions took place, but Batista considered himself secure in his job and would not make any real concessions to the opposition. Once again Batista blocked a return to democracy, and it disheartened Luis to see such an opportunity wasted.

Studying for the last seven law courses and his relationship with Laura occupied most of Luis' time. As a result, he saw less of his classmates at the university and his friends at the HYC. Laura had become the center of his life.

In June, Luis finished law school after writing a noncontroversial dissertation on the unconstitutionality of the rent tax law. Because of his father's connections and his ability to speak English, Luis immediately found a job with Biosca, Uría, and Brage, a large and prestigious law firm in Havana.

At the end of the month, Luis and Laura had a formal engagement party at the Ramírezes, and preparations for the wedding started immediately. Since Laura's family wanted to make the wedding an affair to remember, attention to proper social protocol was essential.

Friends of the couple organized several pre-nuptial parties. The two families sent out eight hundred invitations to relatives and friends all over the island. Luis did not particularly like all the planned pomp, but knowing it pleased the Ramírezes, he spent the last few weeks of bachelorhood observing this conspicuous display as a half-amused, half-annoyed bystander.

Such extravagance contrasted with Mario Ramírez's well-known reputation for stinginess, and as Luis got to know the family better, he learned the tales about Mario's behavior were not exaggerated.

Luis sent invitations to his friends in the U.S., Camagüey, and Havana. He wrote a letter with the invitation to Julio Cubillán in Venezuela and mentioned in it that Laura and he planned to go to Mexico for their honeymoon. Julio had graduated the previous year from West Point and was now a lieutenant in the Venezuelan army. Julio replied right away with the news he was marrying his old sweetheart, Juanita Castillo, on December 7 and they would also be spending their honeymoon in Mexico. Julio suggested the two couples meet in Acapulco. Immediately Luis made plans with Julio so the two couples could spend several days together at Acapulco's Las Brisas Hilton.

In the middle of these pre-nuptial arrangements, the news of the uprising in Santiago on November 30 and Castro's alleged landing in Oriente province two days later, took Luis by surprise. Numerous groups of revolutionaries regularly made the news as violence took place or police discovered caches of arms, but Luis knew the 26th of July Movement was the one that really meant business with this invasion. Castro might have been a gangster at Havana University, but twice now he had shown himself to be the only leader on the Cuban scene who was willing to risk his life for his ideals.

There was something about the elaborate wedding preparations that made Luis uneasy. Every time he went to the Ramírezes, he saw the latest gifts which had arrived. The elegance and extravagance of the many gifts which already filled two rooms contradicted his growing sense of economic inequities in Cuban society.

"What on earth are we going to do with this?" Luis mumbled to himself while looking at a white porcelain vase with two scarlet macaws perched on different limbs of a tree, their long beaks turned toward each other and their multi-colored feathers running the length of the vase.

Luis followed impatiently as his future wife showed him the expensive dinnerware displayed on her bed next to the exquisite Limoge's porcelain.

"Don't you just love it?" she asked as she cuddled close to him with a contented look. Luis nodded with resignation as he slid his hand down her back and tenderly drew her closer to him.

Finally, the day of the wedding arrived. Laura looked radiant on her father's arm, and Mario proudly beamed from right to left as he escorted his daughter down the church's aisle. A sumptuous reception at the Ramírezes followed the wedding mass. Mario and Elsa made this a memorable occasion by renting a gigantic tent under which the guests gathered in the spacious and finely manicured garden. As proof of their generosity, the Ramírezes served Beluga caviar and other delicacies with Don Perignon champagne that flowed freely. In the background, the Benny Moré Orchestra played soft Latin rhythms. Such lavishness suggested Mario was not the miser others thought him to be.

Luis and Laura mingled with the guests until five o'clock, at which time they changed clothes and left for the Rancho Boyeros Airport to catch the flight to Mexico City. The honeymooners spent their first night at the Del Prado Hotel in Mexico City. That night after they toasted with champagne to their love and marriage, they indulged wildly in their new-found freedom. Luis realized he could not distinguish the boundary of his body from Laura's as they consummated their love time and time again. Such was the intensity of their lovemaking. It was more than Luis had ever imagined, and it had been well worth the wait.

"Come, my love," Luis said tenderly to Laura at dawn, "we must get some sleep if we're going to see the sights of Mexico."

A week later they arrived at Las Brisas Hilton, located on a hill overlooking the bay. The hotel was made up of spacious cabanas with individual swimming pools ideal for honeymooners. The sights and sounds of Acapulco fascinated Laura.

Juanita and Julio arrived and moved into a cabana close by. While their wives shopped, Julio and Luis spent hours reminiscing about their days at SMA. They exchanged views about politics in their respective countries and found their situations were quite similar. "You have a Batista, and we have a Pérez Jiménez," Julio summarized, "except our dictator is probably richer because we have oil."

After a memorable week the couples separated, vowing to keep in touch. Juanita and Julio left to visit the Yucatán region, and Laura and Luis went by car to Taxco and then to Mexico City for the return trip to Havana. As Luis drove in air-conditioned comfort across the Mexican countryside, he wondered how things might be going for Fidel Castro in the Oriente mountains.

Chapter 21
Miami, late June, 1958

When his mother and sister arrived two days later, they cried when they saw Luis at the airport. "Thank God you're okay. But you're so thin!" María Luisa exclaimed.

"Mamá, I've only lost fifteen pounds," Luis reassured her with a grin. Clutching Isabel's hand in his own, Luis commented, "What a beautiful ring, but it's not nearly as beautiful as you. Love wears well with my dear sister."

"Oh Luis," said Isabel laughing, "you've always been the charmer, and you're still a master of *piropos*."

"I learned it from Papá Bernabé," he said with a wink toward his mother.

On the way to the hotel, Rogerio surprised them all with an announcement.

"Since Luis must live here until the situation in Cuba changes, I've decided to buy a house. This afternoon we'll have a realtor take us around. This way we'll have a place to stay whenever we come to visit our grandson."

"A wonderful idea," said María Luisa, "we'll have a place where we can all be together."

"We'll have it furnished," said Rogerio, "and even get an interior decorator."

Luis could not take in the difference between what he was hearing now and all he had heard and seen in the mountains. The Sierra was a universe away, and no one in his family could imagine the life he lived there--except perhaps Papá Bernabé. Nearly everyone, he reasoned, is sheltered from reality in one way or another. His parents would be far more baffled by life at Pino del Agua than poor Juan was in the French restaurant in Kingston. One-half of the world had no understanding whatsoever of how the other half lived.

He recalled the visit he made with teammate Joe Williams at SMA to the Johnson's farm near Joe's home and his realization at the gulf between the whites and the blacks until it dawned upon him the polarization in Cuba between the rich and the poor was scarcely any better. He pondered the solution. Was it communism? Not as practiced; however, it was apparent the "haves" in the world were the only ones in a position to make the world better, but he saw no sign they were inclined to do so.

He could not even be sure about Fidel Castro. Would he wind up adding to the ideological polarization of the world, or would he bring change in terms of freedom and quality of life? Luis hoped the latter would prove to be the case, but he was beginning to have his doubts.

After they returned to the hotel, his father took Luis aside and confessed his real intention. "Luis, another reason we're buying this house is our concern for your marriage. We know Laura would be unhappy in a small apartment. The house will provide a place for you two to get to know each other again.

Luis appreciated his parents' generosity and love. While they considered everyone's needs, Laura's tendency was more defined in terms of self-interest. The real contrast of this Revolution, Luis reasoned, is not defined by my father and Fidel Castro, but my wife and Ofelia Ramos.

That afternoon the Recios purchased a Spanish-style house in Coral Gables with a red tiled roof, four bedrooms, two-and-one-half baths, and a central patio with a swimming pool. María Luisa raved about the patio and the flower garden in the back yard, both of which reminded her of her home in Camagüey.

They went with the realtor to the bank where Rogerio wrote a check to pay for the house in full and handed it to the realtor, the words "house for grandson" written in the lower left-hand corner. He made arrangements for Luis to draw from the Miami account as needed.

"I have $350,000 in that bank, Luis," Rogerio said when he had a chance to speak privately. "You have never been an extravagant person, and I trust your judgment with this account."

"Thanks, Papá," Luis said, embracing his father.

Chapter 22

On their return to Havana, the newlyweds moved to a furnished apartment until they decided on a permanent residence. Luis' parents offered to buy them a new two-bedroom condominium by the fashionable Almendares River, but the Ramírezes opposed the idea and tried without success, to convince Laura that she and Luis would be better off living in the Ramírez home.

Laura soon settled into to the pleasant routine of the young well-to-do Cuban housewife. She would get up late and after a light breakfast, spend a couple of hours on the phone talking to her mother and friends. In the afternoons, she was off to the club for a canasta game. This idyllic life came to an end in March of 1957 when she began to suffer morning sickness.

As the days went by, it became apparent to Luis that what mattered primarily to Laura were her marriage and her social life. He rationalized her apolitical nature by telling himself he fell in love with her in spite of her lack of interest in government.

Mario Ramírez, however, had definite political opinions, and they ran counter to Luis' own. Luis discovered their sharp differences one February night while the Ramírezes were having dinner with them at the condominium.

"What do you think of Castro's taking to the mountains?" Luis asked his father-in-law.

"I'd like to see that crazy man and his band of criminals dead," replied Mario without hesitation. "I don't particularly care for General Batista, but you've got to give him credit for ending gangsterism and bringing about economic stability and progress."

"Economic well-being has nothing to do with Batista," countered Luis. "It has to do with the high price of sugar on the world market at the moment. I'll admit Batista has ended gangsterism, but now the government makes indiscriminate arrests, and the police obtain confessions by torture. It's just another type of terrorism."

"Luis, you don't understand how to deal with these rebels. We Cubans need a strong arm, or we are going to have a communist revolution."

"With all due respect, Mario, the Auténticos and the Ortodoxos are not communists, nor are the students. Echevarría is a practicing Catholic. If the government had been reasonable, the situation wouldn't have deteriorated to this extreme."

When the Ramírezes left, Luis and Laura had their first real argument.

"How could you talk to my father that way?" Laura inquired indignantly.

"Laura, I would like for your father to respect my opinions. Your father might be an excellent businessman, but he's out of touch with reality."

"Oh yes, I suppose you think we'd be better off with a leftist government."

"Laura, the opposition is attempting to reinstate our 1940 Constitution and to follow the electoral process. When Batista pulled the coup d'état, he completely disregarded the Constitution. Remember, Batista was head of the Armed Forces when the Constitution was conceived, and he later was the first president elected under that Constitution and served for four years."

"But things are different now," Laura asserted. "In any case, I don't want you involved in this mess."

Laura wanted Luis to be a bystander, but he was convinced the time for action was not far off. Luis wished his wife understood his commitment to political involvement, and it frustrated him that Laura chose to remain uninformed and indifferent to the situation in Cuba.

On the afternoon of March 13, as Luis was discussing a case with Ricardo Brage, one of the junior partners at the law office, an errand boy rushed into the room.

"Rebel forces have overtaken the Presidential Palace! They executed the dictator!" he blurted out.

Luis and Ricardo looked at each other in astonishment. Could this be possible?

"Where did you hear this?" Luis inquired.

"I was at the corner bar getting coffee for the office when Radio Reloj announced the news," the young man said. "Then the radio station went dead. Policemen are all over the streets. Tanks are surrounding the Palace."

Luis and Ricardo hurried to the front of the building and peeped out through one of the second floor windows. Sure enough, agitated policemen could be seen in groups of two or three down the street. The sound of sirens filled the air. Could this be the work of the 26th of July? Luis wondered. Perhaps the *Directorio Revolucionario* was responsible. Regardless, Batista had been assassinated! From the street, a group of policemen shouted profanities and angrily gestured with their guns for Luis and Ricardo to get away from the window. Hurriedly, they complied.

Glued to the radio, Luis and Ricardo stayed at the law office until they heard the news that palace guards, policemen, and soldiers had halted the attack. The information they had received earlier was erroneous; Batista was still alive. Some thirty-five attackers and five palace guards had been killed. Luis admired the bravery of the insurgent group, but intuitively he knew Batista would benefit from the assassination attempt. In the next few weeks, he was proven right when the business community and the members of the oligarchy displayed an outpouring of support toward the government. They condemned the attack as an act of gangsterism by men of disreputable background. It was of no concern to them that the police had killed José Antonio Echevarría, the president of the Havana University's Student Federation, as he tried to enter the university after fleeing the radio station his group had captured.

A certain tacit condoning of an atrocious act apparently committed by the police appalled Luis. The day after the attack, the body of Dr. Pelayo Cuervo, the nominal head of the Ortodoxo Party, was found near El Laguito in the Country Club subdivision.

A few days later while they were having cocktails by the pool, his father told Luis Tony de Varona's theory about the assassination of Pelayo Cuervo. According to de Varona, documents found on Echevarría's body indicated Dr. Cuervo was to become the provisional president if Batista had been overthrown.

"That's no reason to murder someone," Luis replied. "For all we know, Pelayo Cuervo wasn't even aware of the plans for the attack on the Presidential Palace."

"I agree, son, and I'm not condoning the assassination, but understand, violent acts bring about violent reprisals."

"I know, Papá, but how else can Batista be deposed? He had his chance to find a political solution by accepting Don Cosme's plan to hold elections in 1956. Yet he rejected this opportunity which would have given him an honorable way out. Now, I'm afraid there's no real alternative but to topple Batista by force."

Late in March, Alberto Sánchez came to visit Luis in his law office. After a few good-natured exchanges about how fit Luis looked since his marriage, Alberto got down to the real reason for his visit.

"Luis, I'm here to recruit you for the 26th of July Movement," said Alberto, leaning forward with his palms flat on Luis' desk. "I'm organizing the independent cells of the underground. Since the failure of the attack on the Presidential Palace, we've been placing bombs around Havana. We need money for sabotage and arms for the guerrillas. With your connections, you could be a key man in the organization. You could organize a financial drive in Camagüey. What do you say?"

Luis turned Alberto's proposition over in his mind. His previous doubts about armed struggle had been overcome by the realization that even if, as Batista stated, the scheduled presidential elections would take place in November of 1958, the dictator would see to it that one of his men remained in power. Yes, the time to act had arrived.

"All right, Alberto, I'll join. There're a lot of ranchers in Camagüey who are fed up with the situation. I'll see to it that my law office assigns me to some of our clients in Camagüey."

"Thanks, Luis," said Alberto, enthusiastically shaking his hand.

Throughout the next few days, Luis approached friends at the HYC. He first talked with Guillermo Fernández and found him eager to participate. The two of them discreetly talked to prospective contributors and soon had commitments of several thousand *pesos*. Luis even found unsolicited support from some of the workers in the men's rooms. One of them, Torcuato Pérez, had discussed politics with Luis for years. Torcuato overheard Luis and Guillermo talking about Herbert Matthews' article in the *New York Times* that had reached Havana some weeks before. The February 24th article detailed Matthew's visit with Fidel Castro and his men in the Sierra Maestra. The article by the *Times'* senior editor gave a tremendous boost to the 26th of July Movement and denied Batista's assertion that Castro and his force had been liquidated by the army.

"So you and Luis are Fidelistas," said Torcuato, as Guillermo and Luis looked up in surprise. "I knew there had to be some idealistic young men here. I'm on your side. It's time we rally behind someone with the *cojones* to fight Batista and his henchmen."

Luis then asked Torcuato if he wanted to work with them, and Torcuato eagerly accepted. From then on, Luis had a key man at the club who gave him information about the members and their political leanings, which in turn helped Luis assess the prospective contributors and avoid being discovered by government officials and sympathizers who were also members of the club.

When Luis left for Camagüey, he kept the true purpose of the trip from Laura because he knew she would be upset. He simply said he was going on business.

The mission to Camagüey proved to be productive. Among the persons he first talked to was Roberto de Varona, Tony's youngest brother, who was also active in Auténtico politics, having been a candidate for mayor of Camagüey a few years back.

Roberto, a ruggedly handsome, tall man was rabidly anti-Batista and openly expressed himself on those terms. "That worthless son-of-a-bitch has brought this country to its knees," he shouted at Luis as they were having a drink at the Gran Hotel bar in downtown Camagüey.

Luis looked around and motioned to Roberto to lower his voice. The last thing he needed at this stage was to be noticed by the ubiquitous police who were notorious for patrolling Comercio Street to harass young men who went there to flatter the female shoppers with *piropos*. When Luis and Roberto left the Gran Hotel to go to the Liceo, they heard a familiar commotion.

"Here comes Olaón!" a couple of excited teenagers yelled as they ran by the entrance of the hotel. Roberto and Luis watched as a police car slowly passed by. Captain Olaón sat in the right front seat holding a billy stick out of the window while he surveyed the sidewalks and looked for an opportunity to use it. He was a typical police bully who derived pleasure from asserting his authority and harassing young men. In front of the hotel on the other side of the street, stood a defiant young man with his arms crossed who, perhaps to show off to the girls nearby, refused to go inside and hide from the notorious captain.

"Button that shirt all the way up, young man!" demanded Captain Olaón from the car in a threatening voice. When the teenager hesitated, the captain opened the door and ran after him with his stick. In the commotion that ensued, the youngster barely escaped.

"What a son of a bitch," Luis commented to Roberto.

"What do you expect when bastards like him are the law?" replied Roberto.

That afternoon in the privacy of one of the rooms at the Liceo, Luis and Roberto discussed Luis' task at length. Roberto would not commit himself to working with Luis but did give him the names of prospective contributors. "These are cattlemen and sugar cane growers who through the years have been sympathetic to the Auténtico Party," he said. "You know how much Tony and I have relied on your father's support. It's only fair I pass their names to you.

"In one way or another," Roberto added after taking a sip from his drink, "we're all working for the same goal—disposing of our bloody tyrant!"

Aware Grandfather Bernabé, now eighty-four years old, had only a few years left, Luis made a greater effort to spend time with him.

When Luis arrived at Papá Bernabé's spacious home in Camagüey, Caridad, the housekeeper of half a century, fussed over him as if he were one of her own. "How I miss you, my little one! You mustn't stay away so long."

As she spoke, she held his face in both hands, her eyes dancing with light.

"Doesn't your grandfather get a hug?" inquired Bernabé, coming into the living room with a big smile and opening his arms wide to receive Luis with the loving embrace Luis knew so well.

"Come to the dining room, Luis, and tell me about your family. You must be starving. When I found out you were coming for lunch, I told the Caridad to prepare your favorite meal, yellow rice with pork and plantains."

Luis marveled at the solid handsomeness of his grandfather. Although slightly corpulent, he was a picture of health with his tanned face under a full mane of white hair. Looking at him, Luis fully understood how young women could be attracted to this older man.

As Bernabé led the way to the dining room, Caridad grabbed Luis by the arm and whispered, "Luisito, you must talk to your grandfather. Since your Grandmother Celia's death, he has reverted to his old ways. He has lately taken to pinching our young cleaning lady, and he goes out on the town like a slick, perfumed young rooster."

Amused, Luis would have sworn there was a tinge of jealousy in Caridad's complaint.

As soon as Luis finished the legal errands which had served as a pretext for his trip to Camagüey, he drove by his parents' home in the Garrido subdivision. The old mansion looked deserted. Benancio, the faithful gardener, guarded the house with the natural possessiveness of someone who had been around forever. He and his wife, Nena, stayed in the house when the Recios went to Havana. Benancio rushed to get Luis' luggage out of the car, and when Luis told him he was staying with Papá Bernabé, the old gardener was disappointed.

"You would be more comfortable here, Luisito," Benancio said with a reproachful voice.

"I know, Benancio, but I promised Papá Bernabé I'd stay with him."

As Benancio proudly showed Luis the flower garden, Luis noticed Enrique Bueno coming toward them from his house across the street.

"Well, well, so the big shot Havana lawyer is honoring us with his presence in provincial Camagüey," Enrique greeted Luis with a big smile as he opened his arms to give his friend an embrace. "Let me take a look at your face, Luisito. I want to see if it is true you're now a man." Luis gracefully accepted Enrique's teasing and replied in turn,

"My, how you have shrunk! I remember when you used to be taller than I."

It had been not quite a year since they last saw each other. Luis invited Enrique for a drink, and while they reminisced in the large rocking chairs in the front porch, Nena came by with a tray full of snacks and *mojitos*.

"Ah, Nena, you always know how to please me," said Luis as he happily took a pork rind and handed a *mojito* to Enrique.

"How are things in Camagüey, Enrique?"

"Pretty quiet, Luis. What's happening in Oriente Province and in Havana doesn't affect Camagüey. If it weren't for the periodic confrontations that the high school students have with the police and the isolated acts of violence committed by the army, we wouldn't be aware we have a dictatorship and what appears to be the beginning of a full-scale revolution. You heard about Garabatico Sánchez's murder. A trigger-happy soldier gunned him down. It brought the struggle home and turned a lot of people turn against the regime, but things have been pretty quiet since then."

"Have you seen Senator Betancourt lately?" Luis inquired.

"The old man stays here in Camagüey most of the time. Unfortunately, he still admires Batista. There're a lot of members of Congress who will regret their support for this tyrant. Most of them didn't have any idea of what they were getting into. It's a shame, for a number of them are decent fellows."

Luis confided to Enrique the real reason of his trip to Camagüey and invited him to join the 26th of July Movement.

"You know, Luis, you have convincing arguments, but I have a lot of misgivings about this group. I wish the Auténticos or the Ortodoxos had shown more leadership. Since Echevarría attacked the Palace, the 26th of July is the only organization showing any strength."

"Exactly. That's why I began to work for it," replied Luis. "Believe me, if enough of us participate, we'll be able to have an important say in the future of our country."

It took Luis a week to make the needed contacts in Camagüey, and when he was finished, he left Enrique Bueno in charge of coordinating the financial campaign. As a prosperous businessman, Enrique had easy access to banks, and he could use his Hatuey beer distributorship as a front when needed.

After his last dinner in Camagüey at Papá Bernabé's, Luis confided in his grandfather his real reasons for coming back home. Bernabé was not surprised.

"Luis, I might now be considered a sugar baron, but remember when I was younger than you, I joined the Cuban rebels to fight for independence. So I know what it's like to side with the underdogs, and there's nothing I hate more than any type of dictatorship, whether it springs up here or elsewhere. Luis, you must do what you know is right in your heart. I detest people who sit around waiting to see which way the wind is blowing before they commit themselves. I admire people with convictions even if they're my enemies.

"I must tell you, though, there's talk about this fellow Castro that I don't like. Some of my friends swear he's a communist, but I'm inclined to give him the benefit of the doubt. Castro's willing to live hard and fight hard. So, grandson, if you see fit to help him, you have my blessing."

When his grandfather finished speaking, Luis got up from his chair, walked to the head of the dining room table, and embraced Papá Bernabé. "You're unbelievable!" Luis said with a smile. "In spite of your years, you still carry the free spirit of Cuba within you. What a pity you never chose to go into politics."

"If I had," Bernabé replied with a laugh, "I wouldn't have been a free spirit."

Luis threw his head back and chuckled, and his grandfather joined in.

"Do you include *'El Honrado'* in this statement?" Luis asked humorously.

"No, Luisito," Bernabé replied becoming serious. "Manuel was more of a crusader than a politician. That's why he died."

Chapter 23
Miami, July-December, 1958

María Luisa and Isabel enjoyed selecting furniture, china, silverware, and draperies in order to have everything perfect for Laura's and Luisito's arrival. They took care of every detail, from towels in the kitchen to hangers in the spacious closets.

The family met them on July 2 at the airport. Luis held her and his son in his arms, kissing both in turns. Luisito reacted to this display of affection with an outburst of tears, pushing away from the stranger and clinging to his mother.

"Luisito," said Laura, "this is Papá."

Luisito let out another wail.

"You'll have plenty of time to win him over, Luis," María Luisa said reassuringly.

When Laura saw the house and furniture, she was overwhelmed by all her in-laws had done, and she thanked them profusely. The Recios were relieved Laura was pleased, and to give her and Luis privacy, they rented a car and left that afternoon for a vacation in the mountains of North Carolina.

Privacy was hard to come by since Luisito apparently did not like his new room and cried during his siesta. Finally, he fell sleep in Laura's arms. After putting him into his bed, Luis and Laura made long awaited love, each reaffirming their love for the other.

That night in Laura's arms again, Luis counted his marital blessings. Laura had been a devoted mother while he was away, and the faults he had found in her stemmed merely from her deep love for him and Luisito.

In Miami, Luis had every pleasure a man could wish for--family, home, and a sense of purpose. He no longer felt guilty about being sent out of the mountains by Castro.

Luis found himself a celebrity of the anti-Batista groups in Miami. While others were planning on going to the Sierra, he had already been there and came out alive to confirm the success of the rebels. David Salvador, seeing the propaganda potential for the 26th of July, scheduled talks for Luis in Miami, Los Angeles, Chicago, and New York. Because of Luis' knowledge of English, he was called upon to give press interviews about the rebels and help prepare news releases about the Batista dictatorship and the future of a democratic Cuba, reassuring the Americans that Castro and the rebels were not communists. After the articles by Herbert Mathews and others, sympathy in the U.S. had turned in favor of the rebels, and anything Luis had to say publicly only strengthened the image of Castro as the Robin Hood of the Caribbean.

When Luis told David Salvador that his mother's first cousin, Philip Heymann, worked in the State Department, Salvador urged him to go to Washington and work with Heymann and Ernesto Betancourt, the 26th of July representative, to influence U.S. policy. The U.S. had stopped armed shipments to Batista the previous April and was now turning a blind eye to supply missions to the rebels. Salvador reasoned that since the groups opposing Batista were now united following a meeting in Caracas on July 20, it was crucial to keep the momentum going.

Luis was well aware his absences were not sitting well with Laura, and when he returned from Washington after a two-week trip, her reaction did not surprise him at all. Having left Luisito with the maid, she met him at the airport and stood coldly in his arms when he met her at the gate. As soon as Luis started the car, she gave vent to her feelings.

"Luis, I might as well have stayed in Havana! You're obsessed with overthrowing Batista, and you ignore your son and me. You take me for granted!"

Before Luis could respond to her raving, she continued, "I thought in Miami we might be able to capture something of the early days of our marriage, but just like in Havana, you get strange phone calls from people I don't know and go to meetings you don't talk about. Where will it all end? What about our future, Luis? Tell me!"

The disappointment Luis experienced was as familiar as the arguments. From her perspective, he had to agree with everything she was saying. She wanted a family life but had no interest in politics. Somehow Laura's collection of suitcases symbolized her view of the world. When she arrived at Miami International, she had ten big pieces of luggage, and they had to rent a station wagon to haul all she brought to the house. Luis and his father joked about her limited wardrobe, but to Luis, it was really no laughing matter. Laura argued many of the bags contained items for the house and the baby. Concerning her wardrobe, two contrasting scenes played in Luis' mind: one was the image of ten suitcases stacked in their garage, and the other was of Prudencio and his wife in their barren hut.

Luis knew his own answer was also familiarly boring.

"Laura," he said as they motored down LeJune Avenue, "I know how you feel. I'm sorry to have been away so much. What I'm trying to do is help build a better future for all of us."

"I only know that your involvement in politics is ruining our marriage," Laura interrupted.

Luis had other thoughts he could have expressed, but instead he heard himself say, "Laura, we may be incompatible, but let's not make any hasty decisions. Let's try to make the best of things here in Miami. The situation in Cuba can't last forever, and once things return to normal, we'll have more time for each other."

"Oh, Luis," she said, leaning on his shoulder, "if things could only be as they once were between us."

When they got home they made love, both knowing sex was not the solution to their conflict.

After a week of relative calm, Laura hesitantly told Luis at breakfast that her father had called the night before. Mario said he had been at a dinner party with other businessmen at the Presidential Palace where they were given a briefing by General Batista himself. According to Mario, Batista was one of the most charming persons he had ever met.

Luis shook his head in amazement.

"Laura, I can tell you side with your father. I've shared my disappointment in Castro with you. Everybody knows Batista is charming. So what? Hitler, Mussolini and Stalin were also charming despots. Stalin was even affectionately called 'Uncle Joe.'"

"I might just as well tell you everything," Laura retorted. "Papá has been told the man you work for here, David Salvador, is a communist."

"By God, Laura, David Salvador was a communist when he was a teenager! Why don't you remind your father Batista himself was the presidential candidate of the Communists in the 1940 election he won? What's more, two members of his cabinet, Juan Marinelo and Carlos Rafael Rodríguez, were also communists. What's the point?"

"I was just relaying what Papá told me," Laura said defensively.

"Laura, are you really saying that your father doesn't believe Batista is behind the atrocities?" Luis asked in exasperation.

"Papá believes Batista is the scapegoat for the excesses of the armed forces which he can't control."

"Hell, Laura! Batista isn't a scapegoat. He's a mad bull who has trampled the 1940 Constitution. Without constitutional guarantees, anarchy is what you get."

"I just don't understand what's happening," Laura replied, throwing her hands in the air.

"I wish you would take my word for it instead of your father's," Luis responded irritably.

When Luis came home one August night from a meeting in New York, he heard Laura on the phone in the bedroom. She was crying as she talked to her parents. "I'm coming home" was the phrase that lodged in his mind. He started to rush into the room but paused at the door. "I just can't stand it anymore. These have been the most miserable months of my life. I thought he would settle down since I last called you, but if anything he has been gone more."

When she hung up, Luis stepped into the bedroom and said, "Laura, I couldn't help hearing. If you want to go home to your parents, I won't stop you."

Falling on her pillow, Laura began to cry. "I'm leaving," she sobbed, "I can't stay here anymore. I can't figure you out. You told me you had grave doubts about Castro, that he may even be a murderer from his days at the university, yet you're working day and night to put him in power. What am I supposed to think?"

Luis realized her assessment might have been right. Just what was he doing working for the Revolution? Laura had a talent for stripping everything down to the bare essentials. She hated deception, politics, and war, yet he brought all these things into her life.

He sat down on the side of the bed and gently rubbed her back until she sat up, and, still weeping, embraced him, but as both of them knew, her decision was final.

Laura left in early September, taking Luisito and the maid with her. Luis realized if Batista stayed in power, it would be a long time before he would see them again. When Luis returned to the house after putting them on the plane, he felt abandoned and alone. The two most important people in his world had just left him.

In Laura's absence, Luis threw himself into the work of the 26th of July Movement. His marriage had fallen apart, but the Revolution still had a chance of succeeding.

Before Luis knew it, the Coral Gables house became a hive of revolutionary activities. There was rarely a night when guests did not occupy one of the bedrooms, either destitute exiles who stayed until they found a job or revolutionaries in town for a meeting or rally. Luis had never done so much cooking, but that was also a way of keeping busy and useful. One day when friends were splashing in the pool and enjoying loud Cuban music by La Sonora Matancera, Luis realized that in all honesty he was glad Laura was not around. If she were there, she would not have allowed the house to be used as a club and way station.

One night late in November, Luis and David Salvador were having after-dinner drinks in the living room when David asked a shocking question.

"Luis, why does Fidel dislike you so much?"

Staring at his friend, whose long frame was comfortably at ease in a wicker chair, Luis countered, "Why do you ask?"

"Now that I know you well, I can confide in you," said David, rubbing the rim of his glass with his right index finger and looking down at the motion he was making. " In the letter you brought to me from the mountains, there was a postscript which warned me that although you might be an asset, you were not to be trusted."

Looking at the floor, Luis smiled and shook his head. "Well, I wasn't carrying any letter to García, was I? Would you mind telling me what the rest of the letter was about?"

"Sure," replied David, "it had to do with the matter of getting help from the U.S. government. You've already been involved in this in Washington."

David then asked Luis to tell him about his experiences with Castro. Luis did but saw no need to mention that, while he had been faithful to the 26th of July, he had not been faithful to his wife, either in the mountains with Ofelia Ramos or in Washington D.C., with a starry-eyed Cuban graduate student. Laura was right. He had been far more devoted to the Revolution than to his marriage.

Chapter 24

During the next few months in Havana, Luis solicited contributions for the 26th of July Movement, soon having collected more than he ever expected. Other opposition groups sprouted up around the island. The most important was Civic Resistance, started by Raúl Chibás, which Luis learned was a front for the 26th of July in the cities. Alberto Sánchez informed him that the 26th of July had orders to cooperate with Civic Resistance and that Alberto's task was to organize several cells of ten members each. With Luis' help, he recruited most of the members from the law school, many of whom were members of the Ortodoxo Youth Movement. By July, Alberto had put together three cells. One was in charge of the anti-government propaganda, another of sabotage, and the third one of finances.

The propaganda campaign consisted of publicizing Castro's *History Will Absolve Me* speech, posting anti-Batista slogans, and distributing manifestos calling for the overthrow of the dictatorship. The sabotage cell was responsible for throwing heavy chains over electric lines, cutting telephone wires at random, setting off petards in the cities to create confusion, and starting fires in the cane fields. Hearing the loud retorts of the bombs reverberating through the Havana night and periodically seeing the lights go out in certain sections of the city, Luis was thankful his job was limited to the mundane task of collecting money.

Early in the morning of September 5, Luis received a telephone call from Alberto, informing him there had been a Navy revolt in the city of Cienfuegos at dawn. Luis knew that a group of officers had been conspiring for some time with the Auténticos and the 26th of July Movement. Now they had succeeded in taking over the base, and according to Alberto, the people of Cienfuegos had joined in the uprising. Alberto received orders to contact the leaders of his cells, and Luis was told to round up his men.

"What's going on?" Laura inquired, awakened by Luis' excited voice.

The bulge of her pregnancy showed through her light blue negligee. "The people of Cienfuegos have joined the anti-Batista forces," Luis answered, trying to consolidate his thoughts.

"But what's this I hear about organizing your men?" she asked desperately.

"Laura, please, be calm, and I'll explain," Luis said, as he sat down beside her. "For some time now, I've been working with friends in the underground to overthrow Batista. Alberto is also involved."

"Why didn't you tell me?" she asked hysterically.

"I had orders not to divulge any information."

"No, you did it because you knew I would disapprove. You know I don't want you to mix with those radicals. How could you do this, especially in light of my condition?"

"I'm sorry, Laura, but the cause of democracy is something very important to me. I don't have the same opinion of the people you call radicals. In my view, they're freedom fighters."

"I think you're all risking your lives and those of your families for a foolish cause."

"As you wish, Laura. Please, let's not argue now. If I don't call you or come back by six tonight, please go to your parents' house."

"Go ahead, leave me alone. What do you care? But, I warn you," Laura added waving a finger at her husband, "I didn't get married to live in this turmoil!"

"We'll talk about it when I get back," Luis said calmly as he finished dressing.

Luis left the apartment with Laura's words still ringing in his ears and speeded to his office where he began to call the ten members of his cell. By noon, six members had come to the office. They waited anxiously, pretending to be law students studying one of Luis' cases. Alberto's call finally came at two o'clock. The operation had been cancelled. The naval officers in Havana had not joined the rebels in Cienfuegos. Luis' cell members quietly returned home.

As soon as the last of his friends had departed, Luis called Laura. "It's all right, nothing is going to take place," he informed her. "I'll be home by six."

That night Laura tried again to coerce Luis to cut his ties with the rebels. "Please, Luis, please consider our child," she implored. Luis did his best to reassure her he would not risk his life recklessly, but she would not believe him.

Several days after the uprising, information began to trickle out from Cienfuegos. The rebels had controlled the city during the morning of the first day, but by mid afternoon, tanks and armored regiments arrived from Havana to help the forces of the motorized infantry from Santa Clara, the capital of the province. Some four hundred rebels had participated in the revolt; more than half had been taken prisoner, and many were shot on the spot. Only twelve men had died on the government's side. It had been the largest confrontation of the budding civil war.

Amidst all the killings, life went on in its own mysterious way. It was a miracle how the genes of two people coalesced into a living form that had the features of both parents yet was a being unto itself. These were Luis' thoughts as he looked through the glass into the nursery at the Clínica Miramar at his son, Luis, Jr., born at 6 a.m. on October 17, 1957, a moment Luis would treasure forever. Later in the morning, he watched with pride as Laura fed Luisito. He was grateful to her for having presented him with a healthy son to carry on the Recio name. As he cuddled their son in his arms, Luis wanted to make their marriage work, but he also sensed pressures building around them could jeopardize their joy at this blessed moment.

At the end of the year, there was frequent talk about a national Junta of Liberation formed in Miami with Tony de Varona as president. The 26th of July Movement, however, suspected the motives of the Auténticos, Student Directorate, and the old Ortodoxos. Castro denounced the Junta from the mountains and forced it to accept Dr. Manuel Urrutia, an honorable but politically inexperienced judge from Santiago, as the provisional president.

Luis' life in Havana became more restricted as the political situation deteriorated. Numerous arrests often ended in atrocities, and violence came closer to him daily. One of the members of Alberto's sabotage cell, a freshman law student, lost an arm when a petard he had made at the science laboratory of the Vedado Instituto exploded prematurely near Havana's rail terminal. Finding him bleeding and semi-conscious on the sidewalk, the police proceeded to torture him on the spot in order to get names of accomplices. His funeral told a story in itself: an empty right sleeve folded over his body in an open casket. Bruised, disfigured, swollen lips, and an ugly black circle on his cheek spoke of police brutality. "The assassins even mutilated his face with a cigar!" his mother wailed as Luis and friends respectfully stood before the body of their comrade.

Early one afternoon in March of 1958, Luis received a call from Gaspar Betancourt, the senator's son. Gaspar wanted urgently to talk to him and suggested they play tennis that afternoon at the HYC.

Seated on a bench by the tennis courts, Luis waited for Gaspar to arrive, wondering why Gaspar was in such a hurry to see him. They had not talked since Luis' wedding, and then they had only had time to exchange pleasantries. Gaspar was a year younger than Luis, and they had grown up in the same neighborhood in Camagüey. Luis remembered Gaspar was the youngest member of his baseball team. Their parents had been good friends, even during these difficult times when Senator Betancourt chose to defend the government's unjustifiable policies. It perplexed Luis why a fundamentally decent politician would want to side with such a corrupt dictator, but then he realized his father-in-law, Mario Ramírez, was doing the same thing.

Luis pondered how dictators rose to power. He concluded it had to do with *caudillo* worship which has its basis in charismatic appeal more than in understanding of substantive issues. Machado was a *caudillo* to his people from 1925 to 1933, and now Batista followed in the same vein. Luis hoped someday Cubans would pay more attention to political platforms than to the allure of demagogic leaders. Gaspar interrupted his thoughts as he came toward him.

"Luisito, you indeed look good," Gaspar said cheerfully as he gave Luis the expected abrazo. "Let's play a couple of sets now, and we'll talk later."

After the two sets, they went to a small bar at the club where they could talk.

"Sorry to keep you guessing, Luis, but in addition to needing the exercise, I wanted to legitimize our being seen together," Gaspar said as they sipped their beers.

"I have a message for you from my father. Last week he went to the army headquarters in Camagüey on some business pertaining to his constituency, and he got to talk with Colonel Ruiz. I don't know exactly how the conversation turned to the topic, but the colonel began to complain about how ungrateful the ranchers who were siding with the rebels were. The colonel felt the ranchers should support Batista, who represents law and order. The colonel said the police knew what was going on and shortly they would take some action. He then mentioned your name as one of the underground leaders. Papá was flabbergasted. He didn't know why the colonel gave him this information, but he felt it was serious enough to pass it on to you. Papá didn't want to worry your father, so he asked me to talk to you directly and advise you to get out of the country."

Luis took some time before replying to Gaspar. "Of course I'm involved, and I'm grateful to you and you father for this information. Gaspar, where do you stand in all of this?"

After a pause, Gaspar replied. "I have to be faithful to Papá although you know I don't agree with the government's repression. I've had many arguments with my father, and he's convinced Castro's a communist."

"I respect your position, Gaspar. However, we have acquaintances who are involved, and I'd like for you to help me warn one of them. If he's suspected, his telephone might be tapped."

"I'll do what I can. Who is he?"

"Enrique Bueno, our old teammate. Tell him what you told me and stress that for all we know, he hasn't been identified. However, he must be aware that the police are on to our work."

"Of course, I'll do that for Enrique, but what about you?"

"I don't know what I'll do yet. I have to think things over. I don't believe it would be wise for me to return to Camagüey. Please make sure Enrique knows this. I might need your help in the near future. Can I count on you?"

"Yes, as long as you don't expect me to join the opposition. I can't do that to Papá."

With that exchange, they went up to the men's room to shower and dress.

Luis could not imagine how he would break the news to Laura that it was now necessary for him to either leave the country or go into hiding. She would again argue that his commitment to revolution was greater than his commitment to his family.

Part 2

Havana and Miami
A Tale of Two Cities and One Struggle

Chapter 25

On the afternoon of January 1, 1959, Luis and other jubilant members of Miami's 26th of July Movement landed in Havana in a Cubana Airlines plane. The electric atmosphere at the airport swept Luis up in the excitement. Considering the confusion in the toppling of any government, there was a surprising order in the streets. Revolutionaries seemed to materialize out of thin air to assert their authority and stake their claim on the future of Cuba. Luis noticed the young age of the self-proclaimed guards, who embraced him in acknowledgement of a glorious cause when they saw his 26th of July arm band.

From the airport, he took a taxi into the city. All around, armed young men shouted slogans from crowded cars and open jeeps as the sounds of honking horns beseeched citizens to come out and join in the celebration. The sidewalks were almost deserted, most people uncertain about the direction of events. Still, the revolutionary sentiment was evident in the numerous 26th of July flags hanging from the windows of apartments. The black and red pennant with the number 26 in the center would soon to be familiar to all Cubans.

Luis arrived at the Ramírez's home on Fifth Avenue where the residents in this exclusive neighborhood were keeping a low profile. Upon seeing Laura, Luis felt familiar feelings of love and desire. With her thick black hair and bewitching brown eyes, she was as attractive as ever. As he kissed her warm, full lips, memories of their differences faded away. When Luis saw the nanny appear in the hall with Luisito in her arms, he rushed toward them, and to his surprise, his son reached for him. Hugging and kissing his son, Luis experienced the comfort and satisfaction of returning to his family and homeland.

That evening Laura invited all the Recios and Jorge León, Isabel's fiancé, to a celebration dinner. Late that night, they watched the man of the hour, Fidel Castro, make his first television appearance from the de Céspedes Park in Santiago. His speech was inspirational in its simple but eloquent appeal, and the conciliatory tone of the intrepid revolutionary excited all of them.

After the speech, Mario Ramírez rose and requested everyone's attention, "Well, Luis, you certainly know how to pick a winner. I had my doubts about Castro, but I believe he'll be all right. Let's toast to the end of the dictatorship and the beginning of democracy. May God guide Fidel in his noble cause!"

Mario, still in charge, turned to Luis and looking him directly in the eye, added, "And to you, Luis Recio. For your valiant efforts in the underground and in the mountains, we salute you!"

Full of pride, Luis rose and graciously responded. His father-in-law had been generous in his praise, as would he in return. "Mario," he said, "you do me injustice with your kind words. I only did my duty. The real heroes are the women who endured loneliness while their men were away serving the Revolution. I'm greatly indebted to Laura for her forbearance, and I want to publicly express to her my love and gratitude."

Those gathered raised their glasses in acknowledgment of Luis' way of asking forgiveness for the worry he had brought to those present. How appropriate that this is the beginning of a new year and a new chapter in Cuban history, Luis thought as he looked at his loved ones.

Later that night as he and Laura lay in each other's arms, Luis said, "Our struggle is finally over, Laura. This is a new beginning for us and for Cuba. The man whom they called 'The Horse' is on his way to Havana. In spite of some of the things I've told you, it can only to be good for our beloved Cuba."

Laura remained silent, lying contented in her husband's arms.

On the morning of the following day, Luis went to his old law office where his former colleagues received him joyously. Most of them had expressed skepticism about Batista but had not necessarily supported Castro. After hearing and seeing Fidel on TV, however, they were impressed by Castro's message. To Luis' surprise, Dr. Uría offered him a full partnership in the firm, which he gladly accepted even though he was tempted to disclaim the influence the senior partners thought he would have with the new government. Their display of the old oligarchic principles of inside influence irritated him, but Luis was no fool, and he knew he should not pass up this opportunity.

To celebrate Luis' promotion, he and two members of the firm went to lunch at The Floridita, the famous haunt of Ernest Hemingway, renowned for its daiquirís and *paellas*. On the way to and from the restaurant, Luis saw evidence of sporadic looting of homes which had belonged to Batista's followers, but all in all, a relative calm existed in the city. Castro's appeal for order was already having an effect, and the general strike called by Castro kept most people off the streets. The unsettling news was that the Student Directorate leaders had taken possession of the Presidential Palace and were unwilling to relinquish it to the 26th of July contingent. How Castro would deal with them remained to be seen, but Luis was confident Fidel would resolve the issue. Castro, however, was in no hurry to deal with challenges in Havana; instead, he was consolidating his power as he traveled from East to West, starting in Santiago and winning hearts along the way with his powerful and passionate rhetoric.

Luis was working on his first case on the morning of January 8 when he received the news Castro had entered Havana and was making his way to the Presidential Palace. Aware of the historical significance of the moment, Luis deserted his desk and walked to the palace a few blocks away. Thousands already awaited the triumphant entry of the man who, thanks to his oratorical skill and the magic of television, had become the most famous figure in the history of Cuba in only a few days.

Luis forced his way through the masses to reach the entrance of the palace where he worked his way to the second floor balcony to have an unobstructed view of this momentous occasion. There he saw the recently designated president, Manuel Urrutia, and next to him the last Constitutional president, Carlos Prío. Beside Prío stood his father's friend, Tony de Varona, the former Prime Minister of Cuba. Having met Judge Urrutia before the judge left Miami for the mountains in November, Luis went forward to shake his hand and greet Tony de Varona and Carlos Prío. They all received him warmly, and Luis could not help pondering how resigned Prío seemed playing second fiddle to Fidel, who had never been elected, when, in fact, Prío was the legitimate president whom Batista had deposed.

After exchanging a few words with them, Luis moved away from the group. He did not want to be seen as a member of the committee of distinguished officials receiving their new leader.

From his vantage point on the palace terrace, Luis saw the caravan of jeeps, armored cars, and trucks come slowly into the plaza below as the cheering populace closing up the column opened by the vehicles. All the bearded rebels in fatigues were riding in the procession, and their small number astounded Luis. The role of the Herbert Matthews' *New York Times* article in Castro's rise to power could not be overstated since Matthews had been duped by the numbers. Now Castro had many armed followers, but the newcomers had not had time to grow a beard, the true mark of revolutionary distinction. Batista's forces would have arrested anyone with any semblance of the rebels' trademark.

As he tried to make his way to the palace terrace, Castro, carrying his famous telescopic rifle, was so mobbed that for a moment Luis could scarcely see him. Then, as if by magic, the crowd opened up, reminding Luis of the story of Moses at the Red Sea, and Castro, the victor, strode to his appointed place to shake hands with the leaders with whom Luis had just talked.

Other parallels also came to Luis' mind: Jesus entering Jerusalem, Caesar arriving in Rome, and McArthur returning to New York after his last tour in Korea. However, in each case there was a difference. Caesar was the returning conqueror, Jesus the knowing victim walking into the jaws of fate, and McArthur, a military martyr shorn of power but not glory. Now Fidel had both, all the power and glory little Cuba could muster, and there was no thought he would ever be assassinated, crucified, stripped of power, or forced to live in seclusion atop a hotel like McArthur. In his brief talk, Castro criticized the idea of a presidential palace but acknowledged the necessity of a centralized place that would come to symbolize good government more than a presidential residence.

Luis was marveling at Castro's ability to say the right thing to the masses when he felt a tap on his shoulder. As he turned around, he saw

Alberto Sánchez' familiar face, beaming and bearded. A rosary hung around his neck, and he was dressed in the fatigues that had suddenly become the hottest fashion in town. "Well, Luis, what do you think of my beard?" he asked as they embraced. Luis knew Alberto, like so many others, had been forced to flee to the mountains in the last few months, but he did not know what had happened to his friend.

Smiling, Luis reached up and touched Alberto's epaulets, offering congratulations at the same time. "Yes," said Alberto, "I'm now a captain and a member of Fidel's headquarters' staff. I got to the Sierra about a month after you left and have been with 'The Horse' ever since. These last few days have been unbelievable."

They talked until the thunderous applause signaled the end of Castro's speech. Then Alberto grabbed Luis by the hand, headed toward his leader, and pushed aside the many civilians who were eagerly trying to touch their Maximum Leader. A few feet from Castro, Alberto yelled, "Fidel, look who we have here!"

For a split second, Castro stared coldly at Luis and then suddenly broke into a radiant grin, "Well, I'll be darned! If it isn't Luis Recio. Where in the hell is your white suit? You know you should be either in rebel uniform or in that white suit which you bought with our hard-earned money."

As he spoke, Castro jokingly admonished Luis, pointing at him with his right index finger while some of the rebel guards with inside knowledge of the incident laughed heartily.

"Oh no, *comandante*," Luis replied with a smile, directing his own finger at Castro. "I repaid my debt at a high rate of interest, both in terms of money and my services to 26th of July cause in Miami."

"Damn it, Luis, you have an answer for everything, " said Castro, approaching him and patting him on the back of the neck. Castro then turned away to acknowledge the entreaty of other well-wishers.

After informing Luis the story of the white linen suit had been a topic of humor in the mountains, Alberto told Luis he should wear his lieutenant's uniform, a symbol of honor since he had been in the Sierra when times were hard.

"But I left my uniform in the Sierra," Luis explained.

"I'll take care of that!" replied Alberto. "Tomorrow I'll send a tailor to your home to take measurements. It will be my special present. I want you to wear it proudly."

Though Luis was in civilian clothes, Alberto forced him to ride in the victory caravan to Camp Columbia, the largest military base in Cuba where Castro's presence would symbolize his new role as commander-in-chief of the armed forces. Castro had already displayed a mastery of tactics in the field, and now he was displaying a mastery of strategy in politics as well.

Waiting with Alberto for the caravan to move out, someone poked Luis in the back. When he turned around, he saw his old singing buddy, Major Miguel Ochoa, smiling with his arms opened wide like the Christ on the crucifix around his neck.

"You devil, Luis, how good you look! Things weren't too rough in Miami, eh?"

Before Luis could answer, Ochoa engulfed him in a strong *abrazo* and proclaimed, "Now you and I will have plenty of time to do some proper partying. We'll get Camilo to complete the combo," he added, laughing while he patted Luis on the shoulder before departing for one of the loaded vehicles.

"Count me in that combo," Alberto yelled to Ochoa.

Watching Ochoa get in a jeep, Luis remarked, "I see everyone, Alberto, except Ofelia Ramos. Where's she?"

"She should be here, though she may already be at the camp with others," Alberto answered, looking around as if he might spot her. "We'll probably see her there. I know she wants to see you. We became good friends after she found out you and I were old schoolmates."

If Luis had any doubts about going to Camp Columbia, they were now erased by the prospects of seeing Ofelia again.

Chapter 26

The journey along Columbia Avenue took hours. All the houses and apartments on the route displayed 26th of July banners, and crowds jammed the sidewalks. Often the caravan had to stop to let well-wishers shake hands with the Cuban redeemer. Adulation spilled over onto the entourage, Luis himself feeling surges of pride as Cubans waved, threw kisses, and ran forth to touch their heroes. Most of the rebels wore rosaries around their necks, and no one that day would have denied them sainthood. Luis, in civilian clothes and beardless, felt conspicuous, but everyone looking on knew he was among the chosen or else he would not have been given such a place of honor.

"Well, Luis," said Alberto Sánchez, smiling broadly, "don't you like all this attention?"

"I don't believe I've earned it," Luis joked as he rubbed his chin to show he had no beard.

"Now, you know better," Alberto said. "I was the latecomer to the mountains!"

That night at Camp Columbia, Castro delivered a long speech over television. In it, he attacked the members of the University Student Directorate for arming themselves and claiming a share of power in government. He drew parallels between them and the gangs that followed the overthrow of Machado in 1933. Here Castro first used the phrase, "Why do we need arms?" The implication was that since Batista had been defeated, there was no need for any group to arm itself as the Student Directorate had done.

Standing next to Alberto near the speaker's platform, Luis was still impressed by Castro's political acumen. Here was a man who had been in the mountains on the night of December 31. Though Fidel controlled the Sierra Maestra, the Student Directorate held a sizeable portion of the Sierra Escambray Mountains and fought valiantly in the attack on the Presidential Palace, which was probably the most daring act against the Batista regime. Yet here Castro cleverly discredited them by suggesting the organization might be a new generation of the university gang groups like the one Castro himself had once belonged to! He gave not a hint that either the Student Directorate, the Montecristo Movement, the Auténticos, or even the Communists had suffered casualties but encouraged everyone to rally around the Rebel Army, which had borne the brunt of the fighting.

To Luis, the symbol of the culmination of Castro's ascent to power came when one of two doves released in the crowd landed on Fidel's shoulder. It was an omen not at all unlike the story of the baptism of Christ in which the Holy Spirit descended as a dove with blessings from above: "This is my beloved son in whom I am well pleased." The rebels with their rosaries were like the Apostles, and their charismatic leader was the Savior.

Later at the bar in the officers' club, Luis confided his reservations about Castro to Alberto, also mentioning the postscript of Fidel's letter to David Salvador in Miami. The noise of the celebration was so loud that it would not have mattered had he yelled in Alberto's ear. Never before had there been such a rag-tag band of officers in the club, and never before had there been such cause for jubilation.

Alberto assured Luis that Castro's actions in the mountains were the result of the tremendous pressure on "The Horse" during the early days in June.

"Give 'The Horse a chance to run," he said. "You'll see he'll turn out to be a great stallion. I'm sure he holds no ill will toward you."

The two friends reminisced about their youth in Camagüey, their days in law school, their underground activities in Havana, and their time in the Sierra. They joined in victory toasts so often that Luis got a bit intoxicated before long.

Luis was in a daze when he saw her coming toward him through the crowd and the tobacco smoke. She smiled when she saw him, and his heart told him his eyes were not deceiving him.

"What's the matter, Luis? Don't you recognize me now that I'm a lieutenant?" asked Ofelia Ramos as she hugged him warmly.

"I've had too much to drink," he confessed. "I thought you were a vision from heaven. Ofelia, you look wonderful. How are you?"

On the pretext of needing to get home to his family, Alberto excused himself and left, while Luis ordered a *Cuba Libre* for Ofelia. He felt a surge of passion when she discreetly held his hand and looked into his eyes.

"Let's go out so we can talk without noise," Luis suggested when the drink came.

Outside, they joined hands again as Luis guided her away from the light of the club. It was a cool January night with the moon and stars shining with crystalline brilliance. The night air and her fresh smell combined to dispel the lingering odor of tobacco. When they came to a bench along the walkway, they sat down.

"I'm so happy to see you," Luis said, caressing her arm.

"I've been so lonely since you left the camp. Thank God we're together again."

Luis, fearing the danger of her expectation, interrupted her to make his own situation clear.

"Ofelia, you know I'm married and have a son. Laura and I have our problems, but I want to give our marriage a chance. It wouldn't be fair to my wife or you for us to renew our relationship."

Ofelia did not speak but rested her head on his shoulder. Finally, she measured her words.

"I wouldn't want to be a problem to you and Laura. I'll always love you."

"And I love you very much too," Luis said as he kissed her gently on the cheek.

They sat holding hands and sipping their drinks in quiet reflexion until Ofelia reminded him of a promise he made back in the Sierra.

"I hope you're still going to cook dinner for us," she said buoyantly.

"*Mi amor*, you'll be the first to know."

Early the next morning, Luis and Laura awoke to a phone call from Alberto. "Luisito," he said, "I've great news for you. Fidel wants to appoint you Undersecretary of Justice. It proves what I told you last night was correct, doesn't it?"

"Well, Alberto," Luis replied after a moment of reflection, "either that or it proves you did some politicking late last night after you left the club."

"Not at all, Luis," Alberto said. "You tend to sell yourself short. How many educated men like you were in the mountains in the spring of 1958? A mere handful out of three hundred rebels. You were there before I, and although you might have had confrontations with Fidel, he values your integrity and intelligence. Frankly, he needs people like you to give credibility to the first cabinet of the revolutionary government. Also, I happen to know David Salvador gave Fidel a glowing report of your activities in the United States. Hell, if I were Castro, I'd appoint you to my cabinet!"

After a long pause, Luis answered, "I'm surprised and honored by this offer. I'll accept it. Maybe I can contribute something to bringing justice to this new Cuba."

"Accept what?" Laura asked as she overheard the conversation.

Asking to excuse himself for a moment, Luis put his hand over the receiver and explained to Laura what he had just done.

"You mean to tell me after all we've been through, you're going to stay in politics?" Laura blurted. "You know there's no future in it compared to the money you could make with your law firm."

Glaring at her as she sat in the middle of their bed in her negligee, Luis said coldly, "I'll explain later."

Taking his hand off the mouthpiece, he spoke again to Alberto, "As I said earlier, I'll be glad to accept the position. Please convey my appreciation for this appointment to Dr. Castro."

Alberto told him to report that same day to the Ministry of Justice, adding a final note, "As you and I know, justice is very important now, and we need the moderation you can provide."

After he hung up the phone, Luis turned to his wife and said, "You're aware of the executions which have taken place. It's imperative that due process of law be established so the excesses of these first few days of the Revolution will not continue."

"What I know, is that you've been back in Cuba for ten days, and you're already involved in politics again," Laura continued.

"It's not the same!" Luis insisted. "Before I had to work surreptitiously. Now I'll be in a position of leadership in a legitimate and exciting government."

"Well, I just hope you won't be sorry," Laura said. "Do what you wish. I was under the impression that once the Revolution was over, you would want to concentrate on your family and your career."

"Hell, I'll be putting my training to its best use. I'll still have my job at the law office. Laura, the Revolution is not over. It's just beginning. It has to be cared for and nourished, and if people like us don't try to do that, then we'll have another disaster on our hands. It would be good if you, Laura Ramírez, would decide to help in this process."

Laura was silent for a moment, looking abstractly out the window. Finally she spoke, "Luis, I guess the basic difference between you and me is that you're a reformer and I'm not. I'm not going to be a hypocrite and work for the poor in some run-down barrio just for the sake of appearance. From my point of view, there will always be an affluent class and a large poor class. I just think it would be better if you focused on your own family."

"Laura," Luis replied in exasperation. "What you've just stated is the philosophy that we fought so hard to change. The happiness of families depends greatly upon the nature of their society and government. That's why I believe I must get involved."

"That's it, then," she said. "I would start with the family, but you want to start with government. Let's drop it for now. Go ahead with your new job. I won't try to stop you. I love you in spite of your naïve idealism. I just want to save our marriage."

She wrapped her arms around his neck and began to sob. Holding her, Luis felt pity and love but had no idea how to resolve the differences between them. They were too deep and seemingly irreconcilable.

Luis threw himself enthusiastically into his job at the Ministry of Justice. One of his duties was to weed out "the rotten apples" of the old regime and replace them with men and women of impeccable credentials. He found himself in line with the thinking of Ángel Fernández, his immediate supervisor and Minister of Justice, who was also a moderate. Justice, Luis had concluded, was the essence of moderation since it sought a balance between opposing forces. He loved the universal symbol of justice, the blindfolded woman holding the scales in equilibrium.

One afternoon while reflecting upon his time in the Sierra Maestra, Luis remembered his promise to cook for his friends. Knowing he wanted to invite twenty to twenty-five people to the dinner, he asked his father for permission to use the larger Recio home. "I want to do something special for them, Papá. I want a big table by the pool, a bar, and an orchestra. I'll plan the menu."

Rogerio approved, saying as he had many times before, "Son, as you and Isabel have always known, *mi casa es vuestra casa.*"

Luis told him he wanted his family to be present at the party so they could get to know his friends and vice versa. Rogerio understood, but Laura was less agreeable when he presented the idea to her.

"Luis," she said, "I don't see what you hope to accomplish. I've never heard of having a dinner in which you include peasants, rebels, and educated people."

"That's because you've been raised in Havana's upper crust. Elsewhere it's not so uncommon. I've gone to political barbecues in which people of all classes mingle freely."

Laura then asked, "Is this going to be another political gathering?"

"Damn it, Laura," Luis answered, feeling every topic was becoming more and more a point of contention. "All I'm doing is fulfilling a promise I made to my comrades in the mountains. It has nothing to do with politics. We're just celebrating victory and life."

Laura sighed. "All right, then, I'll go to the party, but the people you describe will feel self-conscious and out of place in your father's home."

Luis responded, "You might be right, but these people are my friends. We're going to make them feel welcome. Cubans of all classes and backgrounds need to get to know each other and work together. You can learn a lot from these people."

"As I said," Laura concluded, "I'll be there."

Working through Sergeant Nasario, who was now a lieutenant in Santiago de Cuba, Luis set the date for the last Saturday in January. The list he gave to Nasario included all the names of the members of his squad and three of his domino friends in the camp. Nasario informed him one of the members of the squad had been killed, but he would try to get the others together. Luis said he would take care of all traveling costs. He also invited Alberto, Miguel Ochoa, and Ofelia, asking Ofelia to bring Ana and the other women who worked in the camp kitchen.

When he mentioned the dinner to Alberto Sánchez, Alberto suggested he also invite Castro, but after brief consideration, Luis replied the party was in honor of his friends from the Sierra. Fidel's presence would make it a political affair. For that reason, he did not invite any of the leaders of the Revolution. It crossed Luis's mind to fix a magnificent French dinner, but on second thought, he decided to prepare a Cuban feast.

As his guests began to arrive, Luis greeted them warmly and introduced each of them to his family. The initial nervousness of some of the guests soon evaporated in the warmth with which they were received. As Ana, Ofelia, and the other women came into the house, Ana opened her huge arms and with a grin exclaimed, "Luis, how I've missed you! Give Ana a big *abrazo!*"

Somewhat afraid of his own emotions, Luis was surprised at the ease with which he introduced Laura to Ofelia. Ofelia made the best of an awkward situation while Laura played the role of the gracious wife. When Luis invited Ofelia, she expressed her feelings about coming. "I want to see where you've lived so I can picture you in the place where you grew up, and I'm interested in meeting your wife because I'm sure she's sophisticated and beautiful."

As the daiquirís from the poolside bar took effect, the guests recalled shared experiences. Luis noticed Laura scrutinizing Ofelia. When his wife had the chance, she looked at Luis with eyes that seemed to say, "This is the best-looking rebel I ever saw. You better not have been involved with her." Laura's glances made him a bit edgy, but Luis was too busy as a host to worry about what she might be thinking.

When dinner was ready, Luis got everyone's attention. "My dear friends," he declared, "this dinner is a fulfillment of my promise. I wanted to make you a meal with all the ingredients we didn't have in the Sierra. One way to celebrate the triumph of the Revolution is to enjoy each other's company with the best of Cuban food. Come and eat to your heart's delight!"

Conversation at the table flowed as naturally as waves on the beach, and Luis could tell his meal was a hit. The aroma of rice, beans, and marinated pork filled the air as they were passed around the table. Ana was amazed. "Luis," she said, emphasizing every word, "these are the best black beans I've ever had in my life!" Finishing the compliment, she brought her chubby fingers to her mouth and blew a kiss which landed joyfully in Luis' heart.

Two hours later with the party in full swing and some of the couples dancing to the rhythm of the tropical music, Luis noticed a commotion by the terrace and wondered what had transpired. Before he had time to speculate, someone shouted, "Fidel is here!" Had someone shouted "Jesus Christ is here!" there would not have been more excitement.

In an instant everyone, including the Recios and Ramírezes, surrounded Castro and his entourage, patting him on the back and shaking his hand. Luis, feeling alone at his own party, slowly walked to the group around the Maximum Leader and watched while his father introduced Laura to Castro. "No wonder he was eager to get back to you," Castro said flirtatiously while his eyes travelled over her body.

Luis could not keep from thinking that even when Castro was on his best behavior, he was still duplicitous, putting Luis on the defensive by coming unannounced to the party and by commenting on Laura's beauty.

"Oh, we're so happy you came," said Laura.

"I came in spite of Luis," Castro announced. "I learned about this fiesta by chance, and I was not about to miss Luis' famous cooking. Don't I get a plate, Luis?"

"Of course, *comandante*," Luis said, smiling as he acknowledged Castro's power of one-upmanship. Since Luis knew he was not one of Fidel's favorite people, there had to be another reason for his presence--his passion for surprise which served his ego so well. Here was the new sovereign of Cuba inviting himself to a gathering in order to spite an insubordinate subject.

Sitting at the table with Ochoa and his wife, two aides, and other admirers, Castro tackled the food with gusto and paid Luis the same type of compliments as others had done earlier, his staff echoing his sentiments on cue.

"Luis, I do believe I made a mistake. I should have made you Minister of Culinary Arts instead of one of my lawyers!" Fidel roared at his own humor.

Before Castro's entrance (B.C.), the mood had been merely festive, but after his arrival (A.C.), it was magical. The Maximum Leader succeeded, Luis concluded, with his charisma. Fidel approached the guests effusively, never failing to mention the name of the person to whom he was speaking. Castro never forgot a face, a name, and, as Luis realized, a grievance.

Observing this powerful man, Luis felt shivers run up and down his spine, and they were, he realized, shivers of fear. Even Laura was behaving differently, hanging on to Castro's every word. Luis felt a twinge of jealousy over all the attention Laura was focusing upon the uninvited guest. The man exuded a charm irresistible to any woman. Fidel had an animal magnetism that had been the prize possession of the dominant male for eons, and "The Horse" was definitely the alpha male.

After finishing dessert, Castro lingered for a while longer, dispensing goodwill before leaving suddenly with as much fanfare as when he had arrived. Two of his aides left with him, but Miguel and Eva Ochoa stayed behind, Miguel and Luis joining the musicians in a few of the sentimental songs they sang in the Sierra.

That evening in bed, Laura was ecstatic and more generous in love than she had been in some time. Afterwards, she commented, "I'm so glad we had the dinner. Isn't it wonderful Castro came? Did you see the way your cute friend from the mountains eyed him? Fidel certainly has a way with women!" Instead of feeling jealous, Luis was grateful to the Maximum Leader for two things: one, converting Laura to the Revolution and two, diverting her suspicions away from him and Ofelia.

For the next few days, they enjoyed what amounted to another honeymoon. Not only was she forgiving of Luis' political past, but Laura was now sympathetic to the changes taking place in the country. Castro did it, he had to admit. Quite by accident, "The Horse" had sparked a political interest in Laura and brought Luis' bed to life again.

Chapter 27

During the first week of February, 1959, Luis, as Undersecretary of Justice, and Laura attended a reception for the diplomatic corps at the Presidential Palace. Laura eagerly anticipated the event and made an unnecessary fuss about what jewelry and clothes to wear. She looked forward to seeing President Urrutia and Prime Minister Miró Cardona again, both of whom she had met in Miami. Of course, she was also very excited to see Fidel Castro. She would report the details of the event to her friends at the HYC just as she had done on Castro's surprise visit to the Recios.

At the reception, Luis and Laura stood in line to pay their respects to the President and to the Prime Minister. Laura was delighted to meet Philip Bonsal, the recently-arrived U. S. Ambassador and the most important foreigner in Cuba. She and Luis talked at length with him about Luis' cousin, Philip Heymann, who would soon join the embassy staff as Vice-Consul in Havana. Ambassador Bonsal had known Heymann for many years and thought very highly of him. Of course, Heymann was a Yale man, which Bonsal joked, gave him exactly the right credentials.

They were chatting with the Ambassador from Holland when Castro, followed by a group of officers, belatedly entered the room. Everyone turned in the direction of the center of power of Cuba with the most obsequious guests scrambling to greet him, almost knocking over some of the diplomats in the process. As Luis witnessed this spectacle, he could not help but wonder how long such a situation would last. Here was the most popular man in Cuba who had chosen not to hold any official title but that of Commander-in-Chief of the Rebel Army. It was merely a matter of time until Castro would become the leader in name as well as in fact. When Castro upstaged both President Urrutia and Prime Minister Miró Cardona, no one realized this more clearly than they.

Castro made his way around the room, shaking hands and greeting old friends with the same singular charm Luis had seen at his parents' home in Miramar. Eventually, he arrived at the spot where Luis and Laura were standing with the Dutch Ambassador, his eye wandering appreciatively toward Laura. Luis could not blame Castro for admiring Laura's beauty. Laura looked ravishing with her black hair and black dress which accentuated the perfect curves of her body. Shaking Laura's hand while he kissed her on the cheek, Castro commented, "Your husband's cooking was delicious, but you were the real treat of the party."

Laura blushed while Luis shook Castro's hand and introduced him to the Ambassador from Holland and his wife. Castro bowed as he shook the hand of the ambassador and his young but matronly looking wife. After an exchange of pleasantries with them, Castro took Luis aside and said, "Luis, I want you to come and visit me. I appreciate people like you who had the guts to be in the underground and later fight in the mountains. Those were the hard times, and now everyone wants to be a revolutionary." Leaning closer to Luis and lowering his voice, he added, "You should see some of the opportunistic sons of bitches now seeking a place in the government."

Turning to one of the aides, Castro stated as if he considered Luis one of his intimates, "Give Dr. Recio my private number, and make sure if he calls me, I'm available."

"Thank you so much, *comandante*," Luis acknowledged. "I appreciate your confidence in me."

The following Monday, Alberto Sánchez dropped by Luis' office in the ministry and soon got to the point of his visit.

"Luis, you're my best friend. I've got to level with you. Do you remember our conversation at Camp Columbia when you told me about your reservations concerning Fidel's character? Remember how I said you were wrong?"

Luis nodded.

"Well, I was wrong. When you said you believed Castro disliked you, I argued otherwise. You were right. Mamá is in the hospital for a bladder operation, and I was unable to attend the reception last Friday at the palace. But Miguel Ochoa was there, and as Castro and his staff were leaving the palace, Miguel remarked what a credit you are to the Revolution. What he said really pissed Fidel off. According to Miguel, as soon as the elevator door closed, Fidel jumped on him with a vengeance, humiliating him in front of the rest of the staff. Castro called him an imbecile for not having any better judgment. Fidel referred to you as a conceited playboy who had the nerve to bring your mistress to your home and embarrass the poor rebels by an obscene show of wealth around a fucking swimming pool. He called you a son of a bitch and a womanizer and stated you were not to be trusted. Furthermore, he said the only reason you had been given a job was to pacify the rapacious oligarchs. He believes you're nothing more than a political opportunist. Miguel was flabbergasted since he had just seen and heard Fidel speak highly of you and your wife.

"From now on, I'll have to be on guard. He knows of our close friendship. As long as I'm on Castro's staff, I'll have to be careful in my dealings with you."

Luis stared at his desk and abstractly turned a pencil in his hands before saying, "I'm not surprised. I've known all along that Castro despises me. He doesn't tolerate the opinions of others. Alberto, I understand your dilemma. I'll not contact you from now on, but you know you can count on me. What really concerns me is the path the Revolution is taking. I don't like the new role the communists have in the government, and from what I hear, Che and Raúl are behind the whole thing."

"Fidel would say that is the type of statement a reactionary would make," Alberto commented and grinned as he slowly twiddled his thumbs, "but between you and me, I don't like the rise of the communists either. They did little to overthrow Batista, although a few of them fought in the mountains. Perhaps Fidel doesn't really know what's going on. Or maybe he does know and is giving the communists positions to accommodate the left."

"Perhaps," Luis said with a note of irony, throwing his pencil on the desk.

Having no more to say, the childhood friends walked to the door and embraced.

With skepticism, Luis watched the way in which the Revolution was being managed. Two unfulfilled promises Castro made in the mountains disturbed him. Fidel had agreed to reinstate the 1940 Constitution that Batista so flagrantly violated, and he promised to call for elections six months after Batista was overthrown. It was obvious Castro was in no rush to implement elections, and even worse, the fundamental law of the Republic, the Constitution, was abrogated on February 7th in order to transfer all legislative power to the cabinet.

Luis could see what was going on. Prime Minister Miró Cardona tried to resign in January because he did not like the ideas of restoring the death penalty and making legal penalties retroactive, both of which violated the Constitution. Moderate members of the cabinet persuaded Miró Cardona to stay on in order to hold the growing influence of the radicals in check.

Castro controlled the cabinet's agenda from his suite at the Havana Hilton with assistance from his allies, such as Armando Hart, the Minister of Education. Though President Urrutia presided at the cabinet meetings with the Prime Minister at his right hand, in reality, Fidel called the shots by proxy through Hart. It was an untenable position for Miró Cardona, and on February 16th, he resigned and recommended that Castro become the Prime Minister.

Castro said he would accept the position if given certain broad powers in order to implement his programs. Among his stipulations, he demanded President Urrutia cease to attend the cabinet meetings. It was obvious Fidel was blatantly ignoring the Constitution since it specified that the President preside at the cabinet meetings. Castro had as little regard for the Constitution as Batista.

At first, Luis could not understand why Castro was not eager to run for President since he would certainly be elected by an overwhelming majority. Then slowly it dawned on him what was happening. If elections were held as promised, Fidel would be elected for four years under the terms of the Constitution, but he could not be succeed himself and would have to relinquish power after only one term in office. Of course, he could get a Constitutional amendment passed to allow a president to serve more than one term along with other radical laws he might desire, but even that process would be democratic. It would also be cumbersome and controversial, and Luis knew Fidel was a man with a mission and no patience.

Luis' worse fears were confirmed early in March. Forty-four pilots of Batista's air force had been accused of war crimes but were acquitted after a trial in Santiago. Rather than releasing them, Castro ordered a new trial while announcing in Havana on television that the acquittal had been a mistake. Luis was visiting his father, and they watched in amazement as Castro justified this unprecedented defiance of the law.

How could a person of Castro's legal background not understand a man could not be tried twice for the same crime? In the Sierra, he had ordered Luis to shoot a man without a trial, and here he was revoking a decision of a court of law. Just what purpose did tribunals serve in Castro's mind? The tribunal was composed of rebel officers who would have reached a guilty verdict had the evidence been there.

"I was afraid something like this would happen," Rogerio said. "The Auténticos would never have done such a thing."

Luis did not respond, but at that instant, he decided to resign. He saw the definite need for moderation in government; however, as Undersecretary of Justice, he thought his resignation would make more of a statement than staying on and quietly trying to deal with what was becoming a vengeful juggernaut.

The next day Luis read the stunning news that Major Félix Pena, the president of the tribunal, had been found dead in his car at Camp Columbia. Everyone presumed his death was suicide. Oh, God, what a waste, Luis thought. That afternoon he sat at his desk and wrote his resignation.

> *Dear Comandante:*
>
> *You and I share many of the same social goals of the Revolution, but we have differed from the start on our attitudes regarding respect for an adherence to the law. I tried to understand your disdain of proper procedure while we were in the Sierra Maestra, but now I cannot condone your decision in the case of the pilots. In the mountains, you might have been in a hurry to deal with traitors, but now you have the time and the legal apparatus necessary for due process of justice. Yet you have chosen to ignore the law.*

As Undersecretary of Justice, I refuse to become an accomplice of this travesty. I, therefore, resign my position effective immediately.

I ask you to remember we fought in the Sierra to overthrow an unjust dictatorship and to restore our beloved 1940 Constitution. Specifically, I challenge you to call for free elections as soon as possible.

Sincerely,

Luis Recio

Luis delivered his letter personally to Castro's secretary, Celia Sánchez, at the Havana Hilton and left after a curt exchange of civilities. In spite of his action, he still held hope for the Revolution if not for its leader.

Luis had not told Laura about Alberto's visit and how Fidel really felt about him; however, he could not keep his resignation from office a secret from her. He broke the news to her after breakfast the day before it appeared in the *Diario de la Marina*.

"Did you consult with your father?" she wanted to know.

"Yes, I did," he answered, "but the final decision was my own."

"I'm not surprised you talked with him instead of me. It's not the first time you've done so."

Luis shrugged his shoulders and sighed, wishing his wife had the insight to understand the reasons behind his decision rather than feel slighted.

"What I fear, Luis, is that you're such an idealist you'll never be happy, no matter who is in office," Laura went on.

"You're right, I suppose, if whoever is in office takes the law into his own hands.

I've defended the Revolution because I believe in it," Luis exclaimed. "Although I didn't feel comfortable with Che's and Raúl's executions of war criminals in the first few days after victory, I understand such actions might have been justifiable under the circumstances. While I still support the Revolution, I have no respect for the man who leads it."

"Luis," Laura replied after several moments, "you're in the right profession, for you sure can argue a point. Maybe the whole thing is a blessing in disguise. Now all we have to do is mind our own business. You can go back to your private practice full time, and we can concentrate on our family."

Luis wanted desperately to believe all she said. Somehow, though, it all sounded too easy. One could not turn a commitment to a cause on and off as if it were a faucet.

The second trial of the forty-four airmen produced no new evidence; however, it did produce a new legal philosophy for Cuba. As articulated by Fidel, "Revolutionary justice is based not on legal precepts but on moral convictions." When Luis read this statement at the breakfast table, he shook his head in disbelief. The second tribunal sentenced the airmen to prison terms ranging from two to thirty years.

Chapter 28

Bernabé Morán was one of eight known illegitimate children of Bernabé Recio, the offspring of Bernabé and Julia Morán. Julia was the eldest daughter of Francisco Morán, the overseer of the original three thousand-acre Recio tract before it became a sugar plantation and a mill. Because of the social differences between their families, Bernabé Recio would never have married Julia, just as he would never have married any of the other women with whom he had premarital affairs. Eventually Bernabé provided monthly stipends for the upbringing of the eight children he fathered and made arrangements for them in his will. However, Bernabé Morán and the other seven were labelled by law as illegitimate because their birth certificate required the initials S.O.A. (without another surname) after their mothers' maiden name.

Julia Morán later married a mechanic and continued to live in the Tamarindo Sugar Mill batey. Though Bernabé Recio offered to send his son to Havana University once the young man finished the *bachillerato* in Camagüey, Bernabé Morán chose instead to follow in his stepfather's footsteps and worked at the sugar mill. Because of his efficiency, intelligence, and jovial disposition, he became the manager of all equipment, including an airplane for which a landing strip was built near the mill in the 50's. Bernabé Morán in a few years became indispensable for the operation of the mill.

Rogerio frequently talked over the phone with his half-brother during his stay in Havana. At first, he thought the call he received from Bernabé Morán early one afternoon in early June of 1959 was a routine business call.

"Rogerio, we have a problem. I found out this morning that a representative from the National Agrarian Reform Institute is coming to the mill tomorrow to announce the confiscation of the Recio lands. Our father is moving back to the house to defend his property and is bringing his guns with him. He says that anyone who dares to take an inch of his land will pay with his life. You and Luis need to come to the mill immediately."

"I can get there tonight, but I don't know if Luis can leave on such short notice," Rogerio replied. "Do we really need him?"

"I think it's wise to bring Luis since he's a member of the Revolution. His presence might give us some leverage with the INRA. I can arrange for our pilot to fly to Havana this afternoon, pick you up, and bring you back to the mill early tomorrow. The meeting is scheduled for tomorrow afternoon at two o'clock."

"Alright, I'll call Luis immediately."

Rogerio had known something like this was only a matter of time since the Agrarian Reform Law was promulgated on May 17. When he first heard about the law, he studied its provisions carefully and understood all too well what might be in store for their beloved mill and land. He would not know for sure until he talked to the delegation about what the exact demands would be, but he guessed that since the plantation produced a yield more than half as large as the national average, his family could keep 3,333 acres. He also knew they could keep the sugar mill.

The rest of the land, some twenty-six thousand acres, would be expropriated and paid back to the Recios over twenty years at 4.5% interest based on assessed value rather than actual value. Anyway he looked at the situation, Rogerio knew the Recios were big losers.

The next morning, the pilot flew Rogerio and Luis from Havana International to the plantation where Bernabé Morán was waiting for them in a jeep. He immediately took them to the main house to see the elder Recio, who was sitting in a rocker on the veranda with one of his guns close by on a wicker table. He appeared calm in spite of the conflict in the offing. Luis felt sorry for the old man who seemed to have outlived his time. If Papá Bernabé were dead, Luis thought, he would not have to witness what was about to happen.

The meeting was scheduled to take place at the sugar mill's office, but the INRA representatives were late. Bernabé Recio launched into a stream of graphic vituperation. "This is typical of those shit-eating brigands," he said. "If they aren't plotting how to steal people's property, they lie around all day in some paper-filled office doing nothing, like all fucking bureaucrats. I wouldn't piss on them if they were on fire. "

When they left the house at 1:45 p.m., Bernabé started to strap on two pistols, but Rogerio and Luis insisted he leave the weapons behind. They could keep him from arming himself, but they could not keep him from venting his rage against Castro and company.

While the three generations of Recios waited at the mill for the INRA delegation, Luis climbed up on the upper platform in the mill to see the sugar production process once again. As a child, he had stood there many times and wondered at the human ingenuity behind all the moving parts. He well remembered how Papá Bernabé had shown him the full sugar-making process from this very platform. The freshly cut cane was taken from the wagons and made into pulp. Then the juice was separated from the waste, and finally the crystallization process yielded the rich brown sugar that his grandfather gave him to taste. "Savor it, grandson," he said. "This is what makes Cuba the land it is." Luis wondered if the new owners of the plantation would do a better job at the operation than his family had done.

Two hours later the INRA representatives had still not arrived. Their tardiness, Luis believed, was not necessarily due to bureaucratic arrogance, as Papá Bernabé charged, but to lack of consideration.

While Luis waited, he chatted with the workers, several of whom Luis had known all of his life. They included Bernabé Morán's sons, who held decent jobs in the mill. So did many of his boyhood chums, among them Ramoncito, who worked as a clerk in the accounting office. When Luis made a point to say hello to him, Ramoncito greeted Luis with an ambivalent smile. As they talked, Ramoncito seemed pleased with the prospect of state ownership, but he was not particularly interested in the memories of their youth that Luis kept bringing up in a deliberate effort at camaraderie. Luis got the impression Ramoncito had already changed his allegiance, regardless of the formal decision of the Agrarian Reform Institute.

The leader of the delegation turned out to be a Lieutenant Fernando Hernández who had been a radical member of the Ortodoxo youth group in Camagüey and a communist sympathizer. As Luis attempted to recall how Hernández had gotten his position, he remembered a conversation he had at the Ministry of Justice with Húber Matos, one of the revolutionary leaders whom Luis had known in the Sierra and who was now military commander of Camagüey province. Matos complained about how communists were being placed in key positions. Like Luis, Matos supported land reform but did not want communization of the agricultural system. Bernabé Recio, however, felt Matos was a communist in disguise. Neither he nor the other cattle ranchers had ever forgiven Matos for remarking that the ranchers took better care of their cattle than of their workers.

When Hernández saw Luis, he deferentially extended his hand, apologized for being late and then said, "It's good to see you again, Luis. I'm happy to have a revolutionary here with me. You understand this is not my initiative. I'm just following orders."

Two armed youths that did not take part in the discussion accompanied Hernández, who stated his purpose succinctly.

"Major Recio, you have the choice of keeping either the sugar mill or 3,333 acres of land, but not both. The Agrarian Reform Law specifically protects the plantation owners by prohibiting the proprietor of the sugar mill from owning any land. Which of the two will you give up? All of your land less the 3,333 acres or the mill?"

The irony of the situation struck Luis with a vengeance. Barely six months after the fall of Batista, here was the son of a truck driver from the slums of Camagüey telling the Recios their land was lost forever. Luis remembered discussing the need for Agrarian Reform with Dr. Sorí Marín in the Sierra, but he had no idea that the law would be this radical. He wondered to what extent Sorí Marín had helped to shape it.

Old Bernabé was livid.

"You son of a whore! I fought battles for freedom for this country before you were conceived, and my grandson risked his life against the bastard Batista. What the fuck did you do in the Revolution?"

Hernández replied calmly, "I was with Che in the Escambray after working in the underground in Camagüey. But that's not why I'm here, Major Recio," he added. "I represent the INRA, and you have no option. You must choose one of the alternatives I've outlined. Which will it be?"

"Hell!" Bernabé shouted, "it's not going to be either! You tell Castro to go fuck himself. If he wants to take land from me, he had better come do it himself—that is, if he's got the *cojones* to do it."

Seeing Hernández' expression turn icy, Luis interceded.

"Grandfather, please calm down. You're not helping anything. As Lieutenant Hernández has told us, he has come here to carry out his orders."

Bernabé, ignoring Luis' words, charged toward Hernández. It took all the strength Rogerio and Bernabé Morán had to restrain their father. As they wrestled him back to the house, Bernabé heaped vile curses upon the Revolution.

When Bernabé was out of hearing, Luis apologized to Hernández for his grandfather's behavior but not without a feeling of guilt. The government official had no sensitivity to what the loss of the land meant to his grandfather.

"You must understand," Luis explained, "he built this place from nothing, and at the end of his life, he finds that all his work has been in vain."

"This is not the first encounter we've had with an irate owner," Hernández said, as if in sympathy. "There have even been a couple of suicides since we began to expropriate land. However, I advise you to have him control his tongue. He doesn't seem to understand it won't do him or his family any good to vent his rage against the inevitable or to insult the leader of this historic change."

Looking up at Hernández, Luis knew that as soon as his father returned from the house, they would make the decision. "Land is no good," Luis concluded, "unless one can use it."

When his father returned from the house, he confirmed Luis' opinion, saying the family would keep the mill.

Hernández informed them the paperwork would be taken care of in a matter of days. Bidding them a good day, he turned away, got in his jeep, and departed with his aides like a good officer who had done his duty.

Chapter 29

The following week, Alberto Sánchez paid Luis an unexpected visit at the law firm. It was the first time Luis had seen him out of uniform since the Revolution. As he entered, Alberto took off his sunglasses and closed the door to Luis' office. "I heard about the takeover of the sugar plantation," he commented sadly as he took a seat.

Luis shrugged and asked, "Do you know who was in charge of it?"

"Of course I know," Alberto responded. "Hernández. He's one of the aides Guevara sent back to Camagüey to expedite the reform."

"You remember," Luis recalled, "Hernández was one of the most vocal anti-imperialists of the young Ortodoxos in Camagüey. As you probably know, Húber Matos is concerned about the role the communists have assumed in the armed forces and land reform. I'm afraid Hernández is head of one of many cadres Raúl and Che are setting up across the country. I'm not that surprised over losing the family lands since we all knew reform of some type was inevitable, but, Alberto, the communist connection really worries me."

"I know," said Alberto, shaking his head. "I talked to Carlos Franqui just the other day, and he's also upset with the role the Socialist Popular Party is being given."

The Carlos Franqui to whom Alberto referred was a Marxist and the editor of *Revolución*, the official government newspaper. Luis had known him in the mountains where Franqui wrote *El Cubano Libre*, the rebel newspaper.

"I'm seeing a number of communists sprouting up in top positions," said Alberto. "It's evident Che's and Raúl's influence is growing. Many of communists didn't lift a finger against Batista, and here they are determining the path of the Revolution. On the other hand, I can't imagine anyone manipulating Fidel. He has to be the one making the decisions.

"So what are we to think about all this? I know Fidel went into a rage when you resigned. He vowed you would pay. I suspect that is what's behind the sudden appropriation of your lands. The new law is one thing, but this personal vendetta disturbs me."

"Alberto," Luis said, looking blankly at his desk with his arms folded across his chest, "I believe we need to re-think our allegiances."

Alberto, toying with a black onyx egg paperweight on Luis' desk did not respond.

"I got the egg in Acapulco," Luis commented.

"Let's take our families and go live there," said Alberto lightly.

"Wouldn't it be nice?" Luis agreed, knowing the solution was much more complicated.

Chapter 30

In the last months of 1959 and the first ones of 1960, the metaphor of a watermelon best expressed the deep divisions in Cuba. In answering the accusations of North American reporters that the Revolution was drifting toward communism, Castro replied that the Revolution was as Cuban as the royal green palms. However, his opponents used a different comparison and likened the Revolution to a watermelon, green on the outside but "red" inside.

The Recios and the Ramírezes increasingly saw the "red" of the Revolution. Rogerio and Mario lamented the decline of free enterprise and the economic chaos that policies such as the nationalization of industries were producing. As the Castro regime enacted one radical measure after another, impacting everything from land distribution to urban housing, Rogerio and Mario took steps to transfer some of their money to the United States. Both realized that sooner or later their families would have to leave Cuba for the U.S., and they wanted them to live comfortably. Unfortunately, the decision to move came with the takeover of the sugar mill and the tragic consequences that followed.

In June of 1960, the Agrarian Reform Institute decided to take over the sugar mills in addition to lands it had previously expropriated. Since the loss of the lands, Rogerio had been spending much of his time at the mill, trying to reorganize the operation. He stayed in the plantation house with Bernabé and patiently endured Bernabé's daily diatribes against the government. Though he agreed with most of what his father had to say, Rogerio remained silent through these outbursts out of fear of intensifying the old man's fury.

Rogerio would later refer to the incident as "the Dark Noon" of the Recio family. He and Bernabé were eating lunch when one of the servants informed them an army officer requested to see them about an urgent matter. Going to the door, Rogerio recognized Fernando Hernández, now a pistol-toting captain. "Well," Rogerio said, "you must be doing your job. It looks like you've been promoted."

"*Señor* Recio," Hernández replied, "I'm not here to display my rank. I'm here on serious business. May I come in?"

"Of course," Rogerio said, guiding him and his two aides, also armed with automatic pistols, into the living room.

"I'll get straight to the point," Hernández began, "I'm here to take over the sugar mill as part of the second phase of the Agrarian Reform. You'll need to give up this house."

Rather than argue, Rogerio, understanding the hopelessness of the situation, decided to keep quiet.

"I'm sure you must be upset, but look at it this way. The right of eminent domain allows governments to acquire lands needed for roads or other projects. Well, this is similar. What the Revolution is doing now is setting up a policy of eminent domain for people, which is what we call historical inevitability or the sharing of wealth. You will be compensated for your own loss at a reasonable rate."

"That may be so," Rogerio said, "but we have yet to collect one cent from our lands seized almost a year ago."

"Well, the Revolution is still green, and we're behind in our paperwork," Hernández responded, taking refuge in the popular metaphor of the day.

Bernabé, who had been listening at the door between the dining and living rooms, finally found his voice.

"May lightning strike you dead, you son of a bitch. This Revolution is not green. It's red and black, just like your cursed 26th of July flag. It's red with the blood of innocent people and black as the pit of hell in its sinister maneuvering to steal everything in sight!"

Rogerio, proud of his father, did not know what these uninvited guests might do when they heard such an inflammatory indictment of their mission, but he did not have to wait long for a response.

"Old man, you'd better learn to control your tongue," Hernández threatened, showing that Bernabé's remarks had hit a raw nerve.

"I can say whatever I damn well please in my own house!" Bernabé interrupted.

"Well, enjoy yourself now," Hernández countered, "because in twenty-four hours we're confiscating this house along with the sugar mill."

"Whoever comes to steal this house will have to walk over my dead body."

"Major Recio," Hernández continued with some effort toward indulgence, "out of respect, I won't arrest you right now. Times have changed. All those mementos there on that wall are meaningless relics. You old soldiers take pride in your role in the War of Independence, but you didn't help free Cuba from anybody. You brought on an arrogant Yankee imperialism and make our island a colony of that colossus to the north. Florida itself looks like a prick ready to fuck Cuba."

While he talked, Hernández pointed to the wall which displayed old photographs of Bernabé in the army, a map of the Caribbean, a framed copy of his commission as an officer, his faded citations, his uniform and medals, a couple of crossed swords, and the Recio coat of arms. As a child Rogerio had looked upon them as sacred symbols of a glorious epoch, and he was stunned by the blasphemy of this upstart captain.

Before Rogerio knew what was happening, Bernabé rushed by him to the wall, grabbed a sword, and turned with it raised high to attack Hernández, shouting, "No one has ever dared to . . . desecrate . . . these . . . you . . ."

Rogerio watched in terror as his father gasped and fell forward on the floor, the sword slipping from his hand as he went down with a thump.

Rogerio knelt by his father, slapping his face in an effort to revive him. He repeated Bernabé's name over and over, but, in the vacant stare of his father's bulging eyes, he recognized the face of death. He yelled to a servant to get Dr. Crucet, the physician of the mill, who arrived within minutes. The only thing left for Crucet to do was to close Bernabé's lifeless green eyes.

Stunned, Hernández started to speak, but Rogerio cut him short. "Get the hell out of here!"

Putting on his military cap, Hernández hurriedly left the room with his aides. As they were getting into the jeep, Rogerio, in the spirit of his father, stepped out on the front porch and shouted at Hernández, "This house, this mill, and this land might be yours now, but not for long!"

Hernández ignored the comment and drove away.

Luis, who heard the tragic details from his father, was glad that he had not been present.

Chapter 31

For two days and two nights, the body of Major Bernabé Recio lay in the ancestral home of the Recios. The Cuban flag and his uniform with his many medals draped the richly decorated black casket in which his body rested. These hours for the family were exhausting ones since tradition held that the casket should never be left unattended during the *velorio*, the equivalent of the North American wake.

Hundreds came in a show of respect and affection for the Recio patriarch, the friends and neighbors close to the family returning repeatedly. The family set up folding chairs throughout the house to accommodate the crowd. Although a somber atmosphere prevailed through the house, laughter could occasionally be heard from one of the circles of men on the central patio or out on the sidewalk as they told stories about the colorful escapades of the old soldier. The mourners recounted tales of Bernabé's exploits in love and war and shared the latest jokes about Castro and the Revolution. In typical Cuban fashion, the women sat close to the casket, reciting the rosary and quietly conversing. María Luisa, Isabel, and Laura stayed near the casket along with other women from the Recio, Betancourt and de Varona families and received friends.

Rogerio and Luis made the rounds to the different groups, accepting condolences and sharing memories. A cascade of wreaths from individuals and organizations, such as Veterans of the War of Independence, the Sugar Cane Growers Association, and the Cattlemen's Association of Cuba, encircled the coffin. Since Bernabé had been a war hero, the younger brother of "*El Honrado*," and president of the Sugar Cane Growers Association of Cuba, his death made news in the *Diario de La Marina* and *Prensa Libre*, the only two newspapers that had not yet been seized by the government. Telegrams poured in from all over Cuba, including one from Alberto Sánchez, which said, "WISH I COULD BE THERE WITH YOU ON THIS SAD OCCASION. YOUR BROTHER, ALBERTO." Alberto's parents, who came to honor the elder Recio, also conveyed their sympathy.

Starting from the house on the morning of the third day, the funeral procession was several blocks long, its destination the Recio mausoleum in the city's ancient cemetery. Four white horses pulling a black funeral cart with the casket covered by the Cuban flag headed the procession. Immediately behind the cart walked Rogerio, Luis, and other male members of the Recio, Luaces, Betancourt, Agramonte, and de Varona families. Bernabé Morán and his sons, Morán's half-brothers and their sons, and Luis' cousin, Philip Heymann, from the U. S. Embassy in Havana, followed the immediate members of the family. After the family came those sugar mill employees who had the courage to publicly express their loyalty, and behind them, practically every surviving veteran of the Cuban-Spanish-American War in Camagüey. Several with canes and one used crutches.

The story of Bernabé's death while confronting Hernández spread like wildfire. The brandishing of his sword at the communist infidel reminded many of General Agramonte's statue in the city park in front of the Liceo and was seen as a fitting ending for a *cojonudo*, a man with big balls. Though a crude term, *cojonudo* was a common adjective used in Cuba to describe anything that was bold, brave, or just right. Even black beans cooked especially well would elicit the expression, "This is *cojonudo*!" So it was with Bernabé, a man who was a *cojonudo* to the end.

It was this very quality of *cojonudo* that the traditional funeral orator at the cemetery celebrated, though the word itself was never used. The speaker, Dr. Marcelino Martínez Tapia, a former congressman from the Liberal Party, was well-known in Camagüey for his oratorical skills. In his eulogy, Dr. Martínez Tapia focused upon Bernabé's productive life, the creation of his sugar empire from nothing, his soaring imagination, and his courage in battle during the War of Independence, epitomized by his famous machete charge. It was fitting that at the moment of his death, he was still charging with sword raised against an enemy more diabolical than the despicable Spaniards a half-century before.

Though outbursts were not customary at Cuban burials, Dr. Martínez Tapia's words so moved the audience of some three thousand that cries arose around the Recio mausoleum of "Viva Bernabé!" "Down with the communists!" and "Long live freedom!" The feelings of sympathy for Bernabé and all he stood for were so intense that Luis feared the ceremony might turn into a political rally. He did not want the crowd to get out of hand, considering the unfortunate consequences that such an event might trigger. He knew members of Castro's intelligence infiltrated the crowd, and he had noticed an unusual number of police and soldiers on the sidewalks as the procession moved through the city.

Luis could not tell whether Dr. Martínez Tapia was aware of the same concerns as he, for his parting words, while not inflammatory, were certainly inspirational. He remarked eloquently on the fourteen generations of Recios who helped to develop Camagüey and all of Cuba. He recalled the integrity of Manuel Recio with nostalgia and wondered how Cuban politics might be today had *"El Honrado"* lived. Dr. Martínez Tapia was proud to look upon the three generations still alive as represented by Rogerio, Luis, and Luisito. In Bernabé, he said, they had an eternal example of one who loved freedom from the core of his being.

"Although Major Bernabé Recio is no longer with us," he ended, "his seeds will bring forth a harvest of fruitful, progressive change wherever they are sown. May God rest his soul, and may all of us find the rewarding peace here on earth that he now enjoys in the Great Beyond." Luis was grateful for the kind words of Dr. Martínez Tapia even if, as in the great tradition of Cuban eulogies, his rhetoric might have incited a riot.

Several days after the funeral, Luis returned to Havana and called Alberto at his home to ask if he could see him. They decided to meet at 9:00 p.m. at an inconspicuous place and they chose "El Laguito." As soon as they were together Luis asked his friend.

"I have to find out whether the confiscation of my grandfather's sugar mill was an act of vengeance by Fidel Castro?"

Alberto was slow in answering.

"Luis, I knew the mill property was going to be taken, and initially I thought I'd tell you, but then I realized that there was nothing that we could do to stop it. Fidel has a vendetta against you. He sees you as a traitor, and you're paying the price. I advise you to be very cautious from now on."

"That's what I wanted to know. My family plans to leave Cuba soon. Do you think we need to speed up our plans."

"I suggest you do," answered Alberto. "I don't know how far things are going to go, but after the incident with Luis Conte Agüero, I'm sure Fidel suspects everybody. He knows even old friends are turning on him. He's paranoid!"

Luis Conte Agüero was a friend of both Luis and Alberto. He had been Secretary General of the Ortodoxos and one of the most prestigious news commentators in Cuba. At the beginning of the Revolution, Conte Agüero ranked one of Castro's intimate associates. However, in March of 1960, he denounced the Castro government on television for curtailing free speech. When, on March 25, Conte Agüero tried to read an open letter to Castro on his television program at the CMQ station, Comandante Piñeiro, one of Raúl Castro's aides, physically restrained him. Using the total control he now had over television, Fidel Castro attacked his former ally for two days, referring to him repeatedly as a traitor. Conte Agüero had no options but to seek asylum in the Argentinian Embassy.

"You plan on leaving the country too, I assume?" Alberto inquired.

"Not if I can help it," Luis answered. "I have a lot business to take care of in the law office, and I'll be moving to father's house to look after it in his absence. Laura and Luisito will go with my parents. I couldn't bear it if something happened to them because of me."

"Luis, let me tell you something about your land. Your sugar mill may have been confiscated early because of Castro's animosity toward you, but, believe me, it would have been taken sooner or later. Plans exist this very minute to gain control not only of all the plantations and mills but also of the telephone and electric companies. The die is cast, and you Recios were merely the victim of the first roll."

Luis did not comment, and Alberto understood the sadness of his silence. "Luis," Alberto continued in an effort to console him, "we're living in tumultuous times. Everything we've known, been taught, and heard about is in a state of chaos. As the days go by, I find myself more ambivalent about the Revolution. I know you feel trapped, but believe me, you have more freedom than those who work in the headquarters of this Revolution."

Moved by his friend's honesty, Luis turned and offered his hand in the darkness of the car. Alberto grasped it and held it for a few seconds.

As Alberto got out of the car, Luis said, "Oh, by the way, you'll never believe who came to Papá Bernabé's funeral."

"I have no idea. I just wish I could have been there," answered Alberto.

"Cachita Ruiz," said Luis, "our favorite madam."

"You don't say," Alberto said, laughing. "My folks didn't tell me. Did it create a scandal?"

"I'm sure a lot of eyebrows were raised, but her coming to pay her respect touched me so much that I took her to the casket and introduced her to the women in the family. Of course, I didn't tell them that she supervised the loss of my virginity."

"Hell, mine too!" chuckled Alberto, and then after a pause, he added, "Luis, we had fun back then, didn't we?"

"We did," said Luis. "We were young and foolish."

As Alberto opened the door to leave, Luis took a twenty *peso* bill from his wallet and said, "Here, take this and buy something for my godson, Albertico. I haven't done anything for him in a long time."

"Luis," Alberto reflected, "I think a lot about what kind of country our kids will eventually live in. We try to make things better for their generation, but I fear more often than not we just fuck things up."

"I know, Alberto, I know," Luis replied.

"Goodbye, my dear friend," Alberto said, as he disappeared into the darkness and the silence which accompanied it.

Chapter 32

A week after their return from the funeral in Camagüey Luis told Laura he had important news. It did not take much imagination for Laura, who was applying facial cream before the mirror of the bedroom dresser, to realize what the topic concerned.

"You want us to leave Cuba, don't you?"

For weeks, they had seen friends suddenly disappear, only to learn later that they had fled to Miami. Since the beginning of the year, thousands of families had left the country. The breakdown of order, symbolized by the nightly bombings in Havana and the organized revolutionary mobs bent on harassment of any opposition, contributed to an atmosphere of near panic.

"Yes," said Luis after a pause. "After the funeral, Papá and I discussed our options and decided the time has come to leave. It was a painful decision, but the confiscation of our properties in Camagüey proves we're a marked family. We talked to Philip Heymann, and he's already at work securing tourist visas. If all goes well, you and Luisito can leave day after tomorrow."

"What do you mean by 'you and Luisito' can leave? What about you?" Laura demanded.

"I'm not going at this time," he said softly.

"And why not?"

"Because I need to look after our families' interests here in Havana, and I have unfinished business in my office. Jorge León, by the way, is staying here to help me. He'll join Isabel and the rest of you as soon as he can."

"Damn, Luis!" Laura exclaimed, "You think I don't know why you're really staying here? You think I haven't noticed the telephone calls from people who won't identify themselves, your late arrivals and sudden departures on the strangest excuses? It's exactly like before--the same old song!"

Catching her breath, Laura went on. "I've had it, Luis! No more! You're killing me slowly but surely."

"Laura, I'm staying in order to help overthrow Castro and . . ."

"I know!" Laura said sarcastically, "for a better Cuba for your son to grow up in! A world safe for democracy and all that bullshit."

Interrupting her, Luis restrained his rage but stated emphatically, "If that's truly the way you feel, we should call it quits."

"You're right," replied Laura as if she anticipated the idea. "As soon as I'm in Florida, I'll start divorce proceedings."

Luis got up from the bed, put on his bathrobe, and walked to the door where he turned to her and spoke, "I only have one request. Would you agree not inform our parents of our situation until you're in Miami? With Papá Bernabé's death and the move to Miami, our parents don't need more worries now."

"That's fine," Laura agreed, "but as far as I'm concerned, we're no longer husband and wife."

Lying on his back on the bed in the guest bedroom, Luis reflected on the weakness of human nature. More often than not, men let their libido rather than common sense dictate their behavior. With Laura, he had yielded too much to the gratification of his desires. When he first saw her, she seemed lovely, seductive, and charming, but now he knew that the charm was superficial. In contrast to Ofelia, Laura lacked depth of character and vision. She was like a pampered little girl; Ofelia, in contrast, was like a wise young earth mother, eager to give birth to the freedom of her people.

On the day of departure, Philip Heymann arrived at the Recio home at 8:00 a.m. in a State Department chauffeured limousine with the word DIPLOMAT on the front and rear license plates and a small American flag secured to the antenna. Philip told Luis that the visibility of U.S. symbols would expedite procedures at the airport.

Luis, Laura, Luisito, and the maid were waiting in Luis' car when Philip arrived. Rogerio, María Luisa, Laura, Isabel, and Jorge León got into the nine-seat limousine while the chauffeur loaded their baggage, some of which had to be placed in the seats up front. From the Recios, they drove to the Ramírezes, where, because of the excessive luggage, Mario had to take his car.

At the departure gate, guards dressed in military fatigues separated those leaving by sex, took them to side rooms, stripped, and searched them. When nothing suspicious was found on them, they were allowed to dress again and proceed. This degrading procedure scandalized María Luisa, but she refrained from saying anything for fear of provoking the guards.

At the final checkpoint just prior to departure, a militiawoman told María Luisa that she would have to leave the three-carat diamond ring on her right hand behind. It was an heirloom that had great sentimental value for her since her grandmother Heymann had left it for María Luisa in her will.

"No, please," pleaded María Luisa to the woman in uniform, who was young enough to be her daughter.

"Let me have it!" the woman ordered and brusquely removed the ring from her finger.

Luis, Philip, and Jorge watched the scene helplessly from behind a glass wall. Luis was furious when he saw his mother hold up her right hand and indicate where the ring had been. Only a few months before, María Luisa had told Philip the story of the ring, but now the theft was more a matter of principle than a personal affront. Among other things, the act belied the communist claim that the government confiscated only private property and not personal possessions. As soon as the Recios and Ramírezes were out of sight and on their way to the plane, Heymann lodged a complaint with the airport security chief.

Sporting a Castro-like beard, the major looked at Heymann, Luis, and Jorge with amusement, and then reciting a memorized regulation, he informed them that the government had the prerogative to confiscate any valuables taken out of the country.

"Individuals leaving the country are permitted to take five dollars and a box of cigars with them. I'm sure your family has exceeded that amount, considering the money you must already have in U.S. banks. The government has actually been generous, and your family should be grateful. After all, the plane is still on the runway, and those departing could be brought back and given a more thorough search," the major threatened with a sinister smile.

"Haven't you heard about all the wealth the Chinese gangsters took to Formosa when they fled the continent before the Revolution of the People and how the Nazis carted off the treasures of Europe for their own private use?" The major continued. "You should see some of the things we've taken from fugitives. We don't want Cuba to be drained of her treasures as the oligarchs flee."

Heymann had never heard such senseless rhetoric before in his life. Philip was on the verge of replying in a very undiplomatic fashion when Luis tapped him discreetly on the coat as a signal to let well enough alone. Heymann got the message and after a second of glowering, said calmly, "Very well, our Ambassador will hear of these practices and report them to your government. The United States deplores such actions."

"As you wish," the major responded, throwing up his hands in jest. "Protest all you like. Our government will see it as a minor complaint compared to the major ones we've had against your country for the last fifty years. I find your complicity typical of the U.S. fondness for oligarchs and all their forms of robbery."

The major sounded like Captain Hernández all over again, echoing the same Marxist rhetoric but adding a sarcasm tinged with hatred and couched in a threat.

On the way back to Havana, Luis rode with Philip in the backseat of the State Department limousine in order to talk with him about the rapidly changing scene in Cuba. After discussing the incident at the airport and its implications, Luis commented, "These recurring departures from Cuba are a part of life now. I never dreamed I would be packing up my own family and sending them away."

"I understand, Luis," said Philip. "In the 1930's, I came to Cuba with my family. Our exile from Germany was because of the Nazis to whom the major at the airport just compared your family and mine. I guess that's what got to me. Until American University offered my father a teaching position, your dear grandfather, Uncle Moisés, sent us a monthly stipend. We've never forgotten his generosity."

"Philip, the mask is coming off, and the true face of the Castro regime will soon be exposed." Luis responded. "Castro wants to set up a Marxist-Leninist state in this hemisphere. I would prefer you emphasize that point to your superiors rather than details about the theft of the ring."

Philip Heymann nodded in agreement.

Even before the episode of the ring, Luis knew Philip was well aware of the radical shift that was taking place in Cuba. The real question, Luis realized, was not whether the U.S. knew what was going on but how far it was willing to go in restraining a Marxist-Leninist regime ninety miles from the Florida Keys. Would the U.S. have the balls to invoke the Monroe Doctrine in the twentieth century?

As they neared the Recio home, having ridden the last several miles in silence, Philip patted Luis' arm and said, "Call me if you need help. I'll do whatever I can."

Part 3

Justice and the Revolution
What Color is the Watermelon?

Chapter 33

In December of 1959, the government's announcement of a twenty-year sentence for Húber Matos for the alleged crime of treason stunned Luis. Matos had written a letter to Castro denouncing the totalitarian turn of the Revolution and resigning his major's commission. Castro could not forgive Matos for deserting the Revolution, and he used Raúl Castro, Camilo Cienfuegos, and Che Guevara to fabricate a charge of conspiracy against their former comrade in arms. Luis was surprised that the happy-go-lucky Camilo had taken the lead in denouncing Matos. A few days after Matos' arrest, Camilo allegedly disappeared on a flight from Camagüey to Havana in a single engine Cessna plane. Luis suspected foul play, as had been the case in the trumped-up charges against Matos. Castro was obviously eliminating potential rivals.

Seeing how cruelly the Revolution was devouring its own children, as well as those of the opposition, Luis began to work for the underground. Through Philip Heymann, he established contact with the CIA chief in the American embassy, Frank Dowler, who informed him that the best organized anti-Castro group was the MRR (Movement of Revolutionary Rescue) which had been started by former officers in the rebel army, several of whom Luis knew. Disenchantment with Castro was rapidly growing.

Among the leaders were two of his friends, Manuel Artime and Rogelio González Corso, both members of the *Agrupación Católica Universitaria*. Initially, Father Llorente had been instrumental in convincing influential church and lay leaders that Castro was not a communist. After Castro had gone to the Sierra, Llorente went there himself to get assurances from Castro on that very point; however,

Llorente later realized how skillfully Castro had deceived the Church, and as a result, he and his group started to conspire against Castro.

Luis never became an *Agrupado*, but in addition to his night classes at San Lorenzo, he periodically attended informal meetings at the *Agrupación* headquarters. At these meetings, he participated in political discussions often led by prominent Catholics, such as Juan Antonio Rubio Padilla, an Auténtico minister in Prío's cabinet, and José Ignacio Rasco, the leader of the Christian Democrats.

Only insiders knew that Luis had never been initiated as an *Agrupado*. The *Agrupación* building was ideally suited for private meetings since numerous rooms for study were located on the second floor overlooking the central courtyard. Luis met with Rogelio González Corso, the head of the MRR underground in one of these rooms. Among the tasks that he outlined, Rogelio proposed that Luis write anti-Castro propaganda for the MRR official newspaper, *Rescate*. Luis began to write articles attacking the communist turn of Revolution and was active in distributing *Rescate*. On one occasion, he even persuaded an MRR member, Armando Zaldívar, to have his girlfriend dress up as if she were pregnant so she could carry anti-Castro propaganda under her clothing as she went by plane to the city of Santiago de Cuba.

In addition to writing, Luis recruited military and government personnel. The goal was to reach important individuals who would, in turn, recruit at least five fellow workers. However, numbers were not as important as the strategic jobs held by the converts. Since there was always the possibility that one of the persons he approached could turn the conspirators in, selectivity was of primary concern.

Through the CIA, the MRR obtained C-4 plastic explosives and caps which it distributed around the country with the help of university students. Once Luis participated in a bombing mission whose target was the power station in Regla, a city east of Havana's harbor. His accomplice, an *Agrupado* and an electrical engineer by the name of Rolando Tarajano, was an employee of the Ministry of Public Works and was familiar with the electrical systems of the city and its environs.

The most challenging aspect of the operation was to keep from arousing suspicions among the vigilante committees located on every block throughout the cities. Luis and Rolando, dressed in military uniforms, solved this problem by taking along two young women, Rolando's fiancée and her best friend, to give the impression they were two officers out on the town with their dates. The girls, Catholic and "reputable," were thrilled by a sense of adventure. Accomplices in sabotage, they were also taking on the roles of "questionable" young women going to a *posada* for a session of lovemaking.

At the *posada* near the power station, Luis paid for the room and ordered four drinks, making sure that the clerk saw his lieutenant's insignia. After the drinks arrived, Luis and his group began an animated conversation to convince the proprietor they were partying. A half-hour later, Luis rang the bell for another round of drinks, winking at the clerk as he paid in a show of male complicity. Some fifteen minutes later, he and Rolando left on their mission.

Rolando carried twenty pounds of C-4 explosives, a timer, detonator, and bolt cutters in an army handbag. Under his coat, Luis had a long-nosed .38 with a silencer. They approached the station, which was approximately two hundred meters from the *posada*, on the side opposite a small wooden guardhouse where a private night watchman was reading the newspaper. Luis was sure the paper was Carlos Franqui's *Revolución*, the main propaganda voice of the government. How ironic, Luis thought, that the guard was reading material the editor himself did not subscribe to.

While Luis stood in the shadow some thirty meters away to ensure that the guard did not stop them, Rolando cut a few of the metal strands of the fence, crawled under it, and began applying the waxy C-4 and timer to the base of a central transformer. The roaring hum of the plant was an ally in their operation, helping to drown out the soft snaps of the bolt cutter and any tinkering noises Rolando might make as he got ready to set the explosive. As Luis watched the stealthy and efficient work of his comrade, he remembered the hum of Castro's generators in the mountains and the soothing effect it had on him.

They left the station as quickly as they entered, Rolando putting the wires back in place to conceal their point of entry. They arrived at the *posada* a few minutes later, where the girls waited inside the car. They departed immediately and casually began the short trip back to Havana on the road bordering the bay, the operation as perfectly executed as one in an army manual.

The two couples stopped at a bar in Havana Harbor and took seats in an open-air upper deck in order to have a good view of the show. They sat facing the calm waters of the bay across which they could see the night lights of Regla. Having their drinks and chatting animatedly, they waited patiently and tried to avoid looking at their watches.

The operation was a complete success. An instant after they saw a huge flash, they heard the noise of the blast loud and clear. Lights went out all along the east side of the bay as if they had been candles snuffed out by a hurricane. Electrical fires followed, giving the impression of a firecracker display with rockets and Roman candles.

The fireworks took place in seconds, and then there was complete darkness on the water as if the eastern part of the world had suddenly vanished. The explosion on the upper deck took everyone by surprise, and the festive mood dissipated as quickly as the lights went out across the bay. After a few moments of startled conversation, the patrons left for the safety of their homes. Luis and his group made a silent toast and departed, knowing that the operation had been fulfilled. It served as a reminder to thousands in Regla and Havana that the government did not have control of essential services and that urban guerrillas could strike with impunity at any hour of the day or night.

Chapter 34

Luis knew Ofelia was unhappy with classes on Marxism that officers were required to take. Even worse, as a teacher, she was expected to conduct a class on Marxism for the enlisted men once she completed her basic courses.

"My idea of the Revolution is not one of indoctrinating the people on class hatred. My parents died because of political hatred, and no matter what excuses are offered, people continue to suffer and die for the same reason," Ofelia explained. "I had hoped the Revolution would bring peace to the island, but instead, all I see are more arms and uniforms than before. I truly believed Fidel when he said, 'Arms for what?'"

"I am deeply disillusioned too," Luis concurred.

"When will it all stop--these weapons and this fighting?" she then asked Luis as they continued their earlier conversation one afternoon in a bar near Camp Columbia. After a long period of silence during which he looked straight into her large brown eyes, he heard himself say, "I don't know when it will stop, but I don't think we'll see the end of the conflict any time soon. As long as Fidel is in charge, we'll never have peace in Cuba." After a pause, Luis asked the crucial question, "Ofelia, do you believe Fidel has betrayed the Revolution?"

"Yes, he has, but Luis, what can we do?" she asked with despair.

Luis reached out across the table and held her hands in his. He knew now her allegiance was no longer with Fidel Castro and the Revolution.

"You can work in the underground," Luis confided. "It's the only way we'll rescue our democratic Revolution! We can no longer deny Fidel's intentions and the unforgiveable acts of his regime."

One night in August of 1960, at the Recio home on Fifth Avenue, Luis met with Ofelia, Julián de la Torre, a captain who worked in the armory at Camp Columbia, and Rogelio González Corso. They arranged a shipment of arms and food from Camp Columbia to Bayamo in order to open a front in the Sierra Maestra. The anti-Castro rebels had already succeeded in opening up a front in the Escambray mountains under the leadership of Plinio Prieto. During their low-toned conversation, they heard the doorbell. Octavio, the butler, entered the office and informed Luis that Alberto Sánchez wanted to see him. After excusing himself, Luis went to the living room where Alberto, in uniform, was pacing nervously.

"Luis, Fidel has issued orders to his intelligence officers to check a number of persons suspected of counterrevolutionary activities," Alberto said, going directly to the point. "Miguel Ochoa informed me just this afternoon your name is on the list. You should leave the country as soon as possible."

"Alberto," Luis replied after a pause, "I appreciate your warning, but what I still want to know is if you're going to come over to our side. We need you and Miguel."

Choosing his words carefully, Alberto answered, "I won't deny that there're many things that disturb us, but we're not ready to give up on the Revolution."

"Alberto, you know Fidel is a tyrant! He's deliberately deceiving the Cuban people. Open your eyes!"

"Perhaps you're right, but right now I believe Fidel is testing Che, Raúl, and Carlos Rafael Rodríguez to find out their intentions, but he'll cut them off if they go too far."

Luis looked straight into his friend's eyes and said, "Alright, take the time you need. If we don't see each other again and you and Miguel decide to join our cause, contact Frank Dowler in the American Embassy."

After a tight *abrazo*, they walked to the door where Alberto reminded him again, "Don't linger. You have forty-eight hours at best before they come after you."

Luis relayed Alberto's news and the group quickly closed the business that had brought them together. As Ofelia rose to leave, Luis told her he wanted to talk with her.

As soon as Rogelio and the captain departed, Luis, looking into Ofelia's eyes, said hoarsely, "I want to spend this last night with you."

"You don't know how much I've waited for you to say this," she sighed as she kissed him, caressing his head.

"We can't stay here," Luis said. "We'll go to my father-in-law's house."

Telling Octavio that he didn't know when he would be able to return to the house, he went to the family vault and took out ten thousand *pesos* in cash and gave two thousand to Octavio and the maid to last them until the Recios returned.

"If anyone should inquire of me, say I've gone to Varadero Beach for a vacation," Luis instructed Octavio.

Luis and Ofelia drove directly to the Ramírez's home with Ofelia cuddling close to him. Even though Luis had a key, he rang the bell to keep from entering unannounced. When Humberto, the butler, came to the door in his robe, Luis explained

"There's an emergency. We need two rooms for the night. Are the beds made?"

"The beds are as they were when the family left," Humberto replied with a questioning look at Ofelia. As Carmen came into the foyer, Luis continued,

"We're hiding from the police." This admission brought fear into the eyes of Humberto and his wife, but Luis knew he could trust them.

Luis guided Ofelia up the curving Carrara marble stairway to the Ramírez' bedroom. As they went along the hall toward the Ramírez' quarters, Luis had the feeling he was passing in review before generations of Ramírezes who stared at him in disapproving silence from the gallery of photographs on both walls.

One of the pictures hanging there was of Laura. It was taken when she was seventeen and in the prime of her beauty, her face radiating under her luscious black hair, her opulent lips inviting, and her large eyes looking into the camera. As he escorted Ofelia to Laura's parents' bedroom, Luis felt that these same eyes spied him and followed him along the hallway.

On the dresser in the Ramírez's bedroom were more pictures, including a group picture of the family made at his and Laura's wedding. While Luis turned all the pictures face down, Ofelia giggled. The only person whose picture he would not have turned down had it been there would have been that of his Grandfather Bernabé, who would have enjoyed the situation more than anyone else.

After turning on the two bedside lamps, Luis went back to the door to switch off the lights of the huge chandelier. He whispered to Ofelia, "We've only made love in the darkness of a cave. Tonight I want to bask in your beauty."

He sat on the side of the bed and tenderly took off her uniform, brassiere, and panties until she stood naked in front of him. He kissed her body with passionate reverie, and she trembled under his touch. Kissing Luis' fingers as he caressed her face, she confided, "Luis, I want to do the same to you. Let me undress you now." Yielding to her request, Luis stood while she took off his clothes, repeating the ritual he had begun with her.

When Luis could contain himself no longer, he lifted her to the center of the bed. As he entered her, all the worries of the night vanished.

When they had rested, he led her to the luxurious bathroom full of mirrors. Luis and Ofelia laughed as they soaped each other all over and looked at a thousand wet and shiny images of themselves. It was a night of passion, pause, and repeated abandonment.

Early the next morning, they ruffled up the bed in one of the guestrooms and went downstairs to ask Carmen to prepare breakfast. Though he knew Mario had left a modest bank account in their names, Luis gave Humberto and Carmen one hundred *pesos* and informed them that he would see them in a couple of days. He guessed Humberto and Carmen suspected that something had taken place between him and Ofelia, but he knew that they would not tell anyone. They had not, like other servants of long standing, kept their jobs by being indiscreet.

After saying goodbye to Humberto and Carmen, Luis and Ofelia left for Camp Columbia. They had fewer than twenty-four hours to begin the mission that would start a counterrevolutionary front in the Sierra Maestra.

Chapter 35

ecause of the chaotic situation throughout the country, the plan was less complicated and dangerous than the transport of the arms Luis had carried to Castro in the Sierra Maestra. The Batista regime was an unpopular government supported by an army of corrupt officers. They knew that with defeat they had nowhere to go but into exile, which they did without a last ditch stand. Hence, an army of some forty thousand men surrendered to a group of 3,000 rag-tag rebels in the mountains.

Under Castro, the situation was different. Having turned the original democratic revolution into a Marxist-Leninist revolution with state control of industry, land, and the media, Castro had alienated important sectors of Cuban society and rendered them powerless. Several members of the first cabinet, such as former President Urrutia and Prime Minister Miró Cardona, had resigned and joined the opposition. Military leaders like Húber Matos were already in prison, and Pedro Díaz Lanz, the original chief of the Air Force, was in exile in the U.S.

Further, in blaming the U.S. as the cause of all Cuban evils, Castro was seen in many quarters not only as a communist but also as a fool. In Cuba, the United States was generally perceived as a progressive ally, worthy of emulation. In contrast to the Mexican War of 1846-1848 in which the U.S. annexed northern Mexico, the U.S. had not kept any Cuban territory other than the Guantanamo Naval Base, which it had leased for 99 years. The U.S. had also been instrumental in shortening the Cuban War of Independence by declaring war against Spain when the battleship *Maine* was sunk. Afterwards, the United States spent four years helping rebuild Cuba, including its educational system, and since then, American influence had never abated. There were not any signs of large-scale anti-American sentiment in Cuba until Castro came to power.

In practical terms, many of Castro's supporters regarded his strident anti-American propaganda, while popular with leftist intellectuals, as irresponsible because of the proximity of Cuba to the most powerful nation on earth. Because Cubans liked to side with a winner and because the U.S. was becoming increasingly anti-Castro, most Cubans were reluctant to take sides. This was particularly the case now in light of the persistent rumor of an imminent U.S.-backed invasion.

Luis earnestly believed that Castro's defeat was merely a matter of time. Because of the ambivalence of many officers in the Rebel Army, there was even a degree of recklessness in recruiting within the underground. Had the Castro government been better organized, Luis would have been more reluctant to involve Ofelia. Her job would be risky enough, but the fact that she would end up in the Sierra Maestra as a supply officer for only a short period eased his conscience. In any case, the final decision had been hers.

The efficiency of the operation helped to assure Luis of the wisdom of opening a second front in the Sierra Maestra. It proceeded as smoothly as the bombing of the power plant in Regla.

Shortly before noon after their night together, Luis let Ofelia out of his Buick two blocks from Camp Columbia, and at 2:00 p.m. she and Daniel, a driver she had recruited, arrived at the armory in a commissary truck which was partially filled with boxes of canned food. Captain de la Torre was waiting as planned with five boxes of M-1 rifles and three of ammunition which they quickly loaded behind the foodstuff for the guerrillas.

The truck was slightly more than half-loaded when Ofelia and the driver stopped at the gate to show the guard the manifest listing food for delivery to La Cabaña Fortress overlooking Havana Harbor. He waved them through routinely, never dreaming that the pretty officer in the right seat had forged this manifest as well as another he did not see. The second contained orders for a shipment to a base in Oriente province in case she and Daniel were stopped on the road.

In his officer's uniform, Luis waited in his car at an ESSO station on the outskirts of Havana as planned. Inconspicuously, he pulled behind the truck when he saw it pass, Ofelia jokingly rendering him a snappy salute as she went by. It pleased Luis to see her keeping a sense of humor in tense times. Although he still felt moments of guilt about involving Ofelia, her enthusiasm softened his recriminations. She had already been recruiting persons at Camp Columbia, and as soon as she got back in Oriente, she intended to get in touch with her brother, Teófilo.

They arrived at the Hatuey Beer warehouse in the city of Camagüey around 10:00 p.m. and parked the truck and car on the street. Enrique Bueno was waiting in his office to receive them when Luis knocked. An athletic-looking young man there with Enrique rose as soon as Luis and Ofelia entered the office. After a warm embrace, Luis introduced Ofelia to Enrique, and Enrique, in turn, introduced them to Emilio Martínez Venegas, whom Enrique had picked up the night before on a secluded beach near Nuevitas. Emilio was a member of several infiltration teams which had landed in the different provinces by sea and air to help coordinate guerrilla activities and the eventual invasion of the island. He brought a short-wave radio set and instructions from the CIA pertaining to the re-supply of food and arms in the Sierra Maestra.

Enrique told Luis to have Daniel pull the truck into the darkened warehouse. Then he made a phone call, the signal to the party at the other end to pick up five other men who would come to the warehouse. These men, along with Emilio, Ofelia, and Daniel would make up the core of the guerrilla group in the Sierra Maestra.

As Luis listened to Carlos, he was struck by the vast underground network of which he was only a small part. Luis was confident of success knowing that the CIA backed them. The Cubans had never been well-organized nor known much about espionage and intelligence operations, but the legendary CIA seemed invincible to them. The fact that Washington directed the entire operation proved U.S. commitment to the inevitable triumph of democracy in Cuba.

At the same time, excitement, a sense of justice, and the possibility of an opportunity to get even with Castro and his thugs intoxicated Luis. One of his recurring fantasies was to confront Castro in a courtroom and charge him with the innumerable crimes he had committed against Cubans in the name of revolution. What a farce the man had become! Nothing would give Luis more pleasure than to be chosen as the prosecutor against Castro after the successful overthrow.

Emilio had already loaded the short wave radio set and signal flares on the truck by the time the five new recruits in army uniforms arrived by car. They quickly transferred their belongings to the truck and climbed aboard, after which Daniel lowered the canvas over the rear opening of the truck. While Enrique opened the door of the warehouse, Luis, standing behind a stack of beer cases, said goodbye to Ofelia. They both realized they would not see each other again until after the projected invasion. Clinging to him tightly as he stroked her hair, Ofelia looked into his eyes and simply said, "Luis, I love you."

"And I love you too," Luis replied, astonished at the depth of his commitment.

They kissed and held each other in silence until they realized Enrique was holding the warehouse door open for their departure. Taking Ofelia's hand, Luis walked her to the passenger's door of the truck where she climbed inside and took her seat. When the truck started to roll, he stepped back and saluted her.

Enrique and Luis watched until the truck turned a corner at the end of the street. The next day Captain de la Torre would leave Camp Columbia with another truck and pick up other fighters in Holguín. "How many silent heroes are there tonight over this land? How many will die?" Luis wondered aloud. Enrique did not reply as he let down the warehouse door.

Luis slipped into the civilian clothes he had in the car. He had donned the officer's uniform in order to assist Ofelia and Daniel in case they were stopped by the military. Now it was time for another disguise since he was in his hometown where word had spread that he was no longer with the government, much less the military. He never dreamed his uniform would prove so valuable or thought there would be the necessity for so much deception.

Luis followed Enrique Bueno in his car to the old neighborhood in the Garrido subdivision, and they silently waved good night through the car windows as Luis turned into the Recio driveway.

With his house key, Luis quietly opened the door of his family home and called for Benancio and his wife, Nena. He waited with the door cracked until they awoke, turned on the light, and recognized him. "Nena, could you fix me a *mojito?*" Luis asked, grinning.

"Luisito!" she exclaimed, coming toward him to give him a hug, "Of course."

Chapter 36

The next morning, Luis had breakfast with Benancio and Nena. They sat on the familiar mahogany chairs with black leather seats and the Recio coat of arms imprinted on the back of each chair.

Normally, the servants would not have eaten at the table with a member of the family, but the protocol of earlier years no longer mattered, and Luis was eager to hear their versions of recent events and insisted they join him.

"Once in a while we hear a petard in the city, and sometimes a blackout happens," Nena said. "Castro's police have been questioning a lot of people, and some have been arrested without explanation."

Benancio added, "Luisito, we're afraid. We don't know what's going to happen to us. What's your family going to do?"

Luis reassured them, "I trust this situation is only temporary. My parents are vacationing in the U.S., and I'll join them soon. I'm leaving four thousand *pesos* with you to take care of expenses here and at Papá Bernabé's. I don't have time to go there. Please help Caridad look after the place."

Luis could detect the relief in their faces, although the three of them intuited life would never be the same.

After breakfast, Luis called Bernabé Morán at the sugar mill to find out how things were going since the expropriation by the government.

"As far as the operation is concerned, there isn't much change," Bernabé reported. "I still hold the same job. A few key people at the mill have been branded as counterrevolutionaries and forced to give up their jobs to communists brought in from outside Camagüey province.

I've been able to keep my position because I'm the only one who knows how to work with the machines and probably because everyone knows I'm only Bernabé's illegitimate son. They figure I hate the old man," Bernabé said, "but you know how much I loved him."

"I know that," Luis replied.

"It's not the same out here, though," Bernabé continued. "The big changes are political. Do you remember when they started to set up vigilante committees a few months ago? Well, they're all over the place now, and if they catch you on the wrong side of town, they'll take you in for questioning. They're forcing everybody to join the militia or else be tagged as a counterrevolutionary. Everybody cooperates on the surface. It's interesting to see how people are responding. I didn't realize that, among those I thought were friends of my father, there were some who resented Papá. The one who criticizes him and our family the most is the new head of the mill-- someone you know very well."

"Who's that?" Luis inquired.

"Your old boyhood friend, Ramoncito Blanco."

"I don't believe it. How did he get such a promotion?" Luis asked, stunned by the news.

"I think the bastard had pro-communist leanings all along but kept them to himself. That's why they have him running the place and holding classes on Marxism." Bernabé added.

"Damn!" Luis exclaimed. "I think I'll just call him up, play innocent, and see what he has to say to me."

"You'll get an ear full," Bernabé said.

His mind racing, Luis hung up and immediately called the sugar mill office and asked to speak to the new manager. Yes, he remembered the earthen floors, the flies, and tin plates of Ramoncito's youth. Luis also remembered how he had helped save Ramoncito's younger brother's life, and that at Luis' urging, Rogerio had persuaded Papá Bernabé to allow Ramoncito to stay in one of the rooms in the Recio home in Camagüey so Ramoncito could study accounting at the *Escuela de Comercio*. Papá Bernabé gave Ramoncito free room and board, a monthly stipend, and a virtual guarantee of a secure future in the administration of the mill. Of all the people at the Tamarindo Sugar Mill, Ramoncito was the one most indebted to Papá Bernabé's generosity, yet Luis had noticed, he was conspicuously absent from the funeral.

When Ramoncito came to the phone, Luis identified himself, "This is Luis Recio. How are you?"

After a pause, the curt reply came, "I'm fine. What can I do for you?"

"Well, I want to know what dividends my family can expect to receive for the past quarter's operation."

"Luis," Ramoncito retorted acidly, "You know damn well that you won't ever receive any more dividends or profits from this mill, though you will be compensated for the property."

"Well, I just thought you might have forgotten because we've never received any papers or money from the government since it was taken from us."

"You will in due course," Ramoncito said irritably. "Just be patient."

"Patient my ass, Ramoncito! Don't give me that shit! I guess you think time is on your side, but let me warn you. Your days in that position are numbered, so enjoy it while you can."

"Listen," Ramoncito stated, obviously infuriated, "I've got all the time in the world, as does this Revolution. We're in no hurry. You're the ones who are finished. You'll never return here, Luis, and if you do, I'll have you arrested for trespassing!"

"You know the worst thing about you, Ramoncito, is that you're an ungrateful son of a whore." Luis said calmly. "There's a saying that fits well here, 'Sailors are we, and we navigate in the sea.' Our paths will cross again, and then you'll get your just due."

"Luis," Ramoncito responded, "you think that because you Recios helped me become an accountant that I need to be forever in your debt. Shit! I cost your family very little. You were going to use me as a wage slave for the rest of my life. Bernabé gave me my education, but he had an ulterior motive. There were scores of others for whom you did nothing! You Recios are . . ."

Unable to control himself, Luis slammed down the phone so he wouldn't have to endure another insult to his family. Now he understood why *"El Honrado"* engaged in duels.

Ramoncito's promotion represented the ultimate irony of the Cuban Revolution. Many young men had opposed Batista, fought in the mountains, and been forced out of the country. Ramoncito, on the other hand, had not lifted a finger either to defeat Batista or support Castro, yet he was now the new manager of the family mill and lands.

Disheartened and angry, Luis left Camagüey after lunch in order to arrive in Havana under the cover of darkness. He had barely gotten to the western edge of the city on the central highway when soldiers who had set up a roadblock in front of the Agramonte Army Base stopped him.

Checking Luis' identification, the officer in charge informed him, "Señor Recio, your name is on our list of suspected counterrevolutionaries. You'll have to come in for interrogation."

"What are the charges?" Luis demanded of the first lieutenant at the headquarters building.

"You collaborated with Húber Matos, a convicted traitor, with whom you had a meeting at the Tamarindo Sugar Mill in April of 1959. Furthermore," the officer continued, "you have lost your property in Camagüey, and your parents have fled the country."

"So what!" Luis shouted. "What specific charges do you have against me? Is there any crime in having a meeting with someone who was then a hero of the Revolution and the military head of our province? Just because my family's property has been expropriated doesn't make me a counterrevolutionary. The only property I own is that Buick outside and an apartment in Havana. Furthermore, I can't be held responsible for my parents' decision to leave the country."

At that moment, a corporal entered the office with Luis' suitcase and proceeded to open it in order to show the contents to his superior. Luis knew his military uniform which he had worn the night before was inside. Taking it out and holding it up, the lieutenant said with an accusing smirk, "I was under the impression you had resigned from the government."

Luis rose to the occasion with boldness and imagination. "I did resign as Undersecretary of Justice, but I never resigned my commission as first lieutenant in the Revolutionary Armed Forces! I was in the Sierra fighting Batista when there were only two hundred men there. Before that, I was a leader in the underground here and in

Havana. Tell me, where were you during this time? When did you go up to the Sierra?"

"I went up late in December of 1958," the lieutenant replied defensively and a bit embarrassed.

"Oh, one of the latecomers," Luis countered sarcastically. "I was there in April of 1958 and fought in the fiercest battle. Therefore, unless you have any specific charges against me, I demand you let me go immediately. I'm an officer and a lawyer. I know my rights!"

Luis knew that righteous indignation was often effective in confrontation. Also he believed that the uncertainty of the political situation made those in positions of authority equivocal because if the government should be overthrown, they would have to answer for their excesses. The only exception to this rule were fanatics, and for this reason Luis realized he was taking a chance. Luis considered Captain Hernández a fanatic, though a relatively civil one. On the other hand, there were opportunists who straddled the fence. Luis was betting this lieutenant would not gamble too much on interrogation and detention.

When he saw a softening of the lieutenant's face, he knew his strategy had paid off.

"Fine, Dr. Recio," he said apologetically. "You know we have to be careful these days. Sometimes the Revolution makes errors. You may proceed. I hope we haven't inconvenienced you."

Continuing to affect an air of indignation, Luis nodded acknowledgement, extended his hand, and said, "I accept your apology."

"Have a nice trip, Dr. Recio," said the lieutenant, smiling.

Back in the Buick, Luis reflected aloud, "My God! That damned uniform, which I thought would do me in, spared me, and I didn't even have it on! Thanks, Alberto, for saving my life!"

Chapter 37

Driving rapidly in his Buick, Luis arrived in Havana in the early evening and went directly to the Ramírez's home. When Humberto and Carmen opened the door, he found them in a state of panic.

"The police came this morning," Humberto blurted. "They accused you of sabotage. A major told us that since the owners of this house had fled the country, the government was going to confiscate the property and that we should begin looking for another place to live. The officer told us any effort we made to help you would get us in trouble. We didn't tell them you had slept here. Octavio called to say they had ransacked your parents' house also."

Luis assured the frightened couple he would leave after using the telephone. He first thought to call Alberto, but he rejected that possibility, realizing how intense the search for him had become. Instead, another friend he had recruited offered him a haven. Having that settled, he then called Philip at his home and told him of his desperate situation.

"I need your help, Philip. Castro's police are hot on my trail here in Havana. I don't dare go to my apartment. I must leave the country as soon as possible."

When he told Heymann where he could be contacted, his cousin said he would get back in touch.

After thanking Humberto and Carmen for covering for him, he drove part way across the Miramar section of town, left the Roadmaster by a small park off Fifth Avenue, and walked three blocks to his destination.

When he rang the bell on the dark porch, Olga Loynaz immediately opened the door and said softly, "Come on in." Senator Sócrates Miranda, who was standing beside her in his pajamas and robe, reached out, and shook Luis' hand. The senator and Olga had begun to conspire against Castro after Luis approached her and persuaded the senator to join the MRR.

During a late dinner, the senator expounded upon the country's misfortunes as well as his own, outlining the social and economic catastrophe of Castro's swift decrees which had left him without income or work. The elder statesman appeared dejected, but Olga tried to reassure him by saying the setbacks to his rental and real estate enterprises were only temporary. Luis shared her optimism. The senator, however, continued his litany of loss throughout the meal and while they had cognac in the living room.

The second Urban Reform Law directly affected Sócrates Miranda. The law stated that no person could own more than one dwelling and that the leasee would be a tenant of the government. After a number of years, the leasee would assume ownership of the property. The former owners would not be compensated over 350 *pesos* per month for their loss. It was a hopeless situation which signaled the end of construction and real estate in Cuba.

Senator Miranda summarized the dismal situation with a diatribe, "This mad man Castro has chosen to wage war on capitalism. He has taken over all of the major American companies like Woolworth and Coca-Cola. Coño! In just over fifty years, Cuba's developed a powerful unionized urban working class. Our middle class is one third of our population and has many successful entrepreneurs.

"We don't have the sharp extremes between wealth and poverty that abound in underdeveloped countries. Our per capita income of $520 ranks as the second highest in Latin America. We're first in ownership of televisions and second in cars, telephones, and radios. We're third in the number of physicians, and our literacy rate approaches 80%. Why would anyone want to destroy these accomplishments? It's damn stupid! I'm convinced the U.S. will not sit still. No one should be allowed to mess around with Coca-Cola!"

"Correct," said Luis, "No one messes with Coca-Cola--or Gene Autry either."

"True," laughed Sócrates for the first time, "I like that. No one messes with Gene Autry!"

Fatigued by the previous day's events, Luis requested to be excused and retired to the upstairs guest bedroom. He did not awaken from his deep sleep until the next morning when someone jumped in bed with him and began to fondle him. Startled, Luis sat up and was shocked when he realized his assailant was his hostess in a very revealing black negligee. Giggling, Olga removed her hand from his awakening penis to signal silence. "I've got you, you devil, and you're not about to escape. I've been hungry for you for too long, and you owe me."

"Are you crazy?" Luis whispered. "What about your husband?"

"He's already left for the office and won't be back for several hours," she replied as her expert hands began to ramble over his body. "He has nothing left to buy or sell, thanks to this joyless revolution, but he still goes to the office. I, myself, prefer other things," she chuckled seductively.

Luis was caught in an unanticipated dilemma. On the one hand, here he was in bed with a most attractive woman at the prime of her sexual maturity, one with whom he had an extended affair prior to his meeting Laura. His body was calling for action as her lips joined her hands in exploratory ventures. On the other hand, he was in the home of a fellow conspirator who was risking his life by hiding him. Was he to repay the senator by cuckolding the old man again? How, though, could any man turn down a woman as appealing as Olga?

Seeing no satisfactory resolution and feeling his body respond to Olga's wise caresses, Luis said to himself, "What the hell," and knowing what Papá Bernabé would recommend, he began to return the pleasure.

Luis and Olga were having coffee on the terrace when Philip Heymann called to let Luis know he was coming over within the hour. When Philip arrived, he had a photographer from the embassy with him and a large box under his arm. "Is there a room where we can work?" Philip inquired directly of Olga. She suggested the library upstairs where, surrounded by shelf after shelf of great books, Luis changed into the clothes Heymann had brought and had several photographs taken for the forged passport.

After briefing Luis on the escape plan, his cousin departed with the photographer, stating Heymann would return to take Luis to a Spanish merchant ship in Havana Harbor which would leave at six that afternoon for Miami.

Around 2:00 p.m., Olga served a seafood *paella* and a side order of ripe plantains. Before the senator arrived, she said to Luis, "I want you to remember this last lunch with us."

Luis' feelings of guilt were ameliorated when the senator returned to the house in a surprisingly upbeat mood, which increased when he learned Heymann had successfully made arrangements for Luis to leave the island.

"You won't have to be away for long," the senator said. "I went to a realtors' meeting today, and most of my friends there feel Castro's days are numbered. No one is happy with his preposterous reforms. Everybody talks about his demagoguery; even his most ardent supporters are on the defensive. The U.S. is sure to act now. As I said last night, no one messes with Coca-Cola."

Later that afternoon, Philip Heymann returned to the house to pick up Luis and found Senator Miranda and Olga waiting for their guest in the living room. A few minutes later Luis came down the stairs in his disguise, carrying a valise in his right hand. They laughed, Olga putting both hands over her mouth to restrain her mirth. There was her lover, dressed as a priest in black frock, white collar and black felt hat, a serious look upon his face as if he were set to chastise humanity.

"Forgive me, father, for I have sinned," she said, grinning and dropping to her knees in front of Luis as he came down the stairs. "I absolve you, my daughter," Luis replied in a most solemn and theatrical manner to the laughter of Heymann and Senator Miranda. "Go forth, and sin no more."

"You really do look like a priest," said the senator, "except your frock is a little short."

"You should try to find a priest's cassock for a six foot-two man in less than twenty-four hours!" exclaimed Heymann.

After bidding farewell to Olga and the senator, Luis left with Heymann in a borrowed car for the harbor. Heymann left him by the customs building and parked so that he could determine when Luis got on board safely. At the check point, a young militia woman inspected his new passport and visa issued to "Amado Díaz, S.J." Conscious of her position of power, she took her time in examining his passport.

"What a waste," she smirked, shaking her head. "A big, strong *hombre* like you should be keeping some little *señorita* happy and working for the Revolution instead of the Church."

"Perhaps we're both working for worthwhile causes," Luis replied piously.

"Shit!" she retorted so angrily Luis thought she might attack him. "You religious hypocrites cover your manhood under your skirts. Instead of praying all day to a non-existent god, you should be working in the fields."

"My child, why do you speak to me in such a manner when I have done nothing to offend you?"

"Because you piss me off!" she shouted. "Don't call me a child! I'm almost as old as you. You priests think you know everything. You don't know *mierda*. Why are you going to the U.S. anyway?"

Luis had his answer ready, giving her details of "his diocese" in Havana and the one in Miami he would visit in order to gain information about a new meal program for the poor. When he showed her a letter from "his bishop" and several references, she brushed them aside, saying they meant nothing to her. Still trying to make peace, Luis commented that in the effort to feed the poor, perhaps the purposes of the Revolution and Church did overlap.

"Hell," she said, "they never overlap. You and the Catholic Church are despicable; and, though it may take time, you're going to be silenced."

"I forgive you, my child," Luis dared to say.

"Forgive my ass!" she yelled. "Get the hell out of here before I change my mind and have you detained!"

Afraid even to touch his hat in gracious acceptance of her angry farewell, Luis gave a small nod, picked up his passport, and made his way up the gangplank.

On board, Luis signaled Heymann everything was all right, and he stayed on deck as the ship left the pier and got underway. As he was leaving Havana, the evening sunset was never more beautiful.

When the freighter arrived in Miami the next morning, Luis got off wearing his white linen suit.

Chapter 38

As soon as he got off the ship in Miami, Luis caught a taxi and went to his parents' home in Coral Gables. The Recios had not seen him since June, and they were thrilled to find him safe and healthy. His mother cried as she hugged and kissed him. So did Isabel, who badgered him with questions about Jorge León. Although Luis had not seen Jorge in several days, he knew Jorge was working in the underground with Rogelio González Corso.

After giving the family an update on changes in Cuba, including the urban reform laws that would limit the Recios to one home, he inquired about Laura and Luisito. As they walked to the car, Luis was not surprised with the news Rogerio provided.

"Laura filed for divorce. We tried to convince her otherwise. She says she still loves you, but you and she can never have a stable life together. She doesn't want to raise a son whose father is always fighting political battles."

After lunch, Luis called Laura to arrange for a meeting to see Luisito. When she heard Luis' voice, Laura began to cry. "I'm so happy you're safe. When did you arrive?"

"This morning," Luis answered, feeling his heart beat faster. "When can I come over and see you and Luisito?"

"Luis, I don't want to see you again," she said rather void of emotion. "I've already filed for divorce and custody of Luisito. If you want to see him today, I'll ask Papá to bring him over to the Recios."

Understanding her decision was final, Luis told her he would hire a lawyer and try to reach a fair settlement. He agreed that Luisito should stay with her, only requesting to have visiting rights.

As he hung up the phone, Luis realized an epoch in his life had ended. In spite of his love for Laura and his regrets for what might have been, he felt strangely free. Now, no one impeded him in his quest to work for a free Cuba. Now, he could love Ofelia openly.

When Mario Ramírez brought Luisito to the Recio house in the afternoon, memories of his relationship with Mario assailed Luis. As he held Luisito in his arms, he felt some regret that Mario's genes flowed through the veins of his son.

Mario exemplified the meaning of the term "the revolutionaries of the corns," like corns on the feet. "Revolutionaries of the corns" referred to those who supported the takeover of lands, businesses, and industries by the Castro government until the Revolution finally began to affect their way of life--until, that is, the Revolution stepped on their own corns. Mario supported the immediate confiscation of all of the properties of the high officials of the Batista government in January of 1959. "It served those bastards right," he stated in front of Luis and Rogerio, in spite of the fact that he had been close friends with most of those "bastards."

Mario's corns were not stepped on directly until sales in his supermarket chain, including two gourmet markets in Miramar, began to decline by the end of 1959 by as much as 40% because of restrictions on imports from abroad, especially gourmet foods. A new militancy on the part his workers, who now insisted on higher salaries, compounded his troubles. Caught between demands for higher wages and less profit, Mario "cried ouch" and became a "revolutionary of the corns."

"I'm sorry about the marriage," Mario said with a solemn expression, but Luis was reluctant to believe him. Once again Mario could indulge Laura, though Luis would wager, not for long. Laura was too beautiful to stay single. As he looked at Mario, Luis understood the materialistic nature Laura had inherited from her father.

When Luis got to know Mario, he realized the root of Mario's problems was simple stinginess. He was stingy with money, with friendship, and with love. On rare occasions, Mario displayed moments of generosity, especially if they had to do with his daughter, but in Luis' eyes, Mario was at best an extravagant spendthrift. Luis hoped his son would not inherit that Ramírez trait.

Luis knew the feeling was perverse, but he felt no guilt about having made love with Ofelia in Mario's bed and having frolicked in his Roman bath. If restoring the economic prosperity of people like Mario Ramírez was its main objective, then he would abandon the anti-Castro struggle in an instant. He was not fighting for the likes of Mario but for the welfare of the general population.

The next day Luis went to a two-story house in the northwest section near downtown Miami to report to Manuel Artime, the leader of the MRR, and pay respects to Tony de Varona, recently named head of the *Frente Revolucionario Democrático*. There he found numerous old friends, including Pepito Sosa, one of Tony's right hand men who had been a large cattle owner in Camagüey.

At the *Frente* headquarters, Luis found out that training camps had been established outside the United States. Tony de Varona told him, "There's a lot of speculation as to where, but more than five hundred volunteers have already departed to start their training for an invasion of Cuba. The *Frente* is looking for good swimmers to set up an underwater demolition team. Are you interested?"

"Yes, that's what I want to do," Luis replied eagerly. "I was an all-American swimmer in prep school."

"Great!" said Tony. "You need to contact Renato Díaz. He has an office close by."

The next day Luis went to see Renato Díaz, the officer who was in charge of recruitment for what would become the naval element of the invasion. He discovered several swimmers had already enlisted, three of whom, Blas Casares, Gaspar Betancourt and Gregorio Loret de Mola, were friends from Camagüey. Díaz informed him that once the potential frogmen were recruited, they would have to take a polygraph test to weed out infiltrators and unstable personalities, and then those remaining would have to pass swimming tests.

Mysterious Americans only identified as "Friends of the Cuban Cause" administered the polygraph tests to the candidates two weeks later at an old multi-story brick building in downtown Miami. Luis had not the slightest doubt about his allegiance, and the calmness with which he answered the questions about everything from his personal life to his involvement in the Revolution and later the underground did not surprise him.

Three days later, two Americans took the group to a rambling ranch house by the sea, where a no-nonsense, tall, red-headed American, who introduced himself as "Jim," tested their swimming ability on the surface and below the water in an average-size swimming pool. Luis passed the test with flying colors.

In accordance with the military training he had received at SMA, Luis did not question any order regardless of how ridiculous it seemed. He trusted the wisdom of the CIA. Later, he was glad he had followed instructions, else he might not have been chosen. One of the candidates, a well-known Cuban swimmer, was rejected when he swam three lengths of the pool under water. "I don't want you," said Jim, pointing at him. "You didn't do what I asked, which was to swim only one lap. You didn't follow orders." First lesson learned, Luis thought.

Finally, Jim selected twelve candidates, Luis among them. In the next few days, Luis saw just how elite the members of this group were. They were all well-educated and spoke fluent English, having been to colleges such as Georgia Tech or the University of Arizona, or prep schools such as SMA and Georgia Military Academy. From the HYC, Luis knew Carlos Fonts and Jorge and Felipe Silva, first cousins, and with the others, he had mutual friends.

Luis thought every one of the frogmen had joined the invasion force for patriotic reasons. Certainly, the $175 monthly stipend for parents or wives and additional $50 for the first dependent and $25 for each of the other dependents was not the motivation for risking their lives.

Shortly after the group was formed, Jim called a meeting and gave each man one last chance to withdraw. "The decision to stay with the group is literally a matter of life and death," he began. "I can promise all of you aren't going to make it. You'll be doing operations before the invasion, and you'll be ashore when the invasion takes place. I repeat, some of you will die."

Feeling the familiar onslaught of fear he had experienced in the mountains and in the underground, Luis looked at the silent and serious faces around him and wondered who among them would be the casualties. Intuitively, Luis knew he would survive.

None of the frogmen thought of the dangers but focused on the task before them. They were so committed and so filled with righteous zeal that they began to call themselves the twelve Apostles. The role of St. Peter was given to José Enrique Alonso, who, at forty-one, was the oldest of the group by some fifteen years. Luis, at twenty-seven, was the next oldest.

Like Luis, Alonso had been one of Castro's supporters, working in the 26th of July Movement and later serving as an officer in Castro's navy. Since he had started a school for frogmen in Cuba, it was natural for him to recommend the idea of underwater sabotage to the CIA. He envisioned the frogmen's participation in the sinking of Russian ammunition supply ships in Havana harbor and their coming ashore to blow up power stations, creating a blackout of strategic coastal cities. He convinced the CIA that the use of frogmen was the best way to cause damage at little risk of life and reputation to the United States. It was easy to see how José Enrique could be so persuasive. Wiry and articulate, he presented his case logically without knowing at the time a full-scale invasion would take the place of the sabotage operation.

After their selection, Jim told the frogmen to stand by for further instructions, and while they waited, Luis put his talents to use for the *Frente*, writing a few news releases for Tony de Varona and serving as one of the English translators.

As he waited for the start of the training, Luis became more aware of the role of "the Cuban question" in the U.S. presidential campaign of 1960. By the fourth televised debate, he felt strongly that John F. Kennedy had a better grasp of the Cuban cause. Richard Nixon was too ambiguous in his plans to eradicate Castro. Furthermore, Nixon appeared glib and cautious at once, almost like an insurance agent selling his product. Kennedy, by contrast, was young, dynamic, idealistic, folksy, and sophisticated. For Luis, Kennedy embodied the essence of America. Though it was Nixon who used the metaphor of cancer in regard to communism in Cuba, Luis was sure Kennedy was the best surgeon for the operation.

When Luis and Rogerio saw the results of the American presidential election on TV on election night in November, they toasted with champagne. Their joy reflected that of that of the Cuban community throughout Miami. Victory for Cuba, they knew, was just around the corner.

Early in January, before Kennedy's inauguration, Luis and the frogmen were taken by car at night to the *Blagar*, a modified LCI (Landing Craft Infantry) of World War II vintage, waiting for them at the Miami River. As the ship left the channel for the open sea, Luis watched the lights of Miami disappear behind the horizon. He had no idea where the frogmen were going. He only knew the Americans were in charge and John F. Kennedy, president-elect, had in one way or another placed his stamp of approval upon this historic mission.

Chapter 39

During their seven days on the *Blagar*, the frogmen spent several hours a day exposed to the sun in preparation for their mission in the tropics. They soaked their feet in salt water in order to toughen their skin for the use of flippers and practiced holding their breath, starting with thirty-second intervals until all of them were able to do so for two minutes. They did calisthenics and received instruction in underwater navigation conducted by a blond American by the name of "Bob," who smoked Salems and kept the frogmen at arm's length.

In contrast to Bob, the captain of the *Blagar*, Sven Ryberg, was an approachable fellow who seemed more fictional than real with his one glass eye and Scandinavian accent. Though the frogmen knew little about the men training and transporting them, they had unfaltering confidence in the CIA.

Their destination turned out to be Vieques, a small island east of Puerto Rico used as a U.S. Marine training base. Arriving in Vieques on January 28, 1961, the frogmen set up camp on a secluded white sand beach on the south side of the island, doing distance swimming in the bay, handling small weapons, and practicing night reconnaissance exercises and underwater demolition. While the frogmen trained, the crews of three L.C.U.'s (Landing Craft Utility) practiced landings on the beaches.

Luis found himself with time on his hands at Vieques, so started a journal in which he would periodically record his experiences. His thought was to leave it with one of his CIA trainers and ask that it be given to his parents if anything happened to him.

Jan. 30, 1961

The beach where we're stationed is very beautiful. We live in three tents twenty-five feet from the seashore. We use two of the tents for sleeping and the third for supplies, and we sleep on army cots equipped with mosquito nets. Not even in the mountains of Cuba have I seen so many insects. Here the sand flies are very aggressive. For this reason, some of us sleep completely dressed, even with our caps on. For those small areas that remain exposed, we put on a repellent.

All of us long for a priest to be here. We say the rosary every day, and everyone joins in, including a few of the crew from the L.C.U.'s who have never been religious . . .

Feb. 6, 1961

The Frente has just sent me my parents' first letter with Luisito's photos. What a beautiful child! The sweet smile on his face gives me strength. I truly feel I've been chosen by God to play a part in this great undertaking.

Our day starts at 6:00 a.m. We exercise for half an hour and then have an American breakfast of bacon and eggs four times a week and pancakes on the other three days. After breakfast, we have a ten-minute rest and then proceed to classes and exercises. We eat lunch at 11:30, followed by another ten minute rest and more exercises. Dinner begins at 5:30, and later we have night-time swimming exercises which last about an hour. We train in pairs, and I'm lucky to have José Enrique Alonso, the leader of our group, as my partner. At times, we swim a mile under water with an aqualung, using a water compass as a guide. After a shower, we watch a movie. I've already seen Viva Zapata, Stalag 17, All the Brothers Were Valiant, and The Ten Commandments. We're in bed and asleep by nine o'clock. . .

Feb. 14, 1961

Two days ago a priest finally arrived on the Blagar. He's none other than our dear friend, Father Cavero, and he'll be with us for a few days. The first mass he held was a most beautiful and touching ceremony. We gathered around him in a semi-circle. Even José Enrique, the least religious among us, came to mass. Then the priest did an unusual thing. He explained the different parts of the mass to us in layman's terms. Some of the men from the L.C.U.'s had never attended mass, and the Father wanted them to understand the significance of what he was doing. Words cannot describe the sense of reverence the priest's words invoked in us.

Here, religion plays a bigger role than it did in the mountains in spite of the conspicuous rosaries the rebels wore when they entered Havana. Most of the rebels were not religious in the way we are. When they came into Havana, the rebels wore their rosaries for show, but rarely were they used for prayer in the traditional manner as they are here . . .

Feb. 22, 1961

Since Father Cavero arrived, our spirits have lifted. It's not easy for any of us here, but it's tougher for those who are married. I feel my impending divorce will free me from some agonizing concerns. As I begin to put Laura out of my life, my thoughts are of my son and my parents.

The return of the Blagar has given us the opportunity to practice underwater demolition on a ship. We couldn't use the L.C.U.'s because they were anchored on the sand. We take turns putting dummy charges near the propellers. Our most important night operations consist of beach surveying. We have to find the channels through which the L.C.U.'s can move and land the troops. As we practice this operation at night, our rubber Zodiac runs parallel to the coast about a mile at sea, dropping us one by one at intervals of some twenty meters. We then proceed toward the beach as silently as possible, measuring the depth of the water the last few meters with a weight and string. During the exercises, fluorescent lights coming from the animal life in the sea catch my attention. The beautiful and mysterious lights remind us that other creatures might be lurking nearby. It's an eerie feeling to swim so far at night in the Caribbean . . .

March 4, 1961

The L.C.U. bunch is a strange lot. A number of them were enlisted men in Batista's armed forces, and others served under Castro. They get on one another's nerves, and nasty fights break out. Some of them are mad at the Americans because they've been in this secluded place for some three months and don't see any prospect of leaving soon.

I hope the scenes on the L.C.U.'s are not a prelude to what is going to happen once we topple Castro, but I know this L.C.U. crowd exemplifies one of the many problems we will have to resolve. Although all of the members of the invasion force oppose Castro, I'm afraid not all of us have the same reasons for participating. Those on the L.C.U.'s were among the first to be recruited by the CIA, and the record of a few of them is shady.

I wonder what Cuba will be like once Castro is routed. Some of his ideas are good in principle, and even the Agrarian Reform Law has merit. However, it was implemented unjustly and without compensation. The problem is not so much in the number of acres a man owns but what he does with this acreage and how he pays and treats his workers.

We also need to bring more foreign capital into Cuba to start industries which will employ workers before and after sugar cane harvesting. In short, we should learn from U.S. technology and management and encourage investment that will provide improvements for all Cubans . . .

March 8, 1961

By now our operations have become routine, and tempers are getting short. A couple of the frogmen even questioned José Enrique's leadership ability, but he passed a secret vote of confidence. We have affectionately dubbed him "Abuelo," the Spanish name for grandfather, since he is almost twenty years older than the rest of us.

One day José Enrique was telling us we all had to do K.P. (Kitchen Police), working by turns in the kitchen, cleaning kitchen ware, mopping the deck, and peeling potatoes because the L.C.U. people expected it of us. He would not take a shift because it would look bad for a commander to be peeling potatoes. "O.K." I said, "We'll do it, Abuelo!" He laughed. K.P., by the way, is the toughest work I've ever done.

My fellow frogmen call me "Padre Recio." The story is out about my dressing as a priest in order to get out of Cuba, and it looks like I'll never be able to live it down. So I'm "Padre," and José Enrique is "Abuelo!" Between the two of us, maybe we can keep the others in line . . .

March 14, 1961

Before we left Vieques, we had been led to believe we were going to have a few days leave in Miami before coming to our new base here on the mainland. We were very disappointed when we were told at the last moment that plans had changed. We were even more frustrated when the plane that was to pick us up at a naval base in Puerto Rico took several days to arrive. When we finally landed in Louisiana, one of the plane's four engines was on fire!

We have been told by one of our two new trainers here, a man named Gray, that a secret pre-invasion mission to Cuba is scheduled for us in three days. If that's the case, I want to write a letter for my parents to give to Luisito should I not return.

Our other instructor, a man named Rip, is an ex-Marine captain like Gray. Someone told us he played football for Vanderbilt University in Nashville, Tennessee, but when I asked him, he said he wasn't supposed to talk about his past. He did admit with a big grin he knew where SMA was and said he knew some people who went there . . .

March 28, 1961

Once again plans for the pre-invasion mission have been postponed. While there's an air of urgency about our training, there's much uncertainty in the planning. We know now what the American G.I.'s mean by their term "hurry up and wait." We have had periods of intense training and periods in which we vegetate. We're ready to go. I have never seen a group more motivated, in spite of the fact we've had four different trainers since leaving Miami--Bob, Jim, Gray, and Rip, all with different personalities. I must say I'm very taken with Gray who is tough and perhaps a little wild.

I've always been scared of snakes, and as if he were aware of my fear, the other day Gray took us all on what he called a "swamp patrol" near here. I called it "the snake patrol" since he spent so much time trying to find them, turning over logs and poking in clumps of vegetation to flush them out.

I believe Gray was testing us mentally since he knows we don't have poisonous snakes in Cuba. I suspect he might be trying to select the ones among us who will be the first to land with the invasion. I hope he didn't sense my fear. In many ways "the swamp patrol" seemed as crazy to me as the test of putting ice in the swimming pool.

It all boils down to waiting. Another group of 150 men under the command of Nino Díaz, the famous guerilla leader under Castro, is also here. I have several friends in the group, Tatico Pujals from Camagüey, and Jorge Mas and Sergio Fernández from Santiago de Cuba. Through them and Nino Díaz, I've kept up to date on events on the island. They're optimistic about our activities in the Escambray Mountains and in the second front in the Sierra Maestra. In addition, there's a small group of infiltrators who has just carried out an attack in the bay of Santiago de Cuba. The main force remains in Guatemala, but I don't know when or how all the units will come together for the big show. Everyone is ready to go. . .

April 2, 1961

When you read this diary, I will have left for a rendezvous with the main invasion forces. We still haven't been told anything by our trainers. I'm returning my missal, the letters which I've received from you, and the photos, except the two of Luisito which I'll keep. We've been ordered not to take any personal things with us.

Our training base has been an army depot near New Orleans. We had a two-day leave in the city, and we enjoyed a wonderful luncheon at Brennan's. The martinis and the food were great! That city really has class! Someday I'll come back and really sample the fine cuisine. We also saw the Alamo, starring John Wayne. This time Americans will be on the winning side! Please be assured of that! Our spirits are soaring. . .

April 9, 1961

We are now at Puerto Cabezas, Nicaragua, a run-down port on the Gulf in the middle of nowhere. This is the point from where the invasion force will sail. When we left Louisiana, we had no idea we would come to such a place. When we left, we thought we would rendezvous with other ships at sea for the move on Cuba. We came over here on a merchant marine ship named the Río Escondido, captained by Gustavo Tirado, a Spaniard who works for the Cuban García Lines from which the Americans have rented several ships for the invasion. He has a big German Shepherd named Cyclone which we have come to love.

A funny thing happened on the way over here. As we were coming down the Mississippi River, the Río hit something that damaged one of the propellers and slowed our progress. Alonso, a few other frogmen, and I went under the ship and found two of the propellers entangled in wire. Both of them were bent. After we had cleared the propellers, the ship only made about six knots, and it took us six days to get to Puerto Cabezas. . .

April 16, 1961

Tonight we land and the uprising of the Cuban people will begin. I trust that God will protect us. No matter what, I want to thank you, my parents, for giving me life and raising me. Please forgive me for any unhappiness I've brought you. I often think about the good times we've had and regret we took them so much for granted.

I'm enclosing a personal letter to Luisito. Please give it to him along with this diary in case I don't return. You'll know when he is old enough to understand it all. The letter is a statement of what I want him to know about my life and my beliefs. Please stay as close to him as you possibly can; it's very important that he gets to know you and love you. I'd like him to be proud of being a Recio.

The great hour is at hand. May God bless our efforts.
Your loving and grateful son,
Luis

With these final words, Luis closed his journal, not knowing if he would ever see his family again.

Part 4

"Operation Pluto"
Frogmen Looking for Eagles

Chapter 40

The invasion plan, called "Operation Pluto," was not a complicated undertaking. The invasion force, Brigade 2506, under the command of José "Pepe" San Román, was to gain a beachhead so the civilian leaders of the recently formed Cuban Revolutionary Council (CRC) could land and set up an alternative government which would then seek recognition by friendly nations. The CRC, led by José Miró Cardona, Castro's first Prime Minister, had replaced the old *Frente*. Once the civilian government was on Cuban soil for seventy-two hours, according to international law, the U.S. and Spanish-speaking countries hostile to Castro would then be in a position to give the new government all types of legitimate aid and comfort, including assistance from the U.S. Marines.

The objective was to land some 1,500 Cuban fighters by a naval force consisting of six ships (four of the García Lines, the *Río Escondido*, the *Atlántico*, the *Houston*, and the *Caribe*, and two converted LCI's, the *Bárbara J.* and the *Blagar)* that would transport the troops to the landing area. The plan called for the men, ammunition, and supplies to be carried ashore in three L.C.U.'s, two of which had been at Vieques, and four L.C.V.P.'s (Landing Craft Vehicles and Personnel) which were on the *San Marcos*, an L.S.D. (Landing Ship Dock) that would join the fleet on D-Day.

The Americans had promised the crucial air cover. There were to be air strikes on D-2 and D-Day that would eliminate Castro's small air force. On D-2, two B-26's were to land in Miami to give the international community the impression the pilots were defectors who had just bombed Cuban airfields. Diversionary tactics included a landing by Nino Díaz in Oriente Province and a fireworks display organized by the CIA off the northeast coast of Cuba. A parachute battalion under the command of Alejandro del Valle would set up three roadblocks on routes leading into the Zapata Swamp to cut off any reinforcement by the communist government.

Thus with a beachhead perimeter established, the paratrooper roadblocks would hold Castro's main force temporarily at bay. The B-26's would then be brought in to the Girón airfield to carry out raids on troops and tanks which would be like sitting ducks on the roads since there was no other way for them to get through the swamp. The rest was easy to predict. As Castro's casualties mounted, defection would increase, and the defectors would join the 2506 Brigade, especially when the U.S recognized the Revolutionary Council as the legitimate government and began pouring in aid.

To Luis, "Pluto" had no flaws. How could it have been otherwise when conceived by Americans who had successfully invaded Europe and a whole chain of islands in the Pacific against a determined, heavily entrenched enemy? Were not the Americans the masters of amphibious operations?

In Puerto Cabezas, when José Enrique questioned the capacity of the García Lines ships to carry an invasion force, Gray told him these ships did not constitute the entire invasion force and then took the frogmen to the Retalhuleu Air Base to show them the readied C-46's for carrying paratroopers. The frogmen felt confident knowing Cuba would be assaulted by air as well as by sea, and they were further reassured when they saw the B-26's practice runs. When Luis inquired why there were no fighters to escort the B-26's since they did not have tail guns, Rip told him there would be an aircraft carrier nearby with jet fighters and "blond, blue-eyed Cuban pilots" who had no knowledge of Spanish ready to take off at any minute. Rip then winked. During the first briefing on board the *Blagar,* José Enrique questioned the shadows in the water in the U-2 photos, speculating that they were coral reefs. Gray replied that reconnaissance experts in Washington had determined the shadows on the water were those of clouds and there was no need to worry.

Final proof of U. S. support came the second day at sea. To kill time, Luis went to the bridge of the *Blagar* and looking at the radar scope, he saw a larger number of ships than those in the Brigade flotilla. Upon inquiring of Captain Ryberg as to what the blips could be, he learned two of the larger dots were U.S. destroyers and the third, a U.S. submarine. Then Luis knew for sure the Americans would be over, around, and under the invaders, as the Brigade had repeatedly been given to understand by their advisors.

Shored by the confidence of U.S. ubiquity, Luis believed God, too, was with them, as the priest reassured them at a final mass at dusk on the deck of the *Blagar*. A fiery speech by Manuel Artime, the official delegate of the Cuban Revolutionary Council in the invading army and the "golden boy" of the CIA, only added more fuel to the flames of righteousness: "God and destiny are with us. Our cause is just and necessary. That's why we shall be victorious!"

When night came, Luis was more than eager to meet the challenge, practically jumping off the *Blagar* into the catamaran, seeing the rope netting on the side of the ship as a useless contrivance. Before, he had left Cuba disguised in the robes of a priest. Now, he was returning in green fatigues as a dark avenger from the sea, his face painted as black as the midnight in which he moved and the black fish in the waters on which he would ride. With God and Uncle Sam on the Brigade's side, what could possibly go wrong?

Chapter 41

Originally the frogmen were to wear rubber suits, diving masks, and fins. The plan called for them to survey the beach to find the best path for the L.C.U.'s and the L.C.V.P.'s to follow. In Puerto Cabezas, however, Gray, Rip, and the frogmen were given detailed U-2 photographs of the landing site which, according to the CIA photo experts, eliminated the need for an underwater search.

At 11:30 p.m., on a moonlit Sunday night of April 16, 1961, Gray, Luis, and four other frogmen, José Enrique Alonso, Gregorio Loret de Mola, Gaspar Betancourt, and Jesús "Chiqui" Llama, left the *Blagar*, anchored two thousand meters off shore, in an 18-foot catamaran powered by two 75-horsepower motors. Attached to the catamaran was a Zodiac rubber raft with a silent 25-horsepower Mercury outboard motor that would transport them the last two hundred meters to the beach. Their landing site was the beach in the town of Girón, dubbed "Blue Beach" by the Americans. It was near Zapata Swamp and a bay by the name of *Bahía de Cochinos* (Bay of Pigs), named for herds of wild pigs that once inhabited the region. It dawned on Luis that the bay could just as well have been named after black tropical fish called *cochinos* which were common in waters of Cuba. The frogmen, dressed in dark green fatigues, baseball caps, and sneakers and with their faces and hands painted black, left all metal objects that might reflect light on the *Blagar*.

Some two hundred meters offshore the catamaran stopped, and Luis' group boarded the rubber raft for the final leg to Blue Beach. The other group of frogmen under Rip had already left the *Bárbara J.* for Red Beach in the bay at Playa Larga.

"I'm coming with you," Luis and the others heard Gray say, but José Enrique replied, "No, from now on the show is up to the Cubans." Gray paid no attention and boarded the raft with a Browning Automatic Rifle, better known as a BAR. His participation in the landing deviated from the plan, yet the frogmen were glad to have him lead the final approach since he was the only one with extensive combat experience.

Instead of a darkened beach that the frogmen were to scout and mark with their own landing lights, they saw bright vapor lights along the beach.

"It's like Coney Island," said Gray in astonishment. "We need to change the plans," he whispered, and turning to José Enrique, who was holding the stick on the outboard, added, "Head for the dark place in the center of the beach." José Enrique steered as directed, for they did not want to land near a bar where people were drinking and talking.

About eighty meters from the beach, one of the six red beach marker lights on the Zodiac unexpectedly started blinking, creating pandemonium in the crowded raft. Luis quickly succeeded in covering it with his baseball cap until it stopped. When it came on again, Gray cursed and quickly pulled out the wires connecting it to the battery.

If the frogmen were astonished to find the landing area lighted like a seaside playground, they were more shocked when about sixty meters from the beach they felt the engine scrape bottom against the coral reef which the CIA photo interpreters had called "clouds" and "seaweed." In disbelief, the frogmen cursed their luck, rolled out of the boat, and began pushing it toward the shore, leaving only Gray on board with his BAR.

A few meters further, when they were in water up to their waists, they saw a jeep, whose headlights moved along the waterfront, stop directly in front of the rubber boat with a loud squealing of brakes. Instantly, it swung toward the sea, catching the craft in its lights.

"Fire!" Gray barked, emptying his BAR at the jeep. Luis and the others in the water joined in, using the other BAR and four Thompson sub-machine guns. The tracers in every third round marked their own position, as well as that of the jeep whose lights were soon extinguished. In a few seconds, the lights in the town of Girón went out, leaving the beach in blackness. Their arrival was no longer a surprise.

Hurriedly, the frogmen spread out and made their way to the beach, where they set up the red blinking landing lights. Then they ran to take cover behind the rock jetty where they were to land originally. At the jetty, they positioned a white light to identify their location for the *Blagar*. In communication with the ship, Gray learned there was a truck coming toward them. He directed fire at it from the *Blagar's* machine guns and the 37 mm. recoilless rifle on the bow of the ship.

Rather than shooting at the truck, the gunners on board the *Blagar* zeroed in on the white light at the end of the jetty, sending all the frogmen for cover. The bullets coming from the *Blagar* ricocheted and whined all around them, and to compound their plight, militia fire pelted them from the opposite direction.

"*Carajo!*" said Luis aloud, "this one hell of a SNAFU, you know, Situation Normal, All Fouled Up."

"SNAFU, hell!" Gray shouted back, "try FUBAR--Fucked Up Beyond All Recognition!"

Luis chuckled in spite of the coppery taste of fear in his mouth.

As two of the L.C.V.P.'s roared toward the shore, they hit the coral reef which the photo interpreters had failed to identify and which Gray and the frogmen, in the excitement of the battle, had forgotten to warn them about. The reef ruptured the double bottoms of both craft, but the water was still shallow enough for the seventy fighters to wade on to the shore. Another FUBAR was barely avoided when the landing force almost shot the frogmen who did not identify themselves with the password, *Águila Negra* (Black Eagle). It was an inexcusable oversight--they had never been given the password!!

In spite of all the confusion, the frogmen secured the beachhead without casualties and waited for the landing of San Román and Artime who arrived at the jetty in the catamaran. It was a dramatic moment for Luis. "Welcome to Cuba!" he said to Artime. In the pale light by the jetty, Artime gave a quick salute, picked up a handful of Cuban sand, and reverently kissed it. "Well done!" he said to the frogmen around him. "Cuba owes you a debt of gratitude."

Artime's comments moved Luis, and he remembered his father having him stand on his native soil of the U.S. when he first went north to the military academy. Now more than ever, he understood why men have such love for the land of their birth. At SMA, where patriotism was always stressed, he had memorized lines from a poem by Sir Walter Scott:

Breathes there a man with soul so dead
Who never to himself hath said,
"This is my own, my native land"?

How true, Luis thought, as he watched Artime ritualize the triumphant return to Cuba.

Chapter 42

The major problem still awaiting Pepe San Román was how to get the Brigade through the coral reef. Talking to a local fisherman, the frogmen learned that low tide would be at 7:00 a.m. Hearing this, San Román postponed the landing of troops and heavy equipment until daylight so the reef would be easier to see in the shallow water. Granted, San Román was sacrificing time, but there was no need to rush since the local militia was in retreat and Castro's air force was being demolished. The Brigade's tanks and heavy guns would be waiting for the communists.

Exhausted, Luis fell asleep on the floor of the lone bar at the beach, confident that in the Sierra Maestra all was going well with Ofelia and the second front. In a few hours, he and the other frogmen would be awakened to find the best path for the remaining vessels to come ashore. In a crunch, human beings were more dependable than U-2 reconnaissance photography!

At dawn, Luis and the other frogmen went into the water to survey the layout of the reef. Within a short time, they were back on shore re-establishing beach markers and positioning themselves to serve as beach masters for the incoming craft. Gray, assured all was now going well, returned to the *Blagar* in the catamaran.

The moment the frogmen gave the all clear to Pepe San Román, the landing began. Above them, the C-46's carrying the paratroopers to set up the roadblocks came in on schedule. Along the beach, Luis and the other frogmen happily greeted the disembarking troops. Luis, back in his khaki uniform and baseball cap, found a moment of humor in the landing as he saw the frogmen as black-faced minstrels and the Brigade as American cowboys wearing their western hats pinned up in front with a golden emblem of the 2506 Assault Brigade.

"Hey," Gregorio shouted to an old buddy, "Be careful with the ten-gallon hat. That shining insignia could be a hell of a target!"

"Better to be a cowboy than a black frog!" was the reply.

"Who on earth came up with the idea of substituting a western hat for a steel helmet?" Chiqui Llama remarked to Luis.

"Maybe the CIA wants the Brigade to play Teddy Roosevelt and Jeb Stuart!" Luis commented.

Perhaps, though, the planners knew best, Luis mused as he waded in the water and helped those with equipment get to the beach. Maybe they don't really need helmets; maybe the worst of the fighting has already taken place. Such were his thoughts as he looked up at the sky and saw a B-26 dip its wings in salute, a move that sealed his confidence. "Here are our planes!" José Enrique shouted. Everyone waved at their ally in the sky. The entire operation was unfolding as planned. Most importantly, air cover was secure.

As long as he lived, Luis Recio would remember 6:45 a.m., April 17, 1961. After dipping its wings, the "friendly" B-26 opened fire on the troops and craft on the beach. Behind it came another B-26, and after them a T-33 jet and a Sea Fury, all of them blazing away at the landing force.

The attack on Pearl Harbor came immediately to Luis' mind. How could it be that enemy planes would be attacking when they were supposed to have been destroyed? They were told the B-26's would not encounter opposition, and they also were reassured the ships would not need anti-aircraft guns.

Dumbfounded, everyone headed for cover, some toward the buildings on the beach and others behind vehicles, tanks, and landing craft at the water's edge. Luis ran for the rock jetty that had protected him the night before from the *Blagar*'s bullets and those of the militia. A couple of the frogmen fired their Thompsons, shaking their fists at the planes when they were out of range. There was more shooting along the beach, and one of the B-26's caught fire and plunged into the sea to the cheers of the invaders.

At the jetty, Luis saw one of the Sea Furies make a direct rocket hit on the *Río Escondido*. Fire spread along the deck, fueled by aviation gasoline. Along the sides, men in orange vests were jumping overboard, men he had come to know on the long trip from New Orleans to Puerto Cabezas. Luis watched helplessly as three booming explosions sending a huge fireball high into the sky followed one after another in quick succession. When the black mushroom cloud faded, there on the horizon lay the *Río* with its stern up in the air, revealing the same screws Luis and others had cleared of wire under water at the mouth of the Mississippi. Luis watched as the ship slowly sank out of sight. He hoped one of the dots in the water was the head of the dog, Cyclone.

Seeing that planes were strafing the men in the water around the *Río*, Luis ran to the Zodiac to help in the rescue. After starting the motor, he heard Gregorio beckoning him to wait. In an instant, Gregorio jumped on board, and they took off at full throttle, the front of the raft momentarily rising out of the water. Some one hundred meters out, Gregorio shouted, "Look out! Look out!" and pointed toward a T-33 coming in low on the water. "Shit! Luis heard himself say as he urinated in his pants, his bladder as much out of control as everything else around him. Shutting off the motor, Luis and Gregorio dove in and swam rapidly underwater toward the shore. The .50 caliber bullets made a path behind them, creating a sound in the water like the old-timey gasoline engine he had heard at the sugar mill, "thup, thup, thup, thup, thup."

Some thirty seconds later Luis and Gregorio surfaced simultaneously and saw the raft was still afloat. Checking the jet that was climbing and turning inland for more important targets, they scrambled back aboard and set course again toward the frantic arms waving in the water.

By the time they reached the site of the sinking ship, there were only two crewmen left in the water.

"God bless you!" said a stocky Spaniard in his fifties as Luis and Gregorio pulled him on the raft.

"You don't know how glad I am to see you!" said the other. "I can't swim!" he blurted as he coughed to get his breath.

"And the captain?" Luis inquired. "Did he make it?"

"He jumped and was picked up," one said.

"And Cyclone?" Luis asked.

"I don't know, but I didn't see him with Captain Tirado when he went overboard," was the reply.

Luis was saddened, but there was little time for sentiment. Aircraft, with their tongues of flame, still crisscrossed the area, leaving pandemonium in their path. As Luis and Gregorio headed full speed toward the shore, they had a panoramic view of the opening of the bay and Blue Beach. Debris from the morning attack and the failures of the night before now appeared everywhere. Plastic boats, turned upside down, floated absurdly in the water. The landing craft that had lodged on the reefs in the night served as a visible rebuke to the CIA intelligence experts. The saddest sight remained behind them, the flotsam of the *Río* and the lingering smoke from the explosion. The smell of burnt rubber and gasoline hung in the air.

"One fucking airplane could have saved that ship!" Gregorio shouted angrily.

What was evident in losses painted only part of the picture, as Gregorio and Luis learned when they returned to the jetty with other frogmen. The *Houston* had been forced to run aground at Playa Larga even before the *Río Escondido* sank. Three frogmen who landed with Rip at Playa Larga sent word from the *Bárbara J.* that the *Houston* and the *Río* were both out of action! It was unbelievable! Where on earth were the friendly airplanes?

Even considering the absence of air cover, the mistakes, and the unanticipated resistance, Luis still held hope. As far as he knew, the Brigade paratroopers were succeeding with the roadblocks since the troops on the beach were not under any mortar or artillery attack. He imagined people were rising up in arms all over the island, spurred on by the good news coming from Radio SWAN that Erneido Oliva, second in command of the Brigade, was fighting magnificently and inflicting heavy casualties on the Playa Larga front. Even though a landing at Green Beach to the east had been aborted, that sector seemed secure since during the night Pepe San Román had dispatched a battalion to protect the right flank. The Girón Airport, the most important objective, had been secured without significant opposition. In spite of the air attacks, every military objective had been met--except the unloading of the supplies and ammunition from the ships.

The question of the remaining ships concerned Luis. By mid-morning, he noticed they had departed the area, leaving a blank blue horizon at the back of the "Tigers from the Sea," as local inhabitants had described the Brigade. That same blank horizon had loomed more expansively after the *Río* went down. Without air cover and anti-aircraft guns, what else could the ships do if they were to avoid the fate of the *Río*?

Placing themselves at the disposal of San Román at headquarters in Girón, the frogmen were in a position to get first-hand information on the progress of "Pluto." From Jorge Suárez-Rivas, one of the intelligence officers and an old friend from the HYC, Luis learned only ten percent of the supplies from the ships had been brought on shore. Jorge said the fleet would be back later that night to unload.

Luis felt frustrated because the naval arm of the Brigade was not fulfilling its part of the mission. In addition to leading the landing, the *Blagar* and *Bárbara J.* had been commissioned to patrol the shore from Playa Larga to Girón and support the operation with machine guns and recoilless cannons. Later, they were to transport the frogmen around the coast of Cuba to conduct sabotage in the harbors, starting at Cienfuegos and moving to small coast guard depots until they reached Havana, by which time the Brigade would be well on its way to victory.

It bothered Luis that the frogmen had not had the chance to return to the *Blagar*. The disappearance of the ships increased his apprehension that the frogmen might be stranded on shore. He wished they were on their way to wreak havoc in the harbor at Cienfuegos, whose name appropriately meant "one hundred fires." It was not too late, however, since the ships would return at night when they would be safe from the planes. Then Luis and the frogmen would go back to the *Blagar* in the Zodiac in order to begin their mission of sabotage. He consoled himself, rationalizing that few military operations went according to plan.

As the day wore on, Luis became more accustomed to a different type of combat than he had known where only sporadic guerrilla skirmishes occurred. Here, there was a war on land, on sea, and in the air. Aircraft came in rotation throughout the day, and in the distance, guns pounded, coming closer by the hour. The wounded trickled in and were placed in the ballroom of the club at Girón. Blood stained bandages could be seen around the room, and the air reeked with the smell of disinfectant. A young man in his teens on a stretcher tried frantically to look at his mutilated leg as a medic and chaplain worked to restrain him. A hysterical middle-aged woman and two small children appeared as if they had barely survived a tornado, the woman's floral print dress full of bloodstained holes. Her husband had been killed in the crossfire on the beach. In one corner lay three bodies under sheets. Luis had not heard anyone mention the problem of what to do with casualties.

By late Monday afternoon on the seventeenth, it was obvious that without air cover and ammunition, "Pluto" would fail. What air power could do had been evident in the mid-afternoon when two B-26's in communication with Oliva had annihilated almost an entire battalion and scores of vehicles with bombs and rockets. "Not even the cat was alive," reported Máximo Leonardo Cruz, one of Oliva's company commanders. The coordinated air-ground attack was short-lived, for both B-26's, without fighter protection, were shot down by a T-33 and a Sea Fury. Incredibly, two T-33's and two Sea Furies controlled the air over the bay.

Luis had mixed feelings upon hearing the reports in headquarters from Playa Larga. Something in the statement, "not even the cat was alive," made him think not only of the entombed, terrified Cyclone on the *Río Escondido* but also of Alberto Sánchez, who still supported Castro, and believed he was doing the right thing. Could Alberto be among the dead? It was imperative for "Pluto" to succeed, but Luis hated to think about human beings turned into carrion. Yet he was proud of the Brigade, which against overwhelming odds and without air cover, was holding out after a full day.

With the possibility of air cover virtually dismissed by the end of the first day, the success of the operation depended upon the return of the ships. Thus, all eyes turned toward the sea that night after the Brigade's Chief of Supplies (G-4), Roberto Pertierra, with the help of the frogmen, placed the landing lights on the beach and waited for the ships' arrival. Luis and others strained their eyes looking into the night, but there was no sign of them. There was nothing except the great outer dark.

San Román was counting on Gray's promise that the ships would return at night, but after four hours, he took a radio operator and Jaime Varela Canosa, the liaison officer between the Brigade and the Cuban navy, and went in search of the fleet in a catamaran. Luis felt sorry for the Brigade commander who pleaded at sea for help over the PRC-10 radio and futilely searched for a speck of light in the dark of night upon which the freedom of Cuba depended.

The three men left around midnight, went some six miles to sea, and, returned embittered after an hour with nothing to report. Had the ships been sunk like the *Río,* or had they simply fled for safety? The Brigade held onto the belief that the fleet was still out there just over the horizon, waiting for some word that everything was under control. When Pepe asked for volunteers for a second search, Luis and Gaspar stepped forward. It was not a dangerous mission, just a desperate one.

With José Luis Sosa, another friend from Camagüey, Luis and Gaspar took the same course that the earlier group had searched but went twice as far to send out what amounted to their S.O.S., using the code name for the *Blagar.* "DOLORES, DOLORES!" they repeated, taking turns on the radio. "WHERE ARE YOU? WHERE ARE YOU? THIS IS BEACH. WE NEED YOU. CAN YOU HEAR US? DOLORES, DOLORES!"

The message went out for hours. Listening to his comrade from Camagüey grinding out the same appeals over and over, Luis remembered the story Gray had told them in New Orleans after they had seen *The Alamo* with John Wayne.

"Did you ever hear the story of the 'Lost Battalion of World War II?'" he asked.

When no one replied, Gray continued, "Well, they were part of the 36th Infantry Division--the Texas Division--and they got cut off in the Vosges Mountains when the Germans made their counterattack during the last days of the war. Every day for a week or more, they withstood savage attacks, taking heavy losses but holding on. You know what their nickname was?"

No one knew.

"'The Alamo Battalion, and you know who finally got through to them?"

Again, no one responded.

"The Japanese Americans, the 100th Battalion, the most decorated unit of the war. They were something else. I never saw them, but I heard a lot of stories. Because of their size and because they were always fighting and on the move, the army had trouble keeping them supplied and once sent them some WAC underwear because it was all the quartermaster could find that he thought they could wear. Guess what? They wouldn't wear it!" Gray had roared in appreciation of the story. "They're called 'nisei' and were brave men and heroes in the state of Texas, as Rip will tell you."

"How in the hell can you win a modern war without ships and airplanes?" Gaspar shouted.

As for Luis, his own frustration came through in the variation he made on the procedure during his last turn at the radio: "GENE AUTRY, GENE AUTRY, WHERE ARE YOU? THIS IS BEACH. CAN YOU HEAR ME? JOHN WAYNE, JOHN WAYNE, WHERE ARE YOU? WE ARE ALAMO. REPEAT. ALAMO, WE NEED YOU. PLEASE COME. NISEI, NISEI, WHERE ARE YOU? WE ARE ALAMO. GRAY, GRAY, WE NEED YOU. COME BACK. COME BACK. WE'RE SURROUNDED. WE ARE ALAMO. JOHN KENNEDY, JOHN KENNEDY, THIS IS BEACH. WHERE ARE YOU, JOHN KENNEDY? WE NEED YOU. WE'RE ALAMO. DO NOT, REPEAT, DO NOT DESERT US."

Some thirty minutes before dawn, the search party gave up and headed back to Blue Beach. As they returned, they watched the steady flashing of artillery near Playa Larga that filled the sky over Zapata Swamp. It was, they knew, not so much their own guns now as the Russian-made artillery of Fidel Castro, which ironically exemplified the new and much greater dependence of the Revolution on a foreign power. What on earth, Luis wondered, had compelled Castro to align himself with Russia? What possibly did the happy-go-lucky Cubans have in common with the humorless Soviets? Though no one admitted it openly, they all knew that within a few hours the communist counterattack would be unstoppable without air support and ammunition to answer back loud and clear. "U.S.," Luis said to himself, "WHERE ARE YOU?"

Chapter 43

When Luis, Gaspar Betancourt, and José Luis Sosa arrived back on the beach in the raft, they decided to downplay the failure of their search.

"We didn't make contact, but I'll bet you we'll hear from them any time," José Luis reported to one inquiring soldier. "We'll get air cover today, and with air cover will come destroyer escorts and our own ships."

Shortly before 9:00 a.m., José Enrique and Luis went to San Román's headquarters, a concrete bungalow at the main intersection of the roads in Girón. José Enrique wanted to suggest a day search farther out at sea. When they arrived at headquarters, they knew something important was occurring since Pepe, Artime, and Oliva were in conference. Lack of ammunition had forced Oliva to retreat toward Girón after "the Battle of the Rotunda." Oliva even had to free some two hundred prisoners he had taken since there was no way to get them back to Girón. He found out from the captured men that his force of 370 men had defeated over 2,000 men with twenty Stalin and Sherman tanks. Oliva had displayed such bravery in battle his men began to call him "Maceo," after Antonio Maceo, the great mulatto general in the War of Independence from Spain.

At the height of the "Battle of the Rotunda," when some of his youngest fighters, stunned by the pounding of Russian howitzers, started to retreat, Oliva picked up a recoilless cannon, knelt, and faced a Stalin tank in the middle of the road. When the tank stopped and its commander got out, Oliva's men returned to their positions.

"Are you the commander of these troops?" he asked Oliva.

When Oliva indicated he was, the tank commander stated he wanted to join Oliva's troops because of the bravery he and his men had displayed. To Luis, this act exemplified what could happen all over the front if the planes and ships would only come. The enemy too was tired and was ripe for a change of allegiance.

Luis watched and listened as Oliva, moving his hands over the maps, finished his briefing for San Román and Artime and began to state what he considered the only alternative for the Brigade. In light of their situation, Oliva proposed they pull back the troops from the San Blas front, join with their five tanks, form an arrowhead movement, and strike toward the Escambray Mountains. It was risky but far preferable to being captured or killed if they tried to stay near the beach without ammunition and air cover.

When he mentioned the Escambray Mountains, Luis' thoughts turned to Ofelia in the Sierra Maestra. By this time, he hoped that she and others had been joined by Nino Díaz and his men who had landed at Oriente. If all was going well and if Radio SWAN was doing its job, then thousands would have joined the struggle against Castro.

San Román was not receptive to Oliva's plan, seeing the Escambray as too far away and the Brigade too short on supplies and ammunition. He also knew enemy concentrations around Cienfuegos would be strong and difficult to penetrate. San Román believed the Americans would come to their rescue if they could only hold their position for a couple of more days. As commander, San Román's reasoning prevailed.

San Román's decision soon appeared to be prophetic. Shortly after the debate on their course of action, Orlando Cuervo, son of the Orthodoxo leader, Pelayo Cuervo, and one of the radio operators, rushed into the headquarters and excitedly informed San Román he was picking up the *Blagar*. San Román ran to the radio at the ammunition supply point to talk with the voice on the other end. "Where have you been?" he yelled. "You son of a bitch! You've abandoned us!"

Gray answered and informed Pepe they had not been abandoned.

"Six jets and several B-26's will arrive within two hours. The L.C.U.'s will come tonight, and before their arrival, several C-54's will drop supplies by parachutes," Gray reassured Pepe.

Turning to the crowd around him, Pepe relayed the good news with the comment, "Now we'll get them!" All over the front, his words sparked new hope in the hearts of the battered Brigade, "The jets are coming! The jets are coming!"

The jets, though, were slow in arriving. It was not until 3:00 p.m. when two F-86's finally appeared over the beach. Two, Luis believed, would have been enough to take care of Castro's air force--perhaps only one, as Gregorio maintained. Much to the astonishment of the soldiers, however, the two F-86's did nothing except fly over and then leave without firing a shot. Shortly thereafter, Castro's planes were strafing the beach again with impunity. "What in the hell's going on?" Luis shouted in frustration.

Though the air attacks were constant, Luis knew he would never get accustomed to them. Air power was a feature of modern war he had heard a lot about, but no one could know what it felt like to be defenseless under relentless air attacks unless he experienced it first hand as Luis and his comrades had done for the last two days.

Luis had just left a trench following the lull in the strafing and bombing when one of the Brigade's C-54's passed over and dropped supplies on the airfield. Luis' heart leaped as he saw three parachutes open and descend from a low altitude, but his spirit fell just as quickly when he noticed two of the parachutes drifting out to sea. He saw the boxes hit the water, and the parachutes spread out like collapsing tents. "Oh hell," he said, "can't anything go right?"

In a few minutes José Enrique ran up to him and said, "Luis, you and Chiqui are coming with me. I've just told Pepe we'll get the boxes. Let's go."

A few meters from the first parachute, the prop-driven Sea Fury attacked them, and the three frogmen had no place to hide in a rubber raft. Luis was about to dive overboard when he saw Chiqui facing the Sea Fury head on as Oliva had done with the tank at the Rotunda. "Come on, you bastard!" Chiqui shouted.

Luis did not know which came first, the clattering of the BAR or the thudding of the bullets in the water. He only knew they were vastly outgunned. Throwing on his snorkel and mask, Luis went over the side. José Enrique let go of the stick and followed him, forgetting to shut off the motor. When Luis heard the bullets again in the water, he saw a unique sight. Some seven feet down the decelerating bullets suddenly changed their pattern from that of a projectile to that of a wiggling minnow in a dive toward the bottom of the sea.

When Luis and José Enrique emerged, Chiqui was still in the pilot-less Zodiac firing on the tail of the plane, having followed it with the BAR as it made its pass. The Sea Fury was now smoking and Chiqui was yelling at the top of his voice. "I got the bastard! I got him! Watch him go down!"

Leaving a billowing trail of smoke, it hit the water a few miles east of Girón.

Wildly congratulating Chiqui, José Enrique and Luis climbed back on the raft only to realize a bullet had punctured one of the forward compartments. "I heard it before I saw it. It sounded like a tire losing air, but it's no major problem. It'll hold us." Chiqui surmised.

From under one of the parachutes, they hauled in three wooden crates of ammunition and cut the lines from the chute. Slowly they took the cargo to shore where they patched the wounded Zodiac and returned to sea to look for the other parachute. At first they saw nothing, but when José Enrique peered down and noticed a chute spread out some three feet below the surface, they had to put on snorkels, masks, and fins in order to retrieve the boxes.

Descending, Luis thought the chute and its dangling cords looked like a giant Portuguese man-of-war wafting in the underwater currents. All three of the boxes had settled some fifteen feet down.

Shortly after the supplies were unloaded, Castro's planes came once again, but now steady advancing artillery from Playa Larga accompanied their machine guns and bombs. "Goddamn it!" Gaspar Betancourt shouted in reference to the enemy pilots and artillery gunners as the frogmen ran to the trenches one more time, the acrid smell of powder and smoke in their noses.

When Luis returned to headquarters, he discovered the ammunition they had retrieved was clips for Springfield rifles which no one in the Brigade had instead of the bullets for the M-ls! The whole operation had become a tragedy of errors.

Luis knew that Roberto de Varona and Pepito Sosa, José Luis' father, had come with the invasion force to show that civilian leaders other than Artime, the official delegate of the Revolutionary

Council, were willing to fight and die if necessary. It was important that the military not have too much control after the overthrow of the communists in order to avoid the same mistakes the military government of Castro had made. Luis thought civilian control of the military might be the greatest contribution to democracy; however, civilian control of the military did not necessarily mean universal harmony. Luis worried over the factions already contending for power. The original *Frente* had been so divided back in February that it had to be replaced by the Cuban Revolutionary Council, now the official government in exile.

Although Luis was comfortable with all the leaders, he knew they ranged in political ideology from social democrats such as Artime, Manuel Ray, and Miró Cardona, to moderates such as Tony de Varona and Dr. Antonio Maceo, grandson of "the Bronze Titan." All might have had different visions of Cuba, but they unanimously opposed corruption and dictatorship from the left or the right. But, regardless of political ideologies, their plans would be meaningless unless the ships arrived that night.

After dinner, the frogmen positioned themselves near the supply tent and listened for possible news of the arrival of the ships. By 1:00 a.m., the truth was brought home to Luis when Jorge Suárez-Rivas approached him and putting his arm around Luis' shoulder, sadly confided, "We've had it, Luis. The Americans have abandoned us. They're not coming. We're all going to die."

Until that instant, Luis had believed that somehow the Americans would come through at the last moment. The marine assault upon Girón beach would be like Roosevelt's famous charge up San Juan Hill. How wrong he had been! How could he have been so optimistic and naive? All of his faith in the Americans crumbled with that single statement of Suárez-Rivas: "The Americans have abandoned us." Turning away from his friend, Luis Recio walked slowly toward the sea. At the edge of the water, he faced the darkness of the Caribbean and wept silently, tears for Cuba, for the United States of America, and for himself streaming down his face.

Chapter 44

Luis had been sitting by the sea for over an hour looking over the darkened water. The gentle lapping of the surf and the smell of sea water brought him an inner peace. There was no doubt about it; as a former rebel officer and government official, he would be executed for treason if he were not killed in the fighting that would start again before sunrise.

Luis did not see any logic in fighting to the end. Why continue killing when the cause was lost? The Brigade's purpose had been to free fellow Cubans, not to kill them. Men of common sense only fought out of necessity when pushed into a corner.

Some other voice, though, countered his musing, saying, "So what if the Americans didn't come? You don't have to answer for them in the final judgment. You can die with honor, for you've fought honestly for freedom. Face whatever comes with courage."

Luis was saying the rosary when he heard José Enrique call his name, "Luis, come on. We've got work to do."

Luis walked back to Blanco's Bar with José Enrique where the other frogmen were waiting.

"Well, *muchachos*," José Enrique said in a business-like manner, "we've been ordered to set up a perimeter in this area to defend against militia infiltrators. We'll make foxholes some one-hundred meters directly across the road in front of the bar. We have a couple of shovels. We need to dig three foxholes some twenty-five meters apart and stay in pairs as much as possible since someone will have to be awake at all times. Luis, you'll be with Gregorio, Jesús Llama with Gaspar, and since I can't sleep, I'll be in the middle foxhole.

"Gaspar, will you tell them what you heard on the radio this afternoon? We've already shared this information with Pepe."

"Okay," Gaspar began, "When the two F-86 Sabre jets flew over today, I was on the PRC-10 on the jetty, and I happened to pick up a radio conversation between the American pilots and the carrier. I don't remember the exact words, but here is the gist of what they said: 'We can't believe what we're seeing over here. Below us there are some one thousand men on the beach at Girón. On the other side we see tens of thousands of enemy troops advancing--perhaps as many as 40,000. Our friends are going to be murdered! We have no uniform and no insignia on our planes. Why can't we come to their aid? We've never seen such juicy targets. Just give us the word.'

"The reply came immediately. 'You are not to fire. Repeat, you are not to attack or take any hostile action. Return to the carrier after flyover.'"

"*Muchachos*," José Enrique lamented, "we're not getting the support we've been promised. I simply don't know why. I still think if we can hold on for seventy-two hours, the U.S. Marines will arrive. That's why we're digging in for the enemy assault. I assure you all hell will break loose at dawn. There'll be air attacks and heavy artillery. I believe the Americans are simply waiting to make sure they abide by the seventy-two hour stipulation. This means we need to hold out one more day--about twenty-two more hours. We can do it!"

As they parted, Luis took José Enrique aside and said, "I think you're wrong. The Americans aren't coming."

Patting Luis on the shoulder, José Enrique replied, "You're tired, Luis. You'll feel better in the morning."

"When the T-33's come back, you mean," Luis muttered caustically under his breath.

Alternating their shoveling, Luis and Gregorio began to hollow out a trench on the south side of a sand dune in between clumps of roots and vegetation. They dug deep enough to provide protection from shrapnel and air attacks from the sea. While they worked, they saw the sporadic flashing of the artillery in the sky above San Blas some ten kilometers to the north. Luis knew the front would soon crumble as it had already at Playa Larga. There was no way to fight without ammunition.

"You know, Gregorio," Luis said, breaking their silence. "I respect José Enrique, but he doesn't understand the Americans like we do. Fuck! If the Americans were coming, they wouldn't stand on ceremony or the technicality of waiting seventy-two hours."

"You're damned right," Gregorio responded angrily. "When those motherfuckers decide to do something, they do it. Hell, they're just not coming."

Within thirty minutes, they had completed their new trench, and Gregorio carried the shovel over to José Enrique so he could begin a trench of his own.

Luis had never been so exhausted, not so much from the digging but from the loss of sleep during the last few days. Shivering from fatigue and the chill that came from the fresh night air which played over the film of sweat on his body, he fell into a deep sleep with a Thompson sub-machine gun across his chest.

Well before his wake-up hour, Luis jumped straight up from the trench, rapidly twisting and frantically brushing himself off.

"What in the hell's wrong, Luis?" Gregorio inquired anxiously, standing up to help his comrade.

"Something's crawling all over me! Get with your pen light."

Gregorio hurriedly obeyed, cupping his hands around his light so as not to reveal their position. Shining the light close to Luis, he saw nothing, but when he pointed it toward the bottom of the trench, he saw the invaders.

"Luis, these are just crabs that are all over the beach. A few of them have gotten into our trench." As he spoke, Gregorio reached to throw them out.

"Jesus!" Luis exclaimed, visibly shaken. "Look at the color of the bastards."

In the glow of the pen's light, the little creatures were red and black, the same colors as the flag of the 26th of July Movement. It was as if Mother Nature herself conspired against them, sending her tiniest soldiers to infiltrate their positions. The militia could not be far behind them. After slinging them away, Gregorio turned off his light and told Luis to go back to sleep.

Settling back down in a relatively comfortable position at one end of the trench, Luis concentrated on relaxing his body. One could not go to sleep shaking as he was at the moment. Deliberately pushing the images of the crabs from his mind, he focused on all the comforting scenes he could conjure. He recalled his carefree youth at the sugar mill, the wonderful meals with his family, and the fishing trips with his father on the small keys called *Jardines de la Reina* or Gardens of the Queen. Catching lobsters and fish there with his father approached perfect happiness. When Ofelia entered his mind, he pushed the images of her away since the memories of his love for her triggered fears about what she might be going through.

Finally his quivering body became still, and a restless sleep overtook him. There, in a sandy hole near the shore of Girón Beach off *Bahía de Cochinos*, Luis Recio dreamed.

He found himself in the clubhouse in Girón, standing guard at the door to the dance floor where the seriously wounded lay. Dressed in swimming trunks, he wore a black face mask with a snorkel tube that looked like a black snake stuck in his mouth. Instead of his machine gun, he held the M-1 rifle he had used in the mountains. On the other side of the door stood Gregorio, who, when Luis acknowledged his presence, gestured dramatically for him to look at the scenes on the dance floor and at the windows.

A priest, wearing flippers and a cowboy hat with a light that beamed on each wounded man, was kneeling beside the dying and giving them communion, but instead of offering white wafers as the host, he was dropping small black fish into their beseeching mouths. The hosts were actually small *cochinos* which he took from a basket held in the mouth of a huge black German shepherd serving as acolyte. As the men swallowed the fish, they began to choke. Rather than bringing them peace, this surreal ritual threw them into violent convulsions. Behind the priest and the dog, Luis witnessed a Dantesque scene of writhing and contorted shapes screaming silently and then dying after they regurgitated the fish. Petrified, Luis attempted to scream but could not because of the snorkel. He wanted to tell the priest what was happening in his wake, but he knew he would be shot if he left his post.

Glancing at the windows, he noticed another terrifying scene. Black frogs, for whom he felt a strange affinity, were jumping up at the light and slamming against the glass, trying to escape but attracting the attention of the lurking creatures on the other side of the panes. At first, Luis thought they were vultures lusting for corpses, but looking more closely, he realized they were black eagles as intent upon breaking into the room as the poor frogs were upon getting out. The eagles were screaming, pecking the glass, and diving against the windows in vain. The cause of their desperation and that of the jumping frogs became evident when Luis looked at the floor. An army of thousands of red and black crabs were slowly advancing toward the wounded on one side and toward the frogs on the other. Luis wanted to warn the priest and the dog since he was sure that somehow he knew them both. Why was the priest wearing flippers and a cowboy hat? His skin prickled, and he blew on the snorkel with all his might until it launched from his mouth like a projectile and he could shout the words that would save the priest, the dog and the frogs: "Black Eagle! *Águila Negra*! Black Eagle!"

"Luis! Luis!" Gregorio whispered urgently as he shook him fully awake. "You're screaming. You'll give us away. What's wrong?"

"My God, I've had a terrible nightmare," Luis exclaimed, trying to orient himself. "I'm sorry I yelled. I couldn't help it." He rubbed his face with his hands. "Gregorio, you go to sleep now. I'd rather face what being awake has to offer."

For the rest of the night, the reality of pounding artillery on all fronts and the red explosions in the night sky reminded Luis of the crabs. Red and black, the tangible and the symbolic, merged beyond distinction. Dawn brought an even starker reality. Shortly after 6:00 a.m., a B-26 made a strafing run at Blanco's Bar and succeeded in doing what encroaching artillery had not been able to accomplish--waking Gregorio. When he realized what was happening, Gregorio cut loose with a burst of the Thompson at the plane.

"You're wasting your time," Luis said.

"I still feel better for doing it," replied Gregorio.

When the B-26 circled back over the sea to make another pass from the southwest, all the frogmen noticed four members of the Brigade coming back into Girón from the right flank were taking cover at Blanco's Bar without realizing it had just been the target of attack.

"Those fools are going to get killed," Luis cried to Gregorio. "They don't realize the bastard's going to strafe it again."

"I'm going to warn them!" Gregorio shouted, jumping out of the trench and running toward the bar before Luis could stop him.

He had not gone more than ten meters when there was a burst of fire from the Brigade soldiers near the bar. Luis and all the other frogmen watched as Gregorio fell, yelling, "Black Eagle! Shit! Black Eagle!" Realizing the friendly troops had mistaken Gregorio as an infiltrating militiaman, all the frogmen frantically shouted the password.

"My God! Have they killed him?" Luis muttered as he and other frogmen ran toward Gregorio. Seeing their mistake, the soldiers also rushed to the fallen frogman, all converging at a point that would have made a better target than the bar itself except that the pilot of the B-26 decided to attack a truck headed toward the eastern front.

When they reached Gregorio, they first thought he was dead. He had been hit in the head and in the right arm. Blood flowed profusely from his scalp, and he had already lost consciousness.

"Get us a doctor!" Luis yelled in the direction of the clubhouse while José Enrique examined the wounds. "I don't believe the head wound is serious," José Enrique concluded as he noticed Gregorio was responding to their voices. Within minutes, a medic arrived and began cleaning the wounds, applying antiseptics, and putting on bandages. The medic surmised the arm wound was the more serious because the elbow was shattered. As Gregorio slowly regained consciousness, his attackers apologized profusely. They turned out to be some of Roberto de Varona's group who were retreating from the front.

When a truck came by heading west for a re-supply of ammunition, José Enrique flagged it down, and he and others loaded Gregorio on to the bed. Luis climbed aboard to be with his partner while the others stayed to guard their portion of the perimeter.

At the clubhouse, there was good news. Dr. Juan Sordo was at Girón airfield making arrangements for the evacuation of the wounded on a C-46, and one of the medics thought Gregorio would be able to leave immediately for Nicaragua.

"You're a lucky man, my friend," Luis chided. "You got hit in the nick of time. Within a few hours, you'll be eating steak and drinking beer in Puerto Cabezas, and we'll still be here choking down K-rations!"

Gregorio smiled faintly at Luis' humor; however, Lady Luck was not to smile on Gregorio Loret de Mola nor on any of the other wounded that day. Within minutes after his departure, Dr. Sordo, visibly upset, returned from the airfield. The plane had already taken off because the pilot contended it was too risky to wait for the wounded given the heavy shelling and lack of air cover. The damn Americans were not even willing to provide air cover for the evacuation of the wounded, Luis thought bitterly.

Weak from loss of blood, Gregorio feebly joked, "You guys aren't going to be able to get rid of me so easily."

Walking beside Gregorio as he was carried into the clubhouse, Luis felt the horror of his dream again. More wounded had arrived, and the situation was becoming increasingly chaotic as the doctors and medics worked frantically to stop the bleeding of the most seriously injured. Recalling his dream, Luis made a point to look for the chaplain, Father Tomás Macho, and found him along a wall near a makeshift stretcher giving absolution to a bandaged man who apparently had just confessed. They were near the conspicuous row of bodies covered with sheets. The dead did not pose a problem since they would rest in Cuban soil, but what was to be done with the growing number requiring medical attention? Surely the Americans were aware many soldiers had been wounded in this debacle, so why didn't they do something to get them out of Girón?

Luis left Gregorio at the clubhouse and went to the headquarters to find out more about the situation and what his group should do next. Luis did not need a combat map to know the end was quickly approaching. The T-33's and the B-26 were creating havoc among the battered forces of the Brigade. Men were running in every direction without leadership, and the artillery rounds were zeroing in around the clubhouse and headquarters at the crossroads. The silent sea, as depressing as the constant bombardment on the land, served as the looming backdrop to the confusion on the shore.

At headquarters, Luis learned about the bravery of Alejandro del Valle at San Blas, reminiscent of Oliva's grand gesture in front of the tank at the Rotunda. Instead of facing an enemy tank single-handedly, del Valle got on top of one of his two tanks and directed a counterattack with his paratroopers and the third battalion. When he was knocked off the tank by enemy fire, he climbed back on and started the attack again. The startled enemy, though larger in numbers, broke and ran before the unexpected charge. The triumph was only temporary since all along del Valle's line his men ran out of ammunition. When they retreated, del Valle yelled, "All paratroopers back to the lines and die there."

At San Blas in the early morning, one of Castro's top commanders, Major Félix Duque, mistakenly drove a jeep into del Valle's line and was brought as a prisoner to the headquarters at Girón. Luis was present when he told San Román that if the forces at Girón were all that the Brigade had, then they were surely defeated because Duque alone had some five thousand men and fourteen tanks, which represented only a fraction of the total enemy force.

When Luis heard this information, he knew Duque was telling the truth since his information concurred with the same information Gaspar Betancourt had picked up on the PRC-10 from the conversation of F-86 pilots the day before. The scene at headquarters was so hectic that Luis had to wait to get a word with San Román, and while he waited, he listened to the radio messages going out in vain to the *Blagar*. Every few minutes they made the same pitiful appeal: "SURROUNDED ON ALL FRONTS . . . PLEASE SEND AIR SUPPORT TO THESE COORDINATES . . . AIR SUPPORT . . . AIR SUPPORT . . . PLEASE HELP." When San Román had a free moment, he told Luis the frogmen should help hold the perimeter on the east side of town and expect heavy enemy advance from the Green Beach on the right front.

As Luis hurried toward Blanco's Bar, the clattering and booming on every side increased as the mad symphony of battle greeted his ears and his eyes. Two soldiers, carrying a stretcher with a man whose intestines were protruding, were coming toward him. Still conscious, the dying man begged for morphine.

"What can I do to help?" Luis, numbed by the sight of carnage, asked the soldiers.

"Unless you have morphine, there's not a fucking thing you can do, " they replied without stopping.

Near the trenches, a jeep passed by with a young officer strapped loosely in the passenger seat. Behind him, a medic with his arms around the officer, tried to stop the bleeding of a gaping chest wound. Panic filled their eyes.

Toward the middle of the afternoon, José Enrique called the other frogmen to his trench and told them they needed to make a decision.

"We can stay here and die fighting in these trenches or try to escape and join the forces in the Escambray. If we leave the trenches, we either take to the sea in our Zodiac or cut our way through the swamp. We must consider Gregorio, for we won't abandon him."

"Right," said Gaspar, "we're not like the fucking *americanos*."

"I don't think we should take Gregorio to sea with his wounds," said José Enrique. "If the rubber raft were hit again, Gregorio's bleeding would attract sharks, and we don't know how long we would be at sea. I suggest we head east northeast from here and try to stay away from the Cienfuegos beach road. When we reach the Escambray, we'll join up with guerrillas. What do you think?"

Without hesitation or debate, they all agreed to head for the Escambray.

José Enrique told Luis to go to Girón to check on Gregorio and the status of the hopeless battle. When Luis arrived at the clubhouse, he found Gregorio sitting up and talking to the other wounded. A temporary cast had been put on his elbow and his arm placed in a sling. Gregorio agreed to the escape plan without any reservation. "I knew you guys would never leave me," he said, his voice breaking.

At the concrete bungalow, Luis found San Román as calm as the eye of a hurricane. Luis marveled at the man's control in the midst of a barrage of mortar and artillery. Luis did not have to ask what was happening; he had only to listen to San Román talking to Gray on the radio. Gray was telling him to hang on, that help was on the way. San Román informed Gray that enemy tanks were already in Girón and that the right flank was caving in. Luis listened as San Román sent the last message: "AM DESTROYING ALL MY EQUIPMENT AND COMMUNICATION. TANKS ARE IN SIGHT. I HAVE NOTHING TO FIGHT WITH. AM TAKING TO THE SWAMP. I CANNOT WAIT."

San Román then dispatched messengers to his commanders, ordering them to separate, go into the swamp, and fight as companies until reinforcements came. Thinking quickly, Luis caught a ride with the messenger in a jeep going back to the Fourth Battalion, and as they left, he saw San Román's staff begin to destroy the maps and equipment in the headquarters building. The end had come.

At the clubhouse, the other frogmen picked up Gregorio and prepared to set off into the swamp to the east of the San Blas road when they noticed the arrival of Oliva and his men. They heard Oliva inquire about Pepe San Román, and they saw his outrage when he mistakenly thought Pepe had escaped in a sailboat. They saw Oliva tear off his shirt and shake his fist at the sea, swearing he would never abandon his men. When one young paratroop officer, Amado Gayol, worried about possible reprisals against his family, talked about killing himself, Oliva admonished him, "Don't even think about it. You're a man, unlike those trying to flee on the boats."

Inspired by Oliva, the frogmen were glad they had decided to stay, escape, and fight again.

The frogmen's last disappointment took place right before their eyes. Suddenly they became aware of two American destroyers sailing toward the coast. "Look!" Gregorio exclaimed. "They're coming to rescue us!" No sooner had Gregorio spoken when they saw two artillery shells land in front of the destroyers. Immediately, their last hope of rescue turned around and headed out to sea.

The incredulity and rage of the battered men on the beach knew no bounds. "You goddamned motherfucking cowards!" yelled someone in the group close to the frogmen. Two soldiers ran to a tank and fired at the destroyers. Shots were also fired at the sailboat and the rubber raft belonging to the frogmen. Realizing that some soldiers had taken their raft as they tried to escape, Luis now understood that even if Gregorio had not been wounded, it would have been wrong for the frogmen to set out to sea in clear view of the Brigade. They had been the first ashore, and their pride would have made them the last to leave had evacuation been possible. As Luis watched the great American Navy turn and run like a dog with its tail between its legs while the Brigade fired at the Zodiac, he knew there was nothing else to do but to take to the swamp.

The frogmen looked on while Oliva's men shot out the tires of their vehicles, destroyed the tracks on their tanks, and blew up their equipment. When they began to march to the east in a column, the frogmen fell in behind, thinking they would try to stay with the main body of Oliva's remaining force. The troops had not gone far when they came under attack by T-33's and a Sea Fury. After taking cover, the five frogmen broke with the column and headed into the Zapata Swamp on their own.

"José Enrique," Luis said, as they left the beach area, "when I was twenty-one, I had a choice of deciding between my American citizenship and Cuban citizenship. I'm so glad I didn't choose the U.S."

"Luis," José Enrique replied, "I don't know why the Americans didn't show up, but I know there has to be some reason other than fear. The country that took on the German army and the Japanese Imperial Navy cannot be afraid of four or five old rusty airplanes."

"O.K., *abuelo*," said Luis. "I hope we live to find the answer."

Chapter 45

The Zapata Swamp or "the Great Swamp of the Caribbean" encircled the town of Girón. This marshy terrain extended some sixty-five miles east and west and some twenty miles north and south. In the rainy season from May to October, it was virtually impossible to penetrate; in the dry season, it was as invulnerable. Thick mangrove trees with their exposed, humpback roots and *marabú* bushes with their long thorns cut and stung any unfortunate soul trying to move through them. The area was a breeding ground for insects, birds, and non-poisonous snakes. Some of the plants, such as the *guao* were poisonous, but only a botany professor could distinguish one from the other. The frogmen had had no real survival training in swamps.

As in other coastal areas of Cuba, the primary industry of the swamp was charcoal-making because of the abundance of mangrove trees. In recent years, a sporting industry had begun to develop around *Laguna del Tesoro* or "Treasure Pond," so named because of the legend that Indians had thrown gold icons into the water to hide them from the Spanish *conquistadores*. Fidel Castro had loved to fish at the *Laguna* and had added it to his list of prospective developments, intending to construct a Tahitian village in the middle of the swamp.

The new roads around Girón had to be avoided to prevent capture. The frogmen's plan was to walk one behind the other with Gregorio in the middle and follow their compass east northeast which would take them north of Cienfuegos and into the Escambray. They would travel at night, check their compass by pen light, and rest for ten minutes every hour. They would sleep during the day under cover of vegetation, taking turns at guard. Carrying penicillin and disposable syringes for the infection in Gregorio's wounds, they also brought along a first aid kit, K-rations, and canteens they had filled at an overworked well in the fading minutes of retreat from Girón. Of their weapons, they only kept their .45's and one Tommy gun, their intent now not to fight but to escape.

They moved in a serpentine fashion toward the Escambray because of the thick vegetation that greeted them, each man clearing a path for the one behind him. If they weren't fighting thorny limbs and vines with their hands, they were slapping at mosquitoes and other pests. Luis felt sorry for Gregorio who had only one hand to fight bushes and insects, but of all of them, Gregorio seemed to be holding up the best.

While the heavy morning fog gave some protection from the militia, it did nothing to dampen the spirits of the insects. Once the fog lifted, the sound of the helicopters looking for the invaders drowned out the whirring of the insects. The booming of artillery came from every direction as did the clacking of machine gun fire from the hovering choppers, all shooting at random as if to remind the fugitives there was no hope for their escape.

Unable to pinpoint their location, on the second day the group camped near an old road used for hauling timber and charcoal. They were certain every road and path were under heavy patrol. Just as the swamp was alive with insects and reptiles, so too it was with Castro's militia. Vultures joined the planes and choppers in the sky above. Maybe, thought Luis, they're the creatures in my dream working to peck their way through the walls of my flesh.

By Saturday, April 22, a greater problem than pressing forward faced the frogmen. They had exhausted their K-rations, but compared to their thirst, food was a mere afterthought. Why doesn't it rain? Luis asked himself on Sunday morning when he had gone several hours without water. He remembered the rainy season in the Sierra. How could one call this place a swamp when there was no water?

That same Sunday morning, they began a search for anything to drink or eat. Chiqui was the first to meet with success. Finding a small cactus, he cut it with a knife, shaved the thorns from the side, sucked on the severed end, and passed it to his comrades who did the same thing, reminding Luis of the communion service on Vieques. Again and again they sucked on the cactus, Chiqui finally dividing the remaining meat for them to chew and extract every drop of moisture they could. Not one of the frogmen even considered the juice might be toxic. Every action was risky, just as the whole operation had been.

At dawn on Monday, they continued to look for anything edible, pulling at bark from trees and turning up roots and rocks in the hope of finding something. They snatched up insects and chomped them in two, relishing the fluids as if they were delicacies. They chewed on roots and the stems of leaves, their mouths stained green and dark brown as if they had been grazing. If they could find a wild pig, they would take a chance and shoot it to have its blood to drink. To escape, they first had to survive.

Luis found the answer to his unspoken prayer under a decomposing stump. A black snake, or *majá,* coiled up with head erect, was curious about the disturbance around it. Like an eagle, Luis grabbed it and immediately severed its head, sucking the blood so as not to waste a drop. He returned to his comrades with the body of the snake still wiggling around his hand and arm. With José Enrique's help, he cut off equal lengths for their meal as if he were slicing salami. Each tore at his share, grinding the meat, and smacking his lips as if he had partaken of nature's finest meat. Only a few days earlier Luis would never have dreamed of doing what survival required of him now, yet this feast seemed like a primitive sacrament, prompting Luis to silently thank God for his generosity.

Chapter 46

In the early afternoon the fugitives heard the unmistakable sound of a locomotive.

"Let's move in that direction," José Enrique said. "Maybe we can follow the tracks at night."

At dusk, they came upon the train tracks and started to follow them. Further on, a charcoal oven or *horno de carbón* with its teepee-shaped top was giving off smoke. Nearby they spotted the thatched hut of the *carbonero*, which meant food and water were close by. Waiting for the cover of darkness, the men burst into the hut with their pistols drawn.

"Please don't kill me, *mercenarios*," pleaded a soot-faced old man whose wrinkles in the pale light of a kerosene lantern on a crude wooden table bespoke years of hardship. A startled youth, also soot-faced, suddenly appeared at the door that led into the other room. Desperate for water, the frogmen scarcely noticed him.

"Water!" cried José Enrique. "Get us some water."

From a wooden bucket, they dipped with tin cups the old man gave them, gulping, strangling, and then asking for more. While Gaspar accompanied the boy to refill the bucket from the well, José Enrique sought to calm the *carbonero*.

"Listen, old man," he said, " Keep quiet. We just want food and water. We won't harm you. We'll be out of here soon."

On one of the two shadowy shelves in the room, Luis spotted a chunk of coarse cheese and a large tin can of *galletas*. Quicker than he had sliced the snake that morning, Luis divided the cheese into five portions with his hunting knife and emptied the crackers on the table. The famished frogmen crammed the food in their mouths until their cheeks bulged, and they gulped the water Gaspar brought in to wash the semi-chewed balls of bread and cheese down their gullets. Gregorio, stricken by stomach spasms, vomited before he could run out of the door.

"What else do you have to eat?" Chiqui asked with his mouth full.

"Chickens ...a pig," the man said with a trembling voice.

"Kill a couple of chickens," ordered José Enrique, "and don't make any noise."

The frogmen were so ravenous for meat that they killed the chickens themselves, chopping off their heads with their knives in the moonlight as soon as the old man pulled them out of a coop behind the hut. At the same time, they lit two piles of charcoal, one for boiling water to use for plucking and the other for frying the chicken with pork lard in a skillet.

Before the chickens were fully cooked, the soldiers yanked them from the skillet and ate like hungry dogs, cracking the bones with their teeth, sucking the marrow, and then dropping the remains on the earthen floor.

After the restituting meal, the frogmen interrogated the *carbonero* to find out more about him and the boy, their location in the Zapata Swamp, and the proximity of the enemy. The old man's use of the word "*mercenarios*" indicated he was aware of the invasion. In response to their questions, he acknowledged that the militia had passed by searching for fugitives, but he had not seen other *mercenarios,* except some who had been captured and taken by train to the Covadonga Sugar Mill. From the *carbonero's* information, the frogmen figured they were some ten kilometers east of San Blas and about the same distance by rail from Covadonga.

José Enrique estimated they had travelled less than four kilometers and had over fifty kilometers to go before reaching the Escambray. That meant about two more weeks of walking. They were presently located in a long curve of a railroad track that went north to Covadonga and almost due east toward a lumber mill in the heart of the swamp. If they continued eastward, they would have relatively easy going for about three days. According to the old man, a few other *carboneros* lived along the tracks. The *carboneros,* he added, were rapidly decreasing in number since electricity had been brought into the swamp as a "gift" by Fidel.

My God! Luis thought angrily. Castro has already passed himself off as a kind of modern day Prometheus to these pour souls. He appreciated, however, the old man's courage in sticking by his supposed benefactor in front of his imagined enemies.

The presence of *carboneros* and the lumberyard meant the frogmen could resupply themselves along the tracks before going deeper into the swamp. The only problem they foresaw was that the tracks toward the east were dangerously close to the Cienfuegos beach road. Nonetheless, following them seemed like a risk worth taking. Certainly they could not head toward Covadonga and walk into the arms of the militia. Chiqui thought it might be best to stay fairly close to the Cienfuegos road, swim the channel south of the city of Cienfuegos, and enter the Escambray where the mountains approached the sea, cutting off several kilometers from their original plan.

They soon learned the soot-faced boy was the grandson of the *carbonero*. His mother had died three years earlier, and his father was in the militia fighting against the *mercenarios*. To the astonishment of the frogmen, the young boy proclaimed he would be fighting as well had he been allowed. As Chiqui and Gaspar went for another bucket of water to fill their canteens, Luis quizzed the self-righteous youth, Paquito, as amicably as he could.

"And how old are you?"

"Twelve."

"And your grade in school?"

"Third grade."

"How do you get to your school?"

"We don't have classes now because traitors like you and the Americans invaded our country. When I go to school, I ride the train into Covadonga. Before Fidel, I had no chance to go to school."

"How do you know the Americans invaded your country?" Luis asked, curious as to just where in the hell the Americans had come ashore.

"Because they landed at Girón and Playa Larga," Paquito asserted.

"Son," Luis replied wearily, "You're wrong. There are no Americans on our shores. Believe me, I know."

"The Americans have always been here. I saw pictures in a newspaper of dead Americans who had been shot down in their planes."

"Paquito," Luis said patiently in the pale light of the wretched hut. "Let me tell you the truth. The Americans have made a lot of mistakes in this country, but they have done a lot of good things too. You don't know both sides of the story."

"You're *mercenarios*," Paquito stated with an air of finality that gave Luis cold chills. Luis wanted to shake the boy to make him realize the Revolution and Fidel were not synonymous, but he refrained.

How ironic that he was arguing with a twelve-year-old kid in a primitive hut in the swamp in the middle of the night—he, who dreamed of being the prosecuting attorney at the trial of Fidel Castro. Paquito, though, was more than an adversary; he was a judge. Luis had returned to Cuba with his own face blackened, failed in his mission, and now was being convicted by a soot-covered child who passed sentence upon him, labelling him a "*mercenario*."

Luis turned to see his buddies come in from the well with a fresh bucket of water. Filling their canteens and reassuring the old man and his grandson they meant them no harm, the frogmen gave them fifty *pesos* and struck out to the east along the tracks. They intended to make as much time as possible in the swath cut by the tracks through the "Great Swamp of the Caribbean."

Chapter 47

Along the railroad the frogmen passed several *hornos de carbón* not far from the track, some giving off smoke which created a hellish effect in the moonlight. They knew children like Paquito often manned the charcoal ovens, and the feeling of being watched by invisible faces increased their apprehension whenever they spotted a smoking teepee.

Their clothes and shoes told the story of their ordeal. Their T-shirts and pants were torn by thorns and brush, and after a few kilometers on the tracks, their tennis shoes were full of holes. Blisters covered their swollen feet, and the chunky railroad gravel only made walking harder.

To add to his misery, Gregorio twisted his ankle on a large stone and limped as he held on to Luis so as not to slow down the progress of the others. The freshly wrapped gauze on Gregorio's head glistened in the moonlight. Thus, they made their way, fearful a dog would bark, a chicken or goose cackle, or worst of all, a militiaman yell, "Halt!"

When they went into the swamp some twenty-five meters off the railroad to spend the night, Luis volunteered to stand guard, reasoning he would rather be awake than have another nightmare. His exhausted body had other needs, and shortly after his comrades fell asleep, Luis could not distinguish between one world and another.

Once again dressed in his swimming suit and scuba gear, he was guarding the double-swinging doors at the Girón clubhouse, but this time he had a *majá* in his mouth instead of a snorkel. On the other side of the doors, smoking teepees held the fiends he was to guard. The same priest and the dog were still giving communion of black

271

fish to the wounded, and the frogs, less lively now, were still jumping toward the black eagles at the windows. Who was that priest? He had to know! Luis was blowing on the snake as hard as he could when he heard a voice from above him shout, "On your feet!"

That shrouded soul turned out to be no priest at all but a soldier who was wearing a beret like the prisoners at Girón. No longer an obedient acolyte, the dog transformed into a snarling beast lurching at the leash that held him. The fear of the dog and the rifles did not trouble Luis, but the horror that he could not awaken from this nightmare paralyzed his entire body.

All he had to do was wake up. The dog and all those smirking faces staring down at him out of the bush, including the washed face of Paquito, would be gone, as would the man that held him at gun point.

"I told you they were in here," the boy shouted, pointing to Luis." That one! He's their leader!"

"I can't believe that you *mercenarios* stole the old man's food last night," scowled a lieutenant with affected indignation.

With those words, the militia officer brought Luis back into the web of memory in which each scene had a place and time. In the early morning light, he awoke with the same physical agony he had known for days. Pain, like time, continued to delineate the defining line between the surreal and the discernible. Terror lurked in both, but only pain belonged to the real world of human senses.

"We knew you'd take good care of the old man," Gregorio said to the lieutenant with bitter sarcasm.

"*Sí*," replied the lieutenant, his face toughening and his smile vanishing. "We're the only ones who give a shit about poor people like the *carboneros*, and we're the only ones who've done anything to help them. *Vamos, mercenarios*, your time has come!"

Luis started to respond, but a sharp jab in the ribs with a rifle butt knocked the breath out of him.

"Shut up! Don't speak until you're spoken to!" shouted the lieutenant.

Their capture fittingly concluded an operation where nothing had gone right. It was final proof Luis was not meant to be a soldier. He had been told that by his father, who had tried to dissuade him from going to the mountains, and by Fidel Castro, who had banished him from the Sierra Maestra. Somewhere along the way, he should have listened to one of them instead of attempting to emulate his Recio ancestors. In any event, his military venture had now ended. So, too, he reasoned, would his life. It was only a matter of time.

Chapter 48

Trying to ignore the taunts of their captors, the frogmen were marched to a lumber mill in the Zapata Swamp and placed aboard a small cattle car behind an old steam engine. Soot covered the floor of the dilapidated railroad car which was used for hauling charcoal. Four no-nonsense militiamen guarded the prisoners with rifles cocked, ready to shoot. For over an hour, they waited at the lumber mill until the lieutenant signaled the engineer to move out.

After a few miles, the train stopped to pick up three more members of the Brigade who were in worse physical condition than the frogmen. The *milicianos* herded them into the train and harassed them, referring to them as *criminales mercenarios*. Further on, the train made another stop, and two more terrified prisoners were thrown on board. Demoralized and betrayed, the prisoners had to put up with a savage denunciation of the invasion. The railroad track had served as an illusory magnet to the lost, hungry, and defeated invaders whom the militia had been rounding up for days. Instead of a route to freedom, the railroad track had been a trap.

In Covadonga, the *milicianos* separated Gregorio from the others. "Don't worry," José Enrique said to him. "They're taking you to a hospital. You'll be fine!"

Milicianos with *metralletas*, cheap Czech machine guns, forced Luis and his friends into an open truck with fifteen other prisoners. Through the streets of Covadonga, people hurled abuse at the prisoners: *"Hijos de putas,"* *"mercenarios,"* "Lackies of the Yankees," *"latifundistas,"* *"Batistianos,"* "We'll kill you!" "We shit on you," and on and on.

To Luis' surprise, there was one comment directed solely at him. "What a shame that such a good looking *hombre* is going to end up before a firing squad," a teenage girl sarcastically lamented as she stared up at him.

In the spirit of Papá Bernabé, Luis responded purposely, "My dear *señorita*, I heartily agree. It's indeed a shame and a waste." He succeeded in making her laugh.

Their haughty captors transported them to Girón where the now familiar curses from the populace greeted them. Luis was convinced that had things turned out differently, the crowd would have shown the same outrage against Castro and his followers. The sight of the Girón jetty distressed Luis more than the vindictiveness of the people in Girón, for he was sure he would die before a firing squad in front of those rocks.

Around mid-morning, after being ordered to sit on the ground in front of the clubhouse, guards brought the prisoners water, *galletas*, guava paste, and an orange. Thinking this orange was his last, Luis savored every slice as the juice filled his mouth. He had heard stories of condemned men, who, moments before execution, noticed the full beauty of the sky or a field of grass for the first time. The orange brought him that same sense of appreciation.

When Luis had eaten, he noted a carnivalesque atmosphere prevailed throughout Girón, with prisoners as the main attraction. Anyone who wanted to could step up and spill his venom on the defeated. Reporters from Russia, China, and the Eastern Bloc countries moved through the confusion, taking pictures of the victorious militia and the vanquished Brigade. It would all play well behind the iron and bamboo curtains; for the communists, the Revolution had not merely defeated 1, 500 privileged Cubans but also the most powerful and imperialistic nation in the world. This was the beginning of the decline of western colonization; the U.S. was a paper tiger.

The prisoners' arrival at Girón was a perfect time to exploit their vulnerable psychological state and extract hostile accusations toward the U.S. from them. An attractive young reporter, learning the frogmen were among the prisoners, approached them and focused on Luis.

"You are one of the frogmen, I presume?" she asked.

"*Oui, mademoiselle*," said Luis, noticing her French accent.

"Do you feel any remorse for what you did in attacking a peaceful village?"

"Do you want the truth, or do you want me to say what you want to hear?" Luis asked.

Taken by surprise, the woman hesitated before responding, "The truth, of course."

"I didn't know because it's obvious the government brought all of you here," Luis retorted.

"I might be a Marxist, but that doesn't mean I don't want to hear other points of view. In France, we have a free press."

"Well, we didn't come here to fight against the Cuban people. We came to overthrow a communist regime," Luis replied with firm politeness as he restrained the other frogmen when they tried to enter the conversation.

"Aren't you a member of the old oligarchy?" she asked, taking notes.

"Yes, and I'm also a revolutionary," Luis answered.

"How can that be possible?" she inquired.

"Because I fought the Batista dictatorship in the underground and later in the mountains with Castro, and now I oppose the present totalitarian dictatorship."

"It seems to me you people came to Cuba with the help of Batista criminals to get back your properties."

"Not so, *mademoiselle*. While some members of the Brigade used to serve in Batista's armed forces, many of our leaders formerly supported Castro."

"Who are they?" she asked with pencil poised.

"For a start, our would-be president, José Miró Cardona, was Castro's hand-picked first Prime Minister," Luis began. "Our civilian leader in the Brigade, Manuel Artime, fought in the Sierra with Castro and became a regional director in the Agrarian Reform Institute. Both our first and second in command, San Román and Oliva, served in the army under Castro at the beginning of the Revolution. I could name many others. What further proof do you need that our cause is valid?"

"You sound like a lawyer," she said, grinning.

"I am, *mademoiselle*," Luis replied, "I was Undersecretary of Justice until I saw what a mockery had been made of justice in Cuba."

"Well, this is not quite what I expected," the reporter said with a nervous laugh, rolling her head slightly and hitting her thigh with her note pad.

"With all due respect, *mademoiselle*, you're not what I expected to find in Girón either."

Sizing him up and down, she smiled, and added, "*Bonne chance, monsieur*, I think you might be an exception here."

"*Merci, mademoiselle*," said Luis, "when this government topples, look me up in Havana if you're interested in talking about a democratic government."

"Maybe I will. What's your name?"

"Luis Recio, at your service," he answered with a smile.

Writing it down, she turned to wander among the prisoners.

The frogmen waited in the hot sun until noon when they were ordered with other prisoners to board a trailer truck. As guards called their names, they noticed the truck had no ventilation and a number of their comrades were already packed inside. By the time Luis and the other frogmen got within a few feet of the truck, it appeared to be almost full.

Still, the one in charge of the operation, none other than Osmani Cienfuegos, the Minister of Public Works, kept loading the prisoners while he ridiculed them unmercifully. Osmani was the brother of Camilo Cienfuegos who preceded Castro into Havana and gained fame for his easy manner and apparent love of freedom before his mysterious disappearance. Luis remembered Camilo's gesture of freeing the parrots from their cages at Camp Colombia, saying, "These also have a right to liberty!" Luis could not conceive of Camilo taunting prisoners as his brother was doing.

When Erneido Oliva's turn came to step up to the truck, an aide of Cienfuegos, one Fernández Vila, identified Oliva as the second in command. Oliva, like the frogmen, had been captured that morning.

"What do you have to say for yourself," Cienfuegos tersely asked Oliva.

"I'm only required to give name, rank, and serial number. My name is Erneido Oliva, I'm the second in command of Brigade 2506, and my serial number is 2641," Oliva replied in proper military fashion.

Hearing Oliva, Fernández Vila rebuked him for not cooperating. Oliva returned the fire as he had done throughout the battle, "Shut your mouth. I remember you as little more than a petty thief in the Agrarian Reform Institute."

"What *cojones* that man has!" José Enrique whispered to Luis, as the guards escorted Oliva away from the truck.

Cienfuegos kept loading prisoners on the truck even as Fernández Vila objected. "If we put any more in, they'll die," Fernández Vila insisted.

"Let them die!" shouted Cienfuegos. "I'll keep us from having to execute the bastards!"

When one of the *milicianos* called Luis' name, Cienfuegos recognized him immediately.

"Here we have another fucking traitor!" he exclaimed with disgust.

Sure he was going to be shot, Luis replied, "Osmani, you're the traitor. Your brother Camilo would turn over in his grave if he could see the direction this Revolution has taken."

"Don't you dare mention his name, you dog!"

"Your brother never mistreated prisoners, and neither did I when I was in the mountains with him. By the way, where were you while Camilo and I were in the Sierra?"

Osmani started to go for his gun when Fernández Vila stopped him and forced Luis and the other frogmen in the truck. The prisoners were packed like sardines. Some in the front of the truck had already been inside for an hour and a half. "No more!" they cried. "There's no more room!"

Cursing, Osmani forced a few more in. When the side doors were closed and locked, total darkness engulfed the captives.

The men started to beat furiously on the walls and tear off their clothes in the unbearable heat. Some shrieked and screamed, "No air! No air! We can't breathe!" When the truck started to move, they rocked it from side to side in a desperate effort to overturn it so air could get in.

While some begged for calm, others near the walls clawed on the plywood interior with their fingernails and belt buckles. After ripping away the plywood, they succeeded in puncturing the metal where a few tiny rust spots had formed and showed a speck of light and a place to gouge so that life-giving air could reach them. Eventually, the desperate captives opened two holes in the metal, one toward the front about a foot long and six inches wide, the other further back and much smaller.

To those wedged in the middle and far corners of the truck, the light streaming in the openings seemed like faraway suns; the dots where the wood had been ripped away and where rust had eaten through the metal were like faint stars. In spite of the small openings, it was still an untenable situation. Those who were most panicked soon fainted and slid to the floor. It was important to remain calm even calmness did not guarantee survival.

When someone passed out, others pulled him to one of the air holes until he regained consciousness. Sometimes it was too late. After a few hours, the only words spoken came in moments of panic, "He's down. *Pronto*! Get him to the hole!"

Luis had always heard war was hell, but war was nothing compared to this. Gasping for air, he thought maybe this was his end. At this moment, his fate was of no consequence. Paquito had pronounced him guilty, and Osmani Cienfuegos had passed the sentence, throwing him into this hell on wheels. "This is the end. *Dios mío*, Giver of Life, please forgive me for all my sins," Luis muttered as he faded into unconsciousness.

The next thing Luis remembered was someone tugging at him in the awful darkness.

"Luis! Luis! Wake up! Help me get this man to a hole!"

When he came back into the world of sweaty bodies in a bouncing truck, Luis Recio felt the air from a lighted opening, and a voice was telling him to breathe. After Luis had been sufficiently revived, another prisoner was passed to the hole.

The prisoners could judge the coming of darkness outside by the gradual fading of light through the air holes, but those on the sides kept the precious vents identified for those falling to the floor. With the setting of the sun, another amazing thing happened. It "rained" inside the truck, and around their feet they could feel the accumulation of water which sloshed from back to front and side to side whenever the truck stopped or turned. Human sweat and urine had evaporated in the heat, condensed, and now fell upon the bodies. Though the salt had been separated by evaporation, the men dared not open their mouths to the "rain" since it reeked of the foul smell of urine and defecation.

An eternity later, the truck came to a stop, and as they had at the beginning, the men began to scream, stomp desperately, and pound the walls. Voices outside told them they would never get out unless the shouting stopped. When, after another eternity of silence, the doors opened, water ran out on both sides like a waterfall. Men fell out in the same way, the living and the dead together tumbling over each other, their faces ashen and yellow in the battery of lights of their conquerors, their bodies dehydrated but drenched from the foul moisture that fell over them. As Luis gasped, he gave thanks to God for the simple gift of fresh air. Fidel Castro, the Revolution, and all other human enterprises seem trivial in comparison. I can now bear anything, he thought.

When the prisoners were ordered to line up, Luis saw several lifeless bodies being removed from the truck and placed on the ground. Their bodies had contorted into unimaginable postures, some doubled up as if they had died of stomach cramps, others as if their last motion had been a capriole in a death dance. They reminded Luis of frozen corpses he had seen in pictures of the Russian front in World War II. It was the phenomenon of *rigor mortis*. The torn clothes on their twisted bodies were wringing wet, making plain their final ordeal had been in a battle not with ice but with heat. Looking at them in the dim light of the street, Luis wondered if one of those cadavers on the ground was the man who helped him get to the sacred breathing hole, called him by name, and told him to breathe.

Chapter 49

When Luis looked up from the grotesque scene of the stiff and twisted bodies beside the truck, he noticed the number on its side--thirteen! How uncanny could things be? Looking around, he realized they were in front of the Sports Palace in Havana where he had seen so many exciting athletic events as a young boy. It was a huge, circular, indoor arena built during the administration of Carlos Prío, became the pride of sporting aficionados in Cuba.

The guards marched Luis and the other survivors into the center of the arena and ordered them to take a seat in the stands with the rest of the Brigade. Luis learned through whispered conversation that most of them had been in the Palace for several days, sitting on the same hard seats for twenty-one hours a day, permitted only to go to the bathroom. Selected prisoners had been taken in front of television cameras and interviewed to get them to confess and to apologize for their crimes. Castro's government had cleverly orchestrated the spectacle.

Armando Vega, one of Luis' friends from Camagüey who had also been on the truck, sat on the row in front of Luis, a few seats to the left. Luis was apprehensive when one of the militia came over and took Armando away. After a short while, Armando returned unharmed. Luis was curious to find out what had happened to his friend.

Around 11:30 p.m., Fidel Castro made an appearance in the Sports Palace. Taking center stage in his green fatigues, he put on a masterful show for the millions watching television and listening to the radio. The timing could not have been better to discredit the demoralized Brigade. Tired, dirty, unshaven, and bewildered, they sat as errant children before their omnipotent father. Some had already cooperated by writing letters to U. Thant, the Secretary General of the United Nations, condemning President Kennedy for the attack against the people of Cuba. A few Brigade members made tape-recorded statements describing American involvement in the invasion.

It was Castro's finest hour, more glorious than his triumphant entry into Havana following the overthrow of Batista. Then the rebel army had only deposed a Caribbean tyrant; now it had defeated the most powerful nation in the world. American complicity was undeniable as was the valor of the Cuban militia who had risen magnificently to the occasion.

"We have every reason to kill all the invaders, but the Revolution is going to be kind," Castro intoned. "Except for those who have committed crimes under the Batista regime, I'll spare the lives of you *mercenarios.*"

Castro continued to exploit the demoralized and exhausted prisoners. On one hand they feared for their lives and were grateful for the magnanimity of the conqueror; on the other, they still felt a loyalty to their cause in spite of their abandonment by the United States.

In an informal question and answer session, Castro emphasized that for the first time in history, the defeated were given the chance to publicly discuss their grievances. Seeing Tomás Cruz, a black prisoner in the stands, Fidel asked him, "Why did you fight against a revolution that has liberated the blacks and provided you equal opportunity, even in private clubs?"

Cruz, a paratrooper, gave Castro an answer that took him by surprise, "I don't have an inferiority complex about my race. I've always been a brother to white people, and I didn't come to Cuba to go swimming in a private club."

Others were equally bold. Carlos Onetti asked Castro if he was a communist. Castro replied he was a socialist and began a long lecture on the merits of socialism. As Luis listened to the rambling monologue, he wished Castro had been honest enough to admit the vast difference between totalitarian communism and social democracy.

After Castro's speaking marathon, the prisoners were ordered to the concrete floor of the arena for a few hours of sleep on the mattresses provided to them. As Luis was moving toward a space that would allow him to talk to Armando Vega, a captain called Luis' name and led him to a well-furnished office on the second floor of the palace. After the captain left, Luis heard a commotion in the hallway. A moment later, Fidel Castro strode into the room and closed the door. Taking a seat behind a large mahogany desk, he offered Luis one of the soft leather chairs.

"Luis, you look awful," Castro commented as Luis sat down. "You must be tired. How have you been treated?"

Luis answered sarcastically. "We've been treated so well ten prisoners died in our trailer truck."

"That was a stupid accident," Castro replied defensively.

"I heard Osmani Cienfuegos say that if everybody died, it would save the bullets needed to kill us."

"Osmani is a hot-blooded cretin," Fidel said. "You know from your own experience in the mountains how I took pains to be decent to the prisoners. But what Osmani did is nothing compared to what you and your cohorts did to Cuba."

"What we did was a direct result of your betrayal of the Revolution," Luis responded curtly, realizing he had nothing to lose.

"You know, Luis," Castro began calmly, thumping his ashes in a tray, "let me tell you a little story. As Che Guevara and I were looking at all of you earlier tonight, I referred to you as sons of whores and you know what Che said? '*Coño!* There before you is the cream of the crop of Cuba. With men like them we could conquer all of Central and South America.' And you know, I believe Che is right. It's such a tragedy that all of us couldn't pull together."

The direction the conversation was taking puzzled Luis. Here is a man I know to be vindictive, he thought, yet he is sparing our lives, even complimenting us. Why has he singled me out to hear these things since I know he has hated me from the beginning. What is his motive?

"Fidel, you, Che, and Camilo were like gods to some of us at the beginning. You had a wonderful opportunity to build a new Cuba--a just and prosperous Cuba. Instead, you chose to align yourself with Russia, a country which never had anything in common with us."

"It's interesting that you criticize the Soviets, who have never put any conditions on their aid, when all the Americans ever did was to exploit our resources," Castro commented, leaning back in his chair and tapping the ashes of his cigar into a tray.

Luis, knowing the argument would lead nowhere, purposely remained silent, giving Castro the opportunity to continue.

"Of course, I'm not surprised you, as a citizen of the United States, chose to defend its imperialistic policies."

Luis wondered how Castro knew he had been born in the U.S. since Luis had not mentioned that fact in the mountains.

"I gave up my U.S. citizenship when I turned twenty-one," Luis said.

"Then you're a man without a country, aren't you?" Castro laughed, rocking in the swivel chair.

"Yes, but I've only been aware of that since you took over Cuba."

"*Carajo*, Recio! No matter how nice I try to be to you, you always manage to anger me," Castro shouted, pounding the desk. "The only reason you're alive is because we're holding you as ransom. If the Americans dare to land, you're all going to be killed."

Aha! Luis thought, as excitement shot through his body. The Americans are not out of this yet! Perhaps Kennedy will come through after all!

"Furthermore," added Castro, "all your fellow conspirators in Cuba have been taken prisoner or executed. Your sweet Ofelia is now in prison. Recio, I blame you for her fate. You and others are responsible for the sorrow that has descended on this island. You typify everything that was wrong with old Cuba. You weren't born in this country. You're a member of the oligarchy, you were educated in the U.S., and you're a playboy with no interest in the poor . . ."

Castro continued his tirade, but Luis scarcely heard him after hearing the news of Ofelia. What Luis most feared had come true. He had blamed himself for recruiting Ofelia and others, but it was worse to hear Fidel Castro make the same accusations. Luis struck back in a rage.

"You're such a bastard, Fidel! You're a communist because communism is the only way for you to perpetuate yourself in power. You care nothing about the ideals of Marx. You're a slave to your ego. You asked tonight how many of us had cut sugar cane with our hands, and when only one raised his hand, you decided we were oligarchs.

You and I know damn well you hadn't cut cane until you took power, and then you did so only for propaganda purposes. You've ruined Cuba and wrecked all our lives. Go ahead. Shoot me. Get it over with!"

Leaning forward in his chair with the blood drained from his face, Castro threatened, "You've given me an excellent idea! Maybe I'll do the same thing to you that we did to Jorge León, who will never be your brother-in-law and who sang like a canary before going to the *paredón*."

"If he sang like a canary, it was because you tortured him like Batista's henchmen tortured our *compañeros* in the underground. You're no better than Batista!" Luis shouted, glaring at Castro.

Rising violently from his seat and slinging ashes across the desk, Castro left the room cursing and slammed the door as he stormed out of the room. Immediately, a captain appeared and ushered Luis toward the arena. Seeing all of the mattresses taken, Luis lay on the floor staring at the high ceiling, his thoughts on the fate of Jorge León and Ofelia Ramos. If he lived, some day he would free her.

On his second night, Luis moved next to Armando and learned the reason for his exit from the palace. When Armando got out of the truck, the guards spotted him pointing to the dead that lay on the ground and heard him naming some of them. As a result, they ordered him to identify the victims. Among them were three men Luis knew well, two former members of the HYC, José Ignacio Maciá and Cuco Cervantes, and one whom he had known in school, René Silva.

Armando also informed him that the life-saving holes in the truck had been made by two people who had belt buckles, Armando and a black officer named Tamayo. Armando had made the bigger hole near the front and Tamayo the one toward the rear. Perhaps Tamayo was the one who had brought Luis to the hole. A militiaman told Armando there had been some 150 prisoners in the truck.

Lying on his back on the thin and dirty mattress, Luis squinted at the firmament of bright lights that covered the roof of the Sports Palace and contrasted the brilliant rays with the dark moisture inside the truck. When he looked around the room, his sleeping comrades seemed like a sea of corpses. Luis shuddered. This, he thought, is hell on earth.

Chapter 50

After Castro's speech in the Sports Palace on April 26, members of the Brigade settled into a miserable routine. With the exception of their few hours of sleep on the mattresses, they were forced to sit all day. The guards strictly controlled visits to the latrine even after dysentery spread throughout the ranks. Rumors held that the thirty-weight motor oil used to cook the rice they ate caused the dysentery. The only advantage of the intestinal infection, Luis concluded, was that if he could convince the guard he needed to go to the toilet, he could also stretch his legs.

A voice on the loud speaker, monotonously calling out the names of prisoners for interrogation, punctuated the routine. When Luis' time came to go to the table, he gave only name, rank, and serial number, and refused to answer any questions about his family's wealth and possessions. "We already know all about you, Recio. If you refuse to cooperate, you'll find yourself in front of the *paredón*," said an interrogator in an attempt to intimidate Luis.

Luis stared straight ahead, absolutely silent. When he went back to his seat, he felt he had won at least one small battle in a lost war. Others in the Brigade might not need redemption, but he did.

Several days later one of the guards summoned Luis. As he went up to the second floor, Luis wondered if he was about to pay the price for his defiance. As he waited in the same office where he and Fidel had clashed, the door suddenly opened, and the familiar voice of Major Miguel Ochoa shook the walls, "Let me talk to the bastard alone!"

Closing the door behind him, Ochoa started to denounce Luis and the Brigade loud enough to be heard in the corridor, but as Ochoa shouted, he indicated to Luis with his finger in front of his mouth that the expressions of outrage were for the benefit of the guards outside. Siding up to Luis, he whispered rapidly, "Luis, you really angered Fidel. All of you are alive by chance. Those who were captured the first twenty-four hours were taken to Camp Columbia and returned the next day to Girón. Fidel planned to make it appear as if they were killed in combat.

"A few of us talked him out of it with the argument that all of you could be held as hostages. Later, there were too many of you to dispose of. I know some of you are marked, and you may be one of them. Your case could go either way. He has already executed Sorí Marín while his mother futilely pleaded for his life. He has also killed a number of your friends: Rogelio González Corso, Ñongo Puig, and Plinio Prieto in the Escambray. Also, I hate to tell you, Jorge León."

"I knew about Jorge already from Fidel, but I didn't know about the others," Luis answered sadly.

"I'm sorry, Luis. It's been a blood bath. I'm so disgusted by the whole ordeal that I'm already in touch with the CIA. They want me to stay on and get all the information I can. As bad as your situation is, I'd change places with you. Alberto Sánchez wants you to know he feels the same way."

"Is there a chance the Americans will try to rescue us?" Luis asked.

"Perhaps. Fidel's paranoid about the possibility. It's this fear that's saving your life. Even many of his closest followers are waiting to see what transpires. Whatever you do, keep a low profile."

One more time he roared: "The Revolution is trying to be generous with you pigs, but our patience has limits!"

Ochoa left the room indignantly, his curses audible as he walked away.

The good news of Alberto's and Miguel's change of heart did little for Luis considering the death of his other friends. It seemed as if Fidel Castro was going to kill, imprison, or ruin the lives of everyone Luis knew.

With each dragging day, the *brigadistas* slowly recovered from the humiliation of defeat. When it became clear they were not going to be executed, their sense of failure began to diminish. They assumed the Americans had played a role in restraining Castro's vindictiveness, even at a distance. They knew their fate was more fortunate than that of those in the underground who had been arrested and shot before the landing. They knew, too, their food had gotten better without any obvious reason, though they still had to endure the filth of their clothes and bodies. Luis heard through the grapevine that in the first days of capture, some of the prisoners had been forced to eat rice off the floor with their hands tied behind them while the sadistic guards ordered them "to eat like the dogs they were." Now the food was bearable--rice, kidney and garbanzo beans, cabbage, and occasionally, meatballs.

There was a spirit of camaraderie and more than a touch of pride in the effort the prisoners had made. A renewed sense of humor, centering on their lack of hygiene, irregular body functions, and tales of combat dominated their conversations.

The insults of their handlers ceased to bother them as much as they had at the beginning, and they could even see comedy in the extravagant efforts to humiliate them. Two weeks after their capture, a serious militiawoman in Russian boots and dark olive pants and blue shirt walked among them passing out yellow T-shirts and chiding, "Yellow, yellow, yellow." Her words signified the supposed cowardice of the members of the Brigade since Fidel had publicly referred to them as *gusanos* or yellow worms. To her surprise, a few answered back, saying "Red, red, red," like chirping chickens.

With the T-shirts came one towel for every ten men, and with the towel a shower, their first since capture. Depriving the prisoners of a bath was a psychological torture since Cubans, like the Japanese, are notoriously clean. Once the prisoners had showered and put on clean yellow T-shirts, they felt rejuvenated and even playful, telling the guards the yellow worms were ready to dine on "The Horse."

A culminating moment of pride came on May 4 with the surprise arrival of Erneido Oliva and six others of the Brigade headquarters staff. When Oliva entered the arena, the whole Brigade stood to honor him and gave him a thunderous ovation. This unexpected show of respect and solidarity forced the *milicianos* to separate Oliva from the rest of the Brigade. The last thing they wanted was for the head and body of the foe to be united again.

With the news of Ofelia's imprisonment and the death of his friends, Luis was consumed with sorrow and guilt. He found consolation in memories of his carefree childhood in Camagüey and Havana. He also frequently thought about his family and his underground and war experiences. No matter what strand in the web of memory he traced, the pictures in his mind always returned to Ofelia Ramos.

Not only would he free Ofelia, but he hoped to marry her. His love for Ofelia had taught him to abandon his class prejudice, something the idealism of the Revolution had failed to accomplish. When he went to the Sierra, Luis had been in some ways as insensitive as when he was a teenager, unconsciously echoing traditional views on the separation of classes. Liberating her and marrying her would make his own life finally complete, regardless of what happened to Cuba.

Ofelia Ramos became the center of his daytime musings and his nightly dreams in which he came to her rescue. He recalled how the topic of dream premonitions had come up in conversation one night among peasant soldiers in the mountains. Che Guevara ridiculed the idea, insisting that such folklore belonged to the age of myth, not to a new era where logic prevailed over superstition. Anticipatory dreams, Che emphasized, were the first cousin of religious mysticism in which he placed no stock. Dismissing anything inexplicable or mysterious and crowding everything into the narrow box of reason was one of many places where the Revolution and communism had gone wrong. Luis would never dismiss any emotional notion because it was not logical. After all, who in this crazy world could claim to be absolutely logical? Obviously only a tyrant, the most illogical of all.

Chapter 51

In the middle of the night on May 13, 1961, buses transferred the Brigade to the Naval Hospital overlooking the northeast coast of Havana. The hospital, a five-story building of modern design was new and unused; the rooms were bright and clean, each with a bathroom. Each room accommodated twenty prisoners, and each man was given a thin mattress and a pillow. If they so desired, the prisoners could sleep all day long.

For the first time in weeks, the detainees had access to a real bathroom and a private shower. The food, although basically the same diet and portions as in the Sports Palace, improved considerably in quality. Thankfully, the dysentery epidemic was soon brought under control since the physicians of the Brigade had medicine at their disposal to treat it. The doctors also had ample office space to attend to those with minor wounds. Gregorio, who had been transferred from the hospital at Camp Columbia, continued to receive treatment there.

The other frogmen had not seen Gregorio except from a distance at the Sports Palace, and they were relieved to know he was recuperating. The doctors at Camp Columbia who had placed his arm in a cast said he would need an operation sooner or later, but for now he did not complain of pain. Though Gregorio stayed in rooms with the wounded, he and his friends were able to see one another on occasion.

It soon became clear why the prisoners had been moved to the "Hilton" of Cuban prisons. On May 18, Fidel visited the hospital with the news that he was proposing to exchange the Brigade for American-made tractors. In a briefing with San Román and the other leaders, Castro revealed, "I'm going to send a commission of prisoners to the U.S. to negotiate the details of the proposal. The Brigade can elect their representatives, but San Román, Oliva, and Artime cannot be a part of the commission. The Revolution is being generous to all of you since you really are victims, mere pawns of the Americans who are to blame for the blotched attempt at my overthrow. The Americans must pay for their crime against the Cuban people!" As always in front of an audience, Castro orchestrated his words to paint himself as the soul of generosity.

The Brigade rejoiced. Only a few days earlier, they had faced the prospect of a firing squad or long-term prison sentences at best. Now, by one decree from "The Horse," they would be free, presuming the Americans would negotiate. The Brigade was certain the Americans would not let them down a second time. Perhaps, their ordeal would soon be over.

Luis, although more skeptical of Castro than the others, shared in the euphoria of the moment. He could soon be in a position to work for Ofelia's release. The thought of freedom inspired him to renew the fight against the tyrant who now imprisoned him.

Castro had been straightforward in stating his intentions for acquiring tractors, but he was duplicitous in the manner in which he expressed himself before the Brigade. The other side of "the great chameleon" surfaced in his statements on the subject the night before, which Luis discovered while reading a copy of *Revolución* one of the guards gave to some of the prisoners. Addressing the National Association of Small Farmers, Castro referred to the prisoners again as *gusanos*. If the imperialists did not want their "worms" to rot in prison, then they could send tractors in exchange. So, Luis thought, we lowly yellow worms are going to be traded for state-of-the-art yellow Caterpillars.

The day following Castro's tractor announcement, the prisoners were allowed to write relatives in the United States. In a long letter to his family, Luis described the Battle of Girón and what transpired afterwards, sparing them the gross details. He assured them about his well-being and expressed confidence in the tractor deal. He looked forward to his relatives' first visit in a couple of weeks. He also mentioned he had read about Yuri Gagarin's flight around the world on April 12. To the guards, Gagarin's orbit symbolized Russia's ascendancy as a world leader, just as the Battle of Girón signified the collapse of the United States. He devoted the last part of his letter to Isabel in her bereavement and requested recent pictures of everybody, especially of Luisito.

One morning during the last week of May, the prisoners heard a loud noise outside the Naval Hospital. When they looked out, a crowd was cheering and singing the Cuban national anthem. As the visits of relatives began, Luis wondered who among his family members remaining in Cuba would come. Some of the Heymanns probably still lived in Havana; however, the rest of the members of his family, the Recios and the de Varonas, were in Camagüey, and many of them had already fled the country.

Since the visits were organized alphabetically, Luis' turn to receive relatives came late in the week. When he entered the visiting room on the first floor, Luis saw three familiar faces sitting behind the table assigned to him: Uncle Pedro Heymann, Octavio, the family butler, and Olga Loynaz. He was thrilled to see them because they would now be able to confirm for his parents that he was in good health.

"Cousin Luis," said Olga, giving him a tight embrace. Tears welled up in her eyes as she smiled at him.

His Uncle Pedro did not say a word at first but smiled and opened his long arms for an extended and silent *abrazo*. "I'm so glad you made it, Luis," he said tenderly as they stepped back to look at each other.

Octavio first extended a hand and then ended up in Luis' arms, patting him lovingly on the back. "*Señorito* Luis, I'm so happy to see you." Luis had known Octavio all of his life; Octavio had called him "*Señorito* Luis" since Luis was a small child, which made his friends in Havana laugh at this archaic custom.

Tears of joy and excited conversation filled every corner of the room. Even the sour-faced *milicianos* guarding the room showed some hint of emotion at the jubilant reunions. Octavio and Olga brought bags with a few delicacies still available in Havana at that time, as well as razor blades, soap, toothpaste, underwear, and a towel. Pedro filled his bag with several paperback books in English and also a two-volume Spanish edition of *Don Quixote*. Looking at these presents, Luis was moved by his family's thoughtfulness. If there was anything redeeming in all that he had endured, it was the deep appreciation Luis now felt for all those things he once had taken for granted.

Luis learned from his uncle that Isabel was coping with Jorge León's death as well as could be expected and that his parents were in good health. María Luisa, Pedro said, went to the Church of the Sacred Heart in Miami every day to pray and to light candles for him. From Olga he learned Senator Miranda, though deprived of all his business enterprises, refused to leave the country because he believed Castro's end was near. Octavio informed Luis that the government had confiscated the Recio home immediately after the Battle of Girón and that Senator Miranda had been kind enough to give him a place to stay until he could join the Recios in Coral Gables.

While listening to all of them, Luis came to a clearer understanding of this dreadful moment in Cuba's history. After the first air strike, the government rounded up hundreds of thousands of people all over Cuba in baseball stadiums, theaters, and large public buildings. They had been held, interrogated, and released only after the defeat of the invaders was certain. Hundreds had been executed and thousands imprisoned. Castro's supporters had been in a state of near panic before and during the invasion, but now they had become arrogant and abusive toward anyone suspected of being a counterrevolutionary.

"Everyone here today is a marked person," Pedro confided. "I've been told Jacinto and I will have to turn over our jewelry store to the government within a month. Herminia and her family left last December for the States. Jacinto and I are preparing for departure. I believe our exile will be temporary because the United States will never permit a communist regime ninety miles from its coast."

In a low-toned discussion of the Battle of Girón, Luis heard a theory as to why the invasion failed for the first time. According to a letter from Rogerio, Pedro said, Kennedy had backed down in the face of the Russian threat because of his fear of a counter invasion in some area of Europe or even the beginning of an atomic war. Rogerio also believed that Kennedy was too green and naive a president to deal with the communists. Kennedy's tough rhetoric won him the presidency, but, in retrospect, Nixon's election would have better served the Cubans. Luis now understood the ramifications of the invasion; a small war in a tiny country could bring the world to the edge of disaster.

When Luis turned to leave, he realized how anachronistic all of them were--a faithful butler, a successful family jeweler, a decadent socialite and he, a crazy idealist. How appropriate that Pedro had included *Don Quixote* among the books, recommending with a smile that Luis read it first.

On June 23, the prisoners' representatives made a second trip to the United States. They aimed to salvage the faltering negotiations, and again the Brigade was permitted to send letters to relatives. Luis took advantage of the occasion to tell his parents how happy he had been to see his Uncle Pedro, Olga Loynaz de Miranda, and Octavio. He hoped his father could expedite Octavio's move to the U.S. He included details of the June 13 visit of a U. S. agricultural delegation to the Naval Hospital in connection with the tractor exchange, a sign he interpreted as progress toward their release.

In spite of the brave front he maintained for his family in his letter, Luis, like most of the Brigade, alternated between moments of hope and depression, depending upon rumors of their freedom. As the days crept by with no breakthrough on the negotiations, Luis was more and more inclined toward skepticism about an early release. The test occurred at 3:00 a.m. on the morning of July 17 when the guards suddenly awakened the prisoners and ordered them to get dressed and to assemble for a move. Was the move to Miami or to another prison?

The men soon discovered the buses hauling them were not destined for the airport nor the docks. Exactly where they were going did not become clear until they began to go up a hill in the center of Havana. Ahead of them, the infamous Príncipe Castle towered over the city in the Caribbean moonlight. If the Naval Hospital was "the Hilton" of Cuban prisons, then the Príncipe Castle, based upon its reputation, was "the Chamber of Horrors."

Chapter 52

Because of its size and location, the Príncipe Castle, a Spanish fort built in the last quarter of the eighteenth century on the highest hill in Havana, had been converted into a prison over the years. Its meter-thick stone walls and surrounding moat with vertical walls some fifteen meters high made the Príncipe virtually escape-proof.

Intimidating guards hurried the prisoners from their buses across a drawbridge over the moat and through a huge portcullis leading to an open courtyard. Luis' group was the last to get off of the buses, and their captors herded them down a ramp leading into the bowels of the castle. Finally, the prisoners arrived at a huge dungeon called *La Leonera* or "The Lion's Den." All along the way, the guards cursed and poked them with bayonets. Barking dogs, roaming the wet, stone corridors, joined in the chorus of insults.

"The Lion's Den" was a square-shaped dungeon divided into four galleries, each facing a passageway and separated from it by iron bars. Each gallery had a door of bars that stayed open so the prisoners from the adjacent gallery could mingle. A brown stone wall divided the two galleries on each side of the passageway. From the seven-meter high stone ceiling hung several dim electric bulbs that cast only enough light to reveal a dismal scene reminiscent of the most horrific prisons in storybooks. As he looked about him, Luis recalled the descriptions in Dumas' *Count of Monte Cristo*. Only the light bulbs and faucets for two stone sinks bespoke the twentieth century.

The heat and humidity, the crowded bodies, and the moisture dripping from the shadowy ceiling brought back terrible memories of the squalor of the truck. As Luis lay in one of the dirty bunks closely stacked along the walls, he was conscious of the same sinking feeling of absurdity he had experienced about the jetty at Girón. How suddenly one's fate could change! Two hours ago the prisoners thought they could well be on their way to freedom. Now they were in the depths of a dreadful world, chained once more to a wall of rock.

Later, the guards came into the passageway with bags of the prisoners' belongings on carts and proceeded to taunt them by taking out items, such as toothbrushes, and mockingly asking, "Whose is this?" Then, laughingly, they turned the contents of all the bags upside down and spilled them on the floor of the cells. The spectacle of the Brigade scrambling for toilet articles, scattered photographs, broken jars of food, and books sickened Luis.

As in the Sports Palace, the lights stayed on all the time. The small, barred windows near the ceiling that opened on the lower part of the moat provided little ventilation and less light during the day. Since the *milicianos* at Girón had stolen their watches, the prisoners had to rely on the tiny vents and meal times to differentiate between day and night. A few had received watches from relatives on the first visit at the Naval Hospital and found themselves continually giving the time to those around them.

The meals, which the guards delivered in the hallway in 55-gallon drums, came at 6:30 a.m., 11:30 a.m., and 4:30 p.m. and were served on tin plates by designated members of the Brigade. The prisoners used the tin spoons and cups they had been given at the Sports Palace and which they had to pick up from the floor in the hall after the guards dumped their bags. At the Príncipe the food was much worse than it was at the Naval Hospital. In the morning, they drank *café con leche* and ate foul tasting-brown bread. For lunch, they usually had rice and red beans and occasionally a couple of chunks of canned beef. At night, they were given boiled pasta or rice and beans again. A few times, they were treated to yellow grits and bananas. The food was only seasoned with salt, and most of the homemade treats relatives brought to the hospital had been plundered by the guards or trampled in the melee after they had dumped the bags on the floor.

The prisoners passed the long, tedious days reading and playing cards they made from cardboard and chess with pieces made from cigar boxes. In one of the galleries, a prisoner named Carón, who had been a professional percussion player, soon formed a combo and fashioned the instruments from pieces of metal and wood salvaged from the items strewn on the floor by the guards on the first night. The daily "concerts "provided moments of comic relief as the prisoners improvised conga dances in *La Leonera*. With ample time on their hands, the prisoners began to share their combat experiences, and Luis often had to control his laughter at some of the exaggerated tales.

Many of the stories he heard made a lasting impression on him. His friend, Carlos Onetti, who had confronted Castro publicly at the Sports Palace, had been a paratrooper. When his chute got stuck in a tree, he was one of the first prisoners to be captured during the landing. During his interrogation, he told his captors he was one of a thousand paratroopers who had landed north of Girón, a ploy that delayed Castro's counteroffensive for several hours since the commander interrogating Onetti believed him instead of another paratrooper who told him truthfully that he was one of nineteen men who had stalled the advance of a column. The commander did not believe nineteen men could have held that position for an entire day.

The funniest incident, however, happened to a chubby, jolly fellow by the name of Jácome. After escaping from Girón and making it through the Zapata Swamp, peasants took him in and helped him get all the way back to Santa Clara where he stayed with relatives for a few days to let things cool down. He then took a bus to Havana to try to get into one of the embassies to ask for asylum, but while on the bus, he made the mistake of offering a piece of Wrigley's chewing gum to a civilian sitting next to him. Unfortunately, the civilian turned out to be a militiaman who proceeded to arrest him on the spot since no one in Cuba had seen Wrigley's for years. Jácome embellished the tale of his own misfortune, which always brought gales of laughter among his listeners. Jácome's motto became, "Never offer gum to a stranger."

Tony Zamora told the most pathetic story. He had been able to get into one of the ill-fated plastic boats whose motors had never run and drifted from one small island to another for days. A merchant ship, spotting him, sailed close to his boat. The crew on the bridge of the ship which had stopped dead in the water observed Tony in his camouflaged uniform for about a half-hour. Then without a word, it sailed out of sight. It was, Tony speculated, a ship from a

Central American country that did not want to become involved in an international incident. Four days later, he was captured while sleeping on a tiny island near the Isle of Pines. Luis heard story after story of people who, like the frogmen, had eaten insects, snakes, birds, bark, and leaves in the swamp in order to survive. From that perspective, the prison was a haven with its regular meals and plenty of water.

Some of the prisoners from Oriente Province had been friends with Fidel during his youth and were full of tales about his early wildness. That he now championed the cause of blacks in Cuba puzzled them since Fidel and other teenagers had on more than one occasion stuffed rock salt into shotgun shells and fired at the Haitians workers at Ángel Castro's farm, *Manacas*.

All of these stories, regardless of their veracity, helped to make their life more bearable.

Relatives' visits at Príncipe Castle started the first week in August. In addition to seeing family, the Brigade would get an opportunity to get outside of the dungeon for the first time, breathe fresh air, and see the sun. From *La Leonera*, guards marched the captives single file up the ramp to the courtyard where they were stripped and searched. After dressing again, they walked single file through the portcullis, over the drawbridge, and down a stairway on the other side of the moat. As he descended, Luis could see a huge crowd below him in the empty moat, all women and children, and while looking for someone he knew, he heard a familiar voice call his name. It was Olga Loynaz.

"Cousin Luis," she said teasingly, looking up at him. "Come here and give your cousin a big hug."

Luis could not keep from chuckling at the daring playfulness of this exquisite woman. He hugged her in a prolonged embrace. Oh my, he thought to himself, I had almost forgotten how wonderful it feels to have a woman in my arms. While they were embracing, Luis felt a tap on his shoulder, and when he turned, there stood Aunt Ángela, Pedro's wife.

"Luis, it is so good to see you. Give me a big *abrazo*."

Luis opened his arms to his favorite aunt, and while they held each other, she explained, "Pedro wanted to come, but the government only allows women to visit the prisoners here. We learned this news from *Revolución*. Luisito, I brought you a bag with your favorite foods—everything from smoked pork chops to chocolate flan. As Ángela Heymann talked, her grin suggested the pleasures of the palate which awaited him.

After Luis introduced the two women, Olga inquired, "Ángela, were you also stripped and searched?"

"Yes," Ángela replied, "but it was worth the embarrassment to get to see Luis."

"Well, I've never been so outraged," Olga continued. "One of the women guards tried to fondle my breasts when I was undressing. When I pushed her hands away, the *miliciana* called me an imperialistic bitch."

Hearing Olga's story, Ángela related an even more degrading insult. One of her friends, a widow, was forced to take off the artificial breast she wore as a result of a mastectomy.

"I'm not surprised," Luis said. "They're a new breed of monsters who possess a hatred I don't understand."

In their short time together, the two women and Luis talked of a hundred things, and toward the end of the visit, Luis turned to Olga and asked, "Would you do me a special favor? You've heard me talk before about Ofelia Ramos, the rebel officer who was with me in the Sierra. Fidel himself told me she's a prisoner, but I don't know where. I suspect she's at the Guanabacoa prison for women. Would you try to find out for me? We're not allowed to write other political prisoners, but I've got to find out where she is."

Whispering, he added, "If you can't find her, call Alberto Sánchez at home--not at his office--and ask him to help."

"I'll let you know as soon as I can," Olga promised.

Back in *La Leonera,* the guards brought the inmates their bags with food and articles from their visitors, but this time the guards did not dump them on the floor. This seemingly insignificant gesture indicated to the prisoners that perhaps their luck was beginning to change.

In August, the wheel of fortune continued to turn favorably when packages arrived from the States. Rumors of the tractor deal increased, and with their unanticipated transfer to *El Sanatorio,* the men were convinced once again that their release was eminent.

El Sanatorio was much better than *La Leonera* because there was more space and it had a central patio in which the men could roam at will in the fresh air in their shorts or boxer underwear. Located on the top west side of the Príncipe, *El Sanatorio* even offered a view of Havana through the bathroom window. At night the prisoners could hear the *cañonazo*, the nine o'clock firing of the cannon at Morro Castle, an old familiar sound to Luis. In contrast to *La Leonera*, which had only one defecation hole per gallery, his new lodging had a toilet, several holes, showers, and a fountain in the middle of the patio. In comparison to *La Leonera*, it was like a penthouse where the captives could enjoy the sun and daily glimpses of Havana.

Luis looked forward to Olga's next visit and was disappointed when she did not show up along with Ángela in September. When Olga finally visited in the middle of October, Luis knew she brought good news.

"Luis, Ofelia's in the Guanabacoa prison here in Havana," she reported with a smile. "It's a terrible place, but she's all right."

Luis breathed a sigh of relief as he hugged Olga gratefully. As they broke their embrace, Olga said, "I'll tell you the whole truth. Ofelia was slightly wounded in the fighting near Bayamo and taken prisoner on April 22. She was operated on at a military hospital in Santiago, and the doctor did a good job. I visited her last month, and she only has a minor scar on her left shoulder. She was very happy to know you're still alive and well."

"Are you sure she's okay?" Luis asked desperately.

"I wouldn't lie to you," Olga replied softly, acknowledging Luis's concern for the woman he loved.

After a moment, Luis, looking into her eyes, said, "*Muchas gracias*, Olga. You're the most generous woman I've ever known."

Chapter 53

s his days in his Príncipe Prison wore on, Luis again recorded his thoughts and experiences in a series of letters to his family.

October 17, 1961

Dear Mamá y Papá,

Three days ago, Olga Loynaz brought me the news that my dear friend, Ofelia Ramos, was wounded and captured while fighting Castro's forces. She's now at the Guanabacoa prison for women and has recuperated well. I introduced you to her at the party at our house. Over the course of our time in the Sierra, we fell in love, and if we are ever together again, I want to marry her. This might come as a shock, but I want to let you know now rather than later. . . .

October 24, 1961

Dear Mamá y Papá,

According to the grapevine, the communist government has been successful in eradicating the guerrilla forces in the Sierra Maestra and the Escambray. From time to time, I hear about the execution or imprisonment of friends who fought there. Except for the last couple of months in 1958, there were more guerrillas in the mountains--some 3,000--fighting Castro than he had in the Sierra Maestra. How did Fidel succeed when Batista failed?

Castro's forces have been more ruthless than Batista's army, a fact I never dreamed would occur. You might recall Batista's heartless forces slaughtered Ofelia's parents in one of the most notorious atrocities of the war in the Sierra Maestra. From what we hear, the reprisals against the campesinos have been worse. Who would ever have imagined a revolution that began as green as the palms would end up drenched in blood?

November 11, 1961

My dear parents,

We have no more news about the tractor deal, but there's lots of speculation and talk that we might get the tractors through a German company in Argentina. I don't believe it. At Girón, we waited for U.S. airplanes to come to our rescue, and here we're waiting for U.S. tractors! La espera, desespera. Ironically, we're dependent upon U.S. technology whether in war or peace. It will be a shock to Castro when he has to start relying on those Russian tractors that are a generation behind the Caterpillars made in the U.S.

Life is much better here at the top of the Príncipe than down in the dungeon. Even the music has improved and taken on a professional quality. Two of our men, Héctor García and Mario Abril, have managed to get two guitars from relatives and play classical music for us. To give you some idea of the width of the walls here at the Príncipe, some twenty men can stand in the inset of the windows during one of our musical shows. . . .

December 25, 1961

Dear Mamá y Papá,

I hope you had a wonderful Christmas Eve. In our case, we had our first decent meal in the Príncipe. We were given roasted chicken with rice and real black beans and traditional Spanish candies. At 9:00 p.m., we all gathered in the patio and said the rosary with special devotion. While meditating, I'm trying to understand the good that might come out of this experience. I'm now reading the poetry of St. John of the Cross, who patiently spent many years in jail. What I would give to have his faith! . . . .

February 8, 1962

Dear parents,

Since all of the Heymanns have now gone to the States, faithful Olga is the only person who keeps returning to see me. During the last visit, I had a nice surprise when Bernabé Morán's wife, Micaela, came. Her visit at this time of my life means a lot to me.

Micaela--you know how funny she can be--told me a bunch of tales about life at the Tamarindo Sugar Mill. More than half of the working force is new. It seems the government makes a point to transfer workers from one place to another so they won't establish allegiances. She said some of the new workers are so ignorant they don't know the difference between sugar cane and cornstalks. Micaela laughed when she told me the communists have closed all the houses of ill repute in Camagüey and intend to make "honest" women out of the prostitutes. For that reason, the posadas are more in demand than ever.

For the first time, couples stand in line to get rooms in the posadas, and Micaela swears that often you can hear people shouting, "Hurry up!" "Hurry up in there!" Some of the more bashful ladies are ashamed to be seen in public and wear paper grocery bags turned upside down on their heads as they impatiently wait in line. When I asked about Cachita, the most famous madam in Camagüey, Micaela said Cachita told the government she wanted a pension for the years of service she had given to the people of Camagüey. Rumor has it that since most of the new leaders were frequent guests of her establishment, she now lives in comfortable retirement. . . .

February 23, 1962

Dear Mamá y Papá,

Some one hundred of us have been moved from El Sanatorio to two galleries that face each other. We can now take a look at the central courtyard from our second floor windows. There is much more space here and a back patio where we can get sun. All the Sosas, Enrique Toméu, and his son, Pepito, are with me--fifteen people from Camagüey in all. Gaspar Betancourt is the only other frogman here. From now on, we have been ordered to get our families to write us at P. O. Box 6422, Havana. I don't know what this move means, but since it is an obvious improvement, I am happy with it.

I am now reading <u>War and Peace</u> in Spanish. With so much time, it doesn't take long to get through a long book. Though I haven't seen war on the scale described in the book, I've seen my share.

There are rumors here that Ernesto Freyre, a representative of our newly- founded Cuban Families Committee for the Liberation of the Prisoners of War, is coming to Havana to work out details of the negotiations on tractors. Here at any given moment our mood swings from optimism to pessimism. With news of Ernesto's arrival, we're all optimistic. Let's hope this good, gentle man whose son is here with me will succeed . . .

March 19, 1962

Dear Mamá y Papá,

We still don't know why our last visit was cancelled. Guards brought my food bag from Olga and the Moráns. I don't understand why the Families Committee hasn't been able to complete the negotiations.

Here in prison, some of the self-appointed civilian "leaders" are already dividing government jobs for a new democratic Cuba. I wonder how the thousands of political prisoners at the Isle of Pines and those fighting in the mountains would feel if they knew about some plans of *our so-called leaders. I don't know how Cuba's problems will be solved with all the political ambitions already in place even before we get rid of Castro. The more I think about it, the more pessimistic I am about our future. We Cubans, like so many others, blame the United States for our troubles when we ourselves are at fault. The communists are especially adept at exploiting this myth of Yankee imperialism. We're simply jealous of the American character that makes democracy and capitalism work. . . .*

April 9, 1962

Dear parents,

Now that the trial of the Brigade is over, I can tell you what really happened.

We learned about the outcome of the trial in an unusual way. Castro came to our cellblock at about 2:00 a.m. last night with the verdict. He spent more than two hours talking to us as if he were one of our best friends. I wish you could have seen the spectacle! We were sleeping when we were suddenly awakened by guards opening our cells. Then we heard Fidel's voice, "Hola, muchachos, ¿cómo están? Have you been treated well? Is it safe for me to come inside?" He laughed as he spoke and I sensed a certain nervousness in his voice as he joined us.

He proceeded to tell us he had our sentences in his hand. He said we would be happy to know no one would be executed. This relieved me since many of us felt the three leaders of the Brigade and others, myself included, who had crossed Fidel might end up at the paredón. Castro went on to say all of us had been sentenced to thirty years in prison unless the Americans paid for us. The three leaders would be ransomed for $500,000 each. The ransom of the rest of the prisoners was divided according to their socioeconomic family history. Two hundred eleven prisoners were tagged at a value of $100,000, and the others were divided into categories of $50,000 and $25,000. Fidel chose to place the value of my life at $100,000. I guess I should thank him for that. The total ransom package amounts to 62 million dollars.

Castro then began a weird but rather cordial conversation with us. When some of the prisoners told him they doubted we would ever be able to collect that kind of money, he assured us to the contrary. Fidel said that the Yankees felt responsible for us and that he had received letters and telegrams from all over the world, including from the Pope, asking him to be merciful. He offered to wager with us that within a few months we would be out of Cuba.

Our trial started in the central courtyard of the Príncipe. From the beginning, things went wrong for the government. Rather than having 1,180 frightened prisoners to show on television, they found us in high spirits and treating the whole spectacle as if it were a joke. As the men gathered in the yard from the different galleries, there were many abrazos and expressions of happiness since we were seeing one another for the first time after months of imprisonment.

When the three leaders, Artime, San Román, and Oliva, were brought into the yard, there was a tremendous display of affection. This loud and spontaneous outpouring of camaraderie electrified the Brigade and caught the militia off guard. Upset by this turn of events, the guards tried to make us shut up, and when they were not able to, they started poking some of us with rifle butts and bayonets.

Within seconds, several fights began. The militia all around the second floor cocked and readied their rifles and machine guns. Nevertheless, we began to shout obscenities more imaginative than the ones they hurled at us over the last several months. In the middle of this melee, someone started singing the Cuban national anthem, and everybody joined in. I've felt such profound emotion few times in my life.

After the singing, we continued our loud curses, and I believe had not Captain Rodríguez, the communist in charge of us, asked San Román and Oliva to control us, casualties would have resulted. We might have been able to take over the Príncipe by overpowering and holding the five-man tribunal hostage. As it was, several people had to be taken to the infirmary because of bayonet wounds.

San Román finally restored calm when he called the Brigade to attention. Then, Oliva reminded us we needed to maintain our dignity as soldiers.

During this farcical trial which lasted four days, Castro expected the prisoners to denounce the U.S. In the week before the trial, the authorities interviewed a few of the prisoners who had previously made statements attacking the U.S. and threatened them with death if they did not cooperate. Meanwhile, the Brigade decided no matter what happened during the trial, we were not going to say anything derogatory about the U. S.

When the tribunal, composed of five comandantes of the Revolution, called forth the men, who at the time of capture made negative statements about the U.S., all but two refused to say anything negative against the U.S. Some said the only reason they had originally criticized the U.S. was because they had been exhausted and in a state of psychological confusion, but now that they had time to think things through, they repudiated what they had stated before. I was so proud of them. They were risking their lives by this courageous act. Thus, this whole scheme backfired on the communists, and it was never televised to the public as had been planned.

As I've watched the men around me in this process, I've been thinking about courage. Though it's a fine quality to possess, it's not innate or permanent in any of us. I have seen brave men have serious moments of doubt and even panic, and if anyone tells you otherwise, he is not honest.

The communists made bravery an obsession, and they have taken pains to depict our leaders and us as cowards. This is nonsense. Truly brave men do not have to humiliate the vanquished. That in itself is an act of cowardice. There is something fundamentally sick in the vindictiveness of these people. It's true that the militia fought bravely, but so did the Brigade. We weren't mercenaries, as Castro claimed, but ordinary citizens fighting for freedom for our country. If we had been mercenaries, San Román would have accepted the invitation by the U.S. Navy to evacuate us after we had been defeated.

The world would be a better place if we practiced reason and kindness instead of venerating military valor so much. Bravery has nothing to do with being right. It's justice we should always seek . . . .

April 13, 1962

Dear Mamá y Papá,

As part of a goodwill gesture, Castro is releasing sixty wounded or sick prisoners who need medical attention in the United States. Gregorio Loret de Mola is one of these, so I'm sending this letter with him. This move makes me believe negotiations will materialize.

I want to share a couple of other thoughts while the trial is fresh on my mind. At the beginning, there was an incident between the head of the prison, a man named Martínez, and Artime. Martínez became upset when a black man named Carrillo embraced Artime, who had been subjected to physical and psychological torture. Martínez accused Artime of behaving like a politico with a Negro, but Carrillo replied he considered Artime his brother.

One of the aspects that disgusts me about the communist regime is that it has started a campaign of hatred among social classes and races. While I'm the first to acknowledge we do have racial prejudices in Cuba, *communism is only paying lip service to racial equality. The communists have given the blacks in the Brigade a hard time as if they were traitors to their race.*

Another surprise at the trial was the appearance of Osmani Cienfuegos who came as witness to berate us for more than an hour in the most derogatory terms imaginable. Here was a cold-hearted assassin testifying against us. What a travesty!...

Chapter 54

O n the morning of April 14, 1962 Gregorio Loret de Mola
and fifty-nine of his wounded compatriots in Príncipe Prison
prepared to depart for Miami. Permitted to visit all of the
galleries, Gregorio and the walking wounded gathered letters from
the prisoners for relatives in the U.S. As Luis approached Gregorio
to give him his letter and a farewell embrace, he found Fabio Freyre
emphasizing a point to Gregorio, " . . . and don't forget to go to Palm
Beach and tell Silvia that I don't want her to try to ransom me under
any circumstance. I want to remain with the Brigade." Knowing his
concerned parents might also try to ransom him, Luis asked Gregorio
to convey the same message to his parents. Gregorio was elated as he
embraced Luis and everyone else in his cell. "We'll see you soon in
Miami!" some shouted as Gregorio left the thick walls of the Príncipe.

A sense of euphoria prevailed throughout the prison. As soon
as the people in the U.S. witnessed the wounded and the terrible
shape some of them were in, surely they would put pressure on their
government to free the others. As Castro said, "It was only a question
of a few months."

Through letters and newspaper clippings, the prisoners learned the
arrival of their comrades in Miami had been tumultuous. Gregorio,
Enrique Ruiz Williams, and Humberto Cortina had been on the
Today Show with Harry Reasoner and on *The Ed Sullivan Show*. Seven
of the wounded were guests of the Overseas Press Club. They met with
the Archbishop of New York, the Rev. Cardinal Cushing, as well as the
governor of New York and the governor of Illinois, who was himself
wounded in the Second World War. The Cuban Families Committee

had even hired a public relations firm to bring the prisoners' cause to the notice of the American public.

Soon, however, the headlines faded, and the prisoners settled back to the routine they had known for over a year. Some pessimists began to wonder if that first year would count toward their thirty-year terms. Luis tried to remain hopeful.

On the afternoon of May 27, a guard came to Luis' cellblock and began to call the names of all those prisoners whose ransom was $100,000. When he had finished the list, the guard informed the prisoners the ransom money had finally arrived and they would be leaving for Miami the next morning. Luis suspected something was wrong when he heard the militiamen chuckling and talking in a knowing manner as they read the same list to other cells. Luis was not alone in his suspicions. One noted pessimist in his cell block ventured, "Friends, that is a list for the *paredón*."

In the early morning hours of the next day, the loud speaker--the same one which broadcasted Castro's radio speeches since their imprisonment--called out the names of the $100,000 prisoners, Luis included. As each name was announced, the prisoner ran onto the central courtyard with his little bags of possessions. There, the 211 men waited in formation. Luis was even more convinced something strange was going on as he watched the smirking faces of the guards. Had the prisoners' destination really been Miami, another expression would have been on the guards' faces.

From the courtyard, the selected prisoners were marched through the portcullis and over the drawbridge onto waiting buses. At sunrise, the buses took the group and their three leaders to an air base at Camp Columbia where they boarded heavily guarded transport planes. If they were leaving for Miami, why would there be so many guards with machine guns? Where were the representatives of the Families Committee? Luis had no idea where his group was going, but he knew it wasn't Miami, and he feared his captors were playing a cruel joke on them by raising their hopes and dashing their dreams at the same time.

When the plane gained altitude and leveled off on its course, Luis, who had chosen a seat by a window, could tell from the view of Havana they were heading south rather than north. The Isle of Pines!

Luis said to himself. He had first learned of the place while reading Robert Louis Stevenson's *Treasure Island,* whose setting was The Isle of Pines. Later, in the underground war against Castro, he had heard tales of isolation and torture of political prisoners there. Soon the dreaded words passed from mouth to mouth as other prisoners reached the same conclusion.

Holding the distinction of being the toughest prison in Cuba, the *Presidio Modelo,* as it was called, lived up to its reputation. Though the first sight of the *Modelo* to the new prisoners was a pleasant one of flowers and tropical plants, the legendary cruelty of the place soon became a reality to them.

A man named Pomponio, the head of the prison guards, greeted the new arrivals with insults as they got off the buses inside the compound. "So, you're the sons of bitches who came to attack us. We'll see how tough you are! When I say hurry, hurry! If you don't, you'll have a bayonet up your ass. You're going to pay for your defiance at the trial. We'll see how brave you are!" A mean-looking sergeant beside him joined in, "Here are the exploiters of Cuba. Well, we'll see how much you enjoy your stay here with us, you damn queers!"

Starting at a march, the prisoners were soon ordered to double time toward a long, narrow building at the side of one of the six gigantic circular buildings which housed several thousand political prisoners. As they ran and listened to the taunts of the guards, they noticed sheets draped out of the windows of the closest circular with signs on them paying tribute to the 2506 Brigade. Seeing the display of camaraderie, Pomponio cursed, raised his rifle, and shot at the banners, one of which displayed a cross. Luis admired the courage it took for the political prisoners to show their support in such a brazen way. He wondered where Húber Matos was in that gargantuan complex of circles and rectangles and how many of his other friends from the underground might also be incarcerated.

The long, rectangular building was like an empty warehouse with human cargo rudely crammed into it. Inside, the guards ordered the prisoners to strip naked and face the wall with their hands over their heads and feet apart. If they made any movement whatsoever, they were jabbed with bayonets. After a degrading search, the men were allowed to dress and move to their sleeping spaces which were so small they could not even turn over in their sleep without bumping into others.

For the most part, the personal articles they brought out of the Príncipe had been confiscated, so they were left with only a tin plate, a cup, and a spoon. Luis managed to smuggle in *Great Expectations* and two photographs of Luisito.

It soon became obvious their only connection with the outside world consisted of a handful of books and mementos. They could not write, receive letters, or have packages. For a few days, they tried to communicate with the political prisoners in the nearest circular. They stood on one another's shoulders and elevated a radio operator to a barred window near the ceiling where he could be in a position to send messages by Morse code with a small mirror. When the guards realized what was going on, they put a quick stop to it.

An opportunity for the rest of the world to hear about their condition came when one of the guards entered their cell and called Fabio Freyre's name. The prisoners learned Fabio was to be set free in exchange for ransom paid by his relatives in the U.S. While Fabio did not want to leave his comrades, Luis and others insisted he do so since his release would be the only way the story of the horrors of the Isle of Pines could become public. Reluctantly, the aristocratic but now skeletal Fabio agreed to go.

Since there were no food packages at the Modelo, the hostages' diet was far worse than ever. At 6:00 a.m., they were served weak coffee and stale bread. For lunch, they routinely ate beans with rice and worms, and for dinner, rotten pasta brought into the cell in a 55-gallon drum covered with flies. Occasionally, there would be a rancid soup in which Luis was certain he found two dog molars in the portion ladled out to him. That night, as he could have wagered, he had his recurring nightmare, and this time the keeper of the snarling dog was Castro.

The food at the Isle of Pines was so bad that the political prisoners initiated a hunger strike. Though the strike was broken after two days, during which the prisoners were forced to undergo another humiliating stripped search, their meals began to improve slightly, but it continued to be prepared without seasoning. The quantity was never sufficient, and whatever was served caused diarrhea and dysentery.

Within the big cellblock, there was one toilet and one shower for 211 men. With chronic dysentery, the demand on the toilet was constant. Doubled up with cramps, men stood in line while others had to use the drain in the shower to defecate. Since there was no toilet paper, the pages of the paperbacks were rationed. Luis contributed *Great Expectations* to this dire emergency, and Armando Vega donated *The Communist Manifesto*, the use of which brought some humor to this most prosaic necessity. "Which author would you like to wipe your ass with?" the inmates questioned each other, "Charles Dickens or Karl Marx?" Marx was the most popular and not because the paper was smoother. When the paper was gone, there was nothing left to clean oneself with other than one's finger and the water from the shower. Since there was no toothpaste, the prisoners used the crumbled cement between the stone blocks to rub off the grime from the teeth by means of finger brushing. Luis made a point to remember which finger was his toothbrush and which was his ass-wiper.

As hope dwindled through the months after Freyre's departure, humor sustained morale. Among the fantasies the men shared were images of what they would do to those who had mistreated them most, namely Osmani Cienfuegos, "Pinch Ass" at the Príncipe, Pomponio at the *Modelo*, and Fidel. They derived pleasure in describing all sorts of torture, but the best was still the one told to Luis by Roberto de Varona back at the Príncipe. "I would bring all the men who have been tortured and maimed by the communists to a huge arena like the Sports Palace," said Roberto grandiloquently, "and I would say to them, 'Men, in a free and democratic Cuba, we are not allowed either by our government or our Christian conscience to inflict any injury to those who may have mistreated us. So, I'm going to leave Fidel Castro here in the center of this arena, naked and tied to this post. Here are some whips, gasoline, and matches. *Hermanos*, let your conscience guide you!'" Then he would, Roberto said, wink to each side of the arena and leave with a final comment, "Carry on, *muchachos*."

When the men laughed at these fantasies, Father Macho reminded them it was not a Christian notion to think evil thoughts or to consider harming others, even those who persecute you.

One day in late October of 1962, one of the guards shouted to one of the prisoners, "Come here, you bastard," and when the prisoner approached him, he whispered, "Here's a newspaper with interesting information for you." The guard had been one of the workers on the plantation of the prisoner's father. The news in *Revolución* shocked them all. The Russians had put nuclear missiles in Cuba, and Kennedy had demanded they be dismantled, or else they would be forcefully removed. The U.S. Navy had established a blockade around the island, and there was much discussion of an imminent invasion.

Before the Brigade members could fashion their own response to a U.S. invasion, a captain of the militia visited them and bluntly told them if they tried anything in connection with any sort of U.S. activity, they and seven thousand other prisoners would be blown to smithereens by dynamite charges placed under all the buildings. My God, Luis thought, in their sadism they make Batista seem like a boy scout.

The October missile crisis came and went, and the building remained intact. So, too, did the horrible conditions. If the missiles had been removed, the prisoners had no way of knowing it, and since there was no effort to free them, they assumed Kennedy had backed down one more time. From October onward, their morale and health declined steadily. In the emaciated bodies, the protruding ribs, the yellow teeth, and the unshaven faces, each saw a reflection of his own unspoken despair. Luis became so destitute in body and mind that he even lost the capability to dream.

As a result, Luis could not believe the words of a captain who came into their cell as matter-of-factly as a housewife announcing a trip to the grocery store and announced, "*Mercenarios*, negotiations are completed. You'll be leaving in two days." Looking at one another in amazement, the men suspected he was playing another joke on them. They wondered if this was not a transfer to another spot in the growing prison system in Cuba.

"I'm not kidding you," the captain insisted, looking at their incredulous faces. "Here are your bags with food and letters."

When Luis looked inside the bag with his name on it and saw real food, several letters, and a sweater, he knew the captain was telling the truth.

On the morning of December 24, 1962, the members of the 2506 Brigade at the Isle of Pines saw the sun for the first time in eight months, and some fainted from the sudden impact of bright light. As they walked toward buses that would take them to the airport, they saw hundreds of political prisoners waving and cheering at them from the circulars. Their message needed no interpretation—"Don't forget us."

At four in the afternoon they arrived at Homestead Air Force Base near Miami by way of San Antonio de los Baños Airport in Cuba. From there, they went to Dinner Key Auditorium where thousands of cheering relatives and friends welcomed them. Among them were his parents, Isabel, and Luisito. Luis Recio had lost fifty-five pounds and added several gray hairs. When Luis saw his family, he sobbed uncontrollably.

Part 5

Through Troubled Waters
The Final Passage of the Flying Fish

Chapter 55

Christmas Eve, called *Nochebuena* in the Spanish culture, is traditionally a very joyous celebration, and the one of 1962 was the most meaningful Luis had ever experienced. When Luis arrived at the Recios' after the tumultuous reception at Dinner Key Auditorium, he was exhausted from the events of the previous seventy-two hours. Debilitated physically and mentally by the ordeal at the Isle of Pines, he could scarcely concentrate on the moment, much less talk intelligently with family and friends who gathered in the living room to welcome him back. Realizing the awkwardness of his conversation and the clumsiness of his gestures, Luis apologized for his nervousness. He confided he still had trouble distinguishing between dreams and reality. His family members sensed he needed them nearby while he readjusted to life outside of prison.

After months of imprisonment, the constant ringing of the phone unnerved him. Isabel, who took the calls, tried to protect Luis by saying he would return the call when he felt stronger. Isabel only called her brother away from the houseguests to speak with Tony de Varona and Phil Heymann because Luis had mentioned he wanted to talk with them.

Noting that the guests, including Uncle Peter, Aunt Ángela Heymann, and Gregorio, hesitated to ask questions, Luis assured them that in spite of his weight loss, he was feeling fine. "One of the advantages of being skinny as a green bean is that for a while I can eat all I want," he joked.

In celebration of Luis' homecoming, Catalina prepared a Christmas Eve dinner of roasted pork, black beans and rice, and fried bananas. Luis took care not to gorge himself as he had done when he received the package in prison, wanting to avoid painful stomach cramps. It especially pleased him to see Octavio among all the familiar faces. It was like old times except now he appreciated everything and everyone so much more.

After dinner, María Luisa suggested they go to Midnight Mass at the Gesu Church in downtown Miami to give thanks for their blessings. When they arrived at the church, it overflowed with many others in Miami who had come for similar reasons.

On Christmas Day Luis, along with the other former prisoners, went to Jackson Memorial Hospital for a physical and a series of tests for parasites. Later in the afternoon, Laura and her parents brought Luisito over for another visit. It surprised Luis how easy it was to be in Laura's presence after two years of separation. The love he once held for her had vanished, but in the wake of its loss, he felt the pangs of nostalgia and a strange new awareness of her striking beauty, as if he had never known her intimately. Luis could see his physical condition shocked the Ramírezes and Laura, just as it had done when he saw himself in the bathroom mirror the night before.

"Luis, you're so thin!" Laura blurted, having a difficult time controlling her emotions.

"I know. It'll take some time to get back on my feet. Laura, thank you for taking such good care of Luisito."

All of them seemed relieved Luis had no ill feelings over the timing of Laura's divorce.

In an aside, Mario confided, "Luis, we didn't write you because we didn't know what to say to you, but we thought of you often. We admire you for trying to overthrow that bastard Castro."

Accepting the compliment, Luis replied, "I trust we'll be in touch regularly. We'll always have Luisito to share."

After the Ramírezes left, Luis returned to the living room where María Luisa and Isabel were showing Luisito the Christmas tree and the nativity scene under it. Seeing his mother, sister, and son around the nativity scene was a moment that became forever engraved in Luis' mind. When he held out his hands beckoning Luisito, the child smiled and ran to him with his own little arms open wide. My waiting has ended, Luis thought. I am truly blessed.

The full measure of his luck, though, would depend upon freeing Ofelia. Unable to release the thought from his mind, the morning after Christmas Day he broached the matter with his parents at the breakfast table.

"Luis," Rogerio said, fidgeting with a cigarette in his hand, "after the ordeal you've endured, my greatest wish is for you to be happy. I only ask that you give yourself time to think things over and regain your strength."

"Papá, in prison the one thing you have is time to think. I spent many hours sorting through my feelings for Ofelia and my responsibility for her present situation. Beyond everything else, I love her. Ofelia is genuinely good and selfless. She has given of herself to others since her childhood. It's time for me to do something for her."

"I understand, son," said Rogerio. "I just want to be sure that you don't make a hasty decision."

"I don't know how long I can wait. Ofelia's been in prison for almost two years. Until she's with me, I won't be at peace. I love her deeply."

"Luis, how long has it been since you've seen her?" his mother inquired.

"Mamá, I haven't seen her in nearly two-and-a-half years, but during the time we spent in the mountains and in the underground, we got to know each other well. Some people live under the same roof for years without really knowing each other. Laura and I were incompatible from the start, but we didn't realize it until it was too late.

"I would like to ransom Ofelia out of prison as soon as possible. I can pursue this through contacts in Cuba, but before I begin, I know I'll need a minimum of $25,000, and possibly as much as $50,000."

For a moment, his parents looked at each other, and then Rogerio spoke.

"Son, what we have is yours and Isabel's. We would've spent whatever was necessary to ransom you, and we'll do the same for Ofelia."

Luis, sighing with relief, stood and embraced them. "Thank you with all my heart," he said.

Early that afternoon, Luis placed a long distance call to Berta Barreto in Havana. The mother of one of the prisoners and a liaison officer in Havana for the Cuban Families Committee, Berta was also from Camagüey and a friend of the Recio family. Through the efforts of the Cuban Families Committee, Castro had agreed to permit relatives of the 2506 Brigade to emigrate to the U.S. Since Berta had initiated contacts with Castro in April, Luis thought she would be the proper person to present his proposal.

Within thirty minutes, the operator had Berta on the line. Luis introduced himself and thanked her for the role she had played in the prisoners' release.

"Berta, I want to ransom a friend who is at the Guanabacoa prison. Her name is Ofelia Ramos. She was a former lieutenant in the rebel army. Could you try to convince the government to release her? Ofelia will be part of my family since I plan to marry her. Offer Fidel $25,000, and if he demands more, let me know. If Castro accepts, I'll immediately deposit the money in the Royal Bank of Canada."

That night after dinner, Luis informed his father of his initial contact with Berta. Shortly thereafter, their conversation turned to the failure of the Bay of Pigs. As they sat at the bar and sipped brandy, Luis replayed the battle.

"I'm convinced that if we had had control of the air, we could have won," Luis stated. "Looking back, a crucial mistake was to have the first air strike two days before the landing. That strike warned Castro of the invasion, and at that point, he imprisoned anyone he suspected as opposition. Hundreds of thousands were jailed who might have participated in a general uprising."

Luis outlined the running blunders that occurred in "Operation Pluto" until finally he remarked, "In prison I heard people re-fight this battle many times and talk about all the 'ifs' that could have changed it. But what it boils down to is that we lost!"

Father and son talked of men and arms until the wee hours of the morning. "Isn't it something that this failed invasion triggered so many events?" Rogerio commented. "Because of it, Kennedy wants to put a man on the moon to regain the lost prestige of the U.S., and it has opened his eyes to communists' threats in South Vietnam and Europe.

"The Alliance for Progress, which is an excellent assistance program for Latin America, was also born as a result, so some good has come out of the disaster," Rogerio observed.

Luis had forgotten how pleasant and relaxing it was to have a casual conversation over drinks, no matter how serious the topic. That night he slept like a baby, defying the old nightmare images to reappear.

Chapter 56

On Saturday morning, December 29, 1962, Rogerio drove María Luisa, Isabel, and Luis to the Orange Bowl Stadium for the eagerly anticipated address of President John F. Kennedy to the 2506 Brigade. While his family took seats in the stands among the forty thousand spectators, Luis, wearing a short-sleeved khaki uniform that had been issued to all the Brigade members, joined the other frogmen on the field where the Brigade had assembled.

Lined in formation before the platform set up on the fifty-yard line, the 2506 Brigade waited at ease for the arrival of the President and his wife. Once again Luis was waiting in uniform, but this time as a free man who knew what awaited him. Kennedy may have withheld air support at Girón eighteen months ago, but on this happy occasion, he was coming for sure. Like Luis, the Brigade held no ill will toward the president. Their liberation had washed away the bitterness of their experience. Now JFK was coming to honor the 2506 Brigade and receive its banner.

When the white convertible carrying President and Mrs. Kennedy made its entrance into the Orange Bowl, a thunderous roar reverberated across the field and increased as they walked toward the platform. At that moment, the scene that replayed in Luis' mind was Castro's triumphant entrance into Havana, an image that now seemed like a lifetime ago. Thousands of Cuban and American flags waved in unison, reminding Luis of his love for both nations. When the military band played the national anthems of his two countries, tears streamed down Luis' cheeks. He was choked up when John Kennedy walked through the lines and shook the hands of the frogmen and hundreds of others. This man he had once supported and later rejected now seemed a true brother to Luis.

The emotion Luis felt grew with each part of the ceremony. Tomás Cruz, the black commander, broke rank and hugged the President; Rolando Nova, on crutches, handed the Brigade flag to Oliva, who in turn gave it to the President. When Kennedy began to speak, his rhetoric echoed through the stadium.

"Your small Brigade, is a tangible affirmation that the human desire for freedom and independence is essentially unconquerable. Your conduct and valor are proof that although Castro and his fellow dictators may rule nations, they do not rule people; that they may imprison bodies, but do not imprison spirits. . . ."

To the 6,000,000 people of Cuba, President Kennedy extended the hand of friendship and suggested the idea of revolt. He stressed the importance of freedom and spoke about his recently conceived Alliance for Progress. These ideas, he maintained, were the principles of the majority of Cubans, and he was "confident that all over the island of Cuba, in the government itself, in the army, and in the militia, there are many who hold to this freedom faith, who have viewed with dismay the destruction of freedom on their island and who are determined to restore that freedom so that the Cuban people may once more govern themselves . . . Despots may destroy the exercise of liberty . . . but they cannot eliminate the determination to be free."

Kennedy reminded the Cuban exiles that they needed to remain patient. All the great Latin American liberators--Bolívar, O'Higgins, Juárez, San Martín--had suffered exile before victory. Hence, he suggested, they needed to "submerge momentary differences in a common united front and to keep alive the spirit of Brigade 2506."

Time and again Kennedy committed himself to the downfall of the communist regime in Cuba which brought calls of "*Guerra!*" or "War!" from the stadium. He distinguished between the dictatorial governments of Cuba and Russia and the free government of the United States that stood for "the right of every free people to freely transform the economic and political institutions of society so that they may serve the welfare of all." Appealing to the heads of governments throughout the hemisphere, the president demanded "the right of free elections and free exercise of basic human freedoms, the right of every *campesino* to own the land he tills."

"Gentlemen of the Brigade," he said in closing, "even in prison you served in the strongest possible way the cause of freedom, as you do today. I can assure you that it is the strongest wish of the people of this country, as well as the people of this hemisphere, that Cuba shall one day be free again, and when it is, this Brigade will deserve to march at the head of a free column."

The culmination of the afternoon came when Mrs. Kennedy walked to the microphone and stole the show by saying in clear Spanish: "It is an honor for me to be here today with a group of the bravest men in the world and share in the joy that is felt by their families who, for so long, lived hoping, praying, and waiting. I feel proud that my son has met the officers. He is still too young to realize what has happened here, but I will make it my business to tell him the story of your courage as he grows up. It is my wish and my hope that someday he may be a man at least as half as brave as the members of Brigade 2506. Good Luck."

On their return to Coral Gables, the Recios were ecstatic over the stirring words of the President and the First Lady, Rogerio going so far as to say that Kennedy's speech that afternoon would rank with the Berlin speech as one of his finest. "Today Kennedy put to rest the argument that he promised Khrushchev the United States would not invade if the missiles were taken out of Cuba. He has shown that his hands are not tied with respect to Cuba by any promises to Russia," Rogerio beamed.

Luis agreed the speech was an eloquent piece of oratory. "I just hope he means every word."

"He does, son. I'm sure," his father added. "You could feel that every word came from his heart."

That afternoon, Luis hosted a party for all the frogmen and their wives and sweethearts at his parents' house. It was the first time they had relaxed together as a group. Over drinks and grilled pork chops, *tamales*, *yuca*, fried green plantains and other Cuban dishes, they made light of their own adventures.

They recalled Jim's words that some of them would never make it, and they toasted to him as prophet. They were all alive and kicking, though the ex-prisoners, as Carlos Fonts joked, looked like "advance men for a famine." They wondered where their American trainers were, and they wished they could share this moment with them and learn at last what their real names were. Blas Casares told about seeing Rip and Gray again at a secret investigation held by Bobby Kennedy, General Maxwell Taylor, Allen Dulles, and Admiral Arleigh Burke to try to find out why the invasion failed.

Blas told the committee he had no idea who planned the invasion, but whoever did must have been crazy. Allen Dulles, Blas said, stared a hole through him while Kennedy and the others laughed.

The women shared some of their own stories of waiting, one saying she hoped Kennedy, as a consummate politician, would forget right away any idea about returning.

The Orange Bowl celebration and his party only intensified Luis' longing for Ofelia. No matter how happy he was, the expected phone call from Berta Barreto weighed on his mind. He played out a hundred scenes of how Castro might react to his offer, and always in the back of his mind lurked the feeling that Castro's vindictiveness would override any consideration of a deal.

The call from Berta came on the night of January 20.

"Luis, I'm afraid I have bad news," Berta began, getting straight to the point. "Celia Sánchez, Castro's private secretary, called me this morning. There's not going to be any deal."

"Why?" Luis asked in a despondent tone.

"I wasn't given any official reason. Perhaps Fidel doesn't want to let Ofelia out because she fought for the Revolution and turned against it. I found out something else. Three days ago, Ofelia was transferred to the women's prison at Guanajay."

Berta did not need to explain what the transfer meant since the Guanajay prison was the women's equivalent of the Isle of Pines.

"I don't know what I'm going to do next," Luis replied helplessly. "I'll have to think about it. Thank you, Berta, for your help. We'll keep on trying."

Berta's information was a double-barreled shock. Not only had Luis been unable to free Ofelia, but now she was incarcerated in the worst women's prison in Cuba. It was as if demons were trying to frustrate him at every turn. On the surface, it appeared Berta's assessment was correct; the communist government feared negative propaganda, but Luis could not escape the feeling that Castro's rejection was based on a personal vendetta.

After agonizing about the next step to take, the following morning Luis called his cousin Philip Heymann, now head of the Cuban desk at the State Department. He reasoned Heymann would be in a position to advise him since Americans still worked in the former U.S. Embassy in Cuba, which was now run by the Swiss government. Even on this slim chance, Luis' hopes were dampened when a secretary told him Mr. Heymann was in a meeting and not available until following day, but to Luis' surprise, Philip returned his call later that night.

"Luis, the pressures here are unbelievable these days. We still have twenty-one Americans in prison and thousands of family members and refugees who want to leave Cuba. If this weren't enough, we have to make the arrangements through a third party."

Apologizing for taking Philip's time, Luis told him everything about Ofelia's background and her imprisonment in Guanajay. He related his effort at ransom and wanted Philip to advise him.

"Phil, I'm determined to get Ofelia out of Cuba. I need you to come through," Luis reiterated in closing, "She's the most important person in my life."

After a pause, Phil answered, "I understand. I'll do whatever I can from this end. I'll call you as soon as I know something."

In the days that followed, *La espera, desespera* returned with a vengeance. Luis had freedom and comfort, yet he was disconsolate. Even when Luisito arrived at the house every morning at ten o'clock, thoughts of Ofelia intruded with images of the children they would have to play with Luisito. In his years with Laura, he had never dreamed of such domestic bliss. Life with Ofelia would be different. Ofelia knew the value of giving and, God willing, he would have the opportunity to return her love.

The call from Heymann came eight days after their initial conversation. Luis knew the upbeat tone of Philip's voice indicated something good was in the offing.

"I've decided not to pursue the ransom option through the Swiss Embassy," Philip reasoned. "I don't think it would be any more effective than the one you pursued through Berta Barreto. Someone of the highest authority has to make the proposal to Castro. Bobby Kennedy has contacted James A. Donovan for us."

Luis could hardly believe his ears, for it was Donovan who succeeded in negotiating the release of the Bay of Pigs prisoners and U-2 pilot, Gary Powers, with the Soviets.

"I have some other big news for you," Philip continued. "You'll never guess who wants to meet you."

"Who?" said Luis, his mind racing.

"John F. Kennedy. Let me explain. I approached Bobby Kennedy with your problem because I had briefed him as an expert on Cuban history for the investigation he and General Taylor held on the Bay of Pigs. One of your frogmen who did not land testified before that committee."

"Yes," said Luis, "he's my friend, Blas Casares."

"Right," said Philip, "I felt I had established a good rapport with Bobby Kennedy, and knowing of his deep concern for the prisoners, I told him of your plight. Your story fascinated him. The fact you were born in this country, that you were an officer with Castro's forces, and that you later served as Undersecretary of Justice in the new government intrigued him even more. He was particularly interested when I told him you were one of the first five frogmen ashore at Girón. But between you and me, what really touched him was your love for Ofelia. The Kennedys have a soft spot in their hearts for good love stories. Bobby not only wants to meet you, but he also talked to his brother about you, and the President asked to see you too.

"I shook the President's hand at the Orange Bowl, but I never dreamed I'd have the opportunity to talk with him privately," Luis said.

"Well, they both care very much about the Brigade," Philip continued. "The President feels responsible for what happened. As you know, he invited the Brigade leaders to his Palm Beach home before the Orange Bowl event. I think the fact you speak excellent English will give them an opportunity to hear your perspective of the Bay of Pigs.

"So here's the agenda. Hold on to your hat. The President wants you as his guest for dinner day after tomorrow at the White House, and he wants you to spend the night there. Bobby Kennedy will be present at the dinner. Don't worry about the details. I've already made your plane reservations. Pick up your ticket tomorrow at the Delta desk at the airport. So, I'll see you in two days. Bring a suit and an overcoat. It's cold here. Snow's in the forecast."

When he hung up, Luis was speechless. Was this another dream? Was the Attorney General of the United States really going to pursue his case, and was he really to be a guest at the White House? How could it be that in less than a month one could go from the horrible Modelo Prison on the Isle of Pines to the White House as the guest of John F. Kennedy? It was the whimsicality of fate, he concluded.

Chapter 57

The next morning Luis and Rogerio went to Rich's Department Store in downtown Miami to purchase a gray flannel suit and overcoat for Luis. Seeking out the same friendly salesman who had outfitted him for his modest wardrobe the first week after his return, Luis told the man he had an important meeting with President Kennedy at the White House and needed proper attire.

"No kidding," said the salesman, certain Luis was joking. "Winston Churchill was in here yesterday for the same reason."

Luis and Rogerio laughed and knew better than to try to persuade the clerk otherwise. Luis carried on the humor by adding, "There's a considerable difference between Winston Churchill's girth and my own."

Luis commented he did not know if Rich's could suit him up for a cold climate, but the salesman, reminding Luis that Rich's was the Harrod's of Miami, found a suit that fitted him well right away. The clerk had difficulty coming up with the right size cashmere overcoat but guaranteed Luis he would have one ready by noon the next day.

As he boarded the plane the next afternoon, Luis carried his suit coat and the tan overcoat over his arm. Although the shirt was loose around his neck, he had regained a decent appearance. As the plane took off, Luis was exhilarated.

When the plane reached cruising altitude, Luis picked up the February 1, 1963, issue of *Time* with Mortimer Caplin on the cover. He began to flip through the pages mechanically, and what should jolt his eyes but an article on the Bay of Pigs Invasion. With pictures of Manuel Penabaz and Bobby Kennedy set opposite each other, the piece revived the debate about whether or not air cover for the invasion had been promised. Penabaz, Luis recalled, used the frogmen's Zodiac to escape from Girón.

To Luis' surprise, the article contended that even if a score of B-26's had been promised, the air cover at the Bay of Pigs would still have been woefully weak. Luis agreed that several additional planes might have been needed for interdiction and close air support in strikes against tanks and troops, but he remained convinced a single navy jet could have controlled the air over Girón. Castro's few planes would have been no match for a navy jet fighter.

Returning the magazine to the pocket on the seat in front of him, he noticed another issue of *Time* and began to scan it. At the very end of the issue, Luis read a review of Mariano Azuela's classic, *The Underdogs*, which the author wrote in 1915 while serving as a physician for the Mexican rebels. The article could very well have described the more recent Cuban Revolution: "At first the rebels are content to kill only their oppressors who, by and large, deserve it. But before long, they are making no distinctions, shooting down and stringing up the innocent and guilty alike." To Luis' knowledge, there had been no hangings in Cuba, but the firing squads had been merciless on the perceived enemies of the Revolution.

Ready to dismiss his thoughts of man's inhumanity to man, Luis placed the magazine in his lap, rested his head against the back of the seat, closed his eyes, and concentrated on relaxing every muscle in his body as he had learned to do in prison. Soon he fell asleep.

The voice of the pilot announcing the preparation for landing at Washington National Airport awakened him. As Luis fastened his seat belt, he looked out the window and saw a breathtaking scene, the city of Washington blanketed with snow. Luis loved the tropics, but he had to admit snow had a special magic of its own.

Upon arriving in Washington, Luis remembered that he had not worn an overcoat since he had gone to New York in December of 1959 to collect money for the 26th of July, and he had forgotten how burdensome it could feel on one's shoulders. As he reached the door of the plane and descended the steps, the cold air hit him in like a slap in the face, reminding him of those endless winter mornings at SMA when he stood outside at attention for breakfast formation. There seemed to him to be something fundamentally Anglo-Saxon in that bracing rush of air, and it had always been a mystery to him how the pioneers had survived the hard winters on the vast American plains.

Philip Heymann was waiting inside the terminal and embraced him affectionately.

"You look better than I thought you would!" he exclaimed, delighted to see his cousin alive and well.

"I'm recuperating," Luis replied. "It's a wonderful problem to have to gain weight!"

They inquired about each other's families, Luis saying he looked forward to seeing all of the Heymanns once again. He remembered he had not seen Uncle Heinrich and Aunt Rebecca since he was a child in Havana. He would spend tomorrow night as Philip's guest.

"It won't be like a night in the White House," Philip said, "but we're looking forward to spending time with you in our home."

Chapter 58

On the drive to the White House, Philip briefed Luis on what to expect during the gathering. Philip saw the invitation not only as an act of kindness toward a Bay of Pigs prisoner but also as a way to obtain a perspective on Castro by someone who had fought with him and served in his government.

"It's for these reasons that the president has asked some of his advisors to be there," Philip explained.

"I just can't imagine myself getting this VIP treatment," Luis remarked.

"Luis," his cousin said, "you're too unassuming. You have an impressive background, and the President has the wisdom to see that. Right now he's quite disenchanted with rank and officialdom."

As they talked, Luis about his time in prison, and Philip about the complexity of life in Washington, Luis could not keep his eyes from the snow-covered landscape as he contrasted the dark, chilly looking water of the Potomac and Tidal Basin with the warm, blue Caribbean.

To the left across the snow-covered Ellipse, Luis could see the Washington Monument standing against the dark, gray horizon and the thin snow that fell lazily through the air.

"Philip, this is an incredible moment for me," Luis admitted.

"I'm very excited too," Philip said. "The only time I've been to the White House was when I brought my children on a tour. Most of my service has been overseas."

At the South Portico, Philip turned the car over to a valet for parking, and a waiting White House aide escorted them to the Red Room on the first floor. Luis noticed the elegant simplicity of the house. The residence of the most important man in the world was less pretentious than the Presidential Palace in Cuba.

The Red Room, with its comforting fire, was cozy and inviting, creating a lived-in effect. Following the instructions of the aide to make themselves at home, Luis and Philip stood by the fireplace and admired the portrait above the mantel, unsure of how long they would have to wait for the president.

"That's Angelica Singleton Van Buren, President Van Buren's daughter-in-law. The painting was finished in 1842."

They turned and saw Jacqueline Kennedy approaching them with a bright smile.

"You must be Mr. Recio," she said, extending her hand toward Luis.

"And you are Mr. Heymann," she added, turning to Philip. "We're so pleased to have you visit with us."

"I heard you speak excellent Spanish at the Orange Bowl," Luis said.

"I'm not fluent in Spanish. I was just reading from notes. I may be a little better in French. I do wish our country would pay more attention to foreign languages."

Pausing for a moment, Mrs. Kennedy asked, "Would you like a short tour of the White House before meeting with the President?"

"We would be honored," they responded in unison.

"Well, let's begin here in the Red Room. Here President McKinley wept over his decision to declare war on Spain."

With this beginning, she led them through the other four state reception rooms, describing the furniture and other contents and telling brief anecdotes of former presidents and their families. In the Blue Room, she pointed to the portrait of Thomas Jefferson by Rembrant Peale and mentioned that even the third president of the U. S. had keen interest in Cuba.

"It's a pity he didn't buy it!" Luis commented.

Mrs. Kennedy smiled and pointed to two other portraits on either side of a white Carrara mantel that enclosed a softly crackling fire.

"The one to the right is Mrs. James Monroe and is still owned by the Monroe family. The one on the left is President Monroe who has been in the news a lot recently because of his famous Monroe Doctrine."

Mrs. Kennedy was describing the gilded chairs with golden eagles emblazoned on the backs when she stopped short and asked Luis solicitously, "Mr. Recio, have I said something wrong?"

"No, ma'am, I beg your pardon. Do you see that black eagle above the mirror between the two Monroe pictures?"

As he spoke, he glanced at the anxious Philip who, with Mrs. Kennedy, turned his eyes in the direction where Luis pointed.

"The password for the Bay of Pigs invasion was '*Águila Negra*' which means 'Black Eagle' in English. You can imagine my surprise upon seeing this bird next to James Monroe."

"I think that's another strange story for the White House," Mrs. Kennedy said softly.

Gracefully, their hostess led them to the Green Room, noted for its golden eagles. There, Philip remarked that John Quincy Adams, for whom the Green Room was named, called Cuba "the apple that had to fall by gravity into the hands of the United States."

Mrs. Kennedy continued, "This carpet on which we're standing has a little story. The head of the eagle here, as you can see, points toward an olive branch. On the previous rug, the head was turned toward the arrows. President Truman ordered this change and decreed that henceforth the eagle on the U.S. seal would be an unmistakable symbol of peace with the eagle's head always pointing in the direction of the olive branch."

After a short trip through the State Dining Room and Cross Hall, the First Lady led her guests through the Entrance Hall to the West Wing and on to the Fish Room, so named because Franklin Roosevelt kept an aquarium as well as mementos of his fishing trips there. It provided a warm atmosphere for informal discussions. Telling them the president would be by soon, Mrs. Kennedy said goodbye and offered them her hand. Luis and Philip gratefully assured her they would always treasure the memory of the tour.

A butler then entered with a portable bar and took their orders for drinks. A conference table, sofa, and several chairs made the room seem smaller than it was, and a thick red carpet and the roaring fire provided a sense of comfort. Looking around, they saw mementos everywhere, not so much of a fisherman as those of the most famous hunter to inhabit the White House, Teddy Roosevelt.

"This should be called the Teddy Roosevelt Room," Philip said. "Look over there on that table. Do you know what that piece is called?"

Luis looked at a sculpture of a cowboy riding a bucking horse and said, "No, I've never seen it before."

"That's 'The Bronco Buster,'" Heymann replied. " Its creator, Frederic Remington, presented the original to Teddy Roosevelt as a tribute to the Rough Riders."

Studying the statue, Luis commented, "I don't think Teddy would have been bothered by which way the eagle's head is turned!"

"That's probably true, but remember they didn't have the atomic bomb in those days," Philip answered.

With drinks in hand, they sauntered around the room and examined the memorabilia of both Roosevelts. They stood before an equestrian portrait of Teddy riding triumphantly in Rough Rider uniform.

"Teddy did do some charging in the hills outside Santiago," Philip pointed out, "but not the hill the blockhouse was on, which is not to say he didn't show bravery. The so-called San Juan Hill was taken by black troops, but Teddy got the credit. One humorist said the title of his book should have been called 'Alone in Cuba.'"

While they were talking, they heard the door open and saw the President of the United States enter with four other men, all of them laughing with their drinks in hand.

"I'll just bet you wish that man was still living here," the President said genially to Luis as he pointed to Teddy Roosevelt's picture.

Luis grinned sheepishly as he commented, "Mr. President, I wouldn't touch that comment with a ten-foot pole."

Chapter 59

After introducing Luis and Philip to Attorney General Bobby Kennedy, John McCone, Director of the CIA, Edward R. Murrow, head of the U.S. Information Agency, and General Maxwell Taylor, a senior military advisor, the President suggested they sit around the conference table. Taking a seat at the head of the table, Kennedy placed Luis on his right and Philip Heymann on his left. He let it be known that though the subject at hand was serious, the setting was informal.

"Maxwell," he said with a grin, "you might want to push that large bowl of chrysanthemums out of the way so you and John can see each other. It's important we not have any artificial barriers between the constituencies you two represent." Laughter rippled around the table, and Luis could understand why the President had a reputation for wit.

"When Bobby told me your story," the President began, turning to Luis, "I wanted to meet you and get your views on the little country that almost started a world war. Tell us about Fidel Castro. What makes him tick?"

The President's voice had a raspy edge, and the way he said "Cubar" with an "r" reminded Luis of his roommate at SMA. Taking a deep breath, Luis replied deliberately.

"Power, Mr. President, power drives him. Castro is an egomaniac who can't reconcile himself to being the leader of only six million people on an island the size of Tennessee.

"Pepe Andreu, a friend of mine in prison, describes Castro as having a classic Oedipus complex in that he tried to kill his father, that is Uncle Sam, whom he envies because of his power, and marry Mother Russia, supposedly the unselfish parent of all oppressed orphans. I believe his alliance with Russia is a ruse since he leans more toward fascism than communism. He grew up reading and memorizing the speeches of Hitler, Mussolini, and José Antonio Primo de Rivera, leader of the Falangists in Spain."

"Still, he became a communist," John McCone interjected, leaning back from the table.

"He's never really been a true communist, Mr. McCone. He had no alternative once he made the U.S. the scapegoat for all of Cuba's problems. Had he made his move in the late thirties or early forties, he would have become a national socialist like Juan Perón in Argentina.

"Castro has a pathological hatred of the United States and will do anything to bring your country grief. President Eisenhower was prepared to help Castro, but when Castro visited the U.S. in 1959, he ordered his staff not to accept any aid offered by the U.S."

"Let's hear a little more about the Freudian connection," the President said. "I've often wondered what his hang-ups are."

As everyone laughed, Luis spoke, "Ángel Castro, Fidel's father, acquired some 10,000 acres of land; some say by dubious means. While Fidel enjoyed the fruits of Ángel's wealth, he despised everything that wealth stood for since Fidel could see his father getting richer while ignoring the poor. Thus, his hatred of the U.S. coincides with the hatred for his father."

John McCone started to interrupt, but the President, looking intently at Luis, raised his hand and signaled for Luis to continue.

"Lina Ruz, Castro's mother," Luis explained, "came to Ángel Castro's house as a cook. While Ángel was married to his first wife, he fathered several children by Lina, among them Fidel. Fidel's inferiority complex began with his illegitimacy. To compensate, Castro rebelled against authority in order to gain attention, and this gutsiness made him a natural leader. His victory in the Revolution didn't satisfy his appetite for power; it only whetted it. Once he was the leader of Cuba, he wanted more."

"Mr. Recio," Edward R. Murrow began, raising his eyes toward Luis and speaking in the clear, bass voice for which he was famous, "a Marine Corps General by the name of Smedley Butler said the military defending the interests of American corporations abroad was nothing but gangsterism. So doesn't Castro have a case when he accuses the United States of the same kind of brutal exploitation?"

"Mr. Murrow, American corporations behaved very badly abroad in the earlier part of this century. However, with FDR's Good Neighbor Policy and now with President Kennedy's Alliance for Progress, things have changed for the better. I can tell you American companies paid the highest wages in Cuba. I'm not only talking about a few high-paid executives but also about blue collar workers. By the beginning of the Revolution in January, 1959, Cuba had a growing middle class and the third highest standard of living in Latin America in spite of an oppressive dictatorship."

"You present a good case Mr. Recio," said Murrow as he looked around the room and humorously added, "Perhaps I should try to get you on my staff."

"Mr. Recio, do you see any chance Castro might look for a rapprochement with us?" Bobby Kennedy asked as he went back to the bar for a drink.

"I think he would love to have commercial relations with you. Cuba needs U.S. technical know-how, replacement parts, and tourism, but I don't think he's going to reject communism."

General Taylor then asked, "Why do you think there's such a deep sense of hatred toward the United States in Latin America?"

"General Taylor, many countries have a love-hate relationship with the United States," Luis replied. "Latin Americans love American music, movies, sports, and fashions. On the other hand, Mexicans may hate Americans because they lost half of their territory to you during the Mexican War. Some Spaniards hate you because in the Spanish-American War, they lost Cuba, Puerto Rico, and the Philippines. In Cuba, in contrast, you helped us free ourselves from Spain and later granted us our independence. Thus, the Cubans were never anti-American until Castro began a campaign to discredit the U.S.

"Mr. President, may I say one more thing?"

John Kennedy nodded, indicating he had come to listen.

"Much of the anti-American rhetoric," Luis continued, "comes from left-wing writers and journalists in Latin America. The majority of the intellectuals in Latin America aren't in the center of power. Often they work for newspapers or hold sinecures from the government, barely making a living. If you compare them with the intelligentsia in the U.S., you'll find most U.S. intellectuals are well-paid and hold influential positions in the best schools, government think tanks, and the media. Though well established, they're still as leftist as their counterparts in Latin America. Two individuals come to my mind, Arthur Schlesinger and Norman Mailer."

"I wouldn't equate those two," Murrow interjected with a laugh.

"I don't know exactly where they stand politically," said Luis, "but they're both intellectuals, powerful, and affluent. In Latin America, intellectuals are mostly poor, frustrated, and powerless. In their bitterness, they become radicals and blame the U.S. for the conditions in their countries. I don't say the U.S. is without fault, but it's not the primary cause of the problems in Latin America."

"You must know, Mr. Recio," said Maxwell Taylor, "there're no plans for the United States to invade Cuba. The only other possibility for overthrowing that communist regime is a general uprising by the Cuban people. Realistically, do you think that will happen?"

Pondering the question, Luis put his hands on the table and answered, "No, I don't think so since there are vigilante committees on every block in the cities, but if Castro were to be assassinated, the whole scene would change rapidly."

"Are you saying that assassination is a real possibility?" John McCone inquired.

"Anything can happen in volatile Cuba," Luis replied. "My own great uncle, a well-known political leader, was assassinated in his prime. Castro has always been a lucky man, but no one's luck lasts forever."

"You know, we almost had paratroopers rescue the Brigade during the missile crisis," General Taylor said.

"If President Kennedy had sent troops to rescue us, there would have been wholesale death," Luis replied. "The buildings at the Isle of Pines, where there were seven thousand prisoners, were wired for destruction in anticipation of U.S. intervention.

"What a contrast our situation was to Castro's when he was in prison. By his own admission in letters to friends, Castro's two years at the Isle of Pines were like a stay in a hotel. He had a private cell, books, space to roam in, a toilet, a cooking stove, fine food, a radio, and Cuban cigars."

"Well, let me ask Mr. Recio one final question," said the President. "In your opinion, what's the great lesson of the Bay of Pigs Invasion?"

Luis answered, "With all due respect, Mr. President, the lesson is simple. If a nation risks an adventure such as the Bay of Pigs, it needs to do whatever it takes to win. In Cuba, thousands of people have been killed or put in prison because of the failure of the invasion."

"Exactly, which is why we should never have tried to execute it," Murrow agreed.

"But the United States, as the leader of a free world, cannot be like an ostrich and hide its head in the sand," Luis countered.

"Mr. Recio," continued Murrow, "as you might guess, I'm partly playing the devil's advocate though I opposed the operation which led to your imprisonment. I have the highest regard for your courage and for your convictions. However, I don't want us as a nation to fall into clichés about the role of the United States in this world. It's a very complex matter. Some intellectuals hypothesize that before the Bay of Pigs, Castro had to turn to Marxism in order to bring about social justice in Cuba. How do you respond to that notion?"

"Mr. Murrow, that argument was dismissed in Cuba long before it became fashionable with U.S. intellectuals. A friend of mine said it took American intellectuals thirty years to discover that the Marx Brothers were funny and that Stalin was a bloody killer."

Luis' unexpected response produced laughter around the table, Maxwell Taylor saying that was a line he wanted to remember. Luis dared not tell them the person who had made that statement was Philip Heymann, who had suddenly turned pale and was only beginning to regain color as Luis continued. "There's no proof anywhere a Marxist government will improve the quality of life of people.

"It puzzles me," Luis went on, "why American intellectuals did not embrace the 2506 Brigade with the same zeal with which they embraced the Lincoln Brigade during the Spanish Civil War. I understand the circumstances were different since the Lincoln group was composed of Americans helping the Spanish Republicans against the Falangists. In Cuba, we were fighting communism. The point is, though, we were both trying to preserve democracy."

"Perhaps, but, in the first case the people were all volunteers, and in yours, the CIA was your sponsor," Murrow contended, looking squarely at John McCone as he spoke.

"We were also volunteers," Luis sighed, looking sadly down at the table as if he had finally run out of steam.

There was an awkward silence around the table and Murrow, as if he were feeling sorry for a frustrated debater, said, "Mr. Recio, please understand that nothing personal is involved in my remarks. We're just talking about one of the touchiest issues of our time."

"Well, my last short question evoked a complicated response, didn't it?" the President commented. "It might give Mr. Recio some idea of what we faced in those trying days of April, 1961, and October, 1962."

At that point President Kennedy rose from the table and said,

"Gentlemen, we're already running late for dinner, and we can continue the conversation there. So feel free to bring your drinks if you like."

As they got up to leave, Edward R. Murrow came to Luis to shake his hand and to make sure there were no hard feelings as a result of their exchange.

"Mr. Murrow, what the world needs is for people to be able to respectfully disagree with each other," Luis concluded.

Murrow, nodding and smiling, agreed.

Chapter 60

When they entered the President's Dining Room on the second floor, recurring symbols again surrounded Luis. Between two large windows hung a gold-framed mirror guarded by a golden eagle. The drapes over the window were gathered at the top by gold medallions reminiscent of the emblem on the felt hats of the 2506 Brigade and tokens of American victories, all of which reminded Luis of his own defeat. To the left of the windows hung a painting of General Washington triumphantly entering Boston in 1776. Luis recalled the glorious arrival of Castro in Havana in January of 1959. On the mantle, he read Oliver Perry's words after the Battle of Lake Erie: "We have met the enemy, and they are ours." How wonderful it would have been if they had been able to send that same message to President Kennedy from Girón!

After they were seated at the Sheraton pedestal dining table with the President at the head and Luis at his right, Luis glanced at the menu, and his mouth watered:

> Cream of Chestnut Soup
> Sole en Papillote with Champagne Sauce
> Parsley Potatoes
> Fresh Broccoli
> Champagne
> Bitter Chocolate Mousse.

Once at the table, Philip Heymann said to the President, "My cousin is rumored to be an excellent cook."

"Is this true?" the President asked with a smile, looking at Luis.

"Mr. President, I've always loved good food," Luis replied a bit awkwardly. "We had a great cook in our house. When I got interested in cooking, I made a habit of befriending chefs at restaurants in order to get their recipes, excluding, of course, the recipes at the Isle of Pines Prison."

The President laughed appreciatively.

As the champagne flowed throughout the dinner, the conversation turned to lighter subjects. The President described his trip to Cuba in December of 1957 while his old friend from Palm Beach, Earl Smith, was ambassador. Learning of Luis' interest in swimming and baseball, the president talked about sports and inquired about Castro's own athletic background. "Was he really an outstanding athlete?"

"Castro was an excellent athlete in high school but didn't participate in sports at the university. He was too busy with politics," replied Luis.

From sports, the conversation moved to education in Cuba, and finally to the President's space program. "Mr. President, I've always wanted to know if the failure at Bay of Pigs really played a part in your decision to land a man on the moon before the end of the decade," Luis inquired.

"It certainly did. I felt that a successful space program would prove to the world that America was capable of achieving any goal it chose to undertake," President Kennedy responded.

When the meal was finished, the host and their guests retired to the Red Room for after-dinner drinks. There, Bobby Kennedy spoke first. "I'd like to propose a toast to Luis Recio. We're delighted to have him in this country and hope that someday soon he'll be in a position of leadership in a free Cuba. We pray his loved one will be permitted to leave prison and join him in this country."

Glancing at Philip as if for approval, Luis offered a toast of his own, "Mr. President, I feel very privileged to be here with you. I'll remember this visit all my life. On behalf of the 2506 Brigade, I'd like to express our gratitude for your efforts to free us. Had you not made your commitment to us clear to Castro, I'm sure we would have been killed. I thank you for saving our lives, and I toast to your re-election."

"Do I have to drink to that last item?" John McCone asked jokingly.

"We'll excuse you this once, John," the President replied.

After they were seated, a butler placed a large wooden box on a silver tray by the President, who, as he opened it, spoke with pleasure. "Gentlemen, I have a treat for you which is especially appropriate because of Mr. Recio's presence. Shortly after the beginning of the Alliance for Progress, President López Mateos of Mexico gave me a box of Number 4 H Upmann Cuban cigars. Since I enjoy them so much, he has continued the tradition. Recently, he sent me another box in celebration of the successful negotiations on the Bay of Pigs prisoners.

"Of course, you know Cuban cigars cannot be brought into the U.S., but since they're a gift of our fine neighbor to the south and came through diplomatic channels, I think we have an obligation to enjoy them. I believe they're all safe, but since John is the head of the CIA and a Republican to boot, I think he should be the first to try them out."

There was hearty laughter in the Red Room and general agreement on the fine quality of the Upmanns.

After a while, the President, exercising his customary prerogative, decided to close the evening. As the guests were leaving, Bobby Kennedy took Luis to one side, shook his hand warmly, and said, "Luis, when I saw Fabio Freyre back in August, I was shocked to learn of the condition of the prisoners at the Isle of Pines. I couldn't believe how thin he was. The stories he told me were heart wrenching. The President and I then made up our minds to work as quickly as possible to get the prisoners out. I hope we'll be successful in getting your fiancée out as well. We'll be in contact with you soon."

John F. Kennedy escorted Luis Recio from the Red Room to his sleeping quarters, and while they walked, the President spoke softly, taking Luis by the arm, "I want you to know how much I regret not giving the Brigade the support it needed at the Bay of Pigs. When we realized what the consequences were, it was too late."

"Mr. President, I know it must have been painful to you," Luis replied, grateful for his confidence.

When they reached the quarters assigned to Luis, the President said, "You'll be sleeping tonight in President Lincoln's Bedroom."

Luis was spellbound. He had read about holy places, and this was one of them. As Luis looked at the somber furniture, the President's next words brought him back to reality.

"I want to share another reason you were invited to the White House. You recruited a number of CIA agents for us, in particular Major Miguel Ochoa, our highest agent on Castro's staff. He has provided us with invaluable information in corroborating the construction of Russian missile sites in Cuba. It was Major Ochoa who told us Castro himself pushed the button on the Russian missile which shot down our U-2 plane and killed Major Rudolf Anderson. It was an extremely tense time for the world. We're grateful for what you've done."

"Mr. President," Luis confided, "I don't think people ever realize the sacrifices that persons like Miguel Ochoa make in the cause of liberty."

"I do," the President said, "and I hope someday we'll be able to repay them."

After shaking hands with the President and saying good night, Luis walked around the Lincoln Room, reverently examining the pictures on the walls and admiring the dark Victorian furniture, especially the eight-foot rosewood bed with its towering ornamental headboard. He looked into the faces of Andrew Jackson and young Mary Todd. Above the walnut bureau hung a picture of the man himself, "the American Christ," as someone once called him. Cautiously, Luis sat down in the rocking chair which duplicated the one in Lincoln's box at the Ford Theater. He thought of how the Cubans, in defiance of Spain and slaveholders, wore mourning bands for a week following the death of Lincoln, the most revered of all U.S. presidents.

Castro too revered Lincoln--Castro, who at first had seemed like a national savior. Luis recalled the dove landing on the shoulder of "the Maximum Leader" during his first speech to Cuba at Camp Columbia. The image became a familiar picture on Cuban postage stamps that parodied the descent of the Holy Spirit in the form of a dove that landed on Christ's shoulder following his baptism. There it was for all to see, the dove and Castro's bearded face, the suggestion that Christ and the Holy Spirit had somehow failed the first time around since they had not initiated the true revolution.

Then it had happened again--many had seen it--this time of all places at the Lincoln Memorial during Castro's U.S. visit in 1959. As if noting the presence of a visiting dignitary, doves descended onto the monument, and one, after landing for a moment on Lincoln's hand, flew to Castro's shoulder as he paid homage to Lincoln. Such is the story of saints and saviors, Luis thought, but in Castro's case, Luis was sure the dove had been looking for the most appropriate place to defecate.

On a dark round table in the center of the room, Luis found a large book of paintings and photographs. The title, LINCOLN, was etched in black on a field of dark blue. After getting ready for bed, Luis sat down in the rocker and leafed through the book. Enveloped in sadness, the book began with Matthew Brady's full-face photograph of Lincoln and a portrait in profile of the great emancipator by Allen Topper True, the eyes in both collecting shadows.

A series of pictures depicting Lincoln's life followed. Luis froze at the picture of Lincoln under a black eagle whose wings in the front were tinged with gold. Shivers ran up Luis' spine, but the more he studied the picture, the more details he noticed. It was not the same black eagle that was in the Blue Room. In this eagle's eyes, Luis saw the same sorrow as in those of the man the majestic bird honored and protected in the star-filled, oval-framed picture he held in his claws.

After a picture of Lincoln's funeral train, Luis' eyes were drawn to a scene of a large-winged angel and Father Time lifting Lincoln from his tomb as a great beam of light from above shone upon them. It was called "The Apotheosis of Lincoln" and was, the notes said, an adaptation of a painting of Washington with Lincoln's head placed on Washington's body by an engraver following Lincoln's assassination. Not a black eagle, but rather a bald eagle looked down upon the ascension. It held its shield, emblem, and olive branch to the side as it looked up in gaping sorrow at the martyred president.

There at last, thought Luis, is the answer. The real American eagle, one with a head that can be turned and a heart that can feel emotion, was capable of soaring, but its feet remained on the ground. It was the eagle of the people, an eagle of diplomacy, reason, and cooperation.

It flew in every human heart and had a secret place of honor in every government on earth. The imperial and inflexible black eagle, in contrast, was always perched, poised to go straight for its prey.

Gently closing the book and placing it back in the center of the table, Luis climbed into the great bed and immediately fell asleep.

The next morning at ten o'clock, Philip picked Luis up at the South Portico, and as soon as Luis was in the car, he told his cousin, "Philip, this house is haunted, and so, I fear, is my mind."

"What do you mean?" Philip laughed.

"All the coincidences and symbols," Luis explained. "It's the same type of thing that's happened to me all my life. In our meeting yesterday, I mentioned Castro having fine Cuban cigars while in Batista's prison, and what should the President offer after dinner? Also, I spoke of the Lincoln Brigade, and guess where I slept last night?"

"The Room," Philip said, smiling.

"You're right."

"Did you see his ghost?"

"Yes, in a dream, but I have no idea what it meant."

When they arrived at the home of Philip's parents, Luis embraced Uncle Heinrich and Aunt Rebecca affectionately. He wouldn't have known them except for the photographs he had seen in Miami. He had not been with the Heymanns since childhood when they had returned to Cuba for a visit, and they talked into the wee hours of the morning.

Chapter 61

After his return to Miami, the euphoria of the trip to the White House did not last long. Ofelia's predicament weighed too heavily on his mind. As he lay in the sun by the pool at his home, he created a dozen different plans for Ofelia's rescue. If Castro had intended to let Ofelia go, he would have done so when Berta Barreto made the request. Luis wanted to exhaust all official routes before taking matters into his own hands.

The time he spent with Luisito relieved his anguish over Ofelia's situation. They spent hours playing in the pool and reading children's books. Luis knew his family worried about his sister and him, and on more than one occasion, he caught his mother watching him as he played with the little boy. Isabel would often join him and Luisito in the pool, and her struggle with the loss of her fiancé helped him keep matters in perspective. They understood the depth of each other's suffering, but Luis knew that there was no comparison in their grief. Ofelia was alive, but his sister had lost the man she planned to marry. The two of them took long walks, and it was in the bond of their sorrow that they began to help each other heal. Who would have dreamed that children with wonderfully carefree, happy childhoods would ultimately experience such heartbreak in their adult lives?

One day after taking Luisito to the Ramírezes, María Luisa met her son at the door and told him Dr. Uría, the head of his Havana law firm, had dropped by and left him a package. Luis unwrapped the small box with curiosity, and inside he found the black onyx egg paperweight he had bought in Mexico on his honeymoon. Holding the egg in his hand, Luis smiled at the memento of his marriage and the Revolution. In both enterprises, the outcomes were not what he had anticipated. The egg was hard and unforgiving, a symbol of fate which followed him like a shadow and sneaked up from behind when he least expected it. Thankfully, he had kept a sense of humor. "Fate, your time to give me a break has come," he announced throwing the egg up in the air and catching it.

The long anticipated call came on a Wednesday morning toward the end of February.

"Luis," said Bobby Kennedy, calling him by his Christian name, "I'm afraid we've failed. Castro stated emphatically to Donovan that 'Recio never learns.' The dictator insisted he was not about to permit Ofelia Ramos to go free and join another traitor without paying for her crimes against the state. Donovan told me he had never heard Castro so inflexible. I'm sorry," the Attorney General apologized. They chatted a few more minutes, and Kennedy closed by saying, "Luis, you know you have friends in the White House."

The moment Luis hung up, he felt a hatred for Fidel Castro he had never experienced before, not in the truck, the swamp, the Sports Palace, the Príncipe, or even the Isle of Pines. "Coño," he swore to himself, "That vindictive bastard won't stop me from getting Ofelia out of prison."

In the morning, all the plans he previously considered played around in his head. Restraining his emotions, he began to eliminate impractical schemes, including a commando attack on the prison. By noon, he had what he thought was a feasible plan, and he called two of his fellow frogmen to his house to get their opinion. He chose Blas Casares and Carlos Fonts because they were both unmarried, had not been in prison, and most importantly, had experience in clandestine operations and rescue missions.

Sitting beside the swimming pool, Luis laid out his plan to Blas and Carlos, and when they studied it, they came to the conclusion that it was feasible if Ofelia could get to the coast. Over the next couple of days, Blas took it upon himself to locate Gray and to draw upon Gray's expertise to secure the equipment they would need. They all felt confident Gray would accompany them. Carlos and Gray would then take care of securing a crew. After Carlos and Blas left, Luis called Philip Heymann who said he would see to it the CIA got Luis' letter to Alberto Sánchez.

The following afternoon Luis was on his way to Washington, D.C. with a letter that read:

> *My dear Alberto,*
>
> *I feel very strange writing you from the U.S. again after almost a quarter of a century. I've learned, as the Americans say, "What goes around, comes around." But this time I'm a free civilian, and you, my friend, are in uniform on an island prison.*
>
> *This letter is a matter of life or death. I'm asking you to do whatever is necessary to get Ofelia Ramos out of the Guanajay Prison so I can pick her up at a designated point on the coast. How you arrange her escape is up to you. I'm prepared to pay a substantial sum to anyone who can help me free her.*
>
> *I tried twice to ransom her, and Castro turned me down. Since he knows we're friends, we have to face the fact that should Ofelia disappear from the prison, he might suspect you're involved. I recently received a call from Olga Loynaz telling me her permission to leave the country had been held up after she had been interrogated concerning her visits to Ofelia at Guanajay. She asks me to try to get her and her husband out of the country, and I'm committed to doing so.*
>
> *Therefore, dear Alberto, I offer to bring you and your family to freedom as well. I know I'm asking a lot of you. Your prompt response should be returned by the same channels through which you receive this. Please inform Olga.*
>
> *Un abrazo,*
> *Luis*

Riding in the cab at dusk to deliver the letter to Philip at his home in Virginia, Luis reflected upon the irony of his plan. Here he was offering to terminate the usefulness of one of the most important CIA agents in Cuba, and he was asking his cousin, a member of the State Department, to work against the best interests of the CIA.

He rationalized that Alberto was a marked man anyway. Even if he had not gone through Alberto and had succeeded in bribing someone at the prison through Olga or Berta, Castro would have suspected Alberto because of their longstanding friendship. In a sense, Alberto and Ofelia's futures were inextricably bound together because of their relationship to him. His only realistic option rested with Alberto. When he handed the letter to Heymann, he was at peace with his conscience.

The next morning he returned to Miami for the most anxious period of waiting in his life. That night, Blas Casares came by with Carlos and Gray.

"Luis, I'm so glad to see you!" Gray exclaimed, throwing his arms around him.

Whatever else had changed in Luis' life, Gray had not. There, to Luis' pleasure, was the same exuberant person.

After a nostalgic replay of the Bay of Pigs with the American who fired the first shot of the battle, Luis outlined his plan again. Gray thought the plan would work since similar missions had been carried out before. As for weapons, Gray spoke with the knowledge of experience.

"In the catamaran, we'll put a .50 caliber on the bow and a .30 caliber on the stern. For the PT boat, I recommend a 2.5 inch rocket launcher and a 60 millimeter mortar so we can give them a shrapnel shower if need be. For lighter stuff, we'll get some BAR's."

Luis was delighted to hear Gray speak with such authority. That Gray would be with them increased his confidence immeasurably. He had often remembered what a steadying influence Gray had been during the landing in April of 1961. Whatever else went wrong at Girón or Playa Larga, no blame could be placed on Gray or Rip. Castro considered them soldiers of fortune, but to Luis, they were American patriots.

Like everyone else involved, Gray was again risking his future. If the CIA found out about this episode, he would surely lose his job, and should the whole thing go wrong, it would be an international incident with unpredictable ramifications. Without Gray's American contacts, this small group would not have a chance of pulling off the operation since all of them were Cuban refugees on parole in the U.S.

The Cubans had not the slightest idea about how to go about getting a surplus PT boat, a catamaran, small arms, ammunition, and other accessories needed for a clandestine operation.

"Luis," said Carlos, "let's talk about the crew. We need a captain, a pilot, a mechanic, and three gunners. Gray has volunteered to be the captain, and the pilot and the three gunners are--brace yourself--your old buddies from prison, José Enrique, Chiqui, Gaspar, and Gregorio."

"Oh, no!" Luis responded, "I don't want Gregorio and José Enrique to be involved. No men with families. I won't agree to it."

"I'm afraid, Luis, you have no choice." Carlos replied. "They won't take no for an answer."

Luis tried to argue, daring not to tell anyone of his nagging premonition that something would go wrong. In spite of his efforts to avoid it, a repeat of history was taking shape here before his eyes; the very same group that landed ashore first at Girón, the same men the American advisors said would be killed, were going back for another night invasion.

Later in the evening, Luis, mellowed by several drinks, took Gray aside and said to him, "Old man, I think it's about time you told me your name."

"Grayston Lynch," he said laughing, "but all my friends do call me Gray."

"And Rip?" Luis questioned.

"William Rip Robertson," Gray divulged. "He's a hell of a guy."

The next day Luis called Chiqui, José Enrique, Gregorio, and Gaspar, and tried to convince them not to take part in the mission, but there was no changing their minds. They were all committed to the rescue operation.

Knowing he had to be in good shape, Luis started a rigorous physical training routine. He ran and swam every day, quickly gaining strength and endurance. By the middle of March, he weighed 175 pounds and felt as strong as he had on Vieques Island. He was ready to go; all he needed was the opportune moment.

One day Rogerio came to him by the pool and said he wanted to talk. He looked concerned.

"Son," he started, "we need to level with your mother. She suspects something is going on. She talks about your exercising, your absent-mindedness, your friends' visits, and your trip to Washington. She thinks you might have become a CIA agent, and she's getting nervous."

"Papá, if you think it best, I'll tell her the truth," Luis replied.

The following morning he told his mother and sister of the rescue mission, purposely leaving out the details. María Luisa reluctantly gave Luis her blessing, knowing it did no good to argue otherwise.

On the night of March 19, the call came from Philip. He asked Luis to come to Washington. He had urgent news. When Philip met him at the airport, he handed Luis a letter. Luis sat down and read it immediately.

> *Dear Luis,*
>
> *I've been ready to get out of Cuba for quite a while but couldn't come up with a plan to leave with my family. I don't know yet how I can get Ofelia out, but I'll come through.*
>
> *The pick up point will be the nightclub of the Hotel Internacional in Varadero on Saturday, April 13, at 11:30 p.m. It's far enough from Havana, and the beach is not well-patrolled. On a Saturday night, there are a lot of people enjoying the beaches, and the club will be crowded.*
>
> *You said it's a matter of life and death for you. It's the same for me.*
>
> *Un fuerte abrazo,*
> *Alberto*

After checking with Gray, Blas, and Carlos, Luis sent Alberto another message through Philip saying everything was ready, according to plan.

The day of the mission, Luis got up early and went to mass with his mother. Blas and the others were not scheduled to arrive until 10:00 a.m. When the time came to depart, Rogerio, María Luisa, and Isabel saw Luis to the door, his mother embracing him last and whispering, "I'll say a *rosario* for your safety. May God watch over all of you."

The seven frogmen left Miami on Highway One for the trip south. Luis measured their progress by checking the names of the keys, Key Largo, Plantation Key, Long Key, Marathon, and finally Big Pine.

Gray was waiting at the dock with another American.

"Hey *muchachos*," he welcomed them, shaking their hands, "this is Dallas Cummings, our mechanic, better known as Dub."

The frogmen greeted a pleasant, thin but strong, graying man in his early forties who casually threw up his hand.

"He'll keep those Packards going," said Gray.

Chapter 62

The PT boat set sail from Big Pine after dusk in order to minimize the chances of being investigated by the Coast Guard. The catamaran with its two machine guns was placed in the bow of the PT boat and covered with a tarpaulin.

As the Big Pine shore line receded, Gray, in a flamboyant cross-anchored captain's hat tilted to one side, steered the boat while he described the glorious history of the PT boats.

"This motherfucker here," he explained, "is an ELCO, the same kind as John F. Kennedy's PT-109. It'll do forty knots, and it's in good shape to be twenty years old."

Gray went on to describe John Kennedy's encounter with the *Amagiri* and his heroic efforts to bring his capsized crew to safety. Gray said he admired Kennedy's courage as a PT boat commander but wished he had shown the same guts at the Bay of Pigs. "Then again, he held his ground with the Russians during the Missile Crisis," Gray added.

They continued to sail southeast over a glassy sea, going by the Dog Rocks and around the Cay Sal Bank. Past the Cay Sal Buoy, they steered back to the southwest in order to follow the shipping routes to Havana. Over the flat moonlit sea, they saw the lights of ships making their way between the Bahamas and Havana.

Two hours out of Cay Sal they slowed to fifteen knots and stayed close on the starboard side of a freighter heading toward the Gulf. At 10:30 p.m., they saw the lights of Varadero and steered toward the point of the peninsula. The seriousness of the operation increased with each minute, and Gray became the no-nonsense commander. Five miles out he cut the motors and ordered his crew to put the catamaran and the Zodiac overboard.

At 10:45 p.m., Gray ordered the start of the 200 HP Mercury engine of the catamaran, captained by Gaspar. After some two hundred meters, Gaspar checked the PRC-10 and found it workable. Five minutes later, Gray gave the command to approach the beach.

Slowly, Gaspar guided the catamaran towing the Zodiac toward the lights of the Hotel Internacional located in the center of the peninsula. When he was some five hundred meters out, he stopped the motor and ordered Blas, Luis, and Carlos to board the Zodiac.

Carlos immediately started the silent 25 HP Mercury engine of the Zodiac and steered cautiously toward a point some three hundred meters to the left of the hotel. A hundred and fifty meters from the beach, he ordered Luis and Blas in the water.

Luis and Blas swam the remaining distance without ripple or sound, coming ashore fifty meters apart. After surveying the beach, they signaled Carlos with the small infrared light to come on in, blinking five times as agreed.

Within seconds, Carlos and the raft materialized in the moonlight. Silently, he got out of the raft and handed each of them a plastic bag containing civilian clothes, a towel, a comb, loafers, socks, and a .45 pistol. After dressing, Luis and Blas placed their .45's under their belts in the hollows of their backs where the weapons would conveniently be covered by their *guayaberas*. Carlos then took a bottle of rum and two glasses out of a second bag and poured a drink for Luis and Blas. After making a silent toast to the adventure at hand, they signaled goodbye to Carlos and headed with drinks in hand toward the front of the beach entrance of the hotel some 250 meters away.

Except for a couple in a passionate embrace on a blanket in the sand just past the light of the back entrance to the hotel, the beach appeared deserted. Strangely, the couple's amorous explorations reminded Luis not of Ofelia and Olga, but of Laura and the virginal days of their romance at the HYC. At the steps, they noticed two couples seated at a table and drinking. This would have been the perfect place for a rendezvous with his friends, except he did not know if there would be tables outside or how many people might be around.

Greeting the couples at the entrance to the hotel with a friendly *"buenas noches,"* Blas and Luis set their glasses on an empty table and entered the lobby of the Internacional, passing a large picture of Fidel Castro and a prominent slogan which read, ¡*PATRIA O MUERTE, VENCEREMOS*! or FATHERLAND OR DEATH, WE SHALL TRIUMPH!

As Luis and Blas passed the desk, they were chatting in a lively manner. They stopped at the door of the nightclub where a host met them and said,

"Good evening, *compañeros*, do you need a table?"

"No, *gracias*. We're here just to have a drink," Blas replied.

Following the signal of the host, they moved toward the bar. Luis looked at his watch and felt relieved they had arrived at 11:30 p.m. sharp.

They ordered rum and sodas while both strove to acclimate their eyes to the semi-darkness. On the lighted stage, several dancers swayed to a Latin rhythm while a woman in skimpy clothes sang *"Quiéreme mucho."*

At the crowded bar, Luis and Blas listened to two slouchily dressed Caucasians talking loudly in Russian. One of them had prominent gold teeth and a short haircut that made the top of his head look like the skin and hair of a mangy dog. "These apparatchiks now live in our homes," Luis whispered to Blas.

Anxiously, Luis began to survey the crowd. When he spotted Alberto Sánchez getting up from a table, his heart skipped several beats, but then when he gazed at the table, it almost stopped with disappointment. Everyone was there but Ofelia. Trying to appear nonchalant, Luis waited calmly as Alberto approached and casually extended his hand, saying, "Good to see you again, *amigo*."

"Where's Ofelia?" Luis whispered.

Alberto, in his major's uniform, took a sip from the drink and answered softly, "I have her, Luis. She's outside in a car with the children."

Luis sighed thankfully and strove to keep a lid on his surging emotions. Of all the steps in the mission, he had just learned of the success of the most important one for him.

"There's only one problem," Alberto added. "I had to bring two other people. I didn't need to bribe anyone. I'll tell you later, but I knew the head of the Guanajay prison, and I persuaded her to defect with her husband. Do we have space for them?"

"That's no problem," said Luis. "We needed to make two trips in any case. Where's the car?"

"It's in the front. Let's go."

"Okay," said Luis, "here's what we'll do."

Following Luis' instruction, Alberto returned to his table, paid the bill, and with his wife, Marta, Olga and Senator Sócrates Miranda, the woman militia captain in uniform and her husband, joined Luis and Blas in the lobby. There, Luis greeted the people whose fate depended on him. He kissed Olga and Marta on the cheek and shook hands with the Senator and the others. The militia captain, Mercedes, and her husband, Justo, were delighted to meet the man whose mission allowed them to escape. They all simulated a festive, party-like mood as Luis outlined the plan of escape to them.

As they left the nightclub, the group politely acknowledged two militia guards at the front entrance. Alberto told the guards to carry on, and they continued their lively exchange as they walked toward the parking lot. When they approached Alberto's '58 Ford sedan, Ofelia opened the front door, fell into Luis' arms, and began to cry softly.

"Now, now, *mi amor*," Luis whispered, stroking her short hair, "we're together. Everything's going to be all right."

"I can't believe I'm here with you!" she said, holding him tightly as she looked at him with her tearful eyes.

"Ofelia, my love," Luis replied, overcome by emotion, "I've been waiting for this moment for an eternity."

In a carefree manner, the group walked out of the parking lot and down to the beach, laughing and exchanging jokes as if they were having fun by the seaside before returning to their rooms in the hotel.

The plan was proceeding without a hitch until Blas noticed a distant boat slowly approaching from the south, scanning the beach and sea with a rotating light.

Instantly, Luis ordered Blas to use the radio in the Zodiac to call the catamaran and tell the crew not to fire and pull back out of the sweep of the light. Then he sent Justo and Alberto to help Carlos and

Blas bring the Zodiac toward the hotel so it could be hidden behind the sand dunes. His third order was to direct the women, children, and the Senator to take cover behind the dunes.

When the patrol boat, a medium-sized cabin cruiser, finally passed their position, the beach appeared deserted. All was quiet, and seeing the rays of light sweep over the ridge of sand above their heads, Luis thought to himself, perhaps luck is with me this time.

After the patrol boat had passed, Luis instructed Olga, Ofelia, Marta, Mercedes and the three boys to board the Zodiac. Instead of following the others, Ofelia ran to Luis and whispered in his ear, "I'm not about to leave you this time. From now on, I go where you go!"

Deeply touched, Luis could only give her a quick hug as he quietly ordered Carlos to pass the Thompsons and the BAR.

The silent engine started instantly, and the children waved to the men on the beach. Luis knew Albertico would never forget the night he escaped from Cuba. Seeing them in the departing raft, Luis quietly offered a prayer for their safety.

Luis estimated it would take six minutes for the Zodiac to reach the PT boat and return to the beach, but after some four minutes, he noticed a disturbing sight. The patrol boat, rather than circling the tip of the peninsula, was turning around in a large arc and coming back toward the International Hotel. Then it dawned on him they had not brought along another radio for those on shore while the Zodiac was at sea. Whatever measures that might have to be taken now were beyond his control. He trusted the good judgment of his friends, knowing they would not fire unless they absolutely had to. His main concern was whether Carlos' boat would be caught in the fan of the searchlight that spread out several hundred meters in front of the boat.

Realizing the Zodiac would be spotted if Carlos had left the catamaran for the second trip, Luis ordered as he prepared for the worst, "Blas, aim at the light on the patrol boat with the BAR and shoot immediately if it spots Carlos. I'll cover the rear with the Thompson." Luis also feared if the catamaran fired with its tracers, it would draw fire in return and endanger the women and children.

Again hiding behind the sand dunes, they waited as the patrol boat got closer. Suddenly, their fears were realized, for there, in the reflected glare of the light, was Carlos in the black raft not more than twenty meters off shore. When the spotlight suddenly reversed, Luis knew the Zodiac had been spotted. He did not have to wait to give the order. Blas cut loose with the BAR, rattling the night and simultaneously triggering the two machine guns on the catamaran. Red dashes of the tracers flashed over the water. Within seconds, the spotlight was blown out, and the boat itself was out of control, zigzagging toward the beach. Luis ordered the firing to stop, and Gaspar, in the catamaran, soon followed suit.

"That fucker won't search for anybody else," exclaimed Blas. "He's picked up his last refugee."

Hysteria broke out in the hotel, and at the same time the lights went out, shouts echoed along the shore.

"It's another invasion!" someone yelled, and amid similar cries, Luis distinctly heard from one of the balconies on the seaside "Hurray for the Americans!"

"Let's get to the Zodiac!" he urged the group, covering with the Thompson as they scampered over the dunes.

Carlos was waiting in the Zodiac with the engine running, and Luis could hear him talking excitedly on the radio, "Tell Gaspar to come on in with the catamaran and have Gray bring the PT closer."

"Hurry! We don't have much time," Carlos shouted.

When they got to the Zodiac which was parked sideways on the beach, Carlos helped Ofelia and the men on board, and Luis started to push the raft to sea. He had his right leg inside the Zodiac when he felt two sharp blows that knocked him face down into the raft. He had been hit in the chest and the left thigh. Around him Luis heard the familiar sounds of bullets thumping the water and the clattering of machine guns back on the shore.

"I see them by the hotel steps!" shouted Carlos. "Get 'em!"

Blas, zeroing in on the shadowy figures Carlos pointed to, showered them with the BAR. Luis, conscious but bleeding profusely, weakly passed his Thompson to Alberto, who joined Blas in the return fire.

"I've been hit!" shouted Justo as he grabbed his left shoulder, and no sooner had he spoken, they heard the hissing sound of air escaping the Zodiac. Numbed by pain, Luis saw a front corner of the raft collapse. Ofelia was crouching by Luis when her head snapped sideways and she fell to the bottom of the Zodiac. "Oh, my God,

Ofelia's wounded!" shouted Blas. As in a dream, Luis impotently watched the tracers of the catamaran sweep the sea front of the hotel and silence the enemy fire.

In a moment, the catamaran joined them, and Carlos passed the line to Gaspar amid the chaos.

"We've got three wounded, including Luis," Carlos yelled to Gaspar, "Ofelia's in bad shape. She got hit in the head. One of the Zodiac compartments is ruptured. Take us out!"

While Alberto applied pressure to Ofelia's wound, Carlos ordered the transfer of the wounded to the catamaran.

Blas understood Carlos' concern. With water splashing over the ruptured raft, the blood would inevitably attract sharks. "Let's get Ofelia first, she's unconscious!" Carlos shouted. As soon as Ofelia was transferred, Justo and Luis were quickly lifted on board the catamaran and placed next to Ofelia. Luis held Ofelia tightly, their blood mixing with the tragic waters of the Straits of Florida. Luis mumbled in desperation, "Oh please, blessed Virgin of Charity, don't let her die! Ofelia, Ofelia, don't die on me!"

Slowly moving north, they saw their PT boat rapidly coming toward them, but Gray sailed on by and turned toward Varadero without stopping. In a moment, they saw the reason; another boat, just as fast, was approaching them from the south. As Luis felt himself losing consciousness, an explosion of water rose in front of Gray's PT boat. Within seconds, more cannon fire followed as a sea battle began. José Enrique turned their PT to the east and made a quick 180-degree sweep so Gray would have a side shot at the enemy vessel rapidly approaching the catamaran.

What followed would have reminded Luis of the night he blew up the power station at Regla. An explosion from the 2.5-inch rocket fired into the enemy boat, and subsequent secondary explosions from gasoline and ammunition sent sparks shooting upward. The scene looked like a speeding comet skipping on the water with a ball of fire and a long trail of white vapor. In a blink of an eye, the comet was gone, its head and tail quenched.

"Hang on, Luis! We're going to make it!" Alberto shouted.

In a moment, the PT boat was beside them, Gray barking orders as they carefully transferred the unconscious Ofelia and Luis, followed by the wounded Justo and the children. When everyone was on board, Gray gave a command to move out, "José Enrique, takes us home!" The Packards roared, and the boat lurched, throwing spray toward Cuba.

Alberto and Gaspar gently moved Ofelia and Luis, stretching them out on the padded seats in the cabin. "My God, Gaspar, she's dead," Alberto realized as he failed to find any sign of life in Ofelia. He summoned his wife, Marta, to his side, and together, the two of them gently covered Ofelia's limp body with a blanket they took from a nearby trunk. In her death, the tranquil expression on Ofelia's face reflected a peace she would never have known had she remained in Cuba. As Marta quietly prayed over Ofelia's body, Alberto and Chiqui turned their attention to Luis.

Chiqui grabbed the first aid kit and shouted, "He's alive! "Damn, he's lost a lot of blood! Alberto, help me!" As Alberto rushed toward the lifeless Luis, Chiqui was cutting off Luis' clothes around his wounds.

"The shot here in his chest took out muscle tissue. I just hope he's not hemorrhaging inside. I'm going to plug the wound so his lung won't collapse," commented Chiqui.

"What about his leg?" Alberto anxiously inquired.

"I don't think it's serious. Let's just get it bandaged."

They carefully cleaned the gaping holes in Luis' upper chest and left thigh, and when they had finished, Alberto sat down by Luis, tenderly gathering his childhood friend in his arms, as if he were comforting one of his children. He began to console Luis, speaking as though his unconscious friend could hear his words.

"Luis, Ofelia didn't make it . . . She died instantly, without suffering . . . I'm sorry, my dear friend, I'm so very sorry," he said as he wept unconsolably.

At that moment, Luis squeezed Alberto's hand as if to assure his friend he understood.

On deck, Gray radioed his CIA contacts in Key West to inform them of the situation and requested that an ambulance be waiting for them at the pier. When Alberto joined the others out on the deck two hours later, the string of pearly lights of the Florida Keys glistened in the distance as they headed for Key West in the glimmering Caribbean moonlight.

Epilogue

As weak and confused as he was, Luis Recio remembered a naval officer, who in Luis' blurred vision might have passed for an angel in white, standing by his bed in the Naval Hospital in Key West. Luis had a vague memory of arriving at the hospital in an ambulance and being immediately rushed to the operating room. Now, as he attempted to turn toward the officer, excruciating pain in his left thigh and chest halted his movement.

In his torpor, a sleep that rose and fell like the waves on the monitors at the head of his bed, Luis Recio drifted to other times and places. He felt afloat on a tranquil sea, looking upward at a bright sky. Above him soared several golden eagles, their graceful wings reflecting the sun's rays.

"Where are the airplanes?" José Enrique shouted repeatedly. "We need airplanes! Where're the goddamned Americans? One fucking jet is all we need!"

As he drifted, Luis could detect nothing in the expanse around and above him. The sea was as empty of ships as the sky was of planes. "We're alone! All alone!" Gregorio was saying, "We're all going to be killed. *Los americanos* have betrayed us!"

A woman's voice responded, "You're not alone." It was, Luis knew, the voice of the one dearest to him. "Luis, don't worry . . . I'm with you . . ." From somewhere, the comforting, familiar voice was softly speaking about freedom and hope.

Gradually Luis Recio faded into deep sleep, conscious of images of eagles, of a woman deeply loved, and of the boundless feeling of freedom soaring within him.

Afterword

Some of the characters in this novel are real, and some are fictitious. Luis Recio never existed, though the surname is well known in Camagüey, and he may be considered as a composite hero of the upper class. Similarly, some of the scenes are based on historical facts while others are imaginary, though representative of various aspects of Cuban and American life.

This book has been many years in the making, and we owe a debt of gratitude to many people for their assistance in the writing and research. To ensure accuracy of historical events, we had many conversations and interviews with witnesses of and participants in several of the scenes described. In particular we are grateful to Húber Matos for his insights of Fidel Castro in the hills, to José Ignacio Rasco for information on Castro's after the triumph of the revolution, to Mario Abril, Miguel Uría, Armando Vega for accounts of their experiences in prisons, and to Carlos Fonts and Grayston Lynch for certain episodes of their CIA experiences. We are also indebted to Governor Manuel Eduardo Zayas-Bazán Recio for verifying a number of historical facts concerning political life in Cuba. We wish to thank the following persons for reading portions of the manuscript and making helpful suggestions: José Enrique Alonso, Erneido Oliva, Antonio Zamora, Juan López de la Cruz, Blas Casares, José Andreu, Juan Cosculluela, Laureano Batista, Ted Cobun, Gloria Oster, Katherine Hall, Virginia Runge and particularly Tanya Shook-Wilder, who was invaluable in editing the manuscript.

In regards to published material, we wish to acknowledge the indispensableness of Lord Hugh Thomas's *Cuba: The Pursuit of Freedom*, the virtual bible for any serious examination of Cuba. The works of Che Guevara and those of Colonel Ramón Barquín helped in constructing battle sequences in the Sierra Maestra. In addition to the personal experiences of one of the authors, four books, *The Bay of Pigs: The Leaders' Story of Brigade 2506* by Haynes Johnson and others, *The Bay of Pigs: The Untold Story* by Peter Wyden, *Decision for disaster: betrayal at the Bay of Pigs* by Grayston L. Lynch and *Bay of Pigs: an oral history of Brigade 2506* by Víctor A. Triay helped in describing the famous battle and the prison scenes. The official communist version of the battle, the four volume, *Playa Girón: Derrota del Imperialismo* was also consulted. *A Thousand Days* by Arthur M. Schlesinger, Jr., and *Kennedy* by Theodore C. Sorensen served as reliable sources for knowledge on the role of John F. Kennedy in the affairs of Cuba.

Finally, we are deeply appreciative to the many hours that Reny Higgs and Lourdes Abascal devoted to polishing and typing the manuscript. Their generous assistance and encouragement were crucial for completion of the project.

About the authors

D r. Eduardo Zayas-Bazán is a native of Camagüey, Cuba. He has an M.S. in Foreign Language Education from Kansas State Teachers College, Emporia, KS, and a Doctor en Derecho degree from Universidad Nacional José Martí, Havana, Cuba.

In April of 1961, Zayas-Bazán participated in the Bay of Pigs Invasion of Cuba as a frogman. He was wounded in his right knee, captured, and spent one year in prison before being ransomed with fifty- nine other wounded prisoners that needed urgent medical attention in the United States.

Zayas-Bazán is a Professor Emeritus in Foreign Languages from East Tennessee State University where he was chair of the Foreign Language Department from 1973 to 1993. Throughout his notable career he has been the recipient of ETSU's Distinguished Faculty Award; Sigma Delta Pi's Premio Martel, the Tennessee Foreign Language Teaching Association's Jacqueline Elliot Award, and the AATSP's Robert G. Mead Distinguished Leadership Award. Zayas-Bazán was the first Cuban-American elected president of the American Association of Teachers of Spanish and Portuguese and of the National Association of Cuban-American Educators. He has also been President of the Municipality of Camagüey in Exile, editor of its periodical, *El Camagüeyano Libre,* and vice president of Cuban Cultural Heritage.

Professor Zayas-Bazán was associate editor of *Hispania*, the journal of the American Association of Teachers of Spanish and Portuguese. In addition to writing numerous articles in regional and national journals, he is the co-author, co-editor and translator of eighteen books. Three of his textbooks, *¡Arriba!, Conexiones*, and *Fusión* published by Pearson Education, are being used at some 150 colleges and universities in the U.S. and Canada.

Professor Zayas-Bazán is married to Lourdes Abascal. He is retired and lives in Miami, FL since May of 1999.

Dr. Robert J. (Jack) Higgs was born on a farm in Middle Tennessee. He attended Vanderbilt University before entering the United States Naval Academy where he graduated in 1955 with a B.S. degree. He entered the U.S. Air Force, specializing in photo-radar interpretation. In 1963, he resigned his captain's commission to enter graduate school at the University of Tennessee where, in 1967, he received the Ph.D. in American literature.

After a year of teaching at Eastern Kentucky University, he came to East Tennessee State University where for twenty-seven years he taught courses in American, Southern, and Appalachian Literature, the Literature of Sports and Great Books. He has written, co-authored, or co-edited nine books, including *Laurel and Thorn: The Athlete in American Literature* (UP Kentucky, 1981), which was reprinted in Japanese in 1995, and *God in the Stadium: Sport and Religion in America* (Kentucky, 1995) which was nominated for the Pulitzer prize. He is co-editor of *Voices from the Hills*, which was recently reprinted in a 25th anniversary edition, and of *Appalachia Inside Out: A Sequel to Voices from the Hills* (University of Tennessee Press,1995). Both texts are widely used in the Appalachian region.

Professor Higgs has been honored with ETSU's Distinguished Teaching Award and the Foundation Research Award. In 1984, he was named one of eight finalists for National Teacher of the Year sponsored by CASE (Council and Support of Education). He is the author of over thirty articles on Appalachian/Southern culture, American humor, religion, and sports. He has given over four hundred lectures at professional organizations, universities, libraries, and civic clubs.

Printed in the United States
By Bookmasters